BATTLE FOR THE WASTELANDS

MATTHEW W. QUINN

Thank you for reading! If you
like it, check out prequel
novella "Son of Grendel" and
sequel novel Serpent Sword.

Matt

P.S. online reviews good
and bad appreciated

IN THE BEGINNING, A HUNT

The punishing July sun glared in the cobalt sky above lean Andrew Sutter. He stared down the sights of his rifle, tracking the gray-furred ripper ambling across flat, rocky ground below the desolate brown hills. The heat pulled sweat from his thin face, darkening his straw-colored hair.

The men of Carroll Town went out that morning, each alone to cover as much territory as possible. They'd strip the countryside, right down to the kangaroo rats. If game were plentiful, they could survive until harvest without eating their livestock or their seed grain.

Just his luck he, who'd only hunted meek pronghorn or mule deer, faced the biggest predator roaming the badlands between the river valley and the desert. He'd considered skedaddling, but the growl of an empty stomach stopped him dead. A ripper meant a *powerful* amount of meat.

He'd laid out the scraps of his meager prairie dog breakfast before tucking himself behind some rocks on a nearby hill. The smell brought the ripper into rifle range soon enough.

The predator bent its lupine head and sniffed the meat. Andrew aimed for its flank just behind the ribs and pulled the trigger.

The rifle kicked against his shoulder just as the ripper stepped forward. His shot cut across the ripper's back. The beast threw back its head and howled.

His ears still ringing, Andrew flipped the rifle's lever, ejecting the spent shell. The ripper looked up. Andrew flattened himself against the hard ground behind the rocks, but their eyes met. It roared. Andrew swore and aimed again. The ripper bounded toward him, long forelegs and short, muscular hind legs kicking up dust behind it.

Andrew's bullet caught it in the shoulder. The ripper kept coming. *Oh shit!*

Andrew scrambled back and fired again. The bullet carved a deep furrow down the ripper's side. The wound slowed it but didn't stop it. *Shit!* His stomach boiled. The damn things liked to go for the soft parts, the guts or even the balls.

Andrew made it to the bottom of the hill by the time the ripper crested it. It fell like a lightning bolt. He aimed for the ripper's red right eye.

CRACK!

His bullet punched through the cheek and erupted from the other side of its skull. The ripper tumbled. Its momentum slammed it into the ground beside him.

Despite his shaking hands, Andrew kept his rifle leveled on the dead ripper. He circled it, breathing heavily. He jumped forward and kicked the creature as hard as he could. Something cracked beneath his boot. The ripper did not stir.

Andrew whooped. "Thought you'd be eating me today?" Andrew taunted the corpse. "Looks like it's *you* going on the stove!"

The ripper weighed at least one hundred pounds. Between the meat and what Andrew could trade for, his mother, sister, and himself wouldn't need to worry about food for awhile. He laughed.

Holding on his rifle with one hand, he pulled one of the beast's forelimbs across his shoulders. His back protested. Once he'd have gutted it or at least bled it to reduce the weight, but these days offal and even blood had uses.

Andrew bore his prize from one brown stony hilltop to another, never lingering in the low areas watered by the dying stream. Though the sun wrung rivers of sweat from his body, he wanted to see any predators coming from a long way off.

On his fourth hill, something moved below amid the sea of dying vegetation cloaking a rusted Old World rail line. His gut clenched. Rippers mated for life.

A roar announced the second ripper's attack. The creature surged up the hill, murderous eyes locked on Andrew. Had they been hunting *him* like he'd been hunting *them*?

Andrew twisted away at the last possible second. The blow that would have sliced him open from breastbone to crotch tore only his white shirt and brown trousers.

The ripper's momentum bowled him over. He and the dead ripper tumbled, the live one atop both. They broke apart as they rolled down the hill into the dead grass. Luckily he'd kept hold of the rifle.

Andrew scrambled away as the beast recovered. The ripper lunged. He shoved his rifle forward, the stock catching a blow meant for his throat. He struck the beast's bony brow with his rifle butt. It stumbled back on three limbs, clawing at Andrew with the fourth.

Andrew wasn't going to lick the ripper in close combat. He had to find a way to shoot the damn thing.

The predator slashed again. A claw caught Andrew's left shoulder. Andrew retreated, blood already darkening his shirt. He raised his rifle as it lunged. The barrel touched the ripper's forehead in the instant before he squeezed the trigger. A cone of blood and brain erupted from the back of its head. Some ended up on Andrew's face as the ripper slammed into the brown earth.

He wiped the gore onto his sleeve. Not wanting to waste anything, he picked a large bit off his arm and swallowed it whole. The foul taste gagged him, but it'd silence his stomach.

He looked at his kills. No way could he carry *both* home. He dragged the first carcass over to the second, drew his knife from the sheathe on his leather belt, and opened the arteries on both necks. He scowled as the red blood drained into the dust. *There goes some sausage.* Next he opened both bellies, wrinkling his nose when the hard, fecal scent slammed into his face. He cut the organs free, stuffing them into the bag. Next came the thighs and calves. By the time he'd sawed *those* from both rippers, his arms ached. For a moment, he considered burying the rippers and coming back later.

He shook his head. He'd be damned if he let anything snatch what he'd won. And he wasn't going to risk his family going hungry because he took the easy way out. He wiped the sweat away from his sun-reddened face and returned to work.

He spent hours butchering the two rippers beneath the burning sun, all while keeping his eyes peeled for predators. Fortunately the wind from the Iron Desert blew his scent toward the river valley his folk farmed, an area the rippers and sand snakes had learned to avoid.

When he'd finished, the bag almost *overflowed* with meat. Blood dripped from the saturated leather. He hoisted the ponderous bag onto his back. The straps bit into his shoulders. Andrew leaned forward.

Bent beneath the load, he made his way through the badlands toward Carroll Town. He did his best to ignore the warm ripper blood soaking through his shirt and trickling down his back. His mother and sister Sarah would be glad he came home alive, but his clothes would right horrify them.

As he followed the sun, he pondered how he'd be received. The others likely bagged pronghorn, mule deer, or prairie dogs, if they'd gotten anything at all. He'd landed something bigger, something that ate the game the men wanted. They'd *cheer*. His sweetheart Cassie Wells would want to hear more about it. Hopefully somewhere cozy and private. He smiled.

His heart leaped with delight as the skeletal iron mooring tower, a gift from James Merrill upon his ascension in Jacinto two years before Andrew was born, came into view from the hilltop. The tower was empty — dirigible visits had been rare even when the Merrills ruled, before the tyrant Grendel threw them down and raised up the murderous Flesh-Eating Legion. But it still reared into the blue sky like a huge finger. And though most paint had peeled away, it still bore scraps of the Merrill green.

Eventually the ground sloped downward toward a white wooden fence. Beyond, parched fields of stunted wheat clawed their way from the black earth the river had laid, earth left dry by the drought. A horse-drawn iron reaper, huge and skeletal, sat amid what promised to be a poor harvest.

A voice startled him. "Hey Andy!" Sam Cotton, his friend since they were both six, called out in a voice drawling somewhat more than his own. "What you got?"He approached from the north, following the hills. Sweat plastered dark hair to a head that came up to Andrew's chin, and his skin, fairer than Andrew's, had burned worse. He carried his rifle under his arm. His hands were empty.

"Oh, howdy Sam. You not get anything?"

Sam's thin face fell. He shook his head. "Couldn't find anything. Anything *living*, that is. Found a dead mule deer, but it was half-rotten. Would've sickened anyone who ate it."

Andrew winced inwardly. Sam had two brothers and a sister, all younger. He'd give Sam some of his kill. There was more than enough for Andrew's kin.

Sam's gaze fell on Andrew's burden. "Looks like you got something." A moment passed. "Need any help?"

A twinge of ache crossed Andrew's back. "Yeah."

He set the heavy bag down and tightened the straps holding it shut. If he got one end and Sam got the other, it'd be just their luck if the bag split open in the middle. He tucked his rifle under one arm to keep both hands free.

Sam came over, holding his rifle the same away. He picked up the end of the bag. "You got the other end?"

Andrew nodded. "On the count of three. One —"

"Two," Sam added.

"Three!" both said together. They lifted the bag. Andrew's arms protested but they didn't yell as loudly as his back.

"Okay," Andrew said. "Let's get this down."

Sam nodded. He scooted backward down the hill, Andrew close behind. They soon found the dusty path that would take them the last mile home. The sun was low now. Fear set its teeth to the base of Andrew's spine. Best not be out at night, especially smelling like they did. "Let's get a move on." Sam nodded.

It didn't take more than half an hour to reach the white-painted wooden arch marking the entrance of central Carroll Town.

And just inside were a trio of strangers on horseback. The towns-folk gathered between them and the town's white clapboard buildings.

Through the crowd he saw they wore the red jackets and black trousers of the Flesh-Eating Legion beneath their brown dusters.

The hairs on the back of Andrew's neck stood at attention. His gut clenched. His hands trembled.

Nothing good ever happened when the Flesh-Eaters paid a visit…

ULTIMATUM

Andrew locked his eyes on the trio. The Flesh-Eaters usually came for tribute or conscripts. Those few who returned began their stories with forced consumption of human flesh...

Andrew wasn't *that* hungry.

Sam stepped forward. "What's going on?" Andrew nodded toward the gate. Sam's hands tightened on his end of the bag. "Flesh-Eaters. Goddamn it."

One Flesh-Eater – a ranker based on his simpler uniform – turned straight at them. Andrew hoped they weren't looking for young men. They knew he was here, and he wasn't going to run and risk them burning Carroll Town.

The Flesh-Eater looked them up and down, snorted, and turned away. Andrew prickled. That son of a bitch!

Soon curiosity rose alongside his fear. If they weren't conscripting, why *were* they here? Andrew set the bloody bag down. He edged closer toward the gate.

Sam's eyes bulged. "Andy, what are you *doing*?"

"Just going to get a closer look."

The most elaborately-uniformed Flesh-Eater — he wore a red sash over his buttoned black jacket and red epaulets peeked out from under his duster — sat confidently on his horse. An ugly smile illuminated his blunt features. His two mounted bodyguards, both carrying shot-guns, flanked him. The chief Flesh-Eater spoke imperiously to Arnold Emerson, the short mayor whose hanging skin folds indicated he'd once been heavier.

"I require the usual tribute," the bossman growled as Andrew came into earshot. Andrew could detect the stronger drawl of the hill trash from well north of Jacinto. "One hundred gold dollars, or the equiva-lent in trade or farm goods. Value to be determined, of course, by me." The emissary grinned. Andrew caught a brief glimpse of two filed front teeth, the mark of the cult. "If the money doesn't arrive within three days, there will be consequences."

The insane demand struck Andrew like a blow. Before harvest the people of Carroll Town had little enough to feed themselves, let alone the Flesh-Eaters. That jackass *had* to know.

Fearful muttering snaked through the crowd. "My lord," Arnold protested. "We're in the middle of a drought." He gestured toward the townsfolk, all bearing the pinched look of hunger. "We can't pay now. In a few weeks, when harvest comes, we'll at least have *something*. I doubt your bossman wants *dirt* for tribute."

The emissary locked eyes with the older man. "Pay up, or I'll tell the fort they've got a rebellion on their hands. They wouldn't like that much." He dropped from his horse. His dark eyes swept the crowds. "You know, there might be *another* way out of this."

His gaze fell on Lily, Arnold's pretty dark-haired daughter. Her brown eyes caught his. She paled and recoiled.

Andrew gritted his teeth. Lily was a friend of his sister. His grip tightened on the rifle, but he didn't dare move. Anyone who raised a hand to a Flesh-Eater official doomed himself and his kinfolk too.

The ugly man continued. "One of the officers at the fort delights in young women." He kept his gaze on Lily. "It gets powerful lonely up there sometimes. He might be willing to exempt Carroll Town from tribute *entirely* this year — and maybe even the next — if you give him someone…appropriate."

Arnold swallowed. "My lord, she's only fourteen —"

The Flesh-Eater snorted. "I said *young* women."

Arnold's face reddened. Then he purpled. He twitched.

One mounted man turned to the other. "That one's a bit young, but she'll probably sprout well." The guard, a thin-faced man with cold blue eyes, spoke *entirely* too loudly. A salacious smile spread across his face. "I wonder if there're any older ones?"

Andrew ground his teeth. That description covered Sarah, Cassie, and most of the girls he knew. His fingers clenched harder around the rifle.

The second bodyguard, black-haired and one-eyed, shook his head. "The older ones are a bit more fun. If they've already had kids, they know what they're doing."

That description happened to cover Andrew's mother. The hand enclosing his rifle trembled.

The mayor's impotent rage purpled his face further as the emissary approached Lily. He reached toward her in a manner courtly in anyone else. She stumbled backward. Andrew almost raised his rifle right then and there.

"Your folk are in great danger," the bigwig said. "But if you cooperate, I can save them." Lily kept retreating. The foul man kept coming. The townsfolk pulled away around them. "Nobody needs to die, if you come with me. I'm not asking you *that* much." He looked around disdainfully. "Fucking him's a better life than living in *this* dump."

"All right!" Anger broke into Arnold's voice at last. He advanced on the emissary. "This is damn well —"

The emissary wheeled. "Do you want your town to burn?" he snarled. Arnold retreated. The emissary turned back toward Lily. "What say you? Maybe you have more sense than your pa."

"Leave Lily alone, you piece of shit," Taylor Welborn growled as he pushed his way through the townsfolk standing behind Lily. The Flesh-Eater was not a small man by any stretch, but Taylor had a least a foot and thirty pounds on him, even after the long hunger. Anger lit his broad face beneath the shock of curly brown hair.

"Taylor," Arnold stammered. "Stay out of this!"

The emissary laughed. "Listen to the old man." He shifted his gaze back to Lily, pointedly ignoring Taylor. "You're young," he continued, still playing at being charming. "*Malleable.* He could learn you things, interesting things. You'd be much more fun than any whore —"

Anger lit up Lily's face at the word "whore." She slapped the Flesh-Eater. Her blow did little beyond provoke chuckling from the guards. The emissary silenced them with a glare, a glare that soon fell on Lily.

Oh shit.

He backhanded her, knocking her onto the ground. "You imbecile!" the Flesh-Eater snarled. "I gave you the chance to save your worthless town!"

With a shout, Taylor charged. The emissary turned away from Lily and took a massive fist straight on the nose. Blood spattered both men. The Flesh-Eater staggered.

"Kill him!" His screech was comically nasal despite the volume.

The farthest bodyguard's shotgun snapped up. Thunder cracked. The pellets grazed Taylor's face and shoulder, breaking the skin but doing little real damage. The blast shattered a window — and put down an old stray dog nobody'd eaten yet — behind him.

Many townsfolk fled screaming. Others rushed the three men. Shock and growing horror kept Andrew rooted to the ground.

The bodyguard who'd fired spurred his horse. He thundered toward Taylor, chambering another shell as he rode. The second body-guard, closer to Taylor, raised his shotgun. Before he could fire, the townsfolk tore him from the saddle. The first bodyguard wheeled and fired, felling one man and driving the rest back before they could swarm his fallen comrade.

The emissary grabbed for his pistol, but Taylor seized him before the weapon got halfway up. The emissary pulled the trigger. His shot punched through a woman's leg, drawing blood and a scream. He fought to raise his weapon, but Taylor grit his teeth and kept the gun firmly down.

The crowds closed in. All Andrew could see now were fists and knives rising and falling. Many came away bloody.

The bodyguards fired, blasting townsfolk away from the fallen emissary, but it was too late. The emissary laid spread out on the parched earth. The ground drank blood pouring from a second mouth beneath his chin.

The guards aimed for Taylor. Gunfire cracked. The dismounted bodyguard sank to his knees. The mounted bodyguard surged for the wounded man. Another shot missed. The bullet passed painfully by Andrew's ear. The mounted man dragged his compatriot onto the saddle behind him and spurred his horse straight at Andrew. Andrew threw himself out of the way. He slammed into the stony ground, rocks biting through his clothes.

Sam stood paralyzed in the fleeing Flesh-Eater's path.

"Sam!" Andrew shouted. Andrew's voice snapped his friend into action. He jumped out of the way of the oncoming horse, but the Flesh-Eater's boot still caught him in the chest. The blow toppled him onto his back.

You son of a bitch!

By the time Andrew reclaimed his feet, the two Flesh-Eaters were a fair distance away. The crowd's eyes fell on him. "Kill them!" shouted sharp-featured and balding James Emerson, the mayor's brother and Andrew's old schoolteacher. "You've got the range!"

Andrew raised his rifle. The closer the butt got to his shoulder, the slower he moved. His heart raced. He'd never killed a man.

His gaze shifted to Sam, unmoving on the ground. Anger growled within him. His grip on his rifle tightened.

"Shoot!" someone else shouted. "Shoot him!"

His rage and their words gave energy to his efforts. He brought the butt all the way to his shoulder. He sighted the back of the head of the man holding the reins. He nearly pressed down on the trigger. He hesitated again.

"Andrew, goddamn it, kill them!" roared craggy-faced John Horne, who'd been a sergeant in the Merrill army. "We're all dead if you don't!"

Andrew tightened his finger around the trigger. He still couldn't fire.

"Shoot! Now!" a woman's voice called from the crowd.

Anger flared at the demand. Some of them had guns — why the hell couldn't they shoot? Did they want all the Flesh-Eaters' wrath to fall on *him*?

"Shoot!" James screamed. "He's getting away!"

Andrew looked back to Sam. Sam still wasn't moving. His hesitation blew away. He squeezed the trigger.

CRACK! The Flesh-Eater toppled sideways, pulling the reins with him. The horse slewed. The other Flesh-Eater dragged himself over his wounded comrade to take the reins himself.

"Again! Shoot again!"

As if I need you to tell me that!

Andrew aimed at the man's head. Too far. He shifted the rifle downward. The horse represented a much bigger target.

He squeezed the trigger. Nothing.

"Shitfire!" Andrew hissed.

"What are you waiting for?" someone demanded. "Kill him!"

This was too much. "It's empty!" Andrew roared. His words silenced the crowd. He yanked the ammunition tube out of the rifle butt and reached toward his coat for his cartridge box.

Horne rushed forward. "Use mine!" Andrew chambered one of the older man's rounds and pulled the trigger.

He missed. The Flesh-Eater disappeared into the distance. The townsfolk groaned, but Andrew had more immediate concerns.

He rushed over to Sam. As Andrew got close, Sam moved. "Damnation," he moaned.

Thank the Good Lord!

Andrew knelt by his fallen friend. "You all right?"

Sam winced and nodded. "Hurts like hell, but I think I'll live." His eyes narrowed. "You get the bastard?"

Andrew's stomach churned. "No."

The magnitude of what happened hit him. Men were calling for horses, but the survivor had too much of a head start. He'd get back to the fort.

He'd tell his bossman what had happened.

———————

"I'D SAY we give them Taylor," James said from the front of the room. "It's his fault all this happened. Hell, he likely *killed* that son of a bitch. Blame him and we *might* survive."

The men, both those from Carroll Town proper and from surrounding homesteads, crowded into the large building that served as both a meeting place for the town council and a courtroom. Lit only by the caged flames of kerosene lanterns, the room stank of tension and fear.

Andrew stood in the rear with Sam, who still winced when he moved. Nobody asked for his opinion. *Thank the Good Lord.*

"The hell with that," Taylor's burly father Taylor Sr. growled from the front of the crowd. His blunt face glowed with anger. The wart beneath his left eye seemed even bigger. He glared at James, then Arnold. "You saw what the son of a bitch was doing to *your goddamn daughter.* At least my son isn't a goddamned *coward* —"

Arnold flinched. "What Taylor did was admirable." He paused. "But he might well have gotten us all killed."

The mayor glanced at the younger Taylor, who stood scowling in the corner. Taylor glared at him. James glared back.

"Andrew, what do you think?" asked skinny Jack Welborn, a cousin of the elder Taylor who'd known Andrew's father when he was mayor.

Damn it.

Many gazes fell on Andrew. Just because Pa was mayor once didn't mean *he* had something to say. He forced himself to at least not scowl. "Well," he began. "We're in trouble, aren't we?"

James frowned. "Thank you for that unique observation. Do you have anything helpful you'd like to contribute?"

Andrew's fingers closed into a frustrated fist. "How much food we got?"

"Barely enough to last until the next harvest," Arnold said. "And what we get from the fields won't last."

"I don't suppose you're suggesting we give all our reserves to the Flesh-Eaters," James interrupted.

Andrew shook his head. "I mean, couldn't we hide the food and us outside of town? They might just burn the houses."

"And they'll burn the fields. We *still* starve. And it'll be hard to hide from their dirigibles."

"Perhaps someone could palaver with the Flesh-Eaters," Arnold suggested. "They could tell them this was all an accident, come to some kind of arrangement —"

"The surviving one's got a bullet in him," James interrupted. "The

Flesh-Eaters aren't stump-stupid. And what kind of arrangement would they accept? Handing Taylor over would be the least of it. They'll want even *more* tribute, and we can't pay what they wanted the first time." He fell silent for a moment. "Hell, they might even impose direct control. You want this town crawling with their goddamn deacons? You want their officers taking our land and making us their *cattle*?"

Arnold's jaw worked. "At least it's worth a try." He turned to the rest of the crowd. "What do you all think?"

Thomas Daley stepped forward. He was a little older than Andrew and had red hair, one of the few in Carroll Town who did. "This is fucking stupid!" His words raised a dull roar. "Two of them are dead. They'll want to set an example. I say we fight."

"This isn't like getting a posse together to run down some bandits," John interrupted. "The Flesh-Eaters outnumber us thousands to one. Even if we *could* threaten them, they'll bring in Grendel. Grendel! A man whose lowest privates carry *repeaters*. Grendel'll come just like he did when he threw down the Merrills. We'll all die."

Andrew swallowed. Repeaters. They looked like rifles, but fired much faster and farther. A common rifle fit a few rounds into its ammunition tube, but a repeater had *magazines*. A whole army carrying these would destroy all before them unless their enemies buried them in bodies. And Carroll Town didn't have those.

Thomas wheeled on John. "They're going to kill us anyway. Might as well at least hurt the sons of bitches instead of begging for mercy we won't get."

Someone cleared their throat. The group's attention fell on Eric Tan, who'd come to the town when the Merrills had fallen. Eric had a round face, amber skin, and angular eyes, something even more peculiar than Thomas's red hair. "How about this?" Eric asked. "I'll go and talk to the Flesh-Eaters." He gestured toward a leg crippled in some long-ago war he refused to discuss. "If they kill me, it's not like I'm much use anyway."

"Don't say that," Arnold said weakly. Despite himself, Andrew had to agree. Eric wasn't much of a hunter or a field-worker, but he *was* a decent barber.

"Send him," Taylor's father said. "It's not like we have anything to lose."

The crowd muttered its agreement.

"Why don't you go?" James demanded. "Perhaps they'll take the father instead of the son."

Horror erupted across the younger Taylor's face. The elder Taylor narrowed his eyes thoughtfully. More muttering broke out. Many opposed fighting the Flesh-Eaters — the word "suicide" came up a fair bit — and supported negotiations. Others — mostly around Andrew's age — didn't.

Andrew grit his teeth. He didn't cotton to cravenly giving up other townsfolk, no matter the stakes. "All right." Andrew raised his voice. The noise in the room tapered off. "The Flesh-Eaters are bastards, we know that. If we send Taylor's pa with them, what's to stop them from killing him anyway? If they want anyone, they'll ask. Why give them ideas?"

James leaned forward, locking eyes with Andrew. "It'd show our sincerity. You've got a lot to learn if you think dealing with this kind of folk's easy." He glared at Andrew as if he were cutting up in class. "Besides, we wouldn't be in this pickle if you'd done *what* I told you *when* I told you."

Before Andrew could react, Arnold intervened. "If you ever want to be a leader like your father when he lived —" he showed far more gumption than he had with the Flesh-Eater emissary — "you'll need to know sometimes you have to make sacrifices."

The word "sacrifices" got Andrew thinking. "Why don't *you* go? You're the mayor. They'd be more likely to listen to you than folk they've never seen before."

Some people in the crowd gasped. James purpled with rage. Arnold's jaw worked silently. "That's…that's a good idea."

James's eyes bulged even wider. Andrew smiled. He'd put the older man in his place — and his jackass brother besides.

The jackass brother, however, wasn't out of the fight yet. "Why should we listen to this *greenhorn*? If he'd made sure he'd had enough ammunition, we wouldn't have this problem."

"Greenhorn?" Andrew spat. "How many rippers have *you* killed?"

"Just one." James paused. "But that doesn't make you any less a failure."

Andrew saw red. Before he could retort, Arnold stepped in. "Greenhorn or not, he's got a good idea." He looked at Eric. "We'll leave tomorrow, first light."

"I HATE IT," Andrew said, shutting the front door behind him. The smell of burning wood and cooking meat engulfed him. "Just because Pa was mayor don't mean I know everything. Why don't they bother Arnold as much? He's got the blasted job."

"Probably because this whole situation started when Arnold tried to negotiate," Ma said, looking up from the stove on which she and Sarah prepared cuts of ripper. Sweat shone in her silver-streaked blonde hair. "Young as you are, you've got the Sutter name, and your father was mayor when times were good. Folk *remember* that."

"Thanks." He scowled. "And I've got more of a backbone than that bastard —"

"Andrew!"

"But it's true!" Andrew ignored the guilt from cursing in front of his mother. "James wanted to give Taylor to the Flesh-Eaters! And he *listened!*"

He looked around the room. What might they have to buy off the Flesh-Eaters? There was a brass kerosene lamp. A shelf of books, old and worn. Someone with greater resources than Carroll Town might be able to use *Introductory Mining Engineering*. They even owned a painting of the river before the drought had dried it.

Andrew's family was among the richest in Carroll Town. They owned grain fields by the river, a real house that kept out the wind and, out back, chicken coops. Although little feed meant no eggs in a right while, the chickens could be eaten if the alternative was starvation and given to the Flesh-Eaters if the alternative was massacre.

Other folk weren't so blessed. They worked fields belonging to others, lived hand-to-mouth in shacks, carefully measured out their stored grain and hoped it lasted until the next harvest. He scowled. Trying to buy off the Flesh-Eaters wouldn't work.

Maybe Ma would have an idea. "Why don't they ask you for advice?" He looked at Sarah. "You're his kid too."

"I think we both know the answer to that," Sarah replied pointedly. She turned away from the stove. Annoyance crossed her face. "Besides, you didn't mind being the mayor's son when Cassie wanted to hear about the time Pa and the others helped the Carsons fight the Lees, or when they killed those big wolves."

Andrew reddened. Sarah knowing was bad enough — he did not want his mother finding out.

The corners of Sarah's mouth turned slightly upward. "She didn't ask me." Her smile broadened. "I wonder why?"

"Andrew, what's she talking about?" his mother cut in.

Andrew tensed. "Nothing."

Sarah continued. "She wanted to know all about what Pa did, and she thought the Jacksons's barn was the best place to —"

"Andrew!" his mother erupted.

"Gee, *thanks* Sarah," Andrew hissed. He looked straight at her. "You jealous?"

Sarah made a face. "Eww. No." She shrugged. "Be glad her pa doesn't know about that, little brother, or he'd be showing up here with a shotgun."

Andrew bristled at "little brother" — she was only a few minutes older — but he *was* glad Cassie's father didn't know. If he disliked her, he wouldn't have spent a couple of hours getting acquainted with her in the barn. But he didn't like the idea of getting *hitched*.

He shook his head. "I assume you want to know what *happened* at the meeting." Both his mother and sister leaned forward. Andrew told them about the plan to send Arnold and Eric to palaver with the Flesh-Eaters.

"You really think that's going to *work*?" Sarah asked, face pale.

"It can't hurt," Ma said. "Considering the alternative."

CARROLL TOWN PREPARES
FOR WAR

Andrew watched the mayor and Eric ride out beneath the sun rising over the white arching gate. James's words about how it was his fault the Flesh-Eaters now threatened Carroll Town still stung. It felt right he be there when the two men set off toward the Old World blacktop road. Though much had eroded away and been patched with crushed stone, it still provided the best route.

The men did not return that afternoon. Nor did they return that evening, though James spent half the night watching.

When the men did not return the next day, James and John called the men together for war.

"IT LOOKS like we'll have to fight," John said. Andrew groaned. So did many other men gathered beneath the mooring tower in the town square. "We don't have the kit to attack the fort and we're not fighting them in Carroll Town. We'll meet them where the Old World road crosses the arroyo."

Good idea. The crumbled blacktop cut between two hills before crossing the rust-gnawed bridge over the stony gash that ran with water after it rained. If the Flesh-Eaters stayed on it, they'd hit a choke point. If they moved off, they'd be marching uphill and visible.

"The Flesh-Eaters'll focus on the road and the hills. They weren't much for subtlety back when I rode with the Merrills." He paused. "However, the arroyo's dry. We'll defend it too."

Andrew had been to the arroyo before. Twenty feet at its deepest, it grew shallower as it rose behind the hills. If left unguarded, the enemy could march into their rear.

"How'll we know when they're coming?" the elder Taylor asked.

"And what about the women and children?" his son added.

"Aye." Andrew did not want Ma and Sarah falling into the man-eaters' hands. Nor anyone else, for that matter.

"We know where the fort is," John replied. "James has been keeping an eye on it. An infantry column takes a spell to get anywhere, and we should have time to ride out to meet them. About the women and the children, we can always send riders looking for the Merrill."

Andrew raised an eyebrow. Alonzo, James Merrill's son, still harried the Flesh-Eaters from the high plains. Perhaps he could do more than serve as a refuge. "If we can find them, why not try to bring them here? The Merrills would have a better shot at licking the Flesh-Eaters than we would by our lonesome."

John shook his head. "*If* we find them in time. And we don't know where they are, if they will help us, or if they *can* help us." Andrew gulped. "So here's the plan. We split up. I'll command the gap between the hills, while Clarence Jones will hold the hill to my right. Jack Welborn will hold the hill on my left. James will command the arroyo. When I'm through, we'll divide you up. Any questions?"

Andrew couldn't think of any, but a young man with curly brown hair and bright blue eyes raised his hand. It was tall and skinny Elijah Welborn, Jack's son and Taylor's cousin. He was a sharp one, so it'd pay to listen.

"How long do you reckon we've got to prepare?" Elijah asked. "If we've got time, we should lay traps."

John nodded. "What kind of traps do you have in mind?"

"Well, we could start with holes with jagged metal on the bottom, nails and the like. *Dirty* jagged metal. The outhouses will be right help-ful." He smiled, a thin scar on the right side of his mouth widening his grin.

John laughed. "I like the way you think. We'll need shovels." He paused. "The ground out there is hard. In the old days, they used giant powder to get anything done, but we used the last of ours fighting the Carsons."

Andrew smiled. That was Pa's doing. Bury the giant powder — something the more learned called "dynamite" — and trick the Carsons into marching onto it. *That* ended their scheme to carve an empire out of the imploding Merrill realm.

"Besides shovels, we'll need flammables," Elijah added. "If we set fires, the smoke might hide us and disorient the enemy."

John nodded. "Aye. I've used that trick myself."

Right clever, Eli. Put both together and the enemy would stumble blindly through traps, all while eating bullets. Elijah often found excuses to visit the Sutter home. Sarah denied any interest, but her vehemence confirmed Andrew's suspicions.

You'd make an acceptable brother-in-law, if we don't all die.

"Any other suggestions?" John asked. A moment passed. "Good. Everyone get home. Gather all your ammunition and anything that can be used as a weapon, as well as any shovels and flammables. Come back here and let me know what you've got. We'll need everything we have and then some."

Andrew left the square with the rest of the men. He didn't make it ten feet before he heard a young woman crying.

Lily sat on the steps of her father's spacious home on the edge of the square. Sarah sat beside her, arm around her shoulder. Lily wept despondently. Sarah handed her a handkerchief so the younger woman could wipe her reddened eyes.

Lily's desolation reminded Andrew of Pa's death, how painful that was and how long it was until the tears stopped. And *his* father had been only thrown by a horse and broken his neck. Arnold likely suffered far worse.

Andrew sat on the steps next to Lily, opposite Sarah. He put his arm around her.

"Thanks," Lily said through her tears.

Then Taylor appeared. Andrew ceded his spot. The bigger youth nodded and took Andrew's place. Andrew sat a step below Lily, near Sarah's feet.

Andrew did not know how long it had been before someone coughed, jerking his attention away from the despondent young woman. He looked up. James stood there.

"Thank you," he said. Though his expression was hard, there was softness in his eyes. "I'll handle this from here. You boys get back to getting supplies."

Asshole. Your brother's dead and your niece is grieving.

Taylor glared at the older man. James stared right back, not blinking. Taylor looked away first, then rose and left.

James sat on the steps where Taylor had been. Lily hugged her uncle. He stroked her hair. "There, there," the older man said kindly, his face softening along with his eyes. He turned to Andrew. The hardness reclaimed his face. "You've got supplies to check on too. Your sister and I can look after Lily."

"Don't *you* have work to do?" Andrew accused.

"I went through my kit earlier. And I've got kin to look after. You don't."

Andrew opened his mouth to retort, but Sarah sighed. "Andrew. Andrew, listen to him."

He sighed but obeyed. "All right."

NOT LONG AFTER sunrise the next morning, James rode back into town. The Flesh-Eaters were leaving the fort. Their horsemen chased him away, but he reckoned there were at least one hundred and fifty infantry. The enemy moved south along the ancient road, heading straight for Carroll Town.

Andrew's heart sank. No time to build any but the poorest defenses. The only good news was the Flesh-Eaters only had infantry and cavalry. No dirigibles, no big guns.

Though he couldn't keep the grimness from his face, John took up his position beneath the mooring tower. "Men of Carroll Town. We all know the odds're against us. The enemy is numerous and fierce, well-trained and well-armed." He paused. "But they fight because other men make them or because they believe their false god smiles down on them. *We*, on the other hand, are fighting for our homes and our *lives*." He paused again. "Even if we lose, we'll win. We're buying time for our women and children to find safety elsewhere."

Andrew swallowed. The riders looking for Alonzo Merrill found tracks of what might have been a raiding party but no army to defend Carroll Town or shelter the non-fighters. The women and children would follow the tracks and hopefully find the Merrills before their food and water ran out. Better a slim chance than none.

"Yes," Andrew said aloud. The eyes of those assembled fell on him. *Oh shit.*

The townsfolk would no doubt expect him to give a rousing speech. Andrew scrabbled for words. "I agree with everything he just said." He forced the quavering from his voice. "We *do* have more to fight for than those bastards." He paused. "Those ugly, man-eating savage *bastards*."

John laughed. "You're just like your old man." That didn't bother Andrew this time. John returned to the crowd. "Remember the plan. Don't let fear fuck it up."

The men who would fight formed up in front of John and James near the gate. The women and children remained close to the square. The horses were divvied up. There were barely enough to carry everyone in opposite directions, even with many doubling up.

"We move out in five minutes," John ordered. "Say your goodbyes."

The thought this would be the last time he saw his mother and sister nearly sent Andrew to his knees. He grit his teeth and forced himself to remain upright. His stomach churned.

All around, the men embraced their womenfolk and youngest sons. Much weeping broke out.Andrew walked over to his mother and sister like a man going to the noose. They freely wept. Tears stung Andrew's eyes. He blinked them back.

I'm the man of the house. I can't cry, not in front of them.

The trio held each other for a long time.

Andrew felt the sudden urge to confess. If this was the last time he'd see his family again, he didn't want anything to go unsaid.

"Sarah," he began, pulling away from his mother and sister. "Do you remember that doll you had when we were seven? The one the pikeys brought, the one with the red hair?"

Sarah looked oddly at Andrew. "Yes. That's a queer thing to ask right now."

"Well…" Andrew paused. "It wasn't Taylor who'd filched it. It was me."

Despite the gravity of the situation, Sarah laughed. "I figured that out right quick."

Someone tapped Andrew on the shoulder. It was Cassie, her brown eyes wet with tears. She pulled him into her arms, hard. Andrew hugged her back.

As he and Cassie embraced, Andrew felt eyes on him. Vernon Wells, Cassie's tall father, looked appraisingly at Andrew. Appraisingly, nothing more. If Vernon knew what Andrew and his daughter had done, he didn't show any disapproval. A quick glance showed Elijah talking to Sarah and Ma.

Andrew returned his attention to Cassie. The two held onto each other for a long time. Then they were interrupted.

"Now," John's voice rang out. "Now we ride!"

Andrew forced himself to pull away.

"Goo…" Andrew's voice failed him. He swallowed. "Goodbye."

Cassie started crying again. He wanted to hold her, to comfort her, but the men were mounting their horses.

He turned away from Cassie. He took one step, then forced himself to take another. His mother and sister receded from his vision. Cassie moved to follow him. Her father stopped her.

"Go to your grandfather." He pointed at a one-legged old man with the women and children. Tom Wells would make a poor infantryman, but he could ride and help protect the ones who couldn't fight. Cassie cried, but obeyed.

"Andy!" Sam called from atop his horse. "Up here!"

"Thanks," Andrew said, climbing up behind his friend. He'd given his gelding Clinton to his mother and Sarah for their escape.

The mounted men streamed out beneath the blazing sun, heading for war.

ONSLAUGHT

As the dust column announcing the coming Flesh-Eaters rose high, the militia spread out. Most marched up the hill, shovels in their hands to at least dig *something*. Andrew and several other young men under James's command descended into the arroyo behind the hills, beneath the skeletal and rust-streaked Old World bridge. They hunkered behind a heap of rocks and waited.

The distant, quiet, insistent tramp of the marching Flesh-Eaters thundered in Andrew's ears. Despite the bridge's shade, the burning sun and Andrew's own fear pulled beads of sweat from all over his body. He unscrewed the top of his canteen and took a swig. "See anything?" he called up to Thomas, one of the two atop the ancient bridge.

Thomas looked down from his perch and wiped the sweat from his red head. "Nope."

Andrew's gut clenched. When they came, he'd have to kill again. Elsewise, *he'd* die.

He grit his teeth. He'd hesitated before. *That* let a Flesh-Eaters escape. *That* may well have doomed everyone. Not again. Never again.

But if the enemy did not attempt to flank the hills, if they stubbornly pushed up into the townsmen's teeth, it would be a spell before Andrew had to fight them. He and the others would sit in the gash in the ground and *wait*.

Of course, if the others were doing the fighting, the others were doing the dying. Andrew swallowed. He didn't want to die.

Distant rifle fire shattered the quiet. Andrew jumped, the sweat from his forehead running into his eyes. The fight was starting *already*? He wiped his eyes with a bandana and took another swig from his canteen.

Elijah fidgeted beside Andrew. "I hope John didn't bollix it leaving us down here."

Andrew shook his head. He was no general, but he recognized John's wisdom. If the enemy came and the arroyo wasn't guarded, they could attack the militia on the hills from two directions.

Elijah rose. "Someone should go see if anyone's coming. We might not be needed here."

Andrew could see his side. If they joined their rifles with the men on the hills, they might make a difference. If the Flesh-Eaters took the hills, they were all dead.

But John was a real soldier. And if Elijah went investigating abis-selfa and ran into Flesh-Eaters, he'd die alone without doing jack shit. Although their chances of returning alive were right small, the man his sister fancied wasn't going to die on him.

Andrew shook his head. "No." He looked away, terminating the argument.

"All right." Elijah rose. "I'll be back in two shakes of a lamb's tail."

"No, you won't," James interrupted. He locked eyes with Elijah, using all the intimidation skills decades of teaching had imparted. Elijah knelt back behind the barricade.

"Let's hope they don't send their fanatics our way," Elijah grumbled.

The mention of the fanatics enlarged the lump in Andrew's throat. The Flesh-Eaters had drafted Jacob Burns two years before. He'd deserted and had run home. Before the Flesh-Eaters dragged him off again — along with two more young men for harboring him — he'd said there was *another* Flesh-Eater army. The regular forces would pin the enemy down and let the crazy ones tear into them. The fanatics believed the souls of everyone they killed hand-to-hand would serve them in the hereafter. Andrew reached again for his canteen, then shook his head. He might need it later.

"Don't you worry. They probably don't think Carroll Town's worth it."

Down the arroyo, a horse whinnied. Horseshoes clicked on stone. James's gaze snapped toward the sound. "They're here!" He ducked behind the barricade. "Get down!"

The young men obeyed. Seconds later, three men wearing Flesh-Eater colors beneath their dusters skulked around the bend four hundred feet ahead. All carried short-barreled carbines. Andrew's hands trembled on his rifle. He pressed lower to the ground.

"Wait," James whispered.

Andrew didn't need the encouragement. The trio drew closer.

"At them!" James shouted. His rifle cracked. The older men fired, followed by the younger men. Bullets buzzed down the arroyo like a swarm of lead bees. White smoke gathered around the defenders. One Flesh-Eaters went down. The others fell back, firing as they moved.

Andrew aimed for one Flesh-Eater's chest. His hands trembled around his rifle. He ground his teeth. He'd already killed one man. What was one more?

A bullet threw sparks inches from Andrew's head. If the Flesh-Eaters weren't killed, they'd hit one of the townsfolk sooner or later. The people whom Andrew had known his entire life...

If only they'd brought their horses! A panicking, wounded horse could wreak havoc among the Flesh-Eaters. Then it would be the horse's fault, not his. He sighted on a Flesh-Eater. His finger tightened on the trigger. But he couldn't pull it.

That Flesh-Eater fired his carbine. Elijah toppled. Hot gore spattered Andrew's clothing and face. Andrew remembered the ripper, but this wasn't a ripper. It was a *man!* The man Sarah fancied, the man Andrew wanted to protect! An echo of the pain his sister would feel stabbed him in the chest.

Elijah's corpse slumped beside Andrew. Bone and brain decorated the ground around his head.

The Flesh-Eater laughed. The sound echoed in Andrew's head over and over again. The man raised his gun, hunting for more targets.

Andrew's eyes bulged. *Not again!*

He fired. Thunder cracked. A matchstick smell filled his nose. The bullet punched through the Flesh-Eater's mouth. The man's lower jaw hinged low, chin nearly touching his throat. Streaming blood framed shattered teeth. He screamed.

The bread and ripper bacon Andrew ate that morning returned to his mouth. He swallowed, forcing it down. He aimed his rifle again. He'd silence that screaming forever.

CRACK!

His shot struck the man's breastbone, slamming him into the arroyo wall. He slid down, tracking blood on the red-brown stone. The surviving Flesh-Eater ducked around the bend. One last shot buzzed past.

Andrew repressed a triumphant snarl. They'd stopped the bastards! A small voice in the back of his mind reminded him they'd killed Elijah, but he forced it away.

Maybe they'd come out of this alive. If the Flesh-Eater flanking move was so pathetic, their attack on the hilltop might fail too and…

Then something else whined overhead, deeper and louder than bullets and lingering on the air.

An explosion cracked above them. The bridge shook. Metal and asphalt rained down. Another explosion bloomed before the barricade. Andrew ducked behind his sheltering rock, but a piece of hot metal clipped across his cheek. Somebody screamed beside him.

More whining. Something exploded behind the defenders. More heat and flying metal. More screams. Andrew pressed himself harder against the ground. Somehow he'd survived this one unscathed, but the next one would almost certainly kill him.

"Mortars!" someone shouted.

Andrew had heard of mortars, but he'd never seen them in action before. Now he wished he hadn't.

Bugles rang. Andrew's gaze leaped to the sound. His heart sank. New Flesh-Eaters poured out of the smoke.

These men carried sabers and pistols instead of rifles. They wore uniforms brighter than the rest. As they got closer, Andrew could see scarred-over ritual cuts along their cheekbones from their noses to their ears. Among them was a man in black robes with a white collar looking just as mad as the rest.

The fanatics!

A hard, fecal stench from Andrew's left stung his nose. Something large and wet stained the back of blond-haired Ken Daniels's jeans. At least Ken was still *alive*. Others lay mangled behind the barricade. Blood pooled on the stone around them.

"Son of a bitch!" James shouted. The older man, bloodied but still hale, fired into the oncoming swarm. Gunfire replied. As the bullets whined overhead, Andrew thumbed bullets from his cartridge box into his rifle before risking a momentary glimpse above the barricade.

The fanatics were almost on top of them, their war-cries and pistol shots gouging Andrew's ears. Andrew emptied his rifle. Amid the smoke, Flesh-Eaters fell. *Good.*

All this was too much for Ken. He ran. "Damn it!" James screamed. "Get back here!" But Ken was gone.

James dropped another fanatic. Something moved on the bridge overhead. Andrew's gaze snapped upward. How could anyone be alive up there?

Thomas tumbled from the bridge onto the arroyo floor. His rifle was gone. Gaping wounds stitched his entire left side. Blood soaked his red hair. A shard of metal emerged from his left eye. His appearance set Andrew's stomach roiling. He landed hard on his hale side and groaned.

Son of a bitch! Andrew rushed over to him. "Tommy!" he snarled. "Tommy, can you hear me?"

All Andrew got was a weak moan. At least he still lived. *For now.*

"Sutter, get him the hell out of here!" James screamed. "I'll slow them down!"

Andrew nodded frantically. He pulled Thomas's right arm over his shoulder and dragged him away from the barricade to where the arroyo curved out of sight. Bullets crackled. Thomas jerked against Andrew as one found him.

As they approached the curve, a thought occurred to Andrew. How was *James* going to get out of there? He looked back over Thomas's shoulder. James knelt behind the barricade as the first fanatics surged toward him. Rather than rise up to meet them, the old teacher pulled a round, bumpy object from his coat.

Hell's bells! Where'd he get a grenade?

The explosion sent the oncoming fanatics tumbling. Most did not rise again. One fanatic lay bloodied before the heap of shrapnel-scarred rocks, not far from the twitching wet meat that used to be James.

Andrew snarled. Before he could put Tommy down to finish the wounded enemy, a bullet nipped his left ear.

"Run," Thomas whispered in Andrew's ear. His breath was hot and wet. "Too late!"

Andrew obeyed. The ground rose as the flat lands behind the hills opened up. The harsh stink of spent gunpowder grew stronger.

"Okay, we're safe now," Andrew babbled. He looked for a safe spot to put Thomas down. "John might have people to spare. We'll be able to keep them down in the arroyo and —"

Men spilled down the hill to Andrew's left, some not even armed. They ran toward where they'd left their horses. Far from being able to help Andrew and Thomas, the other townsfolk were *routing*. Mortar rounds exploded among the few holding the line.

War cries and invocations of the Howling God burst into Andrew's ears. A wave of Flesh-Eater fanatics crested the hill. They streamed from the smoke, tearing into the retreating men like rippers or wolves. Dust from so many churning boots soon shrouded the hilltop.

One fleeing man turned and shot a hairy fanatic in the head. Another fanatic further up replied with his pistol. The townsman fell to his knees. The fanatic loped down the hill, drawing his saber to finish him off.

Despite his wounded companion's weight, Andrew managed to fire from the hip. His bullet caught the oncoming enemy in the thigh and blew the man's leg out from under him. He tumbled to a stop at Andrew's feet. His grin revealed a row of sharply filed teeth.

"He's mine," the man laughed. "He's —"

Andrew silenced him with a boot. Teeth and nose splintered. The fanatic's laugh turned into a scream.

Before Andrew could put Tommy down, a mortar shell whined overhead. It exploded somewhere to the right. Andrew landed several yards away, atop the corpse of a townsman he didn't recognize. A bullet had torn away the dead man's cheek and most of his skull, exposing teeth and gray brain matter the first of the flies had already found.

Andrew looked away from the ruined head before his breakfast could make a return appearance.

Another body landed on top of him. The impact jolted his mouth open and squeezed his stomach entirely too much. He upchucked all over the corpse's face. The flies would love that.

A chorus of joyful howls erupted from the hill above. More Flesh-Eaters were coming.

His only hope of staying off the menu was to play dead.

FOR A LONG TIME, the crunch of the earth beneath the Flesh-Eaters' hobnailed boots and their bloodthirsty marching songs growled past Andrew. He stayed stock-still. The heat, the stench of his puke, and the buzzing flies oppressed him. Hopefully none of the Flesh-Eaters would stop for a snack.

Then no more came. Andrew didn't move. There might still be enemy stragglers.

Minutes passed. The buzzing and the stink grew worse. One fly landed in the puke and flew straight at Andrew's left eye.

Andrew squeezed his eyelid shut and slapped at his face reflexively. He froze. If any enemy remained, they'd know someone was still alive. They'd come and stick him and that'd be the end…

To hell with that. He wasn't going to sit and wait to be dinner. He wriggled out from under the corpse and jumped to his feet, gripping his rifle tightly.

No man moved amid the slaughterhouse below the hill. But there were plenty of corpses, mostly the Carroll Town militia. Blankets of flies seethed over them. Vultures and other carrion-birds circled overhead.

A pair of crows dropped from the sky onto Thomas's corpse. He hadn't died from his wounds. In addition to the number the mortar had done to him, a knife wound grinned across his throat. Mercy or murder, Andrew couldn't tell.

Andrew rushed at the birds. "Get away!" The crows flew away, croaking their displeasure. His anger getting the best of him, he threw a handful of rocks after them.

Andrew looked down at his friend's corpse. Maybe he still had ammunition. He knelt and rifled through the other man's pockets. A cartridge box with some bullets inside. Good.

Someone moved to Andrew's right. He spun, raising his rifle. If it was some Flesh-Eater, he'd blow the bastard to hell and…

"Andy!" Sam gasped. He limped forward, dragging his left leg. He'd lost his rifle, but was still alive.

"Sam!" Andrew shouted. He rushed over and helped his friend stand up straight.

"Thank the Good Lord you're all right, Andy."

"You okay?"

"No. I was up on the damn hill when the fanatics bowled us over. Hurt my leg. They kept going. I played possum until they were gone." He broke down crying. "I shammed while the others died. Damn yellow coward I am!"

"Sam," Andrew said. A lump rose in his throat. Tears began forming in his eyes. "Sam! That's what I did! If we hadn't shammed, they'd have killed us both!"

Sam looked at Andrew for a moment. Then he looked down. "Sorry," he muttered.

"No problem. Let's *get*. Maybe we can find a horse."

That was a *big* maybe. If the survivors of the battle didn't get them, the Flesh-Eaters would. But Sam was a mess. He'd need to do *something*.

Andrew pulled Sam's left arm over his shoulder. Sam gave his injured leg a yank. Andrew winced. Hopefully they wouldn't need to amputate.

The two left the field of slaughter. The road was probably full of Flesh-Eaters, but there were other ways back to Carroll Town. Moving slowly, they crossed a wide expanse of stony ground.

Something moved ahead. Andrew raised his rifle, letting Sam's arm drop from his shoulder. If it was some Flesh-Eater straggler, he'd make him pay!

Ken emerged from what must've been a gully. "Andrew? Sam? Oh thank God! You're —"

Before Ken could finish, Andrew punched him in the face. He staggered. Andrew lunged, fist raised for another blow.

"Andy," Sam shouted. "Andy, stop it!"

Andrew ignored Sam's entreaties. "They're all dead!" He struck Ken again. "If he hadn't goddamn run, maybe they wouldn't be!" He raised his fist once more.

"Please," Ken begged. "Please, I'm sorry. They were shooting —"

"Andrew," Sam emphasized. "We shouldn't fight. Let's just get home."

Andrew looked from his friend to the cowering man wiping the blood from his nose. Slowly, he lowered his fist. "Fine," he spat.

They probably didn't have a home to return to anyway.

ANDREW'S JAW dropped when the trio arrived at the Carroll Town gate. The women and children who were *supposed* to have fled filled the street beyond. All were dirty. Some were bloody. Only about a third were left. There were a couple younger men, bloodied and unarmed.

"What the hell?" Andrew gasped.

Andrew ran through the gate, Ken half-dragging Sam behind him. Andrew spotted Sarah. Dirt streaked her straw-colored hair. She held a bloody rag to her forehead. Andrew's heart twisted at the sight of his distressed twin. He rushed over to her. They embraced fiercely. When Andrew pulled away, blood and dirt stained Sarah's dress.

"You all right? What the hell happened?"

"Flesh-Eater horsemen." She swallowed. Her eyes were wide in her thin face. "We ran right into them." She paused. "We…we're all that got away. The Flesh-Eaters killed or took the rest."

Andrew wondered which was worse. Jacob had described the rituals in the Flesh-Eaters' forts. The bastards believed they gained the power of those they ate. They also viewed those they defeated as theirs to do with as they wished. Andrew knew what that meant for women.

"Where's Ma?" Andrew demanded. "Where's Cassie?"

"Ma's all right. She's helping hurt folk. We've got them in Eric's barbershop. Cassie's back there, too." Sarah drew a breath. "Where's Elijah?"

Andrew drew a breath. If he told Sarah the truth, she'd know Elijah's death was his fault. His mouth worked. What could he say?

"He's dead, isn't he?" Andrew nodded. Sarah's jaw trembled. Tears began filling her eyes. "No." She buried her face in Andrew's shoulder. "No." He held her for a long moment. Her tears soaked into his duster. She pulled away and shook her head. She swallowed. "Come...come on. I'll take you to Cassie."

Andrew, Sam, and Ken followed Sarah to the town square. Cassie sat propped up against the front wall of the barbershop in the cooler combined shadows of the overhang and mooring tower. Her blue dress was torn in several places and soaked in blood. She held a bloody rag to the side of her head.

Andrew rushed over. "What'd they do to you?"

"He killed Grandpa," Cassie moaned. "Tried to take me." She dissolved into tears.

"A Flesh-Eater horseman killed her grandpa with a sword," Sarah explained. Her eyes still glimmered, unshed tears thickening her voice. "He grabbed her. He got her on his horse, but she got free." She gestured to the other woman. "It was a rough landing."

Sarah knelt beside Cassie. She took away the bloody rag and tore a piece from her own dress. She handed it to Cassie, who put it up to her head.

"She *got* him," Cassie spat. "Sarah got the *bastard*."

Andrew raised an eyebrow. "You killed him? Good job!"

Sarah closed her eyes. "*Thanks*." She examined Cassie's head. "Bleeding's near stopped. I might be able to stitch this up." Then she looked at Andrew. "You're a *mess*. What happened?"

"We got whipped. What else is there to say?" That reminded him. "Where're the damned Flesh-Eaters? They should be on top of us by now."

"An army can't move as fast as a single man," Sam said. "Maybe they've still got a ways to go."

That was true, but the enemy had gotten a head start. And helping Sam back took time. Andrew's gut clenched. "Sarah," Andrew babbled. "Sarah, they'll be here any minute. Everybody needs to get out of here and —"

"And go where?" Sarah demanded, voice rising. "We tried! Most of us got killed!"

There was anger in her voice and on her face, but her hands trembled. He didn't blame her.

"Into the houses, then! Or out of the town, but not where you met the horsemen. There are places to hide, rocks —"

The whistling of a mortar interrupted.

INSPECTION

Surrounded by six black-jacketed soldiers of the elite Obsidian Guard and with his pterosaur Alrekr perched on his shoulder, Grendel, lord of Sejera and first lord of the Northlands, strode beneath the concrete archway into Fort Brooks. Jasper Clark, one-eyed overlord of the Flesh-Eating Legion, waited with some troops in the courtyard beyond. The bald cannibal rested his left hand atop a ripper. A black and crimson Flesh-Eater dirigible floated nearby, moored in front of the blazing sun. It cast a long but welcome shadow.

"Welcome, my lord," Clark said, a smile splitting his wide face. Though he spoke formally, his drawl betrayed his mountain origins. Despite the heat and his armor, little perspiration shone on his head. Meanwhile, sweat gathered beneath Grendel's gray-edged dark hair. His black frock coat and trousers had an unfortunate tendency to suck up heat. He grit his teeth against the discomfort while his vassal spun pleasantries.

"It is a great honor for us to host you," Clark continued. "When you have visited our forts, I would like to entertain you at Jacinto."

Grendel smiled back. The expression tugged at the long scar the battle with the Iron Horse had carved into his face eight years before. The smile lapped at his gray eyes, but did not swamp them. "It is a great honor to visit," he rumbled. "However, I have urgent work to do and must refuse."

He checked the urge to snort. He was only here because, four years after the breaking of the main Merrill army and the death of James Merrill, the Flesh-Eaters *still* didn't fully control the old Merrill realm.

Not that Grendel intended to let them keep it, of course. There were richer lands further north, and though these badlands hosted only a few settlements clinging to the edge of the desert, men and taxes could be wrung from them. The Old World ruins — and there were more here than elsewhere — could be excavated for technological trinkets or means of war. Ultimately, they must belong to his blood — his son Havarth by Catalina Merrill, Alonzo's captive sister.

But before he could replace the Flesh-Eaters with his half-Merrill youngest, he had to kill Alonzo, to clear the way for Havarth and show his strength. Ejnar Irontooth came for his family when Father returned from reaving with many corpses and little gold. Grendel had no desire for history to repeat itself.

So when Clark began building a series of forts linked together by the expensive new telegraph and hosting even more expensive dirigibles across the Merrill raiding routes, Grendel stepped in. He had given his subordinate the necessary engineers and Norridge's bankers provided loans.

To his credit, Clark used the resources quickly and effectively. Masses of conscripts raised a chain of forts and mooring towers across the wide lands where Clark's power was weak. The northern Merrill remnants were cut off from their fellows to the south and exterminated, the survivors crucified along the roads. Dirigibles ranged ever farther south, finding more refuges to destroy. A thrust into the high plains would soon finish them.

So Grendel came to see his vassal's achievements and remind him who deserved much of the credit. He would sweep through the new forts, hobnob with the local notables, oversee the execution of some captured Merrills, ensure Clark was not tardy with the first repayment, and then return to Norridge. His subordinates Mangle and Quantrill were at loggerheads over a coal field. Coal fed the factories and the combines that allowed for greater harvests. And the disputed lands lay far too close to Norridge.

"What would you like to see first?"

"Where the dirigibles dock. Then the communications center."

Clark pointed. "You can see the mooring tower from here."

The skeletal mooring tower rose over the concrete bunkers of Fort Brooks's citadel. The dirigible's nose attached to a metal cone at the top, while a metal gangway connected the gondola hanging from beneath the balloon to the passenger platform below the cone. Chains descended from the tower, looping around huge gears. Ragged draftees guarded by Flesh-Eater soldiers stood ready to turn them.

"Want to take a closer look?"

Grendel examined the mooring tower. It resembled a smaller version of the ones in the capital, only powered by men instead of steam engines. The airship the tower hosted was also smaller — it could carry a platoon at most, while his airships could carry whole companies if not more. "How quickly can you launch, with soldiers?"

Clark smiled proudly. "Watch."

He gave orders to a nearby pair of guards. One dashed toward the tower, while the other descended the stairway into the concrete depths of the citadel.

Grendel pulled his silver pocket watch from inside his coat. Adding two seconds to accommodate the order, he began counting down how long it took to launch from a standing start.

At the orders of the guard, the conscripts manned the gear-cranks. The tower groaned. The cone atop began turning. Once the dirigible was in position, the huge engines lining its sides rumbled to life.

Horns blared throughout the fort. Armed Flesh-Eaters spilled out of the concrete barracks behind the citadel. They formed into a single file as they streamed into the great archway in the tower's base and ascended the stairway visible inside the metal skeleton. They soon crossed the gangway into the gondola.

As soon as the last soldier passed through, the gangway retracted. The dirigible's engines roared. Its enormous propellers spinning rapidly, the airship separated from the tower and headed east.

He checked his watch. The boarding and launch took five minutes from the order being given. If there were no need for troops, it could have been under way even faster.

Grendel withdrew some dried fish from a bag in his pocket and flicked it into the air. Alrekr caught it in its fanged mouth and hooted appreciatively. Grendel watched the dirigible vanish into the distance and turned to Clark.

"My bankers will be glad to know how well you used their money." Clark did not respond. Grendel frowned. Money was the sinews of war. Disdaining bankers was a fast road to defeat.

"The communications center is located below," Clark finally said. Grendel nodded. Clark led the way down the crude concrete steps into the citadel. The temperature fell as sunlight gave way to kerosene lamps. Grendel was thankful for that at least. "The communications center is on the second floor below ground," Clark continued, pointing to another stairway. "The Merrills don't have much artillery, but it's best to be safe."

Before the party descended the second set of stairs, a young boy in Flesh-Eater colors rushed from below. The guardsmen's repeaters rose. The ripper leaned forward, teeth bared. The boy abruptly halted. A telegram trembled in his hands. Clark worked his hand into the ripper's collar to restrain it.

"Stand down," Grendel ordered his own men.

The guardsmen lowered their weapons. "My lord," the boy squeaked in Jasper's direction. "A telegram from Fort Vallero."

He handed the telegram to his towering master. Clark's gaze swept across the page. His one dark eye grew wider and his gaze more intense.

"May th' Howling God et ther goddamned souls!" he roared. His rage blew away his educated façade. For a moment he was the rough coal miner Grendel knew he had been long ago. Alrekr hopped off Grendel's shoulder and hooked its claws into its master's back. As Clark raged, Grendel's curiosity stirred. Though the big man was not known for self-control, this apocalyptic wrath was a bit much.

"Hand me the message." Clark obeyed. Grendel frowned as he read the message. Apparently an insurrection had broken out not far from the fort. His frown deepened. His regime brought them peace and this was how they repaid it? He continued reading. The garrison had engaged the rebels on a series of hills. The Flesh-Eaters had triumphed as expected and were marching on Carroll Town itself.

Good. The Flesh-Eaters would make the townsfolk into an object lesson.

Then things took a turn for the worse. The telegram *claimed* a delegation from the Leaden Host had been in the area. The townsfolk deployed an Old World grenade during the fight, delaying the encirclement of the rebel force. Old World weapons belonged to the Host leaders alone, so Alexander Matthews, lord of the Leaden Host, *had* to have been aiding the Carroll Town rebels somehow. Merrill involvement was also suspected.

Grendel snorted. Though he and his top subordinates had a monopoly on Old World military equipment — vigorously enforced — he was not foolish enough to think it infallible. Some farmer probably dug the grenade out of his garden and sold it to a passing merchant, who misplaced it in Carroll Town before he could turn it in for a substantial reward. And *Alex* of all people would not undermine Grendel's laws or connive with the lineage he once helped overthrow.

"My lord," Clark began. "If it's true Matthews is aiding rebels in my lands, *especially* if he's helping the *Merrills* —"

"Alexander has been my right hand since the beginning." He left "unlike you" unspoken. "He would not be stupid enough to break the arms law just to cost you a few men, nor would he be stupid enough to consort with the Merrills."

That didn't stop Clark. "Alexander's men have been nosing around my border. They don't return absconding peasants."

Grendel frowned. The latter issue could be left to the two to work out themselves, but border incidents tended to escalate. Still, he was not going to just believe Clark's accusations. He owed his old friend that much. "To bring charges like this is a serious matter, Clark." His preferences and the threat of his wrath showed in his voice.

Clark nodded. Grendel considered his claim. It was ludicrously unlikely Alexander would attack the Flesh-Eaters, especially when he was in his capital and not close by to supervise the resulting war.

One unsettling possibility presented itself. It had been just over four years since he threw down the Merrills, the last substantial foes between the mountains, the desert, and the seas. With no significant wars to provide loot or land for his supporters to give to *their* supporters, keeping the peace had become a full-time job.

It was in Alexander's interests to keep the general peace, but *not* in the interests of his subordinates. *Their* best chance to improve their position came through war. A local commander could be stirring the pot, hoping for the chance to expand his personal domain.

Clark's accusation *could* have merit. A commander who sheltered runaways and aided rebels could generate a following on the wrong side of the border. Grendel was loath to believe an accusation leveled against his old comrade by a former enemy, but an accusation against his friend's henchmen was an entirely different matter.

And if war came between the Leaden Host and the Flesh-Eating Legion, it would likely require the presence of Grendel himself to stop it.

"I am going to investigate this personally, and I will bring my men. If most of the fort's garrison has left, the fort might be vulnerable to the Merrills."

"Do you think I..." Clark's voice trailed away. He must have remembered to whom he spoke.

"Fifty guardsmen are just outside your gate," Grendel continued. Fifty Obsidian Guard. Fifty of the finest soldiers in the Northlands. Equal to five times their number of Flesh-Eaters, if not more. "They're more than enough to handle the matter."

CARROLL TOWN FALLS

The townsfolk screamed as the first explosions erupted around the gate. The shells fell deeper into the town, smashing windows and spreading smoke. The crackle of splintering wood filled Andrew's ears. Those closer to the entrance rushed into the town square. Others ran this way and that like frightened chickens. The whine of incoming shells and the thunder of their explosions buried the townsfolk's screams.

Andrew closed his eyes and slowly forced the fear away. The enemy may well have licked the townsfolk, but even a hurt dog still had teeth. If he died, he'd take some with him.

"Sam!" Andrew shouted. His friend snapped to attention. "Gather everyone who can shoot. Find guns for the ones who need them."

"Got it!"

Sam limped after those nearest him. Andrew looked around. The first person he spotted was a woman. Though the idea of putting women in harm's way offended Andrew in his bones, Eudora Court *had* killed a ripper menacing her baby nephew with a single shot through the throat two months prior. This despite being two years younger than Andrew himself. "Eudora!"

His words grabbed the big blond girl's attention. "Yes?" Her blue eyes were wide and her voice betrayed her fear. "You armed?" She pointed to the handle of the gun peeking out of the top of her long dark skirt. "Come *on*, then!" She hesitated. Mortar shells exploded in the street beyond the square, getting closer and closer. "Damn it," Andrew snarled. He felt a momentary guilt for swearing in front of a woman, but pushed it aside. "The Flesh-Eaters will kill you, or worse!"

Another mortar shell slammed into the town. Andrew felt its wind. Eudora flinched. "What are we going to do?"

Andrew's mind raced. The men of Carroll Town couldn't face the Flesh-Eaters on the hills. What could *they* do?

Then an idea hit him. "They're going to come through the gate. Perhaps we can slow them there. It's narrow. If they use their mortars, they might hit their own troopers."

Assuming they give a damn. "How many women can shoot and have guns?" Sarah had killed a Flesh-Eater. There had to be more.

Eudora looked around. "There ain't many left."

"How many?"

"Two or three, probably."

"I'll get Sarah. You get the rest. Meet me at the far end of the square."

She nodded. Andrew turned toward where he'd left Sarah.

She was gone. Cassie too. "Sarah?" Andrew called out. "Cassie?" Nobody answered. Panic rose inside him. The Flesh-Eaters were still bombarding the town. They couldn't possibly have taken the two women. If both were gone, they were likely somewhere safe. Maybe. Hopefully.

Another mortar shell landed outside the entrance to the town square. The explosion swept across the porch of the butcher's shop. Lily's two little cousins, who'd been hiding behind old salt barrels left out as decorations, slammed onto the ground in the midst of the square. Some parts traveled farther.

Andrew's gut lurched. He quickly forced it down. The harsh smell of the spent explosives stung his nostrils.

"Sam!" Andrew's voice quavered more than he liked. "Sam!"

"Here!" He had Ken with him. Both had rifles.

Andrew frowned. Just three to fight the Flesh-Eaters, and Ken wasn't exactly reliable.

"Andrew!" a female voice shouted. Sarah? His gaze snapped

toward the sound. It was Eudora and her short, curly-haired friend Amanda Fahner. Both were armed. Five men — townsfolk, rather — to face an oncoming army.

Another mortar round crashed on the far side of the now-empty square. This explosion bloomed over the saloon. Wood and shrapnel flew.

Andrew hoped Sarah, Cassie, and his mother were safe. Other than the two kids, there was only one corpse in the square and that one was male. He shook his head. If he kept standing there woolgathering, a mortar might find them. He counted the others again. Their quintet against hundreds of Flesh-Eaters. They were dog meat. But they wouldn't die alone.

Andrew looked at the gate. "The mortars are getting closer!" He could barely hear himself over his ringing ears. "We move forward, we'll be out of the way!"

He spotted the boardinghouse sixty feet from the gate. The mortar blasts had caved in the roof, but the lower floors *should* still be intact. It would be a good place to defend.

Andrew pointed. "There!" The five rushed forward, Sam barely keeping up. "Hurry!" It would be a real quick fight if the enemy brought mortars to bear before they even saw the foe.

"You said we'd get out from under —" Ken protested.

Andrew's thoughts whirled. "They've already shelled the square! They must be doubling back!"

They had to *move*. The next whistling shell would be their death. Andrew ran for the boardinghouse. The others followed on his heels.

All except Ken. Andrew skidded to a stop, with Sam following. The women kept running. "Goddamn it! You stay there, you'll *die!*" Ken stayed frozen where he was. His mouth moved, but no words emerged. "Move, damn it!" Ken stayed put.

"Come on!" Sam shouted from beside Andrew.

There wasn't time. "Sam! Drag him!"

Sam hesitated. Would Andrew have to pull Ken to safety himself? "Come on," Sam said. When Ken refused to budge, Sam grabbed his left arm. Wincing with every stumbling movement, he dragged him toward the town gate, toward the Flesh-Eaters.

"N...no!" Ken cried out. He pulled away from Sam.

"Goddamn it!" Andrew shouted.

He rushed forward and grabbed Ken's right arm with his free hand. He and Sam dragged Ken toward the boardinghouse. Beyond the smoke rose clouds of dust. The Flesh-Eaters were near.

Whistling filled the air. This one would be close. Andrew suddenly needed to shit.

The explosion bloomed atop a building to their left. Splintered wood rained down. One piece knocked Andrew sideways. He barely kept his feet. Sam shouted as something sliced his cheek. But it was the tramp of boots thundering loudest in Andrew's ears.

"If we don't want the Flesh-Eaters catching us out in the open, we have to run!" Andrew shouted. "We might have to leave Ken!"

"No!"

"Keep up, then!"

Andrew ran. Fortunately, so did Ken. Sam brought up the rear. The three scrambled up the steps into the boardinghouse. Andrew slammed the door closed.

"Eudora!" Andrew shouted. "Amanda!"

"In here!" Eudora shouted from Andrew's left. The three barreled into the parlor. The two young women crouched beneath the window amid broken glass. Shafts of sunlight plunged from holes the mortars had torn in the ceiling. Andrew shut the front door behind him and braced it with a chair.

The three men joined them. Seconds later, the Flesh-Eaters passed through the gate.

The first through were the fanatics. Their mad gazes swept ahead, reminding Andrew uncomfortably of rippers. He remembered the arroyo and shivered. They climbed onto the porches nearest the gate.

"You see them?" Andrew whispered, hoping like hell the men outside couldn't hear. The others looked up and quickly ducked down again. "When we shoot, get the fanatics first."

The others nodded.

The ordinary Flesh-Eaters soon followed. Their tramping was the only sound. They fanned out, kicking down doors and rushing into buildings. Two went into the bakery across from the boardinghouse.

They emerged carrying a loaf of bread each. Andrew hoped they'd waste time looting.

A big Flesh-Eater wearing sergeant's chevrons on his collar intervened. Swearing loudly, he picked both up by their uniform collars and slammed them together. They dropped the bread. The sergeant threw it off the porch into the street.

Andrew nearly leaped forward at the sight of food being so casually thrown away. These Flesh-Eaters were so used to living off the sweat of good folk that food — and the work of preparing it — meant nothing to them!

"Andy!" Sam hissed. "Not now."

He checked his movement. His friend was right. He pursed his lips. If it took sergeants keep the regular soldiers in line, what would happen if the sergeants *died?*

He pointed at the sergeant. "See the big man?"

"Yeah," Sam whispered back.

"I'm going to shoot him. If you see others like him and there aren't fanatics close by, shoot them too."

The others nodded. Andrew looked back toward the street. More Flesh-Eaters entered the town. Some drew near. Andrew checked his rifle to see if there was a round chambered.

"Ready?" he whispered. They all nodded, Ken last. "Good. I'll get the sergeant. The rest of you kill the ones heading this way."

Andrew rose into the window. He did not hesitate this time. The man slammed into the porch, the back of his head decorating the wall and doorway.

Sam filled the space next to Andrew. Eudora rose up behind him. Firing together, the three killed both would-be looters and two fanatics. Boots thundered on the porch outside. The enemy pounded on the door to their hideout. Amanda fired through it. The pounding abated for a moment. Then the door exploded inward.

"Kill for the Howling God!" a one-eyed fanatic with a missing ear shouted. He leaped over the chair that once blocked the door onto Amanda and bit her. She slammed into the floor, blood streaming from gashes in her cheek and ear. As she fell she tried to aim, but he batted her arm away and brought a pistol up…

Ken screamed at the Flesh-Eater. The fanatic's mad gaze fell on him. Ken raised his rifle but inexplicably did not fire.

Andrew remembered his own hesitation. *Oh no. He's dead…*

The Flesh-Eater lunged. Ken finally pulled the trigger. The bullet knocked the fanatic backward. He kept his feet, despite blood pouring from his left shoulder. He hissed in anger. His gun hand rose…

Another rifle fired from the doorway. The bullet struck Ken in the hip. He cried out and fell to his knees.

Andrew's rifle snapped sideways. He squeezed the trigger. The rifle thundered in the small room. The bullet threw the Flesh-Eater out of the door into the hallway.

The fanatic turned to face Andrew and laughed.

Then Eudora's bullet caught him in the back. He fell to his knees. He dragged himself toward Andrew, lips moving soundlessly. Despite his injuries, Ken fired. The bullet punched through the Flesh-Eater's head and buried itself in the nearby wall. The fanatic slumped to the floor, *finally* dead.

Another Flesh-Eater appeared in the door. Andrew fired again. The enemy sank gurgling to his knees. Another Flesh-Eater dragged him out of sight.

"We've got to get out of here," Andrew shouted, barely hearing his own words. "Elsewise they'll trap us!" Making their stand in a room with only one door had *not* been smart.

Sam nodded. He dragged himself toward the door. Gunfire cracked in the hall. He jumped back. "Two Flesh-Eaters," he shouted. "Maybe more behind them."

A sick feeling rose in Andrew's stomach. The enemy was outside *and* inside. *Shit.* Although he knew the boardinghouse had a back door, he hadn't planned how they'd *get* to it if they had to run. *Shit.*

Andrew gestured to Sam and to Ken, who lay moaning on the floor in a pool of blood. Then he pointed toward himself and the door. He couldn't believe what he was about to do, but he was damned if he was going to send his best friend and the women into their enemies' teeth alone.

Something clattered on the wooden floor in front of the window behind Andrew. He turned. It was a grenade. That changed things. "Run!" Andrew shouted.

He jumped into the hall, firing as he landed on his side. His first shot missed, but the second hit a crouching Flesh-Eater in the chest. The man slumped onto the ground.

His companion fired at Andrew. The bullet sliced through one of his pants legs and the flesh beneath. Pain flared, but only briefly.

Eudora jumped into the hall behind Andrew and fired. Her bullet caught the Flesh-Eater in the head. Andrew looked back into the room where the other three remained.

"Sam!" Andrew shouted.

"I'm right —"

The exploding grenade cut him off. Thunder cracked in the confined space. Sam fell on Andrew. The weight forced the air from his lungs. For a moment, he saw red.

Luckily it was over quickly. Sam scrambled off. Andrew gulped down air as Sam swore. A chunk of shrapnel stuck out of his friend's left arm. Blood from other wounds spotted his clothes.

"Ken took the worst of it," Sam shouted. "He's dead!"

Ken's body lay just inside the door. The grenade had shredded him from his knees to his head. Jagged metal emerged like quills from a porcupine from the red and white mess the explosion had made of his body.

"Amanda!" Eudora screamed. She rushed into the smoke pouring from the room. Despite his wounded arm, Sam snatched at her dress. He caught a handful of fabric, but she nearly pulled free anyway.

"She's dead!" Sam screamed. Blood welled around the shrapnel in his arm. Despite her struggling, he slowly pulled her out.

"We've got to get out!" Andrew shouted.

"Back into the street?" Eudora screamed. "We go there, we're dead!"

"Back door!" A slim chance was better than none.

The two pulled Sam to his feet, then rushed through a hall into the kitchen. Ahead, beside the old stove, the back door hung open. Through it, Andrew saw Flesh-Eaters gathered on the dirt path behind the building.

"Oh *shit*." Andrew's mind whirled. "I've got an idea. They're going to expect us to run out panicking."

It was Sam who grasped it first. "We run out shooting."

Andrew nodded. "Wish we had a grenade. Our rifles will have to do." He stepped forward. Sam and Eudora followed. Andrew shook his head at her. "Keep an eye out for anyone who comes in the front door."

Eudora scowled but nodded. Andrew and Sam raised their rifles.

"Wait," Andrew said. "Reload!" Both young men reloaded their rifles. "Ready?" Sam nodded.

The two erupted from the back door, firing together. One Flesh-Eater went down. The others retreated around the corner.

"Eudora, now!" Andrew shouted.

Eudora followed, but didn't join them. Instead, she spun and fired. "There're more!"

"I'll handle them!" Andrew pointed back down the alley, toward the square. "See if the way's clear!"

Eudora scampered down the steps. As soon as she was out of the way, Andrew fired twice into the boardinghouse's smoky interior. Someone screamed.

Gunfire roared beside him. Eudora and Sam traded bullets with the Flesh-Eaters around the corner. Smoke stinking of sulfur began filling the narrow space between the boardinghouse and the building behind it.

A Flesh-Eater rifle cracked. A bullet caught Sam in his already-wounded leg. He screamed and fell to one knee. Luckily, he didn't lose his rifle.

Eudora screamed and fired back at the Flesh-Eater, a boy who looked younger than Andrew. The bullet caught him in the stomach and knocked him down. "Ma!" he cried out amid a growing pool of blood. "Help me, Ma!" Tears streamed down his face. His writhing formed corn-kernels of blood and dirt.

Andrew gagged. Gut wounds killed slowly. It would be a kindness to blow out his brains. He raised his rifle, but his hands trembled too much to fire. Just how hard was it to shoot a damn Flesh-Eater?

A short, swarthy Flesh-Eater emerged from the boardinghouse. He aimed at Sam. Andrew snapped his rifle sideways. His bullet caught the Flesh-Eater in the shoulder. The man's comrades pulled him out of sight.

"Cover me!" Andrew called to Eudora. He grabbed the screaming Sam under his arms and dragged him back. A trail of blood lay on the dirt behind them. Andrew hoped the smoke from the gunfire would conceal them.

A Flesh-Eater leaned out from around the corner. With his rifle in the crook of his arm, Andrew couldn't immediately shoot him.

"Eudora!"

She turned. Andrew let go of Sam and scrabbled for his weapon. Sam struggled to raise his own rifle. Before either could fire, the Flesh-Eater shot Eudora in the head. Her ruined skull struck the second step and bounced like a toy ball.

"No!" Sam screamed. Shouting incoherently, he fired over and over. The Flesh-Eater fell, hit three times in the chest. Sam kept shooting anyway.

"Sam!" Andrew shouted. Sam fired again. "Damn it, he's dead!"

Two more Flesh-Eaters leaped out from around the corner. Sam's enraged firing caught one in the thigh. The wounded man staggered out of sight. The second man, however, targeted Sam. His bullet took some hair and part of his ear.

Andrew cut him down before he could fire again. No more Flesh-Eaters appeared. Joy rose in Andrew's chest. They'd killed all the bastards!

Then his gaze drifted over to Eudora's corpse and the smoky boardinghouse beyond. The momentary victory came at a price, and there were many, many more enemies out there. Time to skedaddle...

Holding the rifle in one hand, Andrew grabbed Sam and dragged him down the path winding behind another building. The wound on his friend's leg still bled. The blood on the path would lead the Flesh-Eaters straight to them.

Andrew reached up and tore part of his bloody white shirt away. Then another. He jammed the first piece into the furrow the Flesh-Eater bullet carved in Sam's leg, slowing the bleeding for a moment.

Sam screamed. "Don't touch me!"

Andrew threw the second strip of cloth at him. "Tie this around!"

Sam gingerly went to work. Andrew had his rifle ready just as a fanatic burst laughing around the corner. Andrew pulled the trigger. The Flesh-Eater fell. Andrew returned his rifle to crook of his arm and resumed dragging Sam. Luckily, his friend had the wound covered and left little blood behind.

After passing behind another building, Andrew stopped. He raised his rifle and looked down the sights toward the way they'd come.

No more Flesh-Eaters appeared. They checked their ammunition. Andrew had only two rounds left.

"How many rounds you got left?"

"Three in the tube." Sam searched his pockets. "Got a box, but they're rattling around in there."

Andrew fished in the pockets of his coat. "Got a box too, but it's running light."

"What do we do?"

Andrew looked back once again. No new enemies came. "Hide." A savage anger rose in his chest. "Get ammo off the dead ones. And uniforms too. We'll look for officers." The Flesh-Eater leadership deserved to pay far more than their conscripts.

"This means we don't get out of here," Sam murmured.

Andrew gestured around them. "The Flesh-Eaters control everything to the north, east, and west. South's the desert. There ain't nowhere to get *to*."

Slowly, Sam nodded.

THE JUDGMENT OF CARROLL TOWN

Thirty terrified, dirty townsfolk, mostly women and children, huddled in the town square awaiting their doom. The Obsidian Guard hemmed the captives in, bayonets glittering on their repeaters' muzzles. Flesh-Eaters went from building to building within the cordon, dragging out those hiding within. Clark and his ripper looked on approvingly.

Grendel watched from among the Obsidian Guard gathered in the mooring tower's merciful shade as Fort Vallero's tall, skinny commander stepped forward between two kneeling men who must have been prisoners taken on the hills. The major swept the crowd with an angry gaze before speaking.

"You are accused of many crimes," the officer drawled. "You murdered officials lawfully discharging their duties, then your mayor falsely claimed wrong, all while the rest of you prepared insurrection. Rather than throw yourselves on our mercy, you made war. You killed many troopers, some of whom were your neighbors. I reckon the *Merrills* helped." He snorted. "But just enough to get you whupped."

The captives trembled. Grendel smiled. *Now the boiled pork is fried.*

The commander eyed the survivors. His attentions alighted for a moment too long on a girl not much older than Grendel's daughter Astrid. Grendel frowned. The man continued sweeping the crowd with his hard gaze.

"You know the penalty of disobedience." The commander pointed to one of the few young men in the crowd. "You. Your legs will carry you back to Fort Vallero. If you don't pass muster to work in the cotton fields or the coal mines, your blood will feed the Howling God and your flesh will feed the conscripts."

Ignoring the man's frightened expression, he pointed at another young man, whose hands clamped around a weeping wound in his middle. "You probably won't make it to the fort alive. We'll kill you here." He pointed to the first man. "He'll carry your carcass and get the first bite."

His gaze fell on the women. He smiled, an expression even Grendel found disturbing. "Some of you have skills. Those that don't..." He let his voice trail off, implication obvious.

Then his gaze fell on a little boy sitting all alone. The hard look in his eyes softened for a moment. "He's young enough. He'll make a fine soldier someday."

His gaze swept over the crowd again. "This will be your fate unless you *earn* mercy. During the battle, one of you used an Old World grenade, killing several of my zealots. Having these weapons means death." He paused. "Tell me where it came from. Other than that dead meat over there, you all will be sent into the mountains to mine, but you'll at least be *alive*." He looked up at the mooring tower. "Carroll Town's a good location for an airbase. We'll need to repaint this damn tower." He spat at the concrete piling holding it up.

Grendel stepped between the Flesh-Eater officer and Clark, emerging from the tower's shadow like some monster from the deep ocean. He glowered at the captives, hoping his appearance might loosen some tongues. He wore the battle kit he had not worn since the Merrills fell — black armor and a helmet forged from the skull of the saber-cat he had killed long ago. The durable Old World repeater with its curving magazine hung looped from his shoulder. His axe, whose handle included the spine of Ejnar Irontooth, clung to his back.

"I am Grendel." The crowd shuddered at his name. *Good to know my reputation precedes me.* "Listen to him." He stepped back among the guardsmen, his point made.

Still none spoke. The officer shook his head and turned to the other Flesh-Eaters, a grin splitting his face.

"Wait!" a female voice shouted. Grendel raised an eyebrow. A young woman emerged from the crowd. Her eyes were green and her hair was the color of straw. He leaned forward. This one was dirtier and skinnier than he preferred, but she was easy on the eyes and still had all her teeth. And she was more spirited than the others.

"Where did the Old World grenade come from?" the Flesh-Eater officer demanded. His smile became a leer.

"I don't know," she protested, her accent more clipped than the Flesh-Eaters. "None of us knew anything about Old World weapons!"

The officer scowled. "There was an Old World weapon here! Maybe *you* didn't know anything about it, sweetheart, but one was used."

The woman scowled and drew herself up taller. "That's Sarah to you. And how hard do you reckon it is to hide anything from anybody in a town like this?" She paused. "And we *tried* to find the Merrills and couldn't." She glared. "Maybe if they'd come, you wouldn't be here."

The officer's scowl deepened. Grendel allowed himself a chuckle. He could claim any captive he wished. This one had spirit. Knowing Jessamine Keith, the dark-haired concubine and former citadel telegraph girl traveling with him, she might welcome the prospect of sharing his bed on the way home. She was a strong woman. She would bear him strong children, so the bloodline that nearly went extinct when Ejnar Irontooth fell on his family's hall forty years ago would survive.

He shook his head. If he had too many concubines, he would not be able to devote the proper attention to each. They would seek affairs with his guards, try to pass off their bastards as his. He was not interested in that, not at *all*.

You do not know just how unlucky you are, girl.

The officer did not respond, instead turning his attention to the wider crowd. "Perhaps an object lesson will loosen some tongues." He turned to a pair of soldiers flanking a shirtless man with a black bag over his head. "Bring the prisoner forward."

They dragged the man forward. Blood from hamstrung thighs

trickled from beneath his ragged pants to stain the ground. They tore the bag away, revealing a bloodied man with unfocused eyes.

"This is your mayor. If you do not tell us the truth, we will butcher him in front of you!"

A dark-haired girl cried out amidst the crowd. She rushed forward, only for the other women to pull her back.

Clark stepped forward to stand beside his officer. "I once butchered hogs for friends of the goddamn Merrills who thought they were better than me. Now I butcher *men.*"

Grendel would have left the task to a subordinate, but this was Clark's business. He would see how the townsfolk reacted.

"Hold him still," Clark growled to the two soldiers. "Chicken breasts are good. *Man* breast is better."

He drew a long knife from his belt and went to work. The mayor screamed and thrashed as Clark cut into his chest. A sharp cuff to the side of the head stilled him. Blood poured down his chest to soak his pants and feed the ground.

Clark tore away the pectoral muscle and held it above his head. His soldiers shouted and cheered. Grendel kept his disgust away from his face. Even at his most desperate, hiding in the bog from those who had murdered his kin, he had never resorted to cannibalism.

A young man near the edge of the captive crowd trembled, face red with fury. Grendel frowned. That one could be trouble, but nobody seemed to notice.

Clark sliced apart the muscle in his hand, the knife no doubt biting his palm with every cut. He turned to the Flesh-Eaters behind him. "See how your master favors you!" He threw chunks of the raw meat to the soldiers. Still keeping hold of their rifles, they snatched the flying flesh from the air. Some stuffed it still-dripping in their mouths. Others pocketed it for later.

The angry prisoner lunged for Clark. Though his hands were bound, the blow nearly toppled the Flesh-Eater overlord. Clark recovered quickly as the prisoner tumbled forward onto the ground. Flesh-Eater guns snapped up, but Clark waved them down.

"You've got more spirit than the rest of these dogs here." He stepped over to the prisoner as he wormed on the ground and cut his bonds. The man glared at the Flesh-Eater chief. "What's your name?"

The prisoner spat on the ground. "Taylor Welborn."

Clark grinned."I like you. I'll cut you a deal. If you can beat me, I'll spare this one's life." He looked at the bleeding mayor. "Assuming he doesn't die first."

"If I beat you," Taylor growled. "I'll *kill* you."

Clark shrugged. "We'll see." He threw the boy one of his knives. "You can keep this if you win."

Grendel rolled his eyes. Such bravado. He would have immediately killed any man who dared attack him. He was not in so weak a position he had to prove his mettle at every opportunity.

Taylor rose to his feet, knife in hand. Clark did not draw any of the other knives in his belt, clearly choosing to face an armed opponent bare-handed. Grendel nearly snorted.

With a shout, Taylor charged. Clark stepped aside, letting his opponent rush past. He kicked the boy in the rump before he got too far. He tumbled to the ground. The Flesh-Eaters and even some Obsidian Guard laughed.

Taylor rose, murder in his eyes. Blood trickled from his wrist where the blade must have bitten him as he fell. This time he approached slowly, holding the knife like he knew how to use it. Grendel raised an eyebrow. He did not recruit flatlanders into the Obsidian Guard, but he was momentarily tempted to make an exception.

Taylor lunged again. Clark stepped aside once more, but Taylor turned to match his movement. The blade flashed. Clark shouted. Blood flew. One Flesh-Eater raised his rifle, but Clark waved him to a stop. The cannibal overlord wiped blood away from his split cheek and held his wet hand high.

"Blood for you!" he shouted at the sky.

Taylor lunged again while Clark made his invocation. Clark's huge fist snapped forward, striking him in the throat. He fell to his knees gagging. A swift kick followed. Bone cracked. Taylor's head rolled at an unnatural angle.

"A pity," Clark shouted to the townsfolk. "He would have made a fine Flesh-Eater." He laughed. "In a way he will. We'll feed him to our most promising men so they will have his spirit." He stepped over to the fallen mayor and kicked him. The man did not move. Clark looked at the townsfolk. "Your mayor's dead. Anyone want to spill their guts? Last chance."

The dark-haired girl erupted from the crowd, shaking off the restraining hands of other women. She glared at Clark, enraged eyes bulging in a tear-stained face. "You dirty murderer!" she cried.

Ignoring her, Clark turned to his men. A grin sprawled across his face. "They belong to you now!"

The Flesh-Eaters fell on the captives like rippers. The townsfolk screamed as the soldiers separated the hale from the injured and the women from the men. The wounded man batted with bloodied hands at one Flesh-Eater and got his throat slashed for his pains. The Obsidian Guard remained behind, weapons ready in case of trouble.

"Take anyone you don't want over there," Clark ordered, pointing toward a barber's shop. "Make an offering of their blood."

Grendel nearly smiled. The Flesh-Eaters played right into his hands. Havarth would someday claim the Merrill inheritance. Clark would trumpet his suppression of the Carroll Town revolt far and wide hoping to cow his subjects, not knowing he sowed the seeds of his own doom.

WEARING Flesh-Eater uniforms already stiffening with blood, Andrew and Sam made their way toward the square. Andrew led, rifle up, while Sam limped behind. He'd since stopped bleeding, but the leg wounds slowed him considerably.

As they drew near, a Flesh-Eater sergeant's gaze fell on them. Andrew tensed. Hopefully they were far enough away he wouldn't see bullet holes or the lack of filed teeth.

"You two lost?" the sergeant shouted. "What the hell are you doing here?"

"We were fighting the holdouts near the boardinghouse." Nerves sped Andrew's tongue. He gestured to Sam. "He got hurt. Had to patch him up a bit."

The sergeant didn't *seem* to notice anything abnormal. "Did you get them? Bastards killed good men."

"Yes, sergeant," Sam said. Andrew forced himself not to look incredulously at Sam. "We got them."

The sergeant nodded. "Good." He pointed toward the gap between two buildings to Andrew's right. "The bossman and *his* bossman are in the square dividing up the survivors. Git."

"Yes, sergeant."

"The bossman and *his* bossman?" Sam whispered once they were away from the sergeant. "Who do they mean?"

Andrew pondered that. Fort Vallero had a commander — a right pervert, based on how his man talked about Lily. Perhaps the man in charge of the bastard had come along to oversee the judgment of Carroll Town? "Flesh-Eater bigwigs no doubt."

A faint smile crossed his face. Flesh-Eater bigwigs. Just the kind who deserved to die.

They approached the alley. The first thing they heard was a cruel shout from the square.

"Take anyone you don't want over there. Make an offering of their blood."

Screams erupted from the square. Andrew's heart jumped into his throat. He quickened his pace, almost jogging. Only the need to avoid revealing himself to the Flesh-Eaters slowed him. Sam staggered after, every step bringing grimaces and hisses of pain.

"Please!" Andrew's mother shouted above the din. "Stop! We can't hurt you! We have skills! We can —"

Then she screamed. Her cry lasted for a terrible second before fading back into the chorus of terror erupting from the square.

Andrew nearly screamed but quickly bit his tongue. What came out resembled a groan he hoped the sergeant couldn't hear. He rushed toward the gap between the two buildings, Sam barely keeping up. They were in such a hurry they nearly collided with a Flesh-Eater.

The man's blue eyes — beneath which were half-done fanatics' scars — locked on Andrew's. Andrew skidded to a stop, barely avoiding colliding with the Flesh-Eater.

"Looking to get in on the action?" The man's grin churned

Andrew's stomach. "There're some pretty girls there." Andrew barely avoided snarling. Before he could devise a good lie, the man locked eyes with him. "I've seen you before," he growled. "You're one of the Carroll Town rebels!"

The Flesh-Eater opened his mouth to shout a warning. Andrew leaped forward, slamming the man's head into the wall and cutting his words off. The Flesh-Eater bounced back, aiming right at Sam. Before he could shoot, Sam yanked the weapon down. Although the enemy still held onto the weapon, he couldn't reach the trigger.

At the end of the alley sixty feet away, Andrew saw more soldiers in the square. The Flesh-Eaters still struggled with the surviving townsfolk. And soldiers wearing unfamiliar black uniforms stood between them and the alley. Andrew's stomach clenched. They must be Obsidian Guard. Grendel's men.

"Keep him quiet!" Andrew hissed.

Sam nodded. He reached toward the soldier's mouth...

And that left an opening. A long knife appeared in the Flesh-Eater's free hand. Before Andrew could react, the Flesh-Eater buried the knife below Sam's ribs.

Andrew bit off a scream. Sam's mouth worked, but no sound emerged. Blood soaked the soldier's hand. Its metallic stench filled Andrew's nostrils.

Anger as red as the hot blood clouded Andrew's vision. He couldn't fire without catching the attention of the Obsidian Guard, but the rifle butt would make an effective club.

He spun the weapon in his hands. The Flesh-Eater turned, ripping the knife out of Sam's body. He slashed at Andrew as the younger man struck him in the face with the rifle butt.

The Flesh-Eater missed Andrew's shoulder by an inch. Andrew's blow caught him in the mouth. The Flesh-Eater screamed around the rifle butt. Andrew glanced left. The soldiers on the square looked none the wiser.

Andrew yanked the rifle free, broken teeth flying like popcorn. The Flesh-Eater slashed once more. The blade caught Andrew's elbow, drawing blood.

Andrew struck again. The Flesh-Eater moved too quickly. The blow meant for his head instead caught him in the left shoulder.

The Flesh-Eater snarled. He slashed again with his knife, the blade biting Andrew's collarbone. Andrew bit off a scream, his teeth digging into his tongue.

The Flesh-Eater recoiled, knife up like a rattler about to strike. He lunged for Andrew's throat. Andrew knocked the blow aside with his rifle and kicked the Flesh-Eater in the kneecap.

With a shout, the cannibal fell to one knee. Andrew hammered his head into the wall behind him with his rifle butt. The man toppled forward into the dirt.

Andrew's head snapped back toward the square. The enemy still hadn't noticed!

He turned his attention back to the Flesh-Eater. The man lay there, dead or unconscious. For a moment, Andrew pondered taking the man's knife and making sure the job was done.

The screams coming from the square reclaimed his attention. He took a step forward. The Flesh Eaters would be busy terrorizing helpless women, children, and wounded men. They wouldn't see their deaths coming. He could reap a mighty harvest before they felled him.

Then he remembered Sam. Andrew forced himself to look away from the square toward his wounded friend.

Sam trembled on the ground, his shirt from ribs to belt soaked in blood. His breathing came shallow. Bright red blood spattered his lips. "Sam!" Andrew knelt by his friend's side. More blood. The blade must've pierced one of Sam's lungs. "No." Tears formed in his eyes.

"Andy," Sam gasped. Blood bubbled in his mouth. He grabbed onto the sleeves of Andrew's coat. "Andy, don't die." Sam's grip tightened. "There are too many to fight." Blood poured from his mouth. "Don't throw your life away. Run, find the Merr..."

Then he stiffened. His eyes bulged. His hands slid free as his body slumped to the ground.

Sam Cotton was dead. Andrew's oldest friend lay in the alley, his lifeblood pooling around him. Just like the Flesh-Eater boy behind the boardinghouse.

"No." Tears dripped from his eyes. "No."

A yawning emptiness opened in his chest. He remembered growing up with Sam. The ball games, cards, the times they got caught eavesdropping, all the things boys would do in a town on the edge of the Iron Desert. All that was over now — Sam's death ensured that more than the fall of Carroll Town.

Despite his efforts, the tears kept coming. "Sam," he hissed, shaking his friend's body. "Sam, wake up. Sam, please don't die!"

Nothing happened. The tears came faster now. Andrew laid his head on his friend's chest and stopped trying to fight his emotions. He simply wept, his tears soaking the stolen enemy uniform.

Then something else emerged from his sadness, transfiguring it.

Anger. White-hot killing *rage*.

"I'll kill them for you, Sam." His hands trembled. "I'll kill them *all*."

His grief and the momentary consideration he should run vanished like straw before a firestorm. His mother and his best friend were dead. His sister and his girl were in the rough hands of the Flesh-Eaters.

The fallen enemy moaned, blood bubbling in his mangled mouth. Andrew's gaze fell on him. He grit his teeth until they hurt. Everyone in Carroll Town, including himself, would die. Or worse. But it wouldn't come cheap. For the sake of his mother and Sam, if nobody else.

He knelt and took the knife from fingers offering little resistance. Although Andrew had a knife of his own, it felt more fitting to finish the Flesh-Eater with his own weapon. His and Sam's warm blood trickled onto his hand from the blade.

The Flesh-Eater moaned again. Andrew shoved the man's arm away and buried the blade in the man's neck. Hot blood stung Andrew's eyes. Wiping his face with his left hand, he pulled the blade across the Flesh-Eater's throat. The man's trachea and other artery parted. He gurgled. Blood pulsed from the open wound in time to the enemy's fading heartbeat.

Andrew picked up his rifle and returned to his feet. He wiped the last blood from his face with his sopping sleeve and looked toward the square.

The Obsidian Guard *still* looked away. *Damned deaf idiots.* He raised his rifle and crept forward. The one standing directly in front of him would make a good first kill.

As Andrew raised his rifle, the soldier stepped left. Now Andrew saw three men beneath the mooring tower. One wore a Flesh-Eater uniform, but his was significantly cleaner and had something shiny on each collar. The second, heavier than the first, had a shaved head and a brown patch over his right eye. He wore a long jacket extending to his knees colored the same as Flesh-Eater duds. When he moved, the glint revealed it was actually metallic armor.

The third didn't look like a Flesh-Eater at all. Like the second man he wore a long armored jacket, but it was solely black. He wore the skull of a big cat with two long fangs forged into a helmet. Could that be *Grendel*? But why would he *bother* with Carroll Town? It had to be some Guard bigwig.

All three had the hard eyes of men who killed for their bread. The first looked about the square, obviously approving of the atrocities taking place. The second did as well. The third seemed like he had his mind elsewhere.

Andrew pressed himself against the wall. If they chose to look closer, they'd see the fresh blood on Andrew and the bodies in the alley. They would *not* see him coming for their lives.

He raised his rifle. He'd start with the man in black. Even if he wasn't Grendel, he was *special*, he had to be with that crazy getup. He looked down the sights, lining up against the man's gray left eye.

Then the first man turned to the second. He said something Andrew couldn't figure. Laughter crossed his cruel face. That sparked rage in Andrew's soul. Andrew's breathing came harder and faster, to the point he feared they'd hear him.

Damn him, damn him, damn him, damn him!

Andrew shifted his aim away from the dark-clad man onto the one with the ornamented collar. Before he died, he would make sure that laughing bastard went into the dark with him.

Andrew took a breath, then squeezed the trigger.

CRACK!

A bullet seized the commander of Fort Vallero and sent him sprawling, minus the side of his head.

Grendel was halfway through unslinging his repeater when his guards clustered around him. The Flesh-Eaters turned their attention away from the captive townsfolk, most of whom were now hogtied. Alrekr leaped away from a corpse it was nibbling on to circle the square.

"Some holdout, no doubt," Clark said quickly. "Don't worry, we'll find him. What do you want us to do when we've got him?"

The Flesh-Eaters would vie among themselves to subject the holdout — assuming they caught him alive — to the most hideous tortures they could devise. Currying favor, hoping he would overlook the fact someone got within shooting distance of the first lord of the Northlands.

He shrugged. What did one townsman matter? "Do as you will."

The Obsidian Guard and some of the Flesh-Eaters returned fire. Amid the crackling, Grendel's gaze fell on the fallen commander of Fort Vallero. Fitting he died as a result of his own failure to properly secure the town.

Grendel whistled for the guard captain. The short man came rushing over, his fellows parting before him.

"Yes, sir?"

"The commander at Fort Vallero —"

"His name was Major Thomas Marshall," Clark added helpfully.

"Major Marshall did not *fucking* clear the surrounding area well enough. I want the guardsmen to clean out every goddamn building touching this square, in case there are any more holdouts."

"Understood, sir." He paused. "But what about the one who shot Marshall?"

"Let the little bastard run. The town is crawling with Flesh-Eaters. If they do not catch him, the desert will eat him alive."

INTO THE DESERT

Bullets sliced around Andrew. The repeaters' insane chattering chorus shattered his resolve to drag his enemies down with him. He flung himself out of the alley into the street.

He landed on his hands and knees and looked up. The sergeant who'd let him and Sam pass minutes ago loped toward him, two younger Flesh-Eaters close behind. Murder burned in his eyes. Andrew aimed and fired, hitting the sergeant in the gut. The man fell screaming. Andrew scrambled forward through the dirt. The gunfire that kept him on the ground also kept the two other Flesh-Eaters off him.

Andrew pulled himself onto the porch of the chandler's shop as bullets whined overhead. He crawled through the open door and kicked it closed behind him.

Behind a counter newly-scarred by Flesh-Eater bullets was the door to the workroom. A way out!

Andrew was atop the counter when the door banged open. He rolled off and landed arm-first on candles he'd knocked over. Snarling and rolling onto his backside, Andrew scrambled away. A Flesh-Eater loomed over the counter. The man aimed…

Andrew fired twice. The first missed entirely, but the second didn't. The man staggered out of sight. Andrew bolted into the work-room and kicked the door shut. Despite his pain and exhaustion, he seized a shelf with a few candles on it and hauled it in front of the door.

Safe for the moment, he looked around. There was a back door. He could reach the fields outside town. If the Flesh-Eaters had all their men in the square, he could escape that way and look for the Merrills. Better if he could find a horse, but going back was suicide.

He seized the handle of the back door. It wouldn't open. He'd probably only wounded the Flesh Eater. The man was going to batter down the door and shoot him in the head...

Then he saw the deadbolt above the doorknob. He tore it free of the lock, yanked open the door, and ran for it.

Outside lay open space bounded by a white picket fence. Beyond, acres of sickly and stunted grain. A Flesh-Eater emerged from around the building. Andrew fired, the bullet snapping by the Flesh-Eater's head. The man shouted and retreated.

Andrew had to skedaddle before more showed up. He bolted across the open ground. The pointed fence-posts bit as he dragged himself over. Fabric tore as one caught on the Flesh-Eater jacket.

Andrew rolled off the fence onto his back. He momentarily lost his grip on his rifle. Biting off a scream, he snatched it back. His eyes locked on the back door of the chandler's shop. Nobody emerged. He felt like laughing. Had the townsfolk killed so many cannibals that they couldn't surround *and* occupy the town at the same time?

Slowly, Andrew's breathing returned to normal. As it did, his limbs grew heavier. His eyelids drooped.

He shook his head. This was not a good place to rest. If the enemy found him, he was dead meat. Literally.

He looked across the field. Beyond lay a footbridge and after that, rough, stony country. He'd be safe in the ravines there.

Holding the rifle in the crooks of his elbows, Andrew pushed his way into the grain and looked back.

The grain did not pop back up after him. His movement left a trail likely visible from the chandler's shop.

"Damn it!"

He pulled himself to his feet, hunching over so the wheat hid him as much as possible, and ran. His growing fatigue slowed him and reddened his vision, but he soon came to the wooden bridge. He looked back. More Flesh-Eaters beyond the fence!

His gut clenched. His limbs felt lighter. He stooped and dashed across, over the drought-stricken stream, and off the path into the rough country.

Across the dry, stony ground lay a ravine some long-ago waterway or digging had cut into the brown earth. He and Sam had played there long ago. He spotted the trail they'd taken where the wall wasn't as steep and shook his head. That was the obvious way.

Instead, he ran and jumped. He stumbled when he landed, the hard ground tearing through his pants and the skin beneath. When he rose, the ground was bloody.

It had been years since he'd been here. Was the overhang to the left or right? Left. He stayed on the rocks as much as possible. The Flesh-Eaters were right good hunters from the northern hills. Leaving even the smallest track would be cutting his own throat. His limbs and eyelids grew heavy, but he bit his lip to keep fatigue at bay. He could rest hidden beneath the overhang.

There! There it was! Ahead the earth extended over empty space, roots dangling from some plant long since dead. A large rock lay below. Andrew climbed over and slid down the other side. He was safe. For the moment.

Now that he wasn't standing, darkness pressed against the edges of his vision. He forced his eyes open and pulled the ammunition tube out of his rifle. Four bullets. He pulled the cartridge box from a coat pocket and thumbed three bullets into the tube. Between the rifle and the box he'd lifted from the bastard who'd killed Sam, he had eighteen rounds to give the Flesh-Eaters hell.

He shoved the tube back into the rifle. Here, with no sign of pursuers, he could close his eyes. Just for a minute…

SOMETHING TICKLED Andrew's face and shoulders. It felt like Cassie's blond hair. For a moment, he thought it was Cassie climbing atop him. He smiled.

Harsh buzzing dragged Andrew into full consciousness. It wasn't Cassie's hair touching his face — it was a swarm of black flies! They crawled all over him, thickest at his wounds.

Andrew shouted in disgust, slapping at his face and body. Flies pulped beneath his hands. Others leaped away, their buzzing angry in Andrew's ears. A snarl curled across his face. They wouldn't be nibbling on *him* today.

He closed his eyes. Cassie was dead, or would soon wish she were. He'd failed to protect her. She was his girl, and he'd let her down. He sighed, closing his eyes and clenching his fists. He was weak. He was a failure.

Nearby voices seized Andrew's attention. Three Flesh-Eaters descended into the ravine sixty yards away. Two were ordinary enough, while one stooped and twitched when he walked.

Andrew held his breath. If they saw him, they'd attack. If he somehow defeated them, the noise would attract more Flesh-Eaters. Either way, he was dead.

He grit his teeth. He was dead the moment he shot the Flesh-Eater bossman. He'd at least choose how he died.

He raised his rifle. One of the Flesh-Eaters pointed and shouted. *CRACK!* The man paid for that with his life.

The two survivors ducked behind the remains of a small rockslide and returned fire. Andrew scrambled behind the rock and threw a glance back. The ravine curved out of sight twenty yards away. It wouldn't take long to run, once he had killed them.

Andrew risked a look. One Flesh-Eater peeked above the rocks. Andrew fired, but the bullet sparked off the stone. The man ducked back unharmed. The other Flesh-Eater popped up and fired. His bullet struck the rock perilously close to Andrew's face.

Andrew took another shot. No effect. He couldn't keep wasting ammunition like this. He looked around. Rocks lay everywhere. He couldn't hit the Flesh-Eaters head-on, but what if he got something *over* their heads?

He snatched up a rock and hurled it. The stone landed halfway between the enemy position and his. "Shit!" He threw another, harder this time. It landed a few feet farther. His arm already hurt. This wasn't going to work.

A Flesh-Eater bullet slammed into the dirt beside Andrew. Andrew shouted and let his left hand sprawl. He kept his right hand on the trigger. Time to sham again.

Nothing happened. His left hand trembled. He forced himself to remain still. Still nothing. *Shit.*

Then one Flesh-Eater ordered the other to stay behind. Andrew grinned and waited, ears pricked. Seconds passed slowly, cruelly. Perhaps the Flesh-Eaters were onto his trickery and wanted to fool him into moving first?

Boots scraped on stone. *Almost there. Come a bit closer, you man-eater.*

The steps came closer and faster, faster than Andrew had reckoned. The Flesh-Eater clearly wasn't being very cautious.

Andrew raised his body and rifle above the rock. The Flesh-Eater was halfway between the rock pile and Andrew's hiding place. He had his rifle up.

CRACK! CRACK!

The Flesh-Eater's bullet slammed into the stone near Andrew's face. Rock bit Andrew's forehead. Andrew's shot hit the Flesh-Eater in the stomach. The man sank to his knees screaming.

Andrew grit his teeth. The man's screams sounded like those of his mother before the Flesh-Eaters had killed her.

Andrew's vision turned red at the memory. He aimed at the fallen man, ready to put one between his eyes.

"Tom!" the Flesh-Eater sheltering behind the rock pile shouted in a distorted voice. The stooped enemy rose, spraying bullets at Andrew. Andrew retreated behind the huge stone, avoiding the gunfire but not the wounded man's screams. Andrew scrambled toward the curve, shooting as he moved. The man staggered and shouted, his cries joining his gut-shot buddy's.

Andrew ran until he was out of the ravine and atop a hill. There he stopped short. His eyes bulged. Though his mouth worked, no words came.

Something huge floated in the air ahead. For the first time in years, he saw a dirigible.

This was much bigger than those the Merrills had sent to take the census and collect taxes. Its watermelon-shaped balloon bore the Flesh-Eater red and black instead of the Merrill green. The blocky engines lining its length were bigger, as was the boxy metal gondola hanging from its belly.

His gut lurched, but there wasn't anything left to upchuck. He couldn't fight this...this *thing*. Maybe the Flesh-Eaters had sent the troopers to force him toward the dirigible, like hunters driving birds into a net.

A bullet punched through the side of his stolen uniform, tearing his shirt and drawing blood. Other bullets slammed into the ground nearby, throwing up dust. Andrew threw himself back down the hill, barely holding onto his rifle. A sound like fabric tearing, only far too loud, stabbed his ears. The ground where he'd been exploded. Rocks and dust rained down on him. Hot metal stung his left hand. The offending debris landed in the dirt nearby. Gray bullet fragments mixed with the dust pouring down the hill.

His mind whirled. The dirigible had some kind of rapid-fire gun. Going up the hill meant death. He looked back. The last Flesh-Eater hadn't pursued.

Thank the Good Lord.

He couldn't see the dirigible. It probably couldn't see him. He looked ahead. The hills ran for a long distance.

He laughed. If he kept behind the hills, he'd stay out of the dirigible's line of fire. He rose into a crouch and bolted. His back protested, but better that than a bullet.

Eventually, he risked taking a gander. The dirigible floated in the distance. He was far from where it had shot at him. He looked frantically around. Gray-brown sand interspersed with the occasional plant stretched away to the horizon.

Some of those plants were big enough to hide a man. Andrew rushed forward and threw himself behind an impressive-looking shrub. He lay on his belly for a long time. No bullets stabbed him or the ground around him.

He looked back. Streaks of dust rose from the hills behind him to mar the blue sky. Andrew rolled over and raised his rifle. A blunt head emerged, followed by a gray, furry body.

The ripper looked down. Its brown eyes locked on his. Muscles played beneath its fur. It was tensing to leap, it *had* to be.

Andrew kept his rifle up, despite the exhausted trembling in his limbs. He could shoot the ripper if it charged. He snorted. He'd barely managed it last time, and that was *before* the Flesh-Eaters had run him through the wringer.

The ripper didn't attack. It just stared at him. Andrew narrowed his eyes. Was it waiting for him to die?

"I'm not going to die anytime soon, you furry bastard!" he shouted. "If you're waiting, it'll be a right while!" His words did not provoke the beast. It just stood there waiting. "Come on! Do something!"

The ripper eyed him for a moment longer. Then it turned and shambled away.

Andrew's jaw dropped. He was tired and bloodied. Easy prey. He shook his head. Now wasn't a time to ask why. He should get gone before the ripper changed its mind, or if its mate — if it had one — showed up.

He looked to the dirigible. It was still there. If he moved, he might attract its attention. He looked back toward the top of the hill. The ripper wouldn't have gone far. It could still return.

It would be better to die quickly in a hail of rapid-fire bullets than be torn to pieces by a wild animal.

He rose to his feet. The dirigible still didn't move. He took one step, then another. There was no reaction from the enemy airship.

He quickened his pace. The high plains lay somewhere to the southwest.

SWEAT TRICKLED into Andrew's eyes. He wiped it away, again. He'd been walking for an hour beneath the sun, now high overhead. He still couldn't see the beginning of the high plains where the Merrill still ruled. He kept walking.

Then the ground wasn't there anymore. Andrew's left foot sank into empty space. His weight carried him forward. His right heel scraped against the sand and against something curving and metallic.

The ground bit Andrew's knees, reopening the old wounds. Andrew screamed. He sat there on the ground for a moment before looking back. What had appeared to be a small hill was really...

A house.

A house buried in the sand with only its front showing. Cracked as it was, the siding was still far more refined and smoother than anything Andrew had ever seen in Carroll Town. The gutters that had nearly caught his foot still held, despite being filled with sand. This had to be from the Old World.

In the center of the structure stood a green wooden door with a tarnished brass knocker and doorknob.

A momentary grin flickered across Andrew's thin face. If he'd found this earlier, he and Sam could have gotten inside, found something valuable...

Sam. Sam was dead in an alley in Carroll Town, torn open by a Flesh-Eater's knife. Andrew would never see him again. Tears came to his eyes. He swore and blinked them back. He wouldn't cry, not now.

The back of his head grew hot as the sun beat down. Andrew's hand fell to the hot doorknob. He could hide from the sun. He could rest and set off again at night. And if there were valuable artifacts — he'd heard of can openers running by themselves on something called "electricity" — he could barter them with the pikeys. They'd drive a hard bargain, but they *might* help him.

He shook his head. That assumed he could get inside for the goddamned can opener. He tried the door. It was locked.

He shook the handle, hoping time had weakened the lock. That didn't work. He shook the door harder. The ancient deadbolt rattled, but the door still would not open.

As Andrew worked, beads of sweat rolled down his arms and his neck. He stopped and raised his canteen to his lips.

Nothing. He raised the canteen higher, hoping for more water, but none came. He kept rattling the door. It *still* wouldn't open. With his remaining strength, he slammed the butt of his rifle into the door. His blow left no marks. He struck the door again. His heart leaped at the sound of cracking wood.

He'd barely chipped the wood. *Goddamn it!* He struck the door a third time. Wood cracked, but it wasn't the door. His gaze dropped to his rifle butt. There was a fine crack, below where he'd inserted the bullets. Not only was he not getting in but he was destroying his weapon! He was too far out for rippers, but the desert had its own perils. Twenty-foot sand snakes. Bandits pushed south by the Flesh-Eaters.

He could worry about animal and human predators later. Right now his enemy was the sun. He grit his teeth and struck the door again and again, shouting each time. On the fourth blow the wood cracked. A manic grin split Andrew's face.

Sand trickled from the damaged door. The house's roof must have collapsed, letting the desert in.

Andrew screamed and kicked the door as hard as he could. He sank to his knees, the hot sand burning the exposed skin. "Damn it! Damn it, damn it, damn it all to hell!"

He sat beneath the cracked door for a long time. He shook his head. He wouldn't wait for death. He would keep going.

He rose and took off walking. Maybe if he found some pikey traders, he could barter the location for food, water, or transport to where the Merrills laired. The pikeys loved their coin, but they loved Old World artifacts more.

The house fell away behind him.

His FOREHEAD BURNED beneath the merciless sun. Andrew looked down, the light hurting his eyes. He'd been marching southwest for hours and the horizon remained the same. Sweat stung his eyes. Andrew wiped it away. Dried blood flaked off his sleeve.

He looked back. His tracks stretched out behind him, a long line reaching toward his destroyed hometown. He brought up his right hand to shield his eyes from the sun. Only desolation lay before him.

He might be able to make it to the ruined Old World building. Its bulk would provide at least a little shade.

He shook his head. He'd slump down halfway there and fall asleep. The sleep from which none woke. His only hope was to keep walking. Maybe he'd find an oasis? Maybe Merrill soldiers?

He took another step. His foot caught on something. He jammed the business end of his rifle into the ground to keep his feet. He'd need to check it later. Hopefully he hadn't clogged the barrel or broken something important. If there even was a later.

Using his rifle, he forced himself up. He took a few more steps. The sun pounded on him like a hammer on a forge. His skin burned. The world around him spun. He shook his head. The world righted itself. For a moment at least. Red began creeping from the edges of his vision. He trudged on. Each step left him dizzier. He sweated less and less now. He stumbled again, catching himself once more with his rifle.

I'm going to die.

The thought came unbidden to his mind. He might well be the last man from Carroll Town to fall, but fall he would, abisselfa in the desert. Dead just like that Flesh-Eater boy.

He shook his head. He'd hold onto life like the biggest goddamn leech ever spawned. To hell with the Flesh-Eaters.

His willpower kept him going another few yards. He slumped onto his bloodied knees. His grip on his rifle kept him from falling onto his face. He put one foot under him and tried to do the same with the other, only to find he couldn't.

"Damnation."

He slid down the rifle until his cheek touched the hot sand. The world grew dark as unconsciousness swallowed him.

ALONZO MERRILL

A line of horsemen and a few cattle stretched out beneath the tan bluffs marking where the stony badlands met the Iron Desert. Third in the line, behind two bodyguards and ahead of two more, rode Alonzo Merrill, the last man of the direct Merrill bloodline.

A mounted man broke from the line and rode toward Alonzo. His guards stirred, hands tightening on their repeaters. As the man drew nearer, they relaxed. It was Captain Gerald Ralston, commander of one of the cavalry companies. "Sir, I think you need to know about this." Alonzo nodded, sweat dripping from under his brown hair. "Per your orders, I've been questioning them about what happened at Carroll Town." Ralston gestured toward the civilians the Merrills had rescued from the Flesh-Eater column scattered among the mounted soldiers.

"And?"

"From what they've told me, I reckon Grendel and Jasper Clark were there."

Alonzo yanked on the reins, bringing his horse to a dead stop. Pain lanced from his left wrist to his elbow where a Flesh-Eater saber had caught him two hours prior. He clenched his fists around the reins, the three clockwork brass fingers the Shoemaker underground smuggled from Jacinto digging into his left palm.

"*Both?*" Alonzo demanded, forcing the pain from his voice. His lips pulled back around yellow teeth. Ralston recoiled but kept speaking.

"Aye. This might be our chance. Not just Clark, but Grendel himself!"

Alonzo's hands shook, the pain from his wounded arm fueling his anger. Grendel, the tyrant that ground his family underfoot. Grendel, the one who'd fed his brother John to the monsters of the Blood Alchemy Host and transformed the Flesh-Eaters from a rabble of man-eating hill trash into a dangerous army. Grendel, who'd claimed his little sister as a war prize. He remembered what the one faithful soldier who returned from captivity in Norridge told him, how Grendel threatened prisoners' lives to make Catalina spread her legs for him...

Alonzo's right hand flew to one of the two chest-length braids snaking from the back of his head onto his shoulder. He would cut one when he killed Clark. The other when he killed Grendel. Whenever those glorious days came.

"How many troopers they got?"

Ralston grinned. "Not many. The numbers don't add up, but I'd reckon no more than one hundred. Mostly Flesh-Eaters."

Alonzo looked back over his men. If he abandoned the civilians and the cattle and made straight for Carroll Town, maybe he could blitz the relatively small enemy force and get a shot at Clark and Grendel. He grinned at the thought of tearing the two bastards apart.

He forced himself to slow his breathing, to ponder the *wisdom* of the suggestion. Grendel likely came by dirigible. He'd need a lot more than the twenty horsemen he had on hand to face even *one* airship. Even at full gallop, it would take hours to get there. Grendel and Clark would be gone when they arrived. And he *needed* the cattle taken in the raid and the civilians.

Alonzo shook his head. "Not risking it." Ralston nodded. "Keep asking questions. Find out all you can. We might be able to get *something* out of this."

"Understood, sir."

Ralston returned to the column. Alonzo returned to his brooding. Unless the two overlords were so kind as to come visiting with

minimal protection another time, the chances of him ever getting his
final revenge dwindled.

The Flesh-Eaters tightened their grip on the desert fringe every day.
They increased the tribute exacted from the towns they didn't govern
directly and rounded up folk to build forts cutting the region off from
the richer farmlands to the north. Many raiding parties had already
been repelled and most of those getting in didn't return.

He looked back toward the rustled cattle. They'd help feed his
people for awhile. The nails digging into the wrists and ankles of his
cause had pulled away, but only just. The steel points were still there.

A mounted man appeared ahead. Alonzo's guards stirred once
more before it became clear the newcomer was friendly. "Sir," the
horseman said. "We've found another group of survivors, a fair bit
south of here."

"How many?"

"About a dozen. They're in a poor state and say they're from
Carroll Town."

"We're right far from there."

"They were mounted. Women and kids."

Alonzo nodded. The survivors they'd rescued said the Flesh-Eater
cavalry circled Carroll Town and caught the women and children leaving. Given how the Flesh-Eaters craved *live* women and kids, it made
sense they'd burden their horsemen with prisoners. That'd allow a few
mounted survivors to run.

"Where are they?"

"Right behind me, sir."

The timing brought a small smile to Alonzo's face. Behind the rider
appeared another scout, followed by several bedraggled civilians.
Most were terribly sunburned. Some slumped down on their horses'
necks. The conscious ones had the wide, staring eyes of those who'd
seen horrors. The horses' nostrils flared, breathing like blowers on a
forge. Their bodies glistened with sweat. If the scouts hadn't found
them, they'd probably be dead within hours.

Alonzo winced. They'd need to get back to the refuge quickly. He
gestured toward the main body of horsemen behind them. "Get them
in the column. Give them water."

The scouts obeyed, guiding the women and children forward. As the survivors filed past, Alonzo counted out eight women and four kids. He doubted the new arrivals would bolster the battle line but he had other work for them. "Anything else?"

"We also found a Flesh-Eater." Alonzo pursed his lips. He knew how the Flesh-Eaters recruited their troopers. Perhaps he'd used the chaos of the battle to desert? "He was a lot closer to Carroll Town than the rest. He was on foot."

Alonzo snorted. "Definitely a greenhorn if he thought he could cross the desert abisselfa. Was he one of the fanatics?" The rider shook his head. "Good."

Although some would gladly kill anyone wearing Flesh-Eater duds, Alonzo knew most Flesh-Eaters didn't want to be soldiers anymore than his people wanted to be refugees. Deserters made good rebels, and he had a harsh and, thus far, foolproof way to ensure their loyalty. Fanatics, of course, were to be killed out of hand.

The horseman nodded. "Understood, sir."

This Flesh-Eater, whoever he was, would be taken care of and given the opportunity to join the Merrill army. If he refused, bayonets wasted no bullets.

A REASON TO LIVE

Andrew's eyes cracked open. His head pounded. His weight bore down uncomfortably on his lungs. His tongue felt huge in his mouth. Through vision gauzy and tinged red, he saw the yellow sands of the Iron Desert moving several feet below.

That was strange. He didn't know what he believed about what happened after death — beyond the fervent hope the Flesh-Eaters got theirs — but he didn't reckon he'd drift in the desert forever. That'd be an improvement over some stories he'd heard. Legend had it those who died alone in the Iron Desert became ghosts that sought to quench their endless thirst with travelers' blood...

Andrew realized his mouth was wet. It had been dry when he'd slumped down to die. He licked his lips, getting the last of the moisture. His lips stung as his tongue touched the sun-cut cracks. The droplets he gleaned tasted like blood.

Then he realized the ground below him rose and fell. It took a moment to realize he lay across the back of a horse and *he* was bouncing up and down. His side pressed up against something broad and hard and warm. A rider.

He forced his head upward. The man wore a brown duster, which could conceal red and black Flesh-Eater uniforms or ordinary clothes.

Andrew cleared his throat. Though he tried to put some volume into it, he could barely hear himself. He shook his head. "Hey." He raised his voice as much as he could. What emerged from his mouth wasn't much louder.

Andrew tried to reach over and tap the man's leg, only to find he couldn't. Rough rope bound his hands behind his back, rope that scratched his wrists when he moved even slightly.

He tensed. The pikeys loved money, far more than they loved any outsider. If this were a pikey, chances were Andrew would be sold as a slave!

And who *bought* slaves? The Flesh-Eaters!

Andrew thrashed. The Flesh-Eaters would conscript him into their armies or put him to work in the fields or mines. He'd rather goddamn die.

Something cold and circular pressed against his temple.

"Hold still, you little bastard," the rider ordered. He spoke with a slow drawl much like a Flesh-Eater. Andrew froze. "That's better." The gun remained pressed against his head for a moment longer and then vanished.

The man turned in the saddle, his body pushing against Andrew.

"You were in a bad way when I found you. Drink this." A rough hand holding an open canteen appeared in Andrew's face. "Drink."

Water! Andrew wrapped his mouth around the canteen's opening. The man tilted the canteen, pouring enough to fill Andrew's mouth but not so much it spilled. There was something odd about the taste, something Andrew couldn't quite place.

"That'll keep you out for a spell."

Andrew's world began spinning. It was slow at first, so much Andrew didn't notice it at first. As it grew faster, the yellow-brown sand and the blue sky swirled together, like some insane, colorful version of the swirling in the river after a rain when the water was high and fast.

He only had a moment to wonder just what he'd drank before the whirl grew too intense to bear and he spun away into unconsciousness.

ANDREW'S HEAD still hurt when he woke. The first thing he heard was nearby voices. One might be a neighbor, but the other two had northern drawls. *Flesh-Eater* drawls.

Andrew looked from side to side. He lay on a simple cot, looking up at the canvas ceiling of a tent. The three people he heard were in the tent with him.

"He's awake," one Flesh-Eater said. "Let's see what he has to say."

Say? I'll do more than say!

Andrew swung in the direction of the one who'd spoken. A hand caught Andrew's fist. Weakened as he was, he couldn't get free.

The hand belonged to a large man in brown trousers and a plaid shirt. Beyond him stood another large man whose clothes hid beneath a duster. None wore obvious Flesh-Eater uniforms.

Relief flooded through him. The first thing awaiting recruits to the Flesh-Eating Legion was a week of living only on the flesh of prisoners sacrificed to the Howling God. He'd been spared *that*, at least.

Of course, just because he wasn't in the custody of the Flesh-Eaters didn't mean he was safe. These men could be slavers or common bandits.

Then he spotted a short young man with a crudely-stitched wound on the right side of his round face. It was David Court, one of Eudora's cousins. Like the others, he bore a holstered pistol on one hip.

Oh thank the Good Lord.

Chances were he was in friendlier hands if someone else from Carroll Town was there and armed.

"This one's feisty," the man who grabbed Andrew drawled. "Maybe we'll keep him."

"Sergeant, that's a damn sight better than he deserves." The other stranger's voice combined equal parts drawl and gravel. "He's a damned Flesh-Eater."

"Not a Flesh-Eater," Andrew moaned. Pain crackled across his lips. He smelled blood. "Stole uniform."

"A right likely story," the second man snapped. "If you said you were one of their conscripts who deserted, maybe we'd believe that —"

"He ain't a Flesh-Eater," David declared. "That's Andrew Sutter."

He's from Carroll Town like me. He was born the same month as me, his dad was the mayor in town, his family owns fields near the river I used to work in, and —"

"Why's he wearing their duds then?" the second man interrupted.

David paused. "Good question." He turned toward Andrew. "What's with the getup?"

"Sam and I stole it off a Flesh-Eater we killed."

That got the sergeant's attention. "I'd like to hear this." He handed Andrew a canteen. "Drink and tell me more." The man paused. "I'm Sergeant Ezekiel Thaxton, Second Pendleton."

After drinking most of the water, Andrew told him what had happened, starting with the Flesh-Eater tribute-gatherer and his body-guard. The three listened to his tale patiently until Andrew arrived at the death of Eudora.

"She was with you?" David demanded. He stepped toward Andrew's cot. "You led her against the *Flesh-Eaters*?"

"Yeah." David's tone irritated him. "I needed anyone who could shoot and she took out that ripper, remember? The ripper that —"

David recoiled. "I know about the ripper. I was actually going to *thank* you. Better what happened than what the Flesh-Eaters would've done if they'd got her alive."

"Enough." Zeke silenced David with a glance. He turned back toward Andrew. "Continue."

Andrew continued his tale until the part where he had the bald man and the man in black in his sights.

"Hold it," the second man — Wyatt — interrupted. "You saw a big, bald man and a man in black, a man who wore a helmet made of a tiger skull?"

"Yeah," Andrew said guardedly. His scalp tingled. Those men must be important, somehow.

"That was Jasper Clark and Grendel!"

"Jasper Clark?" Andrew's eyes widened. "And *Grendel?*"

Wyatt nodded. Andrew abruptly fell silent. He had the chance to kill the Flesh-Eater bossman and the man who held his leash? And he *didn't? Well shit.* He'd killed a lesser officer when the biggest target of all was right there! He had a right great opportunity and blew it!

Shit.

Wyatt leaned forward, blue eyes wide in his narrow face and his stained teeth showing. "Did you get them? Did you get both of them?"

Andrew closed his eyes. He could feel himself turning red. "No," he whispered. "I shot an officer with them." When the man's expression darkened, Andrew's voice hardened. "I didn't know who they were, okay? I got one of their officers, though. Must be a high one, if he's consorting with them!"

"You dumb goddamn kid!" Wyatt roared. "You could have killed Jasper and Grendel and you *didn't?*" He stepped forward, teeth bared. Andrew's hands trembled. He couldn't have beaten the man even if he'd been hale. "I ought to whup your ass for being so goddamn stupid!" Wyatt raised his fists. "You fucking —"

"Rein it in!" Zeke barked. He stepped between them. As he moved, Andrew spotted an old manacle encircling one wrist.

Wyatt immediately backed away, but kept his eyes locked on Andrew. "Boy, you could have won us the war right then!"

You're a right fool, *Andrew Sutter.* Jasper Clark, ruler of the Flesh-Eaters? And Grendel, a man so powerful even the Flesh-Eaters truckled to him? And he'd skipped the chance to kill one or both to kill some brown-noser?

That officer had *laughed* about his mother's death. Grief and anger welled up from inside him. He grit his teeth. "The man I killed, he was laughing about what they did to Carroll Town! Laughing about killing my ma!"

"A lot of people lost their mas *and* their pas to the Flesh-Eaters," Wyatt retorted. "If you'd laid Clark or Grendel in boot hill, there'd be a lot fewer mas and pas getting killed." He spat on the dirt floor. "Dumb, idiot kid."

"Andrew ain't dumb," David interrupted. "Maybe he's ignorant, not knowing who those people were, but —"

"Hobble your lip, greenhorn," Wyatt retorted. "I'm a goddamn corporal. If I want to say someone's a right dumb shit and he ain't a sergeant or an officer, I damn well *will.*"

"Both of you, can it," Zeke ordered. "Squabbling won't put either of them in boot hill." Wyatt scowled. Zeke turned back to Andrew. "All right. Once you're rested up, we're gonna need to find something for you to do."

Then someone pushed the tent flap open. "The Merrill approaches," a new voice said. The three stood to attention, David a little slower than the others. A slender man stepped into the tent.

He was tall, at least six feet, and wore a shabby duster that looked a little too large. Brown hair peeked out from under a slouched hat whose crown was encircled by tattered gold braid. Two long ponytails hung over his right shoulder down to his chest. White bandages spotted red emerged from his left sleeve. Three fingers on his left hand were made of metal.

Andrew's heart leaped into his throat.

Alonzo Merrill!

He sat up a little higher. It was the best he could manage.

"At ease," the rebel chieftain ordered. The others relaxed. He looked at Andrew. "I wonder what the desert brought us today? It looks like we've got a young Flesh-Eater."

Andrew looked down at his clothing. Although his red jacket was gone, he still wore the black trousers of a Flesh-Eater infantryman. "What were you thinking, running off into the desert?" Alonzo asked. "If I hadn't been raiding your people, you'd be food for the vultures or a sand snake."

Andrew was right tired of people thinking him a Flesh-Eater. "They're not *my* people."

Alonzo raised an eyebrow. "If you're not a Flesh-Eater, what are you?"

"I'm from Carroll Town," Andrew declared. "There was a revolt. We were hoping you could help —"

Alonzo turned to the others. "Is this the same story he told the rest of you?"

"Aye," Zeke said.

"Andrew's no coward," David spoke up. "He's right brave and right smart. There's no way he'd ever join the —"

Alonzo raised his hand, silencing David. He looked at Andrew for a moment. "You look familiar. What's your father's name?"

Andrew sighed. Why did everything keep coming back to Pa? "Maxwell."

"Maxwell," Alonzo repeated. "Are you related to Maxwell Sutter?"

Andrew groaned. Alonzo cocked his head. Andrew's stomach lurched. Hopefully he hadn't pissed off the rebel leader. He didn't want to end up bunking with a ripper.

"He was my pa."

Alonzo smiled. "I remember him. He led the delegation from Carroll Town when my grandfather died and my father became the Merrill. You look a lot like him." He turned to Zeke. "He's not one of them, so we won't need to put him in the pen."

Andrew sighed in relief. If they locked him up with Flesh-Eaters, he doubted he'd come out alive.

The rebel leader turned and left the tent. Zeke gestured to Wyatt and David to leave likewise. Wyatt stepped backward through the flap, scowling at Andrew the whole time. David stayed put.

"There're chores to do, Court," Zeke said. "Get."

David flinched, like he suddenly realized something. "Got it, sir."

"Don't call me 'sir.' I work for a living."

"Sorry, sergeant. Yes, sergeant." David quickly left.

Zeke turned to Andrew. "The bossman seems to reckon you're on the level, but I want to hear more. What happened after you didn't kill Grendel?"

The man's words stung. Andrew continued his tale, his voice rising to a babble when he described the encounter with the dirigible. He went on about the airship until Zeke raised his hand.

"We know all about dirigibles. Keep going."

Andrew described the rest of what had happened, including the Old World house. By the time he finished, both of Zeke's eyebrows were pretty high. "Pretty impressive, surviving all that. How old are you?"

"Twenty-one."

Zeke laughed. "Not much younger than me when I took James Merrill's dollar." He pulled a canteen from the pocket of his duster and set it by Andrew's cot. "Stay here and drink when you need to. I'll come by when you're rested."

The big man turned away, giving Andrew another glimpse of the manacle, and left the tent. Andrew reached over and took a swig from the canteen. He lay back down and stared at the canvas ceiling.

He was alive. Despite all that had happened, despite the deaths of so many, he was still alive.

He closed his eyes. Tears gathered beneath his lids. He was still alive, while so many from Carroll Town had died.

"Why me?" He kept staring at the canvas ceiling. "Why am *I* here?" Tears rolled out the sides of his closed eyes, sliding over raw, sunburned flesh.

Sam had survived the battle on the hills and even the Flesh-Eater invasion of the town. If that Flesh-Eater hadn't killed him in the alley, he'd have joined his rifle with Andrew's and maybe both Clark *and* Grendel would be laid in boot hill.

But Sam had died. Sam had died because Andrew hadn't reckoned a Flesh-Eater had seen them fighting. If he'd been more careful, they could have gotten the drop on that son of a bitch and Sam wouldn't have been killed. Sam would still be alive, and maybe both tyrants would be dead.

The guilt still lashed his mind when he finally slipped into the dark.

ANDREW SPENT the next four days in the tent, wobbling out only to answer the call of nature in a nearby slit trench. The cot provided little comfort. He constantly pulled the blankets on or off — it was always too hot or too cold. When he did get close to sleeping, trumpets often yanked him back awake.

David brought him water and after a couple of days, food. He also brought new clothes and Andrew's rifle, which Andrew hadn't even noticed was gone. Something metal now hung beneath the muzzle.

Once Andrew had time to ponder anything other than water, food, and sleep, he started picking David's brain about what had happened at Carroll Town.

"Well, after you potted the enemy bossman, they rounded everybody up and took us out of town. They split everyone into groups of around ten. Lucky for us, the Merrills had been raiding north against the forts the Flesh-Eaters are building. The Southern Wall, people call it. They were on their way back and bushwhacked the Flesh-Eaters who had us. They killed all the bastards and set us loose. Afterward, they — we — went south. The scouts went out in two directions. One set found some other people from back home out in the desert, mounted, while the other set found you."

"Who else was with you?" Andrew demanded. "Ma? Sarah? Cassie?"

"Sarah got taken by a different group. I got a look at them going straight north when my group went east." Andrew swore. He was relieved Sarah was still alive, but he was *not* relieved she was in the hands of the Flesh-Eaters. "Before you laid the bastard in boot hill, the Flesh-Eater commander asked her some questions." Enthusiasm crept into David's voice. "She gave him a piece of her mind. It was a hoot."

Andrew grit his teeth. That sounded just like Sarah, but her performance probably pissed the cannibal sons of bitches off. Things would go even *worse* for her, if that were possible.

"What about Ma?" Although he'd heard her scream, that didn't necessarily mean the Flesh-Eater had *killed* her. Maybe the Flesh-Eaters changed their minds. Anybody with half a brain knew older women could be used for more than bed-warming.

David winced. "They damn near cut her head off. She was one of the first."

"Damn it!" Andrew snarled. He pounded his fist on the wood of the cot. David recoiled. Andrew closed his eyes. It wasn't David's fault he bore bad news. "Sorry. Thanks for telling me."

"Got it."

"And Cassie?"

"I didn't see her after they took everybody out of the square."

Andrew changed the subject. "Where are we now?"

"We're at one of the camps the Merrills've got scattered about." He paused. "When you're rested up, I expect they'll make you a soldier. They put me in the Second Pendleton, in Zeke's squad. Every man in this outfit fights, and some of the women besides. Seems a bit peculiar, having women soldiers, but they — we — don't really have much of a —"

Andrew raised a hand. "Okay." He reckoned he'd end up a Merrill soldier. He didn't mind one bit.

"I've never seen you rope cattle or ride with a herd before, so I doubt they'd make you cavalry. I reckon they'd make you a dragoon."

Andrew had heard that term before, but he didn't recall where. "What's a dragoon?"

"A mounted footslogger. You'd ride to the fight and dismount. Best of both worlds, I suppose — mobile like a cavalryman, but can dig in and hold ground like an infantryman." He paused. "That's one reason the Merrills have been able to keep fighting for so damn long. It's a right pain in the ass to feed all these horses, but we can get in and out double-quick. Zeke says one time, the Flesh-Eaters were pulling a noose round the whole army, but there was a gap, just one gap, and all the troopers got out through it. I don't know why the Flesh-Eaters don't mount up their infantry, but —"

Andrew raised a hand. "Okay. I got it."

ON THE FIFTH DAY, Andrew felt well enough to look around. His boots crunched against the stony earth when he left the tent. In areas where few feet had trod, he spotted grass. The camp must be on the high plains, not the badlands or the Iron Desert.

The yellow sun hung to Andrew's right in the blue sky. It was hot, but not uncomfortably so. Maybe it was still morning.

The Merrill encampment lay spread out as far as Andrew could see. Relatively few people moved among the tents. It must be time for training, chores, and the like.

He didn't see David. He'd have to explore on his own.

Directly ahead a vast, brown rock emerged from the tents like a huge tooth from gums. A rickety wooden stairway scaled the stone, culminating in a wooden platform manned by several soldiers. A green flag bearing a yellow horseshoe hung limply on a pole. *Observation point.*

The wind picked up, blowing in from the west. The smell of cattle struck Andrew in the face. Andrew followed the smell through three rows of tents before he found dozens of cattle penned behind a crude wooden fence.

"We rustled them from the Flesh-Eaters just before we found you." Andrew nearly jumped at Zeke's sudden appearance. "The bastards were collecting tribute from all the towns and ranches along the desert and we collected it from them." He smiled. "Now follow me. Since you're walking around, it's time we found you work."

KEEPING THE PEACE

Dressed once more in his black finery, Grendel looked out the window of the *Nicor*. His personal airship floated smoothly over the teal waters of the Buni River and the farmland it watered around the city of Hamari. The Leaden Host's regional seat of power sat in a relatively wet spot amid the dry lands. At last, he was through with the desert.

He turned to his bed where Jessamine lay asleep beneath a black blanket decorated with silver serpents, lions, and bears. She could afford to sleep off the afternoon's exertions. He, however, had work to do.

He sat at an ornate desk bearing carvings of longships and serpents and opened the folder with the intelligence reports about the Carroll Town uprising.

The guardsmen had searched Carroll Town after the survivors had been dealt with. No Old World arms were found. Although the grenade almost certainly came from one of the local trading clans, Clark stuck by his accusation. Per the treaty formalizing his submission to Grendel, Clark had the right to file a grievance. This meant Grendel would have to hold a perfunctory hearing to exonerate his old friend.

His gaze returned to Jessamine. Based on what he knew of the local culture, she would be left with the officers' women while the men did business. If she were still tired, she could sleep there. If not, she could gossip and relay anything interesting to him. He stepped over to the bed.

"Jessamine, wake up." He pulled back the blanket, unveiling the planes and lines of her back and shoulders and the twin hemispheres of her buttocks. Jessamine murmured in protest. "We are at Hamari. I am not leaving you here. Get up."

Jessamine obediently rolled over and sat up, giving Grendel a delightful view. He felt himself stir, but that needed to wait. There simply was not time before the dirigible docked.

Grendel affectionately ruffled her dark hair. "Good girl. I will leave you with the commander's wives if he has any. I want you to see what information you can pick up."

Jessamine's green eyes widened. "With the commander's wives? Do you want me to —"

Grendel's jaw set. It was no problem if he were to spread his seed — all he needed to do was make sure all his children were acknowledged and accounted for. For one of his women to cuckold him, *that* was different. His former concubine Alexandra had slept with a guardsman, hoping he would help her escape. He hanged both before the windows of his harem as an example. And that was merciful compared to his initial plan to send them to Mangle's breeding pits.

"No, then," Jessamine said.

"He would be on his guard, knowing you share my bed. His women, however, might be less careful. Talk to them. Make friends, if not more." Now *that* he had no objection to. "Report any interesting gossip to me."

"What would you find interesting?"

"Anything military. I want to know if the soldiers here intend to attack the Flesh-Eaters or expect to be attacked. I also want to know about relations between Hamari and anyone under Flesh-Eater jurisdiction."

Jessamine nodded. She climbed out of bed, gathered her things — drawers, lacy black Cassandra dress, red shawl, and gold bracelets – off the floor, and disappeared into the adjoining bathroom.

Grendel watched her ass until she was out of sight before returning to the window. The dirigible had passed over Hamari's adobe and wood buildings and now approached the cannon-studded ramparts of Hamari Fort on the large rocky outcrop overlooking the city. Within lay mooring towers for airships, water tanks, silos to hold grain during a siege, and a star-shaped concrete citadel housing even more cannon. Grendel did not envy any men sent to take the place.

The airship slowed as it passed over the thick walls of the fort. Distant hatches clanged open. Guardsmen rappelled from the gondola. Beneath their watchful eyes, the ground crew pulled the *Nicor* toward the central mooring tower. A slight shudder rolled through the dirigible as it docked.

Grendel put the papers in his leather satchel. Many would leave this to a servant, but a sneaky courier could tamper with them. Keeping important things in one's own hands was always the best policy.

Jessamine emerged from the bathroom dressed and no longer smelling of sweat and sex. Grendel stepped over to the brass cage hanging next to his desk and released Alrekr. The pterosaur hopped onto his wrist and then onto his shoulder. He removed the bag of dried fish parts hanging from the cage and put it in his pocket before leaving.

Others joined Grendel and Jessamine as they walked down the corridor running the length of the gondola. First came guardsmen. Next were intelligence personnel and dogsbodies for any unexpected tasks.

Across the gangplank linking the mooring tower to the *Nicor*, flanked by a pair of black-clad guardsmen, stood the local dignitaries. Grendel recognized a tall, dark-haired and beak-nosed man in a white uniform as Colonel Ibrahim Mifshud, the city's Leaden Host governor.

"Welcome to Hamari, my lord. We're glad you have chosen to grace us with your presence."

Grendel forced himself not to roll his eyes at this obsequiousness. "I have come to discuss a matter concerning your relations with your friends across the river." Grendel locked eyes with Mifshud. The man did not flinch, but Grendel discerned a slight trembling in his hands.

"What have they accused us of this time?" Though Mifshud's voice was flat, there was an undertone of anger and longstanding hatred. The man could be useful when the time came to unleash Havarth. Assuming he still had his responsibilities or his life.

"Old World weapons and secretly helping the Merrills. Border disputes and absconding peasants likewise, but those are small potatoes."

Mifshud's breath quickened. He no doubt pondered the devastation of Hamari by the Obsidian Guard and how he would be drawn and quartered like a common criminal if he survived. That was the punishment for allowing Old World weapons to fall into unauthorized hands. And that was not the only accusation.

That is something he should fear. Being loved is optional; being feared is essential.

"Alexander Matthews is on his way," Mifshud said. "He should arrive by supper."

Grendel nearly smiled. The commanders of his loyal Hosts and those smart enough to kneel could govern their territories as they saw fit, provided they paid tribute and obeyed certain rules. Mifshud clearly knew how things worked and invoked his master as a shield.

"Jasper Clark should be arriving soon as well. With everyone here, we will get this sorted out quickly." He paused. "Do you have the maps you use to mark the border between your territories and those of the Flesh-Eaters?"

"Yes, my lord."

"Gather them. We will discuss this matter after supper."

"Excellent." Mifshud was a bit too eager. "I will find a place for you, your lady, and your soldiers while we wait."

CLARK and his entourage arrived next. Grendel paid him the usual courtesies and sent him on his way. He stood with some guardsmen in the shade of the citadel across from the empty tower reserved for Alexander's dirigible, the *Old Epharim*.

The first sign Alexander had arrived was the rhythmic scudding of his airship's propellers. Soon afterward, the flying leviathan itself appeared in the northern sky. Alexander's vessel was as long as the *Nicor* — about six hundred feet — but its balloon was brown, unlike the *Nicor*'s distinctive black. Grendel's dirigible bore the skull of a saber-toothed cat on its balloon, but Alexander's bore the Leaden Host's heraldic grizzly, its chest protected by a pair of huge brass shell casings.

It did not take long for Alexander's entourage to descend from the airship. His guards stopped fifty feet away, leaving Alexander to approach his master alone.

Alexander was shorter than Grendel, with close-cropped brown hair that was starting to thin and brown eyes. He wore a knee-length brown coat and jeans atop leather boots. A large six-shooter hung on his left hip.

Grendel extended the hand he had cut open long ago. Alexander extended his own, which bore a matching scar. The two shook.

"It has been too long," Grendel said.

"You know how it is," Alexander replied.

Grendel knew that all too well. "It is good you came so quickly."

Alexander paused. "I wish I could agree."

"Alex, Clark is full of shit. We both know that."

"Then *why* did you summon me?" Alexander demanded. "I don't have *time* to answer lies from some hill trash cannibal who's gotten too big for his britches."

"If it was just personal preference, I would tell Clark to piss off. However, I need to avoid brother-in-law politics or else the whole thing will collapse."

Alexander scowled. "I understand the need to keep order. But do you *really* reckon Clark can threaten you?"

"Not by himself. But it is no secret Clark is not the only one I dislike. If I start playing favorites, the ones I disfavor will ally and wreck everything *we* have built." Alexander nodded, but his lips were still thin with anger. "Enough. Mifshud prepared us a proper feast. It will be a good dinner, and it will be on his coin, not yours."

"That'd be swell. But don't expect me to have a hog-killing time here."

ONCE DINNER CONCLUDED, Grendel put on his armor and helmet and took the high seat in the vast hall where Mifshud held court. More chairs were brought up for Alexander and Clark at Grendel's right and left. Guardsmen stood on the four corners of the dais and by the doors, repeaters ready. Mifshud stood before the three overlords. Beyond him, local officials and members of the rulers' entourages formed an audience.

"I have come to hear the grievance Jasper Clark has made against the Leaden Host, in particular, Colonel Ibrahim Mifshud," Grendel intoned.

Short and stocky Captain John Anderson, the new commander of Fort Vallero, emerged from among Clark's entourage. "The rabble of Carroll Town had an Old World weapon," he declared. His left shoulder twitched when he spoke. "They certainly didn't get it from us and the Nahada herdsmen hereabouts don't much like us any more than they did the Merrills. The Leaden Host's got the motive to needle us and the Old World arms to do it." He looked at Mifshud. "How hard'd it be to have some pikey smuggle grenades in? Or maybe an agent of the Merrills?"

"I wouldn't know," Mifshud retorted.

Grendel resisted the urge to yawn. The accusation was almost certainly a pack of lies.

Alexander leaned forward, locking eyes with Anderson. "Do you have any proof the grenade came from Colonel Mifshud?"

"He's got the motivation," Anderson replied. "And *we* keep track of our Old World gear."

"Do you have any more evidence?" Grendel asked. Anderson shook his head. "Dismissed."

Anderson withdrew. A big man missing his right hand and sporting a formidable mustache stepped forward. Grendel recognized him from the intelligence reports as Major Thomas Ward, a Flesh-Eater officer who ruled the territory across the river from Hamari. Ward glared at Mifshud before focusing his attention on the overlords.

"I don't claim to know about the accusations Captain Anderson has made about Old World arms, as serious as they are," he began. "But I have another complaint."

"Speak."

"Over the last two years, Mifshud has cost me taxes by not returning absconders from my territory. I'd say a couple hundred have shirked their obligations and hid in Hamari."

Grendel raised an eyebrow. That was a substantial number in the dry country in the southwestern part of his empire, only slightly more hospitable than the badlands around Carroll Town. Clark certainly complained about the situation, but he never even hinted at the scale.

"This is a most grave claim," Clark said. He glared at Mifshud. "Does the little Nahada bastard have anything to say about this?"

Alexander glared at Clark. "I would imagine so."

Mifshud stepped forward. "I will concede Major Ward's accusation." Clark leaned forward, a predatory gleam on his face. Alexander's expression hardened. Grendel's eyebrow rose higher. He did not expect Mifshud to *confess*.

"Although Hamari is wealthier and more populous than much of Clark's realm, we still have more sheep than people," Mifshud continued. "If we want to build, to provide more tribute to our superiors" — he looked at Alexander and Grendel — "we need more people working the land, engaging in crafts, and trading with the *Menceir*. And considering how our neighbors would rather destroy and extort than properly rule —"

"This is irrelevant," Clark interrupted. "And a goddamn lie. We're in the middle of a drought right now, especially in the southern parts."

"That certainly isn't helping matters, but even so, I'd imagine people would still take their chances here. After all, we're not in the habit of *eating* them."

"You're a right liar, you little —"

"Irrelevant." Grendel focused on Mifshud. "Continue."

"We have allowed those willing to risk absconding to remain here if they work and pay their taxes."

"Which they should be paying to *us*," Clark interrupted. "Either where they're at now or somewhere else in our domain, with the proper permission."

Mifshud ignored the Flesh-Eater overlord. "We are, of course, open to the possibility of negotiating a financial settlement."

Ward exploded. "Financial settlement? I offered ransom for my brother when you bastards got your hands on him and you went and cut his goddamn head off!"

"It is not Leaden Host policy to give quarter without good reason," Alexander interrupted. "Your brother obviously wasn't worth taking alive."

"Silence, all of you!" Grendel roared. "I did not come here to mediate a fight over somebody's goddamn brother. Major Ward, you are *dismissed.*"

The chastened Flesh-Eater slunk back into the audience. Grendel returned his attention to Mifshud. "And the Old World weapons?" He let menace flavor his words.

Mifshud narrowed his eyes. "A pack of dirty *lies*. Major Ward and his master are upset I harbored their runaways and hold land on the other side of the river. They're trying to provoke you to destroy me."

Grendel let his silence hang on the air for a moment. "This is my judgment. If Mifshud wants to continue eroding the Flesh-Eaters' tax base, he should pay for it. For every runaway he keeps from now on, *he* will pay two hundred gold dollars to those holding legitimate authority over them."

Mifshud nodded, his eyes narrow. The Nahada officer would be a lot more selective with his benevolence if he personally had to fund it. However, allowing him to continue weakening the Flesh-Eaters would also serve Grendel's long-term goal to replace Clark.

"Is this acceptable, Alexander?"

"It is."

Grendel's gaze fell upon Clark. "Do you agree?"

Clark glanced from Alexander to Grendel. "It's acceptable."

"I have examined the reports from Carroll Town about the Old World grenade," Grendel continued. "Although it appears the grenade came from outside the town, we found no evidence it came from Mifshud. Clark will pay ten thousand gold dollars to Mifshud for this rash accusation."

Clark's eyes bulged. This would mean fifty escaping Flesh-Eater territory before he gained a single coin.

"However," Grendel continued. "In the interest of caution, Alexander will appoint an inspector for Old World arms caches in Hamari. *If* indeed a leak is found, Mifshud will return the settlement to the Flesh-Eaters with interest." That would be the *least* of Mifshud's problems if it turned out there were Old World weapons getting to rebels.

"It will be done," Alexander said.

Clark frowned. Although Grendel made sure the Flesh-Eating Legion would be compensated for runaways, Mifshud would obviously not feel the wrath of the Obsidian Guard. The lord of the Flesh-Eaters needed to learn something was better than nothing.

"Now about the territory on the other side of the river," Grendel said. "Colonel Mifshud, show me the border."

A pair of Leaden Host dogsbodies emerged from the spectators and set up a map on a large stand. Mifshud pointed to a pair of towns on the other side of the river from Hamari. "Terry and McDougal belonged to the Merrills. After you defeated James Merrill, they submitted to us." Mifshud grinned. It must have been wonderful to see his old enemies groveling before him, seeking his protection from the triumphant Flesh-Eaters.

"We beat the Merrills," Clark growled. "All that's theirs is ours."

"You didn't beat them alone," Alexander retorted.

Grendel nodded. When James Merrill defied him, he had first invaded the northeast of the Merrill domain. There the Merrill's writ ran thin and it was Clark who ruled. He had made Clark an offer he could not refuse. It had not taken much — the Merrills had killed his wife and son over a decade before. After the Blood Alchemy Host drew off enough Merrill strength, the Flesh-Eaters struck south and the Leaden Host swept east, crushing the Merrill armies in the center of their realm and paving the way for the final victory at Fairmont.

Clark pointed at Mifshud's map. "Look there. The river makes a natural border. And if you're concerned with absconders, giving *us* Terry and McDougal means they'll have to cross the river rather than a fence."

"A fair point," Grendel said. "But that does not address how the Leaden Host participated in the dismemberment of the Merrill realm. To the victor go the spoils, after all."

Clark frowned. *Hoisted on his own petard.*

"Very well. A trade. In exchange for Terry and McDougal, I'll —"

"I will leave that to you and Alexander." His main concern was that his lieutenants' territorial disputes were peacefully resolved. If they wanted to horse-trade for a couple of towns, that did not bother him.

He rose from his seat. "This meeting is adjourned."

GRENDEL AND ALEXANDER stood beneath the *Nicor*, the Obsidian Guard a discreet distance away. "You see," Grendel said. "That was not so painful."

Alexander nodded. Clark left soon after Grendel passed judgment. Alexander was not interested in making deals, and Grendel figured Clark could tell when he was not wanted.

"True," Alexander conceded. "Perhaps taking a day to travel here means I won't have to spend years fighting a war."

"That is the plan. And if war does come, it will not start on your land."

Alexander nodded. "I'll keep a closer eye on Mifshud. Being a light hand is good for business, but not when it pisses off the neighbors."

Grendel could understand those wanting to escape Clark's dominion. However, his entire regime from his palace in Norridge to the lowest soldier of the lowest commander rested on the those who worked or built providing for the military. Alex and most of his commanders ran ships so efficient they could let those under their thumb move around and still collect the taxes, but Clark could not say the same. If Hamari were as poor as Mifshud claimed, it would not shelter runaways much longer.

One more grievance for the people the Merrills once ruled. One more reason to rise up when my son comes.

Out of the corner of his eye, he saw Jessamine and her bodyguard leaving the citadel. She briefly paused to speak with a dark-skinned Nahada woman.

It looked like Jessamine had made a new friend. If they started corresponding, this gave Grendel a source of information on what went on at Hamari Fort, independent of Alexander or Mifshud. It never hurt to have fingers in many pies.

THE ARMY LIFE

*Z*eke led Andrew through rows of tents to where the Second Pendleton gathered. Andrew was shocked at how small the outfit was. He thought regiments had one thousand men, but this one had barely two hundred. Although they still called it a regiment, nobody had bothered replacing the dead colonel. The last surviving major was in charge, with two captains below him. Zeke's squad and a couple others served under one Lieutenant Jack Hardy, who wasn't there. Wyatt, however, was. *Shit.* The corporal's expression darkened when he saw Andrew.

"Add Sutter here to my squad," Zeke ordered.

Wyatt nodded. "Yes, sergeant." He wrote on a notepad and fixed an eye on Andrew. "Let's hope you work out. Stay out of my way."

Andrew was just in time for the tail end of morning chores, done after breakfast and before drill. That day Zeke's squad was touching up the trenches along the camp's northwestern edge.

Luckily, most of the work had been done when he got there. Andrew spotted David scooping dirt into a wheelbarrow held by a red-haired young man he didn't know.

"So you're the new guy?" the redhead said. "Come here'n take the damned wheelbarrow."

Andrew didn't like the other fellow's tone. "Why?"

The redhead glared. "Take the damn wheelbarrow, greenhorn."

Andrew gritted his teeth at "greenhorn." He'd fought the Flesh-Eaters and even Grendel's men and survived. Could the other fellow say the same?

He looked at the redhead. He could lick him. However, that wouldn't look good, getting into a fight on his first day. "All right." He came over and took the wheelbarrow from the redhead. "What's your name?"

"Will Simmons. Yours?"

"Andrew Sutter."

Will shrugged. "Nice to meet you."

Andrew forced himself to smile. "You too."

Will pointed to some boards forming a crude ramp. "Take the dirt up there. *Hank's* working on the berm."

Andrew frowned. Why had Will said Hank's name so scornfully?

The wheelbarrow pulled at his hands, the rocky soil heavier than ordinary dirt. Andrew bent down and forced the wheelbarrow up the tracks left by previous trips. Above he found a dark-haired young man touching up the elongated heap of rocky earth dividing the bare ground of the camp from the sea of grass outside. He looked heavier than the rest.

"You Hank?"

"Yeah. Hank Evans. You must be the new guy."

He set his shovel down and shook Andrew's hand. There was something odd about how he held his upper lip when he spoke, but he seemed friendly enough. Greetings done, Andrew pushed the wheelbarrow over to the berm. There Hank scraped out the dirt with the shovel.

"Get me some more dirt. The berm's getting a bit eroded."

Andrew made three more sweaty trips between the trench and the berm before Zeke was satisfied. Zeke next ordered the squad to an open space for drilling. Andrew received a bayonet to fit into the new lug attached to his rifle.

"All right," Zeke ordered. "We start off with bayonet drill. My squad, line up here."

Behind Zeke, another sergeant shouted at his troopers, lining them up in front of Andrew and the others. The men did not line up directly.

They instead spaced themselves out, every man facing an empty spot. The ones who had been soldiers for awhile stood with their legs spread apart and upper bodies bent forward like prizefighters. David imperfectly imitated their stance. Andrew did likewise.

The sergeants walked the lines of their men. When Zeke reached Andrew, he stopped. "Feet wider." His arm leaped forward, striking Andrew on the shoulder. Andrew stumbled backward. Somewhere, Will laughed. Andrew turned red. "Keep your feet shoulder-width and you won't be easy to knock down."

Zeke soon returned to the center. "First off is stabbing. Lunge forward, like you want to stick that knife in some Flesh-Eater. Then we'll switch to rifle butt. Begin."

With a shout, the more experienced men surged forward, thrusting their bayonets. Andrew followed a beat later, with David a beat after that. On the second lunge, everyone kept up. The stabbing drill lasted for twenty minutes, leaving Andrew's upper arms, shoulders, and even his hips burning with pain. His arms, already sore from hauling dirt, trembled slightly. Zeke showed no signs of releasing them. Instead he ordered them to practice striking with the rifle butt.

To distract himself from the pain, Andrew imagined his blows cracking open Flesh-Eater heads or crushing Flesh-Eater throats. The rifle felt lighter. He struck his next mock blow with much more enthusiasm.

"Stop!" Zeke called out after several minutes. "Time for water. Next is squad-level drill for closing with the enemy."

After the soldiers drank from their canteens, Zeke and the other sergeants lined up the squads. "All right," Zeke began. "Some of you already know how to fight as a team, but we've picked up a couple of greenhorns. You're good individually, but sometimes we'll go in-close with the Flesh-Eaters rather than just shooting and running. Then you'll need to fight as a squad. Sound off!"

"One!" the soldier on the far left shouted.

"Two!" Hank shouted.

"One!" Will shouted.

"Two!" David shouted.

It was Andrew's turn. "One!" *Good.* He wouldn't be paired off with Will.

"Odd numbers, you'll start with the rifle. Even numbers, you'll start with the bayonet."

The other squads were already moving. Andrew stood on his tip-toes to watch. Around half of each squad stood and pointed their rifle as if they were firing while the other half got down on one knee and thrust with their bayonet. The men with the rifle would lower their weapons and switch positions, only they'd be somewhat forward of the ones who knelt before.

"Begin!" Zeke shouted, interrupting Andrew's pondering.

The squad spent twenty minutes on the new drill. Will, Hank, and Owen already knew it. Andrew picked up on it soon enough. David, however, fell a single movement behind toward the end.

"Stop!" Zeke ordered. "Court, front and center. The rest of you, dismissed for lunch."

Lunch consisted of two pieces of a thick bread called "hardtack," eaten sitting on an empty patch of stony earth near the canvas mess tent. When Andrew first bit into one, his teeth stopped abruptly.

"Ah!"

Will snickered.

"Not a good idea to eat hardtack straight," said Owen Gollmar. "Put some water on it, let it soak in."

Andrew looked at Owen. The other soldier had ruddy skin like a pikey, which put Andrew on edge, but lacked the traders' substantial nose. And he didn't smell. Andrew decided he'd be polite, but keep an eye out lest the other man try to swindle him. "Thanks."

He poured a bit of water from his canteen onto the hardtack and let it work its way in. He took another bite, more carefully this time. The hardtack still resisted, but he gnawed a piece off. It was bland and took awhile to chew and swallow, but he ultimately managed to defeat it.

Andrew had barely finished when David skulked in. "What'd he want with you?"

David scowled. "More drill. I missed *one* movement, just *one*, and —"

"The better-drilled a man is, the better he is in a real fight," Will interrupted. "Zeke'll drill you extra because you damn well need it. We'll make damn sure you learn it, or else he'll make us *all* do extra drill. Got it?"

David glared at Will. "Who made you —"

"Will's right," Owen interrupted. "Fighting as individuals works fine for taking pot shots at the bastards, but if we tried that in a line battle, we'd be their lunch. And one man can be the weak link of a whole squad."

Andrew remembered the men of Carroll Town spilling down the hill, the Flesh-Eaters at their heels. Maybe someone hadn't been quick enough and the Flesh-Eater he could have killed got through, or someone ran and the others followed. Will was an asshole, but he seemed to know his business.

"Yeah," Hank added. "A weak line'll crumble and then it's time for killing."

"Of course he knows," Will sneered. "He's done it before."

The spirit returned to David's face. "Hobble your lip, Will. He didn't have a choice."

Will leaned forward. "Everyone's got a choice, if anything between living and dying."

Andrew's gut clenched. Hank had been a Flesh-Eater! That business with his lip must've been to hide the filed teeth!

Andrew looked at Hank. The other man had been pleasant –unlike Will – but he had also supped upon human flesh and helped stomp on the faces of good folk. As far as Andrew knew, Will hadn't committed those particular sins.

Before Andrew could open his mouth, Zeke cleared his throat. Everyone fell silent as he walked among them, glaring at each. "We got enough fighting outside the camp. I won't have fighting in it." His voice rose. "All of you, give me twenty gaspers, now!"

After the gaspers — an unholy mix of squatting, push-ups, and jumping — were done, Zeke gestured for them to follow him. "It's time for target practice and then long patrol."

The second part got Andrew's attention. "Patrol?"

"After target practice. Move along."

Zeke led them to a range at the camp's edge. A line of dummies wearing the red-and-black of the Flesh-Eaters and occasionally the black of the Obsidian Guard stood several hundred yards away. Wyatt appeared with a basket full of ammunition boxes, handing one to each soldier.

Andrew weighed his box in his hand. "That's not a lot of ammunition. How —"

"We don't *have* a lot of ammunition," Wyatt spat. "Bullets are best spent on fighting, not training." Scorn etched his face. "Let's hope you can hit the right targets this time."

Andrew looked at the dummies. He sniffed. He'd hit them easily. After all, he'd been in a real fight before.

Then the dummies started moving up and down and from side to side on their stakes. Andrew nearly jumped. *What the hell?* Soon he spotted the ropes trailing from the dummies. That reminded him of when some pikeys had once put on a puppet show in Carroll Town when he was four. Right clever. Moving targets were harder to hit.

"All right," Zeke shouted. "Shoot these sons of bitches!"

Andrew quickly emptied his rifle. The dummies proved more difficult to hit than he thought. He missed twice.

He frowned. In a real fight, the dummies would be firing back. He'd escaped the destruction of Carroll Town with just flesh wounds, but his luck wouldn't hold up forever.

Zeke stepped forward and inspected the targets. Then he nodded toward Will and Owen. "Perfect accuracy." Owen simply smiled, but Will smirked at Andrew. Andrew scowled back. He'd have to learn the redhead a lesson in manners.

Zeke walked up the line, talking to Hank and David. Then his gaze fell on Andrew. He leaned forward, his face in Andrew's. "All the times you aimed for the center of the target you *hit*. The two times you missed, it looked like you were aiming for the head. *Always* aim for the center of the target. What the hell were you thinking?" Andrew reddened. His mouth worked. Zeke raised an eyebrow. "Well?"

"I've always been good at hitting the center of the target…"

His voice trailed away. Training was a poor time for experimenting. He was being stump-stupid and he knew it.

Zeke sighed. "Sutter, don't be a *fucking* idiot." He pointed at the ground. "Twenty push-ups, now!"

"Yes, sergeant."

Zeke waited while Andrew did the push-ups. Dust mixed with sharp-smelling gunpowder dirtied his hands and chest. When Andrew dragged himself to his feet, Zeke addressed the whole squad. "Long patrol's to the green hills and back. Follow me."

As the squad followed their sergeant, Andrew leaned over to Owen. He didn't want to rely on a pikey, but he was the closest one and he'd been there longer. "What're the green hills?"

"They're out east where the grass thins out and the desert creeps north. Ground's queer, too slippery for horses. We'll ride up, look around, and head home."

The men mounted up and rode through swiftly-drying land for what felt like hours until they reached a cluster of hills coated with green glass. Andrew's eyes widened. A lightning strike in the desert could turn sand to glass, but the hills had to have been struck hundreds of times. Andrew swallowed. He wouldn't have wanted to be there for *that* storm.

"Dismount," Zeke ordered. "Hobble your horses. Court, watch them." The soldiers dismounted and tied their horses to a trio of pickets Zeke hammered into the ground. "All right," he said when everybody was finished. "We're going to circle round and look for enemies. It'll most likely be Flesh-Eaters, but scuttlebutt is Grendel himself was here." A scowl crossed his wide face. "There might be Obsidian Guard. We are *not* to engage unless we're spotted. Got it?"

"Yes, sergeant," the soldiers chorused. The tramp of their feet echoed the march of the Carroll Town militia in Andrew's mind. His grip on his rifle tightened. Would he have to face the Flesh-Eaters again?

For good or ill, there were no enemies. Sliding on the ripples in the strange green glass was the only danger. After circling and probing the hills and finding nothing, Zeke had them remount for the long ride back to camp.

Soon after they returned, Wyatt summoned them to their company's mess tent. The smell of hot potatoes struck Andrew in the face. His mouth brimmed with saliva. His mouth grew even wetter when he saw jerky served alongside the potatoes. It had been *months* since he'd eaten meat he didn't have to kill himself.

"This'll be the last meat for awhile, boys," the frog-faced cook said as he doled it out. "Hope you like it."

Andrew gobbled down the jerky. Part of him wanted to savor it, but most of him was too damn hungry. Most of the squad did the same. Finishing off the potatoes took longer, but not by much.

David chewed his jerky thoughtfully. "Good meat. A bit chewy, but that's jerky for you. Could stand to have a bit more sugar, but —"

"We haven't got a lot of sugar," Will interrupted. "We haven't got a lot of anything. Now shut the hell up."

"Will," Owen rumbled.

David scowled but did what Will told him.

Once the meals were eaten and the cleaning done, Andrew turned to David. "C'mon," he said. "Let's go."

David furrowed his brow. "Go where?" He paused. "You're not skedaddling, are you?"

Andrew frowned. The Merrills saved his life. He wouldn't abandon them. Sticking around would keep him alive and give him more chances to kill Flesh-Eaters.

"I want to look round, see if I can find Sarah or Cassie. It won't be long 'til it starts getting dark." He'd learned night fires were almost forbidden — dirigibles – and he didn't want to stumble around in the dark.

David nodded. Andrew set off, David behind him. They hadn't gotten far when Hank turned up. "You need help with anything?" This time he didn't bother hiding his teeth.

Andrew looked at him without speaking. Hank had been a Flesh-Eater. Who knows what loathsome habits he'd picked up? Did he really want someone like him near Sarah or Cassie?

But Jacob Burns had been conscripted and run away. As David said earlier, Hank hadn't had a choice. It wouldn't be fair to hate him for it. He'd keep an eye on him though, just in case.

"We're looking for my sister and my girl."

Hank nodded. "What they look like?"

"Sarah looks a lot like me, considering we're twins. Hair like mine but longer, green eyes, and a bit shorter'n me."

"Got it. And your girl?"

"Cassie's got brown eyes. Blond hair. She wore a blue dress last time I saw her."

Andrew didn't mention she'd been hurt before the Flesh-Eaters invaded Carroll Town.

THE THREE HAD PASSED through yet another row of tents when Hank stopped and pointed to the left.

"That your sister?"

Andrew's gaze followed his finger. Straw-colored hair flashed as a woman about Sarah's height vanished between two tents.

Andrew's heart leaped into his throat. He turned and ran toward where the woman had gone.

"Sarah?" he called. "Sarah!"

He turned between the tents. He looked right. She wasn't there. He looked left. The woman's hair flashed again as she passed between another set of tents.

Andrew kept running. He was so focused on the woman he didn't notice the tent peg in his path until he was nearly on top of it. His foot caught. He pitched forward, slamming into the dry ground. Through the dust, he saw the woman turn his way.

It wasn't Sarah. She had the same hair, but her eyes were brown, her nose was bigger, and her face rounder. She rushed over and knelt by Andrew, setting aside the basket she'd been carrying. "Are you all right?"

Andrew nodded, pulling himself onto his knees. "Just fine," he muttered. "Thanks." Both rose to their feet. Andrew looked at her for a long moment. She might not be Sarah, but maybe she knew something. "Have you met a Sarah Sutter, from Carroll Town?" The woman shook her head. "She would have arrived here a few days ago. She looks a lot like me; she's my sister."

She shook her head. "I'm sorry, but I haven't."

"All right. If you meet her, tell her Andrew Sutter, her brother, is alive. He's in the Second Pendleton. If you meet a girl named Cassie Wells, tell her the same thing."

"I will." She briefly touched him on the shoulder, then disappeared among the tents. Andrew sighed. He'd thought he'd found Sarah!

Someone laid a hand on Andrew's shoulder. "Sorry," Hank said. "There're a lot of women around here. If we keep looking long enough, I'm sure we'll find her." He fell silent.

Andrew wondered if he should ask what was gnawing on Hank. Then he wondered if this was something he wanted to know. "Thanks." What else was there to say?

"Yeah," David added abruptly. "There're a lot of girls here. Chances are we'll find her."

THAT NIGHT, Andrew lay staring at the ceiling of the tent he now shared with the rest of the squad. Every time he closed his eyes, images from the day Carroll Town died poured into his mind. Bullets tore away most of Elijah's head. Hot blood stung Andrew's skin. Elijah's death was his fault — he hadn't been able to shoot the Flesh-Eater!

And the Flesh-Eaters only attacked because Andrew didn't shoot the emissary's guard. If all three Flesh-Eaters had been killed, the townsfolk could have hidden the bodies. The Flesh-Eater army wouldn't have come.

He shouldn't have survived. Sam or Eudora didn't screw up like he had. He should have died in Carroll Town. *They* should have his place in the Merrill army. They wouldn't hesitate when the time came for killing. Ma should have survived. Maybe she couldn't be a soldier but she could make life easier for those who were.

Tears gathered at the corners of his eyes. He clenched his jaw to stop from sobbing. He looked about the tent. The others didn't seem to have any trouble sleeping.

Andrew relaxed slightly. After all, if they were asleep, they weren't watching him.

Relaxing allowed the first sob to escape. His face burned. He tensed. He looked left to right, allowing more tears to pour down his face. He hadn't woken anyone. He sighed in relief, but that only unleashed another sob. His face grew even hotter. He looked around again, but none of his tentmates moved.

Andrew wiped the remaining tears away from his eyes and shook his head. Weeping was for women. Men did not cry. They fought.

But the men of Carroll Town fought. And for the most part, they died. Tears began gathering in his eyes again. Andrew blinked them back. He wouldn't cry. He wouldn't.

Despite his best efforts, the tears came and would not stop. Andrew bit his lip and barely kept himself from sobbing.

His efforts weren't successful. Another sob burst out. Andrew looked around again. Hopefully the others weren't awake.

His gaze fell on Hank. Although his eyes were closed and he didn't move, his breathing wasn't regular like the others. He was *too* quiet, like Andrew himself had been when he was trying to make his parents reckon he was asleep so they'd go to bed and he could sneak out. He was shamming!

Andrew reddened. If *Will* knew he was crying, he'd never let him forget. Better not let *anyone* see him cry at all.

He lay back down and counted the threads on the ceiling. Surely something that boring would put him to sleep.

Andrew didn't know how long he lay there. Nothing moved in the darkness beyond the tent for what could have been minutes or hours.

The tent flap opened. Zeke poked his head in. "Go to sleep," he ordered. "We'll be up in a few hours and it'll be more of the same unless there's a fight."

"Yes, sergeant."

Andrew closed his eyes. When the blood and horror returned, he thought about something else. The times he'd played pool with Sam. The time he'd poked Cassie in the barn before the Flesh-Eaters came.

Andrew grit his teeth. The Flesh-Eaters destroyed everything he'd known. He would make them pay.

He started thinking of all the ways he could punish the Flesh-Eaters. Bullets worked. So did the bayonet he'd trained with that day.

Sleep came much faster.

AMBUSH

Andrew knelt in the line alongside David beneath the glaring sun. He looked down at hot dirt at the base of the hill, eyes averted from the blazing sun. Despite himself, his hands trembled around his rifle.

A Flesh-Eater company marched on the other side. Their gruesome song about the taste of fallen Merrill soldiers eaten during the siege of Jacinto overpowered the tramp of their boots.

His stomach lurched, but it wasn't because of the disgusting lyrics. Soon he'd face the thunder of the massed rifles, the whistling of the mortar shells. And then there were the fanatics who feared neither and lived to kill.

He closed his eyes. His meager breakfast rose into his throat. He forced it back down with a hard swallow.

The cavalry moving ahead of the company were supposed to have picked off Flesh-Eater scouts and outriders during the long ride down from the high plains. Hopefully the enemy didn't know about the hundred Merrill soldiers. Ambush the column, loot the supply wagons. That'd ball up the Flesh-Eaters' walling off the Merrill army and secure supplies food to boot.

Hopefully.

"Don't worry," Zeke whispered beside Andrew. "It's worse waiting. You'll soon be too busy trying to kill the other son of a bitch to worry." He paused. "Besides, these aren't the Obsidian Guard or the goddamn Blood Alchemy monsters." The sergeant's words were not exactly reassuring, but Andrew nodded anyway. He clutched his rifle tighter. Zeke pushed a flask in Andrew's direction. "Drink this. Liquid courage."

Andrew seized the flask. He unscrewed the top and took a mouthful. The harsh corn liquor burned. He'd drunk it before, but never this strong. He gagged. Some trickled from the corners of his mouth.

"Not so much," Zeke chided. "We don't want you dried out."

Andrew nodded. Tears rolled down his cheeks as it burned down his throat into his stomach.

Zeke retrieved his flask and took a swig himself. Then he passed it to David before rejoining the other sergeants and officers at the bottom of the hill.

Andrew turned to David. The other man had the flask to his lips and pulled down a lot more than Andrew.

"You drinking all that?" Andrew whispered.

David lowered the flask."Heard a phrase once. 'Fighting drunk.' I reckon I'll get that way."

"I reckon I will too," Will hissed from beyond David. "And that's not happening if you drink it all." He snatched the flask from David and took a quick swig before handing it to Owen. "And be quiet!" He gestured in the direction of the marching Flesh-Eaters.

"We're moving," Zeke interrupted. Andrew hadn't seen him come back. "The bastards are in our laps."

Andrew's hand sank to the cartridge box on his belt the quartermaster had given him. Fourteen rounds. Even with his rifle fully loaded, that didn't seem like a lot.

All down the line, the men crept up the hill. The troopers stretched out beyond Andrew's sight, a river of rifles and bayonets that would shred the Flesh-Eater column marching beyond the hill.

Hopefully.

The men stopped below where the Flesh-Eaters would see them. For a long moment, no one moved. No one spoke.

Then Zeke made a chopping motion with his hand.

Andrew leaped forward along with the rest of the squad and

opened fire. The roaring rifles split his ears. An officer toppled from his horse, as did a black-clad man Andrew had learned was one of the "deacons." Enemies fell all along the column. Andrew's fear blew away. He laughed. It looked like they'd taken out a fifth of the bastards at once! There was no way they could lose now!

The Flesh-Eaters turned toward the Merrill troopers as a body and returned fire, the new thunder drowning out the echoes of the old. Andrew looked around, but nobody seemed hurt. The Merrill fire slackened.

"Stop looking around and keep goddamn firing!" Zeke roared, barely audible over the ringing in Andrew's ears. "They're not stopping!"

More bullets flew in the Merrill troopers' direction. The soldiers around Andrew stayed low. None got hit.

Andrew laughed. At this rate, the enemy would be wiped out long before the Merrills. If the Merrill troops were this skilled, how did the Flesh-Eaters lick them in the first place?

Then came the first explosion. Andrew's hands trembled anew. Another shell slammed into the Merrill line far too close. The explosion threw men into the air, their bodies mangled by shrapnel. Harsh sulfur burned in Andrew's nostrils. Curses and cries of dismay erupted.

Another round hit to Andrew's right. The soldiers not pulped lay moaning, bodies dotted with gray shrapnel and limbs twisted by the explosion. Another shell landed to the left, producing the same chorus of pain. The air stank of blood and shit. Andrew's gorge rose. This wasn't the bombardment of Carroll Town that wrecked more buildings than it hurt people. He looked around frantically. If they stayed there, they were dead. They had to *run*.

A man rose from the Merrill line. The other fellow had barely gotten to his feet when a bullet caught him in the back. He slammed face first onto the ground.

Andrew looked back and forth. Running would kill them and staying would kill them. They were doomed…

"We close with them, they can't use their mortars!" Zeke screamed. "Follow me! Others will cover you!" He pulled something from his coat, lit it with a match, and threw it down the hill. It spewed smoke upon hitting the ground. Beyond Zeke, more smoke bloomed on the hillside. Zeke strode toward the enemy. Owen, Hank, and Will followed. Andrew swallowed and joined them, keeping low and hoping a shell wouldn't land on him.

The harsh smoke filled Andrew's nostrils as the squad passed through it. The cloud thinned further down. Gunpowder's acrid stink replaced it. He tried breathing through his mouth, but the air tasted like matchsticks. An occasional bullet cracked past, but the Merrill troopers above kept the enemy below occupied.

For the moment. Mortar rounds fell behind the advancing squad. Clods of dirt pelted his back. Something hot nipped his shoulder. He bit his lip to keep from shouting. All around, men shouted and rifles cracked as the troopers advanced down the hill, covering each other when the smoke wasn't too thick.

Gaps opened among the Flesh-Eaters. Andrew's heart sank. He'd seen this before.

A wave of fanatics erupted. "Kill!" they screamed over the storm of flying lead. "Kill for the Howling God!"

Before he could imagine all the ways the fanatics could do that, Zeke's roar cut through the thunder of the gunfire and the fanatics' mad howling.

"Mow the bastards *down!*"

Andrew's rifle kicked against his shoulder again and again. One shot hit a fanatic in the chest and put him on the ground. Another caught a fanatic in the eye and tore away most of his head. A third struck a fanatic in the shoulder and dropped him.

Although the gunfire swept the oncoming fanatics down like a reaper cutting wheat, the enemy was too close and too quick. The screaming tide slammed into the advancing Merrills. The collision sounded of blades punching into flesh and bodies slamming into the unyielding earth.

Andrew shot a fanatic in the face but couldn't fire again before another one was upon him. A saber flashed in the glaring sun, the curving blade reaching for Andrew's throat.

Andrew shoved his bayonet forward, catching the Flesh-Eater in the thigh. Blood spurted like a spring. The fanatic screamed and swung again, straight at Andrew's left hand. Andrew recoiled, tearing the bayonet out of the enemy. Blood gushed, but the Flesh-Eater's movements did not slow. The saber slammed into the side of the rifle, carving out a chunk of the wood and knocking the weapon aside. The fanatic slammed his head forward. Andrew instinctively looked away and the man's forehead struck him above the eye. Andrew saw black.

"Kill!" the fanatic screamed. "Ki —"

The man's cry became a gurgle. He fell away, blood streaming from his mouth and from a huge wound in the left side of his chest.

Andrew looked left. Owen turned away, aiming his rifle elsewhere. The man whose looks vexed Andrew had just saved his life.

A gunshot echoed loud enough to hear over the din. Andrew's gaze snapped right. A fanatic turned away from the collapsing body of another Merrill soldier, his grin revealing his filed teeth. His pistol rose —

Andrew fired. The bullet sent the fanatic sprawling. The shot that would have split Andrew's face instead went up into the air. There were no Flesh-Eaters nearby. Andrew took the opportunity to reload.

A bullet snapped by his head. Andrew threw himself down. No fanatic came. Andrew aimed at a Flesh-Eater further back. He missed. Andrew fired again and checked the ammunition tube. Four rounds left.

"How much do you have?" he screamed at Owen.

The other man shook his head. "Not much! Let's hope the sons of bitches don't have more than we do!"

In a pig's eye. Andrew fired twice, but he wasn't sure he hit anything.

The ground shook. The Flesh-Eaters began bunching together. Andrew fired, catching a running Flesh-Eater in the thigh. The Flesh-Eaters formed into a square, bayonets facing out.

Onto the scene swept the Merrill cavalry. Their sabers tore into enemy infantry and clashed with those of the few mounted Flesh-Eaters left. Rival horsemen collided with a crunch of flesh and bone audible over the gunfire. The screams of horses and men merged in a cacophony stabbing at Andrew's mind like a multitude of knives.

Andrew thumbed more rounds into the rifle. The squares would keep the horsemen at bay but would also serve as nice compact targets. He fired twice into the enemy formation, felling at least one Flesh-Eater.

A mortar shell erupted within the square and raced over his head. Another crashed somewhere to his left. The different squares were supporting each other!

Some Flesh-Eaters on the left had somehow gotten separated from the square. A pack of horsemen tore through them, then wheeled back through the survivors. The Flesh-Eaters remaining in the square fired. Their volley blew three horsemen down. The cavalry retreated, shooting as they moved.

The front ranks of the square were thin now. Beyond them, Flesh-Eaters loaded a pair of mortars. Andrew fired until his rifle clicked empty. "I don't have any left!" he shouted. "Anyone got more?"

"Who's out of ammo?" Zeke demanded.

Besides Andrew, David had exhausted his ammunition and Hank only had one bullet left.

"We need to take that fucking mortar out!" Zeke screamed. "The three of you, bayonets! The rest will cover you!" Zeke pointed. Andrew's gaze followed the sergeant's finger to the weak spot in the front of the square. "Forward!"

Uncaring of the bullets, Andrew ran. A Flesh-Eater screamed orders. Enemies filled the gap. Bullets whizzed by. Someone screamed as the bullets caught him. A Flesh-Eater pointed his rifle at Andrew but ate a bullet before he could fire. Another Flesh-Eater had his rifle up, but Andrew sank the blade into his gut. The man's chest and head snapped forward and he screamed, spattering Andrew with blood.

Andrew tried to tear the rifle free. Something snagged the bayonet hilt. The Flesh-Eater's writhing nearly tore the rifle away. Andrew's hands tightened on the weapon. The man dragged him forward.

A Flesh-Eater about Andrew's height appeared beside him. He drove his bayonet straight at Andrew's side. With fear-fueled strength, Andrew threw himself forward, knocking himself and his mortally-wounded foe to the ground and tearing his rifle free. The Flesh-Eater swept through where Andrew had been and caught a bullet in the head a second later.

Soaked in the dying man's blood, Andrew rose in time to see a Flesh-Eater aim at David. He lunged, ready to shove his bayonet through the man's throat. The Flesh-Eater wheeled on Andrew and fired. He missed. A bullet caught the Flesh-Eater before Andrew could spit him.

That left a clear path for the mortars. There were only two crew left standing, but one had a shell in his hands. Andrew leveled his bayonet and screamed. He'd rip the man open before he could murder any more Merrills! The Flesh-Eater hurled the shell at Andrew. He barely felt the blow as he plowed into the man, burying the blade in his gut. Ignoring the man's screams, he tore the blade free.

The other Flesh-Eater lunged, a long knife flashing. Andrew shoved his rifle into the man's chest. The blade that would have buried itself in Andrew's flesh instead tore through his shirt and drew little blood. Before the man could recover, a bullet caught him in the side.

Will and Owen rushed forward, Zeke on their heels. Zeke pointed through the clouds of smoke and rushing men toward the nearest Flesh-Eater square. "Simmons, Gollmar, the mortar! Smash the bastards!"

Will oriented the mortar at the enemy formation and cranked down its angle. "There's a shell over here!" Andrew pointed. "Son of a bitch threw it at me!"

Will snatched the shell up while Owen tore a pair of binoculars off a corpse. He gave the enemy square a quick look and shouted instructions to Will. The redhead made the final adjustments, shoved the shell into the mortar's hot throat, and ducked out of the way.

Whistling. A fireball bloomed amid the Flesh-Eater square. Bodies flew. Those left standing soon fell to flying bullets or cavalry sabers. "More shells!" Will screamed. "They're not all dead!"

Owen snatched up another while Andrew knelt by the Flesh-Eater's corpse, thanking the Good Lord the enemy used the same rounds. He thumbed some bullets from the dead man's cartridge box into his rifle.

"Horsemen!" Hank shouted. Andrew turned. Three enemy cavalry surged toward them. One fired his carbine, while the others cut down isolated Merrills with their sabers. The noise and smoke of the battle had hidden their approach — they were only fifty yards away.

"Simmons, keep at it!" Zeke shouted. "The rest of you, to me! Bayonets *up!*"

Zeke, Hank, and Owen stood straight in the path of the horsemen, blades up. David quickly joined them.

Andrew's hands shook. Three horsemen bearing down on the squad would scatter them like bowling pins, crush them beneath their hooves...

"Sutter!" Zeke shouted. The command pulled Andrew forward. He fell in beside Hank, raised his own rifle, and hoped for the best. "Fire!"

The horses veered out of the way as Andrew squeezed the trigger. The bullets threw one rider from his saddle. Others struck the second horse, which screamed and surged away, carrying its rider with it.

"Don't just stand there!" the last horseman shouted as he wheeled his horse back toward the squad. "Crush these termites!"

Three Flesh-Eater infantrymen, their own bayonets fixed, rushed out of the chaos behind the horseman toward the squad. Owen, Will, and Hank lunged to meet them, David close behind.

Andrew aimed at the horseman. He'd bring the proud bastard down —

The cavalryman raised his carbine. Andrew threw himself to the side. *CRACK!* Will shouted. Andrew's heart sank. If the horseman got Will, who'd fire the mortar?

Andrew fired at the horseman. The bullet clipped the Flesh-Eater's waist. The man shouted in pain and turned toward Andrew, murder in his face.

"Heeya!" a woman shouted over the din. The incongruous sound of a female voice grabbed Andrew's attention.

Another Merrill rider appeared out of the smoke, blood dripping from his saber. The long honey-colored hair tied behind the horseman's head and finer features showed the "horseman" was actually a woman. She surged toward the mounted Flesh-Eater. The man wheeled to face her, abandoning Andrew for the moment.

Andrew aimed for the horse – a bigger target — and pulled the trigger. The horse screamed, staggered, and fell. The Flesh-Eater leaped away as his mount collapsed, landing on his feet.

That left him in just the right position for the horsewoman. She swept down like an eagle on a rabbit. He raised his carbine, but was too slow. Her saber flashed amid the dust and carnage as her horse blocked Andrew's view. Her passage revealed the Flesh-Eater sinking to his knees, throat open almost to his neckbone.

THE FIGHT DIDN'T LAST MUCH LONGER. The enemy cavalrymen retreated with the footsloggers they could carry, using the few remaining fanatics as a screen. Once the zealots had been dealt with, the Merrill cavalry pursued. Andrew got a glimpse of honey-colored hair as the horsewoman vanished into the dust.

Now came time to deal with the Flesh-Eater wounded.

Several lay in front of Andrew amid the clearing smoke. One had already been killed for holding onto his rifle too tightly.

"Still got your bayonets?" Zeke asked almost casually.

Andrew looked to the wounded Flesh-Eaters. Some tried to scramble away, blood caking the dirt behind them. Will grinned. "I sure do." Blood still dripped from a long cut across his forehead. He glared at the wounded Flesh-Eaters. "Where's your god now? He going to save your ass, you cannibal sons of bitches?"

Andrew looked from the wounded to Zeke. Though these men likely committed terrible crimes, killing helpless men didn't sit right. Zeke stepped over. "Sutter, the Flesh-Eaters will return. We can't leave them here for the enemy to save and we can't take them prisoner without leaving valuables behind."

Andrew looked over his shoulder at Hardy. The short, tanned lieutenant with a missing front tooth oversaw soldiers from another squad looting a wagon. Maybe he didn't know what Zeke and Will were going to do to the enemy wounded. Maybe he'd stop this.

He didn't. When he saw Andrew's imploring look, he nodded and pointed to Zeke.

Zeke took Andrew's shoulder. The manacle on his wrist glinted in the sun. He steered Andrew's attention away from Hardy and pointed at one of the fallen Flesh-Eaters.

"That one there's an L-T. Probably got a fine estate made out of other folk's land, with the people who used to *own* the land sharecropping. If they're lucky."

A lieutenant — an officer! The incongruous emotion of *hope* surged in Andrew's chest. Maybe he knew what happened to the other Carroll Town survivors! Andrew stepped over to the wounded man. "I've got a question," he snapped. "And I want it answered."

The man snorted, blood spattering his lips. "What you want to know, pup?"

"When your crew took Carroll Town, you marched the survivors some place. Where? What did you do with them?"

"I wasn't there. Probably went to Fort Vallero."

"Then what?"

The officer laughed. "They'll go where they're needed. Mines, the officers' and vets' farms, our beds if they're pretty enough." Andrew's grip tightened on his rifle as he imagined the likely fate of Cassie and Sarah. The man was close, close enough to cut to pieces with his bayonet or just stomp to death. The officer laughed. "Looking for your sweetheart? She might be some lucky *fort's* sweetheart right now."

Andrew saw red. The image of filthy Flesh-Eaters lining up to take turns with a weeping Cassie filled his mind. With a scream, he rammed his bayonet into the man's throat. Blood poured around the blade and the Flesh-Eater's last defiant words vanished in his dying gurgles. Andrew stabbed the Flesh-Eater over and over, tearing open the man's throat and his belly.

"Die you son of a bitch!" he screamed. He raised his blade for another stab before strong hands seized him.

"He's dead!" Zeke shouted. "He's dead! No more!"

Andrew stopped. Slowly, his breathing returned to normal. Around him the others set to their grisly task. Only Hank hesitated. He stood alone as the others' bayonets flashed in the sun.

"Come on!" Will called out, a nasty smile on his face.

Hank swallowed. Gripping his rifle, he stepped forward and joined the slaughter.

Andrew looked at one prisoner who had scrambled away, dragging a broken leg behind him. Andrew's eyes widened. He remembered Sam, wounded in the leg back in Carroll Town. The man was older, but he had the same dark hair, similar enough eye color. Andrew paused.

The wounded man locked eyes with Andrew. "Please," he begged. He scooted away, wincing with every move. "Please. I have gold." He reached into his uniform jacket and pulled out a bloodstained bag.

"That gold won't be yours much longer," Zeke interrupted. "Sutter, finish him."

Andrew looked at the wounded Flesh-Eater. He wasn't Sam. Sam was dead, spitted through the lung!

Andrew lunged. The Flesh-Eater threw the gold aside.

"I have a fam —"

His words turned into a scream as Andrew rammed the blade into his belly and angled it up. Blood poured from his mouth like it had from Sam's. His howling rose higher as the blade sank deep. A second stab finished him.

Once the grisly work was done, the soldiers finished their looting. Besides the wagons, the enemy dead had weapons and ammunition to liberate, gold dollars, flasks of corn liquor, and other necessities. Andrew heard the Flesh-Eaters believed that to the victor went the spoils. It was fitting they end up on the receiving end.

"Once you're done, strip the bodies!" Zeke called out. "Ours and theirs. Pile them over there." He pointed to a pair of damaged wagons the soldiers wouldn't be taking with them. "Burn them."

Andrew smiled. No food for the enemy. He pocketed the dead man's cash and began stripping the corpse. Once he finished, he grabbed the dead Flesh-Eater by both feet and pulled. Pain erupted across his back. Now he'd calmed down, all the licks he'd taken were making themselves known.

Gritting his teeth all the while, he tried to pull the body onto the wagon by its armpits. It was heavy enough when he dragged it. Now it tore at his hands as he tried to lift it. The pain from his hurt shoulders and back grew worse.

Ultimately, he left the corpse by the wagon for the hale prisoners the Merrills put to work. Then he took stock of the dead who hadn't been stripped and heaped.

Most wore the enemy's red and black, but far too many wore the Merrills' mix of day-to-day clothes or ragged brown uniforms. His squad hadn't lost anyone, but that was a right miracle. The Flesh-Eaters had a big country to recruit from; the Merrills didn't. Andrew frowned. At this rate, the Merrills would run out long before the enemy did.

Once they'd piled up the bodies, they put the wagons to the torch. The Merrills rode away, black smoke smelling too much like roasting pork staining the blue sky behind them.

HOME SWEET HOME

Catalina Merrill stood naked in the shallow end of the pool in Grendel's harem, the ends of her red hair just above the warm water behind her. In front of her, under his armpits, she held her three-year-old son. "Hayes" – *Havarth is such an ugly name* – she began. "Do you know what we're going to do today?"

A big grin crossed his thin face, so much like her brother Alonzo's. "We're going to *turn!*" The grin lit up eyes that didn't belong in his Merrill face. Gray eyes. *His* eyes.

Catalina pushed that dark thought out of her mind and returned her son's grin. It didn't require as much effort as before. "Yes!" That was how she was first taught to tread water, in the Grand River in the shadow of the Merrill citadel. *Before he came.* Head to the sky, turn around and around. There was no open sky here, but the clean white ceiling would serve just as well. "You know what to do?" Hayes nodded. "Go!"

The boy began kicking. Catalina let her hands drop to his hips. Hayes sank – her heart jumped – but soon his kicking and the efforts of his arms to keep him spinning pushed him higher, keeping his head well above the water. She kept her fingers on him just enough to gauge whether he was sinking or keeping himself up by his own efforts. *So far, so good.* This time last year she'd started teaching him with a customized piece of cork to keep him floating, but he clearly didn't need it anymore.

Hayes laughed as he spun in the water. Soon Catalina found herself laughing as well. Sometimes this was almost enough to forget.

Then a shadow fell on mother and son. Catalina's gut clenched and she pulled Hayes close. Was Grendel back from his trip already? Did he merely want to check on the progress of his – their – son, or did he have more amorous intentions? She drew her legs together under the water. Not that that would help much if that's what he'd come for.

Nope. It was Lenora Starr, another one of the tyrant's women. One who actually *gloried* in having borne the despot children. Wearing only a white robe, she stood on the pool's red brick lip and looked down on Catalina.

"Getting some swim lessons in?" Catalina nodded, avoiding making eye contact with the older woman. "Good. Logmar was a bit younger than Havarth when I started him on turning." Catalina repressed the urge to scowl.

Then Lenora opened her robe and let it puddle to the ground around her feet. Catalina turned her son's head away. He didn't need to see another grown woman naked. Lenora slipped into the pool and regarded Catalina with disdainful eyes. "It's not like anything he hasn't seen before." She gestured at Catalina. Catalina felt her cheeks redden. Swimming suits apparently weren't common in the tyrant's north-western homeland. And there were other reasons – sometimes when the women were swimming he'd come watch and choose the ones whose efforts pleased him for his bed that day. Often, too often, that had been *her. Old dirty bastard.*

"I heard from Roderick that he's on his way back." Roderick was one of the Obsidian Guard assigned to guard Grendel's harem and in charge of assigning protectors to the women allowed freedom of the citadel. Like Lenora. Not like her. "He left the Flesh-Eater base a few hours ago." She smiled. "He'll be back before supper. I'll be here to meet him."

Then she was off swimming laps, leaving Catalina and Hayes alone.

"Let's get back to turning," Catalina said, pushing Hayes back out into the water. He was soon spinning and laughing like before, but the darkness hanging around Catalina kept his joy from spreading. She looked at the clock on the wall. It wasn't long until supper. "Let's swim to the edge." She took Hayes by the hands and pulled him chest-forward toward the edge of the pool. "Can you kick?"

"Yes!" His voice bubbled the water, but his nose was clear. Catalina slowly drew him toward the cement steps leading out of the pool, Hayes kicking along all the while. Once she got to the edge, she set him at the middling step where the water was up to her chest and quickly pulled on the robe she'd left there. Then she pulled him out of the water. His face fell. "We done, Ma?"

Catalina nodded. "It won't be long until...until your pa is home." Hayes beamed. Catalina's heart sank. It was only natural a boy love his father, and he was too young to know why the man didn't deserve it. "Let's get you ready." She wrapped him in one of the towels she'd brought, and they both set off toward her rooms.

FALKI GRENDELSSON STOOD in the long shadow beneath the mooring towers of Father's citadel above bustling Norridge. The afternoon wind whipped through his black hair. The *Nicor* had just become visible in the south. The enormous airship passed over the two mono-liths topped with the carved skulls of saber-cats marking off where the southwestern railroad left the city and now passed over the chronic smog of the factory quarter. He narrowed his angled eyes, the legacy of his mother Lin Cao. The dirigible — and Father — would arrive at the citadel soon.

He shifted from foot to foot. His long Jiao sword banged against his leg. He frowned. He closed his eyes and breathed in and out, willing himself to remain still. Father controlled both himself and a mighty empire. If he intended to put on the older man's cloak, he would need similar self-control.

"He'll like this," Falki said aloud. His hands tightened on the folder containing the report on the foiled plot against the Obsidian Guard district governor and the death sentences he'd signed. Twenty troublemakers from Hamilton would kneel before the axe, and the damned city council would pay the taxes and shut the hell up.

"Aye," said Lieutenant Thomas Nahed, the dark-skinned Nahada second-in-command of Falki's company. The wind did not seem to bother him, even though being bulkier than Falki, he presented a bigger target. "Hamilton's been complaining for too long. This should cow them for awhile."

"One would hope."

Astrid Grendelsdottir, Falki's blonde half-sister, made her way onto the platform behind them. The wind whipped her blue dress about her ankles, but she walked into it regardless. A teasing smile broke out on Falki's face. "Good afternoon, peanut. You finish your schoolwork?"

Astrid fixed him with a gray-eyed glare. "I have. And *don't* call me *peanut!*"

Falki rolled his own gray eyes. At some point he couldn't quite place, she'd stopped being his sweet little sister who'd always wanted him to read to her and become something else. She'd been at cross words with Signe — her mother, Falki's stepmother — and been forbidden from joining her in a trip home to Sejera. *She wouldn't dare act this way toward Father, but she has no problem taking it out on Signe or me.*

Well, if she thought entering adulthood meant she could be downright rude, treating her like a child would *definitely* piss her off. Falki reached over and ruffled her curly hair.

She pushed him away. "Stop it, Falki!" She smoothed it back into place and scowled.

Falki shrugged. He'd had his fun. And she *was* fifteen, not a little girl anymore.

The sound of the *Nicor's* engines grew loud. He turned to see the airship thread the last columns of smoke and begin the final approach. He fingered the folder with the death sentences. Father would see just how well he could rule on his own.

GRENDEL SPOTTED HIS SON, daughter, and two guardsmen waiting as he and his entourage descended from the mooring tower. Falki, garbed in the black uniform of an Obsidian Guard officer, stepped forward to greet him.

"Father," the younger man said. He was tall like Grendel, but slimmer. He'd fill out. After all, he was only twenty and Grendel himself had not finished growing until he was twenty-five.

Astrid was significantly less subtle. She rushed up and threw her arms around him, pushing him back a step. *"Pappa!"* she exclaimed in Sejer, Grendel's birth tongue. While Grendel untangled himself from his daughter, Falki rose up on the balls of his feet, his eyes sweeping the men — and woman — clustered around his father.

"It looks like you didn't bring home any female souvenirs this time." Falki had switched to Jiao for *that* comment.

Grendel frowned. Not only was his son being impertinent, but the fact his present entourage lacked Jiao did not mean it lacked Jiao-*speakers*. "Not now," Grendel ordered in the same language before switching back to flatlander. "How goes Norridge?"

"Much the same ever." His son fell in beside him as they walked off the platform. Astrid trailed closely. "However, there have been some issues outside the capital. The councils of Riverside and Stirling are complaining *again*."

"Taxes?"

"That is Riverside's problem, but Stirling is whining about the garrison. Some soldiers have been rowdy and the city wants to punish them, but that's the commander's job."

Grendel frowned. Given his experience with young soldiers, "rowdy" generally meant stolen trifles or compensating husbands or fathers. The Obsidian Guard was trained to be better than that, but there was always some fool who got lax with his men.

"And what did you do? I hope you did not raise Riverside's taxes to punish them for complaining."

"I considered that, but Isaac didn't think it wise. He said the goal is to milk the cow, not drain its blood until it dies. In fact, *lowering* taxes can produce a net gain in income."

"To a point. Too high and you kill the cow; too low and you do not milk enough to feed yourself. What did you do?"

"I lowered the taxes three percent to show my benevolence, then rather brusquely sent him home. According to Isaac's sources, the council is now split between those who think I can be pressed further and the ones who fear annoying me. I doubt they'll come calling anytime soon."

Grendel smiled. The boy was a chip off the old block. And Isaac gave good service to the son like he did the father.

"What about Stirling?"

"I fed their representative and let him talk seven cottages full. When he *finally* finished, I told him it was the commander's prerogative to keep his guardsmen in line and sent him home."

"And did you contact the commander?"

Falki shook his head. Grendel frowned and quickened his pace. Falki moved to catch up, while the others wisely fell back. "Falki, I just cut a deal between Alex's boys and the Flesh-Eaters that may have headed off a *war*. You need to deal with the small problems before they become large ones. Having the commander make an example of men who misbehave when they are in their cups is easier than repressing a riot. That costs money and anyone shot or hanged will not pay the taxes needed to keep this" — he gestured toward the fortress surrounding them — "going."

Falki frowned. Grendel narrowed his eyes. He had hoped the boy would understand his wisdom without arguing. "When we are done here, I will take Jessamine upstairs. Contact the commander of Stirling and tell him to keep a tighter leash, or *I* will be the one to know why."

"Yes, Father." Falki was not eager enough for Grendel's taste. "Did anything happen on your trip?"

"Besides that dispute, there was a minor insurrection that had to be put down," Grendel said. He gestured to some of the bureaucrats in his entourage. "They will have more information."

Falki's gray eyes lit up at the mention of a rebellion being crushed. He and his company had gotten good at hunting bandits and armed ex-freeholders where the Guard veterans had been resettled, but there were fewer such opportunities these days. Grendel preferred his son learn to *govern*, not just fight. Ideally, there would be no rebellions at all. Falki and those like him could slake their bloodlust by hunting.

"You will be able to read the reports. Both of us taking the field at once is a big risk. Suppressing some pissant rebellion is not worth it. Do you want some ambitious son of a bitch to think he can kill your brother Arne and take Norridge for himself if we both die?" Falki nodded, once more too reluctantly. "Did anything else happen while I was away?"

"Well, there *is* this."

He handed Grendel a folder marked "Assassination Plot — Gov. Orm Hildasson." Grendel's frown deepened. He switched back to Jiao. "You did not see the need to tell me this *first*?"

"It's been dealt with. Hildasson killed the assassins and sent the other conspirators here for your judgment."

"And he did not deal with them himself?"

"Because several are on the Hamilton city council."

Grendel raised an eyebrow. That *did* change things.

He turned to his entourage. "Return to your duties. I will summon you if needed." He turned to Astrid. "You wanted to see me?" Astrid nodded. Grendel smiled. "I have something I need to work on, but it should not take long after I drop you off."

GRENDEL, with Jessamine and Astrid trailing behind, approached the doors carved with wild beasts marking the entrance of his harem. The two guardsmen entrusted to watch his home, women, and youngest children crisply saluted. Grendel returned their greeting and the guardsmen opened the doors.

The vast space opened up before him. Alrekr leaped off his shoulder and flew beneath the vaulted white ceiling. The complex was quiet — at this time of the afternoon, the eldest children still living there would be with their tutors and the younger ones likely napping.

Grendel headed toward the heavy door bearing the saber-cat insignia that marked his apartment. He walked beside the long pool, watching a nude pink form slice through the water. It was Lenora, the concubine who had once minded Falki, Arne, and Astrid.

Between the lack of physical labor and good food, he and his were in danger of getting fat. Though Grendel did not appreciate famine victims, neither did he appreciate the unhealthy and weak. It took strong women to bear strong children. Swimming was an excellent exercise and to that end, he prescribed courses of swimming to his women and children. He followed this regimen himself in addition to drilling with his men.

He smiled as he watched her swim. Though she was years older than the youthful Jessamine, Cora Wilkes, and Catalina, she was smart enough he could actually *talk* to her. And though bearing two children had left its mark, the exercises were certainly paying off.

At the thought of Catalina, Grendel looked over to the rooms closest to his own, where Catalina and their son Havarth Grendelsson lived. Unlike the others, she did not want to be there. He continued along the edge of the pool and drew close to her rooms.

Through the door he heard her singing, in the high, steady voice one used when singing to a child. "Turkey in the straw, turkey in the hay. Roll them up and twist them up a high tuckahaw."

Catalina told Merrill stories and sang Merrill songs to her son, did her best to inculcate her people's values in him. Her subtle rebellion only played into his hands. After all, the boy would have to appeal to the people of the former Merrill realm to retain their loyalty once he disposed of Clark.

Sometime soon, he would let her take her horse outside the city. He would make sure Havarth rode on a dead-broke pony as well. In order to be a proper Merrill he would need to know how to ride. Although it would be years before he could unleash the boy, one could never begin too early. Catalina would be less melancholy for awhile, less likely to kill herself or, even less likely, try to murder him some night in bed. Havarth needed his mother, her dying by her own hand or his would be counterproductive to his plan, and she was an excellent lay besides.

But first, he would need to see how Falki dealt with the plot against the governor.

Lenora rose from the pool, blonde hair dark from the water and clinging to her neck and shoulders. Water rolled off her full breasts, the breasts that nursed his children Logmar Grendelsson and Lin Grendelsdottir. Although she first looked at Grendel, her attention soon fell on Jessamine. Jessamine met the older woman's eyes for a moment, but soon her gaze fell to the floor.

"Jessamine, put your things away," Grendel ordered. The younger concubine had not borne any children to potentially threaten Lenora's brood, but that would not last. And Grendel had taken *her* on the trip south, not Lenora. Governing his empire took up enough time as it was. Letting his women squabble would add even more headaches.

Jessamine nodded and headed to her room beside Catalina's, pulling her wheeled suitcase behind her. Lenora stepped closer, a smile spreading across her face. Although Grendel had business to attend, she had no way to know. He would need to reward her enthusiasm, but not right now.

He stopped her with a finger to her breastbone. "In a couple of hours." He gently turned her toward the pool. "Finish up. I will meet you in your quarters when my work is done."

She headed back toward the pool, an extra bit of swish in her hips. Grendel's appreciative gaze followed her as she returned to the water. Astrid made a distasteful sound behind him. Grendel snorted. "Where do you suppose those babies you love to play with come from?" He turned to face her. "You know, it is about time I started looking for your husband. You are not much younger than Katie was when I found Egill." Astrid turned beet red. "Now I have some work to do. I should be done in an hour."

Astrid scampered away while Grendel went into his private rooms. Once ensconced in his comfortable chair, he opened the folder. Four of the seven members of the city council were involved. Not only them, but the city manager and several local police, including the chief. They had concocted some bullshit story involving raiding an establishment known to be frequented by gangsters and "accidentally" killing the governor, who had stopped by on his way back to the district capital.

He scowled and marked the files of three of the four members of the city council with his red execution stamp with a bit more force than necessary. Their kin would pay to sharpen the headman's axe afterward. And they were lucky — if they had succeeded in their scheme, he would have had them blood-eagled.

The fourth council member's case was a bit more ambiguous. Even under torture, the man had been consistent about his involvement, or lack thereof. Maintaining the same story while being flogged, branded, and having fingernails torn out was beyond most people.

He set that man's case aside. He would take a closer look later.

He marked the city manager and the police officials involved for death as well. He would have executed the rank-and-file police involved, but the governor and his detachment of Obsidian Guard had already taken care of that.

He paused. That was eight death sentences and one he might or might not spare. His son had sentenced eleven more to die. Two were financial supporters of those implicated, while another owned a local bank. Two were relatives of the councilmen. Two were union organizers. Two others were *scribblers* of all people. And then there were three children, the sons of those slated to die.

The last document brought a smile to Grendel's face. It was a general order to the Obsidian Guard garrisons in every city in the Basin except for Havelock and Colby. In light of the Hamilton plot, a representative of the local commander was to attend all meetings of two or more city council members, public or private, indefinitely. *Never let a good crisis go to waste.* Leaving the two most loyal cities alone was clever — their example would answer any claims that this was a power grab. It would be wonderful if it were a case of like father, like son.

Still, he would sound out his son's reasoning. A calculated purge merited pride. Mindlessly lashing out like Jasper Clark did not. And Falki had committed that sin before…

"THE COUNCILMEN NEED NO EXPLANATION," Grendel told his eldest son. "The police officials likewise." He took another swallow of mead before speaking again. "But the others? I would like your reasoning." Once he had visited with Astrid as promised, he had summoned his heir to an empty office deep within the citadel, well away from his harem.

"One scribbler was part of the plan." Falki drank from his own goblet. "His reporting on the local lowlifes would give the whole 'mistaken identity' charade plausibility."

"And did actual criminals frequent that ballroom?"

"Of course. The plotters weren't idiots. They'd want a plausible explanation for why their police would barge in and start shooting."

"The rest?"

"The other scribbler criticized the local commander and our government in general. The union men were involved in that strike the Guard had to crush in the spring, which is what pushed the council from pissing and moaning into treason in the first place. They somehow hadn't been sent to the mines with the rest, but they're not escaping this time. The rest were allies of the councilmen. Killing their sons means no revenge."

This was exactly what Grendel had hoped for. "I like the way you think. I approved all of your sentences, bar two. The councilman who was not as involved as the others would best serve us alive. That means we will not kill his son."

Falki's fingers tightened on his goblet. "Him? He claimed he didn't think they were serious, but he should have thought again. He's a threat to *your* rule, the same as the others."

Grendel frowned. Time for another lesson. "There is more to ruling than imposing one's will by violence. You have to make friends as well as enemies. Gratitude can be a powerful source of allegiance. If all you have are enemies, soon someone else will sit on your throne." He paused for effect. "It will hopefully be one of your brothers if you botch it when I am gone."

Falki scowled. "That's not much incentive to keep them alive, now is it? You named me your successor, but you keep fathering rivals."

Grendel leaned forward, locking eyes with his son. "That is not much incentive to let you succeed me, if you will murder my other children before my body is cold. I have many sons and I am not *that* old." Falki tensed. "How about this? If any of your brothers die, you die next." That would make sure Falki *protected* them, at least while Grendel lived.

Falki replied more quickly than Grendel expected. "Clever. I like Arne and he knows his place, so you needn't worry about him. And we need Havarth to hold over Clark's head and get rid of him when the time comes." He leaned forward. "However, there is Logmar – "

"Logmar is fifteen and has never commanded men in battle. You are twenty and you have. Your fixation on him does you no credit."

"He is already making friends with people in the capital, sons of the elite and lowlifes both. Probably people who don't want to be ruled someday by a half-Jiao. Building a power base." Falki paused. "Signe is content I succeed you and look out for Arne and Astrid. Lenora, that governess with delusions of grandeur, wants *him* to be the next first lord. You'll need to keep an eye on her."

"I do not *need* to do goddamn anything." Grendel kept his eyes locked on his son. "Having someone plot against you that you cannot simply kill if you want to keep your head might be good practice."

Of course, he *would* keep a closer eye on Lenora. Of all his sons, Falki was in the best position to succeed him if he died tomorrow. Barring treacherous stupidity on the boy's part, he intended to keep Falki alive. Blood-kin were precious.

"While we are still on your brothers, it is in the best interest of our family for you to keep them around once you put on my cloak," Grendel continued. "Even Logmar. Remember what I told you before. One arrow can be easily broken, but many arrows together cannot." Falki rolled his eyes. "And what if you die in battle, some hunting mishap or, say, *get sick*?"

Falki's grip tightened on the goblet. His mother and younger full brother had died in the cholera epidemic that had swept Norridge after Grendel claimed the city. The cholera that had nearly killed Falki himself. It paid to know what buttons to push.

"That's incentive to give you grandchildren."

"That would please me, but they had better be from Nora Matthews before they are from anyone else."

Had James Merrill the good sense to submit, Grendel would have married Falki to Catalina. It would have been a win-win — the Merrill's grandson would rule all between the mountains and the desert and the seas and Grendel's senior grandchildren would have the prestige of the oldest dynasty in the known world, a lineage dating back to the day after the ancient world had burned.

But the fool viewed Grendel as a parvenu and Falki as mongrel, and so it was war. James Merrill's loss was not Grendel's though. Marrying Falki to Alex's daughter would ensure the bonds between the Basin and Sejera and the Leaden Host remained tight long after Grendel and Alex were gone. Although marrying Catalina to Falki after wrecking the southeast meant an enemy whispering in his son's ear, taking Catalina himself meant his own claimant for the Merrill throne. And besides, Catalina was *quite* fetching.

Falki nodded. Grendel smiled. "I am glad we understand each other. Anything else?" The younger man shook his head. "Excellent. Now I have some other business to attend to. Make yourself scarce."

Falki nodded again, turned on his heel, and walked out.

HOW THE MERRILLS DO JUSTICE

Andrew sat at a ramshackle wooden table beneath a dull green tarp, a smile on his face. He fondled a bronze medal etched with the image of a horse and the letter V.

It hadn't taken long for word to get around about what Andrew's squad had done. The captain gathered the whole company and then called the squad forward. After some quick questions, he gave each man the bronze decoration. The others clapped and cheered. Even Wyatt joined in, though his expression soured when his eyes met Andrew's.

It's been less than a month and I've gotten a medal. *Who knows what'll come next?*

Of course, that award didn't exempt him from chores. He pocketed the medal and returned his attention to the disassembled rifle spread out before him. He picked up the bristled cleaning brush and peered down the breech. The three rounds he'd fired during target practice left little behind, but even a little would be too much if it caused him to miss in the next scrap with the Flesh-Eaters.

"Andrew," Will interrupted. "You've *got* to come see this."

What the hell did he want? Knowing Will, probably nothing good. "Can it wait?"

Will shook his head. "No way. The Merrill has decided what Flesh-Eaters we're going to keep. He's going to have them *kill* the rest."

Andrew nearly dropped the brush. "What?"

"Remember the ones we took alive? The ones we reckon are trustworthy join up. Then we have them kill the rest and send the heads back to the Flesh-Eaters. No way they can skedaddle now."

Andrew raised an eyebrow. *Clever.* Any returning turncoats, if they didn't hang for turning their coat, would hang for *that*.

"It's a right treat to watch," Will continued. "With the harvest coming up, it'll be the last fun for a spell. Everybody turns out. Maybe the trading folk will show up and we can swap out some of the loot."

Owen appeared behind Will. It was right fitting he'd show up. "Come on. The ones who're going to get the blade are officers. They damn well deserve it."

Andrew tensed. The pikeys didn't care about anyone outside of their clans, but Owen'd been nothing but friendly. Hell, he'd saved his life during the ambush. He shrugged. Owen was probably half-breed. Maybe he'd been brought up in the towns like anyone else and wouldn't have their attitude.

"All right. Let me put this back together first."

"Fine. But don't dawdle."

THE HOT SUN watched from the bright blue sky as Andrew, Will, and Owen approached the hundreds gathered around a large wooden platform. The crowds kept them back, but Andrew could see six poles standing at one end. Flesh-Eaters were bound to two. David waited there, but Hank was nowhere to be found.

"Figures," Will spat. "They made him do this too."

"I hope Hank's at least getting some work done," Andrew said. "Zeke's going to make us do gaspers until we drop if someone's rifle isn't clean."

"I wouldn't worry about him," Owen said. He looked at David. "Did you clean your rifle?"

David frowned. "Course I did. Did a damn good job, I reckon."

"Good."

Andrew took a gander at the day's victims. One was tall and

swarthy, the other shorter with blond hair. Both still had silver bars on their collars.

"Lieutenants," Will observed. "I thought we only bagged *one* the other day." He shrugged. "Another one to kill's fine with me."

Four men wearing black Flesh-Eater trousers, but not their red jackets, gathered at the other end. Armed Merrills surrounded them. In the center of the platform, flanked by soldiers carrying repeaters, stood Alonzo Merrill. His two long braids trailed behind his shoulder and out of sight.

"Is *everyone* supposed to be here?" Andrew asked. "What if the Flesh-Eaters attack?"

Will shook his head. "It's not required. But most come anyway."

Andrew looked at the pair. The only officers he'd seen were cruel and vicious, men who collected tribute and conscripts. The image of the young Flesh-Eater soldier screaming for his mother as the huge gut wound slowly killed him rose into his mind. Andrew winced and quickly pushed the image away.

"Don't puss out on us now," Will said. "These are *officers*, not some poor body dragged away to be cannon fodder."

"I *know* that!"

"Quiet, both of you," Owen ordered. "The Merrill's going to speak."

"Soldiers of House Merrill," the rebel chief began. "Thanks to your skill and valor, Lieutenants Marshall Pierce and Gabe MacDonald of the Flesh-Eating Legion have fallen into our hands!"

Merrill listed their crimes. Pierce oversaw the killing of ten men in one town in reprisal for the death of a single Flesh-Eater. And MacDonald was even worse — he'd celebrated his platoon's victory over a Merrill raid by building a bonfire of living prisoners. The audience booed. MacDonald — the blond-haired one — cursed back. Pierce remained silent.

"As the Merrill, I sentence them to death." The troopers on the platform escorted the Flesh-Eater rankers forward. Alonzo turned to face them. "These men made you into cannon fodder, forced you to commit crimes against your neighbors and against me. As your first act of service, kill them."

The troopers handed long blades to the former Flesh-Eaters. The four stepped forward, two eagerly and two less so. Those required prodding with bayonets.

"Kill the bastards!" someone shouted from the crowd.

"Cut them open!" added someone else.

The two eager ones approached MacDonald. They raised their knives. Andrew smiled. *Pay the sons of bitches back.* One lunged and buried the knife in MacDonald's gut. Andrew winced. Just like how the Flesh-Eater had stabbed Sam two weeks ago. He hoped MacDonald's death'd be slower and worse.

MacDonald's eyes bulged but he kept his jaw tightly clenched. *Fuck. I wish he'd scream.* The captive kept his mouth shut as his attacker tore the knife free.

The second ex-Flesh-Eater slashed MacDonald across the face. Blood spattered the turncoat's white undershirt. MacDonald still did not scream. The first turncoat struck again, stabbing MacDonald's face a second time before slashing him across the throat. Blood boiled from his ruined neck. MacDonald slumped forward, not even gurgling. The audience roared. Andrew thrust his fist into the air. One less Flesh-Eater soiling the world!

Now the Merrill soldiers prodded the two reluctant Flesh-Eaters toward Pierce. *What the hell is wrong with them?* If they were rankers, their officers probably treated them like shit. Now they had a chance to kill the sons of bitches and they didn't want to do it?

The officer looked straight at them as they approached. His mouth moved, but Andrew couldn't hear him. The prodding grew more aggressive.

"Come on!" Andrew shouted. "Gut the son of a bitch!" He wasn't alone in voicing his displeasure.

Steel flashed in the afternoon sun as the first straggler slashed Pierce across the throat. Twin fountains of blood erupted. The second straggler watched until he received a firm jab from the troopers. He stabbed Pierce in the gut and flinched. Pierce slumped forward.

The audience roared as the soldiers on the platform let the turncoats step back. Andrew shouted until his throat hurt. The cheering went on and on and someone even fired a shot in the air. Beside

Andrew, David flapped his arms excitedly. Will and even Owen looked at him as though he'd escaped a sideshow. David glumly lowered his arms. Andrew remembered he'd done that more when they were children. People'd call him "bird." It was rarely a compliment.

The Merrill raised his hands. "Return to your duties. And know someday this will be done to Jasper Clark and Grendel himself!"

The crowd gave one last cheer as he turned and departed.

Andrew headed back toward where he'd been working on his rifle. As he entered the rows of tents, the jangling of bells pricked his ears. Through the gap between the rows came colorfully-dressed men on horseback, with heavily-laden bulls bringing up the rear.

The pikeys had arrived, no doubt attracted by young men with Flesh-Eater loot burning holes in their pockets. And however they might try to cheat anybody outside their clans, they'd have a lot more to sell than the other troopers.

Andrew followed the traders back toward the platform. Other soldiers peeled away from the disintegrating crowd as the traders halted in an empty spot. Owen was among them, which wasn't a shock. Andrew reached into his pockets and counted the coins he'd taken from the Flesh-Eaters after the skirmish three days before. Four gold dollars and some smaller silver coins too. That might buy some extra jerky or perhaps a patch for when his boots started to thin.

He spotted Owen palavering with a trader as he ambled closer. The trader wore a sneering expression. Owen looked pissed off.

Andrew's jaw clenched. Pikey or not, Owen had saved his life. He wasn't going to let *anyone*, let alone some big-nosed pikey vagrant, treat the other man poorly.

He strode toward the two. A right hook would wipe the sneer clean off the trader's face good and proper.

Another man appeared in Andrew's way. He stood out among the drably-dressed Merrill soldiers like a peacock, his vest crimson edged with gold. The white shirt underneath was cleaner and finer-made than Andrew's. A bright red belt held a dagger to his waist. He stank of the too-spicy food the pikeys loved. A smile crossed his broad face.

"Money burning a hole in your pocket?" Andrew grit his teeth. Did this clownish-looking man know what he had planned? "You look like you haven't been eating," the pikey continued. "Need something to supplement your rations? I've got jerky and flour. I bet you could whip up something better than that awful *hardtack*."

Andrew's stomach rumbled. Breakfast that morning was hardtack, some potato peelings Zeke said would keep scurvy away, and water. And there wasn't lunch, not until harvest. Dinner wouldn't be until dark. There wouldn't be much.

Andrew's gaze drifted. Others had gotten between him and Owen. He couldn't see either man now. "All right." He could deal with the insolent trader later. "What you got?"

"Bags of wheat flour for two gold dollars each. If you're in the mood for bargains, cornmeal goes for a dollar a bag."

The trader pointed to the coarse fabric of the bags peeking out from the saddlebags of his horse. Andrew's heart sank. When times were good, ten gold dollars bought a fifty pound sack of wheat flour. The man's saddlebags didn't look like they could hold that much.

"How much flour per bag?"

"One pound each."

Andrew's eyes bulged. Right ridiculous!

The trader rolled his eyes. "I said bag, kid, not sack."

"I'd like the cornmeal. How about two bags for a dollar?"

The trader sighed. "We have to travel fifty miles straight into the desert to avoid the Flesh-Eaters before we turn west to get into the high plains. If the man-eaters catch us on the way in or out, we're lucky if they just rob us. Do you want me to *starve?*"

The trader reached into his saddlebag and pulled out a roll of paper. "I'll throw this in so you'll see how much of a boil on our ass it is to keep you people supplied. A bag of cornmeal for a gold dollar and you're lucky we've got plenty of maps."

Andrew pursed his lips. That map could have been right useful when he'd fled Carroll Town. "All right. Four bags of cornmeal for four gold dollars." He extended his hand. The trader shook it. When the man turned away, Andrew wiped his hand on his pants leg.

It didn't take long for the trader to bring his goods. "Here you go." The man set the cornmeal on the ground, the map on top. "Knowing army rations, I'd say it'd last you about a month."

That'd be the case if Andrew kept all of it to himself, but he wouldn't hoard his food while his tent-mates hungered. That was something *pikeys* would do. Andrew fished the coins from his pocket, coins that soon disappeared into the trader's coat. There went most of the loot he'd gotten off the Flesh-Eater corpse. The cornmeal would supplement the scanty Merrill rations, but it wouldn't last forever.

Another soldier pushed past. Andrew picked up his goods and stepped out of the way. The crowd had thinned but both Owen and the sneering man were gone. His frown deepened. The bastard had been rude to one of his friends. Letting him get away with it just wasn't right.

Holding the cornmeal bags as best he could, he unrolled the map. His eyes widened.

The map didn't cover just the towns along the desert rim and the high plains. It included much of the desert, cities to the north he'd heard about but never seen, and an ocean in the west. An arrow marked "Everett" pointed out to sea. It even included a city *south* of the Iron Desert.

Andrew didn't know there *were* cities below the desert. Hell, he didn't even know there was *anything* there. He'd thought the desert rolled on and on to the end of the world, a dead land inhabited only by the ghosts of those who'd died there.

Will's face appeared over the map. "So, what'd you buy?" Andrew pointed at the sacks of flour. "Good call. You intending to share?" Andrew nodded. "Good."

Will cocked his head as he examined the map."Hope you didn't waste any coin on *that*. There're plenty of maps around the camp, and you can't eat the damn things."

"How about we not judge too fast?" a feminine voice interrupted. Both Andrew and Will jerked to attention. Was that the horsewoman he'd seen during the ambush?

He turned to see the woman with hair the color of honey approach. She dressed like a man and walked slightly bowlegged like a cowboy, but she stood out from the men like a flower in a mud puddle. And based on some of the looks she was getting, it wasn't just him thinking that.

Remember Cassie.

She walked up to Andrew. She stood far closer than any stranger would. He could feel her warmth even though she wasn't touching him. "Care to let me take a gander?"

Not really noticing what he was doing, Andrew pushed the map forward. She took it from him, her hands sliding across his. She swept it with her eyes and whistled appreciatively.

"You got yourself a good one here. Not just the fringes of the desert and our old country, but down into the desert and the lands beyond."

"Have you...ever been there? Beyond the desert?" A moment passed. Andrew felt like an idiot for even asking, but she *did* seem casual about the "lands beyond."

She shook her head. "Nope. Some of the trading clans around here have traded with other trading clans deeper in the desert who have, but most of that's done out west. I've heard of ships from the south too, but I don't know much." She returned the map. Their hands touched again. Andrew's heart raced.

"I'm Alyssa, by the way. Alyssa Carson."

Andrew tensed. The Carsons. It hadn't been long since the Carsons had attacked Carroll Town. If she learned who he was, she might not be so nice. Andrew wasn't sure if that was good or bad. On the other hand, she *was* comely, and friendly to boot.

"I'm Andrew." They had the same enemy now. "Andrew Sutter."

She raised an eyebrow. "Maxwell's son?"

He was afraid she'd ask. Of course, if she didn't cotton to him because of that, maybe she wouldn't come around and he wouldn't be tempted...

"I suppose so," she continued. "Right clever move your pa did. Taught us not to mess with Carroll Town."

"Th...thanks."

Alyssa smiled. "Course, we're all on the same side now."

Andrew nodded quickly. "Yeah."

"By the way, you boys did good back there with the mortars."

Will finally found his voice. "Thanks."

"Well," she said. "Gotta run now." She looked at Andrew. "Be seeing ya." She slid back into the crowd with a wink. Andrew's gaze followed until he couldn't see her anymore.

"Wow," Will said. "Wow."

Andrew shared the sentiment. It wasn't often pretty girls came out of nowhere that were interested in him. Or at least that's what it *seemed* like. It was all well and good for a man to pursue a woman, but for a woman to pursue a man? He wasn't sure if he should be glad or complain about it being improper.

Behind Andrew, the trader laughed. Irritation flared. *Eavesdropping pikey bastard.* "Pretty lady likes maps," the man said. "Anybody else want one?"

"I sure do!" one soldier shouted. He rushed past Andrew.

Andrew almost laughed. *Copycat.*

Then his scalp prickled. Cassie might still be alive. He hoped she wasn't spreading her legs for some Flesh-Eater — willingly at least. He owed her the same courtesy.

He shook his head. He had to get off this horse lest it carry him somewhere he didn't want to go. He walked away from the trader and Will, passing a group of officers carrying bundles of red and black fabric. The sight stopped him dead. His gaze followed the officers as they disappeared into the crowd.

They were selling Flesh-Eater uniforms?

———

He found Owen beneath the tarp, cleaning his own rifle.

"I saw you with one of the traders earlier. What the hell's going on?"

Owen sighed. "That piece of shit thought I'd joined the Merrills even after most of our Houses — the great families of my people – knelt to the Flesh-Eaters. The heads of the Houses disowned the ones who did, to protect themselves. The ones who left get called 'cast-out.' They don't have a House to protect them, and we're too dependent on the ones trading with us on the sly to make a stink. When he found out I was from House Gollmar, it got worse."

"Why?"

"My pa was part of House Gollmar, but Ma was a flatlander from Pendleton. Most of the Houses would cast out anybody marrying an outsider, but my grandfather thought it a good idea to have ties with the towns."

That would explain the smaller nose. But he'd been brought up among the trading folk, not in some town they'd visited. Andrew's scalp prickled. Perhaps the *Gollmars* weren't so bad.

But the ones who'd joined the Merrills came from other clans too. He paused. He could ruminate on that later.

"And the other Houses didn't approve?"

"That's part of it. The real issue is they're ashamed." Andrew didn't expect that. "We stood by the Merrills even after Grendel killed James Merrill at Fairmont. Most of the Houses switched sides or at least went neutral." Pride entered his voice. "Grandpa kept his word. We beat the war drums all night for Alonzo and sent the Flesh-Eater emissary who demanded tribute and submission back with his boots shoved down his throat. We kept his scalp."

Andrew laughed at House Gollmar's sheer balls. Owen scowled. "Two hundred Gollmar soldiers and maybe one hundred shootists who didn't run away against a whole army of Flesh-Eaters. It was insane, but what's the point of making a promise you don't keep? The other Houses didn't have the guts." He frowned. "Who knows if it would have made a difference?"

Andrew's eyes widened. That definitely didn't seem like something a pikey would say. "What happened?"

Owen's scowl deepened. "What do you think? We raided the forces besieging Pendleton and got our asses *whupped*. We killed a lot of the bastards, but they outnumbered us and had some damn big guns — not just mortars, but the kind that fire from so far away you can't see them. Howitzers." He sighed. "The Flesh-Eater commander thought himself funny. He gathered up all the bodies and made jerky. He sold them around and called them 'Gollmar bars.'"

Andrew didn't laugh. "How'd you survive?"

Owen closed his eyes. "When it was obvious we were losing, Grandpa led an attack on the enemy command post to distract the bastards and sent the women and kids away. I was one of the youngest bearing arms. They put *me* of all people in charge on account of everyone else being needed for the attack."

He sighed. "Everyone else died, but around a hundred got out. The horsemen stopped chasing us once we got out into the sand. That's when sand snakes and rippers showed up." He paused and closed his eyes a moment. "We'd chase them off, but we started running out of ammo. There were maybe fifty of us left when we found a Merrill patrol who took us to where Alonzo regrouped the army."

Owen's words struck Andrew like a blow to the gut. That sounded a lot like what happened to *him*. Slowly, Andrew laid a hand on Owen's shoulder. "I'm sorry."

Owen shrugged the hand off. "Don't apologize. It's the damn Flesh-Eaters' fault." He smiled grimly. "Every time we season some turncoats, I come see if we're using that bastard from Pendleton. Only it never is."

Andrew reckoned now would be a good time to change the subject. "I saw some officers taking enemy uniforms to the traders. What's going on with that?"

"I wondered about that too. Zeke enlightened me." He grinned. "We foul them so the Flesh-Eaters have to waste time and money on mending. And since they buy them from the other *Menceir*, who buy them from us, that means they're paying for our war."

Andrew laughed at the irony. "But couldn't we put those uniforms to use? Spying and the like?"

"I don't think we sell them *all* back. I guess the Merrill uses them that way, but I've never seen it done."

Andrew nodded. If the Merrills had that kind of trump card, it'd make sense they'd keep it close to their vest. It was a gambit that'd work only once.

Owen looked at Andrew. "You clean your rifle? It won't be long until Zeke comes. He's going to be right pissed if you're not finished."

Andrew remembered he hadn't finished cleaning his rifle before putting it back together. "Good idea."

THINGS (START TO) FALL APART

Grendel faced the line of dirty prisoners across the sandy expanse of the Obsidian Guard firing range below the citadel. "If you can get past the guardsmen, I will pardon you. There are forty of you, but only eleven of us."

The prisoners shifted uneasily. Sweat was beginning to glimmer on heads shaved to avoid the lice infesting the capital's jails. It was not every day a man could be dragged from Norridge's dungeons, given a saber, and told they could soon be free.

If they could get past Grendel and his favored trainees. But the guardsmen had only a single ten-round magazine each, not the thirty-round battle magazines. They would have to shoot quickly and accurately or the prisoners could break through to the archway carved into the black stone wall enclosing the range.

"How can we trust you?" asked a fatter man standing apart from the others. From his look and attitude, he had to be a political prisoner, not a cutpurse or other lowlife. He did not look like he was the only political there.

"What do you have to lose? If you are quick, you can be free. If not, death is an improvement over being these gentlemen's girl." The heavier prisoner tensed. One criminal snickered. A guardsman laughed too. "Besides, my men can always shoot you where you stand." His speech done, Grendel stepped back into the line.

"Order *arms!*" the towering blond Sejer sergeant shouted. Grendel lowered his weapon to his side along with his men. These new recruits probably needed to learn how to kill. Grendel had no problem with killing but he was also old enough to be their father. In fact, noting how one wiry Jiao did not look like he had ever shaved, possibly their *grandfather*. They needed to be seasoned; he needed his speed and reflexes kept sharp.

Some prisoners shifted forward. Grendel knew their kind — hard, ruthless men who would kill for what they wanted. They were his kin, but unlike them, he had self-control and wisdom. That was why *he* sat on a throne made from his defeated enemies' most powerful weapon in the greatest city in the Northlands and *they* rotted in a dungeon.

"Come on, you dogs!" Grendel shouted. "You want freedom? Come and get it!"

With a shout, a quarter of the men surged forward. The others, more hesitant or intelligent, fell in behind them. Some did not move at all, obviously paralyzed by fear. One of those was the fat one.

CRACK-CRACK-CRACK-CRACK! The first prisoners fell, blood and brains flying. Bodies threw sand in the air as they hit the ground. The ones who did not immediately die screamed. For a moment, Grendel remembered Jacinto, his last great battle. He took aim and squeezed the trigger. The political prisoner, who had only started to move, toppled forward with paired holes in his chest.

An emaciated prisoner with stringy hair hanging to his waist shouted obscenities. His saber rose high, ready to take Grendel's head.

Grendel let him take two more steps before squeezing the trigger. The repeater kicked against his shoulder. The man went down. Grendel pivoted and shot another, then lowered his rifle. He could always kill more, but who would be left to blood the men?

To Grendel's left, one prisoner managed to close with a guardsman. Unfortunately for him, the guardsmen had fixed bayonets. The wet sound of a blade sinking into flesh told Grendel the prisoner's fate. Some extra drill would be the guardsman's.

The firing range fell silent except for the moans and whimpering of the wounded. With the exception of the bayoneted prisoner, none came within ten feet of the guardsmen. The metallic stench of blood and the sharp smell of gunpowder hung thick in the air. The shadows of the range's resident carrion-birds fell across the sand.

One prisoner cowered at the wall. He had not even tried to rush the guards. "Please!" the man begged. "I'm due out tomorrow! I just forged a signature! Please!"

CRACK! He slid down onto the sand, leaving a trail of blood behind him.

"Finish them!" the sergeant shouted. The guardsmen stepped forward. The moans grew louder before the bayonets silenced them.

Grendel loomed over one prisoner, an amber-skinned Jiao with only one eye. Blood trickled from a wound in his shoulder and his remaining eye was alive with pain. He grabbed onto Grendel's boot as best he could with his good arm.

"I was a guardsman," he hissed. "I took more than my fair share of the loot, but I was there at Jacinto!"

Jacinto, the Merrill capital. That had been a hard siege even with most of the Merrill army butchered at Fairmont weeks before. Grendel shook his head. The rules governing loot distribution existed for a reason. And the man would not have been in the capital's prisons unless he had been drummed out of the Guard and then committed another crime.

Still, the man *had* fought for him.

CRACK!

"Guardsmen, attention!" the sergeant shouted. The men stood straight. "Guardsman, dismissed!"

The men began filing out. Now it was time to finish that painting of Catalina he had been working on. He might send it to Alonzo Merrill, to goad him into doing something stupid.

The sergeant approached Grendel. "Sir, you have a visitor." He pointed to a suited man with spectacles flanked by two guardsmen in the range entrance.

"Bring him in," Grendel ordered. The guardsmen escorted the newcomer onto the sand. Disgust bloomed on the bookish man's face as he took in the heaps of bodies. "State your business."

"My lord, war has broken out between the Blood Alchemy Host and the Legio Mortis."

Though Grendel knew Mangle and Quantrill were at loggerheads, those words cut him to the core. Fear snaked unwelcomingly out of his intestines, rising into his chest like some monster from the deep ocean between Sejera and Everett. He breathed in and out, keeping his expression impassive. He would not show fear in public, especially before subordinates.

The smell of blood and gunpowder on the air vanished from his perception. This was much worse than Alonzo Merrill. This was worse than the friction between the Leaden Host and the Flesh-Eating Legion he had papered over. The two rivals controlled prime coal mining territory only a day's flight from Norridge itself. Norridge, whose factories were the key to his domination, *depended on that coal*. The great empire he had spent decades building could crumble in months if the fighting spread.

Anger soon blew the rising fear to pieces like a well-aimed artillery shell. His jaw clenched. If those idiots wouldn't keep the peace, he would cement the cracks in his realm with blood.

The man winced. Despite his efforts, it seemed Grendel's wrath showed on his broad face. "Give me that." The official handed him the telegram with trembling hands. Grendel scanned it. Just as he had thought, it was that damned coalfield. His frown deepened. There went his planned afternoon of painting Catalina naked and fucking her.

He folded the telegram and pocketed it. Had he been a religious man, he would have thanked Odin neither side had called in allies. Two subordinates fighting could be suppressed quickly.

He turned to the messenger. "Fetch the Guard commanders in Norridge, Isaac Tompkins, and Falki Grendelsson." The man, who looked like he was on the verge of spewing his guts, quickly nodded. "I want to see them in an hour and a half. Send orders to the Firebird Host and the Leaden Host. Describe the situation. They will know what to do."

CATALINA LAY naked on her belly in Grendel's bed, hair damp and clinging to her neck and shoulders. Grendel stood on the balcony mere yards away, wearing his absurd armor and reviewing the lines of Obsidian Guard marching through Norridge. He was engrossed in the array of armed might rolling through the streets below.

They were ten stories off the ground. He'd go out the window if she gave him a good shove and fall, faster and faster. The so-called first lord of the Northlands would end up as nothing more than a shattered mess on the pavement. She'd gaze down on his mangled carcass for a moment and glory in killing the one who'd butchered her family and oppressed her people, the man who'd used her as a goddamn *toy*. She was a Merrill in enemy territory. She'd succeed where her father's and brothers' armies had failed.

Then she'd grab her robe for modesty's sake, fetch Hayes, and run for the doors. She frowned. Right into the guardsmen. Then the men who saw Grendel's fall would arrive. She'd be lucky to get a bullet in the head. If she were kept alive for interrogation, they'd make her beg for death before they finished. And they'd kill her son in front of her. Falki had every reason to order that, to dispose of a future rival. Arne might plead for the life of his little shadow, but he would be on thin ice enough as a half-brother regardless of how close he and Falki seemed now. Her fists clenched around the soft sheets, her nails digging into her palms through the thin fabric.

But the time the old bastard would get his comeuppance was drawing near. Without new enemies his thugs were turning on each other. Jessamine had mentioned how Grendel headed off a war between the vile hillbilly Flesh-Eaters — her stomach twisted at how they tyrannized *her* people — and the merciless Leaden Host. This time he hadn't stopped the war and some new fire could ignite while he put out this one. Should any army enter Norridge, he'd find he had an enemy *inside* his walls.

Catalina found she'd crept to the edge of the bed. She looked at Grendel. He was still there, still looking out the window…

"Yes?" Grendel didn't move a muscle. His deep voice froze her in place. Catalina's stomach lurched into her throat. He must've heard even her most subtle movement.

Grendel turned away from the window abruptly. His gaze fell on

Catalina like a lightning bolt. She tensed, instinctively squeezing her legs together. He was dressed for battle, but that wouldn't stop him from making her please him with her mouth. He locked his gray eyes with her hazel ones.

"For someone who has lived in my house the last four years, you do not know how things work. I can fuck you any time I want, but I do *not* have that flexibility with politics." He scowled. "Or war."

Catalina exhaled and relaxed a little. He'd been gone for over a day and when he'd returned, he was *angry*. She'd nearly hit her head twice on the headboard. The relief she wouldn't have to please him again overwhelmed her anger.

"You will also like this. Between Mangle and Quantrill, I know who is cunning enough to *not* have started this. It is the Blood Alchemy Host that will get the worst of it."

How well the old bastard knew her. She'd been in Jacinto when the first reports of the invasion came. A horde of deformed soldiers spilled out of the Pass into the northwest. Thousands of civilians taken prisoner. Those who escaped reported mutilation and experimentation. Amid the carnage strode a man they called Mangle, garbed in black. One of his hands was made of metal and could crush concrete. The other was black and clawed, the hand of a monster and not a man. The superstitious thought him some unholy amalgamation of a Thirsty Ghost from the desert and the machines from Norridge.

Her father had husbanded his armies to protect Jacinto and defeat the Flesh-Eaters coming out of their hill country before dealing with Grendel's main assault. But there was no way he could leave the people of the northwest to the mercy of something out of a nightmare, even if that meant playing into his enemy's hands and dividing his forces.

He'd sent her oldest brother John north with soldiers who were *supposed* to crush the Flesh-Eaters. Old pain lanced through her as she remembered learning his army had been cut to pieces, with John killed by the monster himself. Without the additional armies barring their way, the Flesh-Eaters poured south. Now John and all the people who'd been killed or mutilated by this "Mangle" would be avenged at last.

"That does please me, my lord." She nearly gagged on the last two words, but they were what Grendel wanted to hear. And she didn't really *need* to pretend. If only he'd kill every single commander who ravaged her homeland. That might provoke a revolt and bring down his whole evil empire.

He threw her robe onto the bed. "Get dressed. Tell the others I should return within a week."

She pulled on the robe, not slowly-slowly to preen for him like the others but not *too* quickly. He'd laugh or, worse, change his mind about making her take him in her mouth…

Back to her rooms, her hideaway he let her decorate with books and other items from her desecrated home. She'd retrieve Hayes from Astrid and tell him again about how he wasn't just the son of Grendel. He was the grandson of James Merrill and through him the descendant of Charles Merrill, who'd survived the burning of the Old World. Lessons that'd hopefully stick no matter what Grendel or his tutors taught him. Maybe if he were a Merrill in his heart, her kin would forgive her.

She'd barely gotten her robe tied before he tramped past, heading off to war. Part of her hoped he wouldn't return, but another part feared what would happen to Hayes if he didn't.

She locked her eyes on his retreating back. His time would come, sooner or later.

THE *NICOR* LED the convoy of twenty black Obsidian Guard airships straight north along the rail line. Grendel stood behind the reedy Sejer captain on the airship's bridge, looking out over the wide lands below. Alrekr perched on his shoulder.

"When should we get to Stilesboro?"

"Three hours, sir," the man replied from his post at the dirigible's wheel. "Six for the trains from Trickum and Martinsburg."

"Excellent."

Grendel would lead the first wave of the Obsidian Guard into Stilesboro, where the rail line emerged from the Basin. He did not expect trouble, but if trouble came, it would be there, where the rail lines in the north crossed. Whoever commanded that juncture would be able to invade both Blood Alchemy and Legio Mortis lands while keeping both armies from moving freely.

Three hours should be plenty of time for the three thousand guardsmen in the army's airborne vanguard to occupy the town and prepare for the main army's first wave.

His gaze followed the railroad back into the city itself. The trains should begin flowing out of the city soon. Falki's company would be among that second wave. If any treachery awaited Grendel, Falki should be far enough away to escape it. And he would be close enough to avenge it once the Guard's Jiao and Sejer generals proclaimed him first lord.

Grendel frowned. He had not had to worry about this nonsense when he was not the sole power in the Northlands. He had strong opponents to keep his sworn men fighting or preparing to fight. There were no such enemies in the Northlands now, only the Merrill dregs far to the south and occasional uprisings. No more loot or land to distribute, no new wars to keep the bloody-minded busy. Grendel missed the battlefield, but administration provided its own set of challenges. Not all of his followers appeared able to make the transition.

His frown deepened. He had survived the butchery of his family. He had lived by the gun since he was fifteen. He had forced his enemies into subservience — those he had not he had simply killed — and shattered empires to make lordships for his friends. The realm he created would ensure his family would not only *survive* but *rule* for generations to come. He was damned if he would let everything he had built fall apart because his subordinates were *bored*.

Enemies. We need enemies who are not each other.

Nobody knew just where the trading city of Everett lay and in any event, he could not successfully challenge them at sea. The Flesh-Eating Legion could be made such a foe, but Clark was too smart to provoke him. Attacking Clark *without* provocation risked a general rising of the less loyal. He would be fighting on multiple fronts, against the Legio Mortis in the northeast, whatever remnants of the Camrose Confederation had not been fully digested by the Firebird Host in the east, and opportunists the length and breadth of his empire. And the once-broken Merrills might emerge from the desert rocks they had crawled under to avenge the death of their chief and the captivity of his daughter.

The desert.

Though the Fall, the fiery end of the Old World, had shattered the trade routes that, according to legend, once spanned the world, commerce with the lands beyond the Iron Desert never truly stopped. A trickle of goods came to the western ports on Everetti ships. The farthest-ranging of the trading clans plying the southern edge of the Iron Desert also brought goods not of Northlands manufacture. Expensive as they were, they showed the desert could be crossed and there was something worth conquering on the other side.

This merited further thought. "I will be in my quarters," he told the captain. "Inform me when we are close to Stilesboro."

HARVEST PROBLEMS

The angry sun lashed Andrew's neck. His squad wasn't among the lucky ones on patrol or sweeping the countryside for game. Instead, they'd been sent with the women and children to cut hay from the grasslands well east of the camp.

Andrew swung the scythe through the waist-high dry grass, the blade cutting through the stalks just above the ground. He looked behind him. It had been hours and the two dozen or so workers had cut only a few acres. The nearby reaper would do the same work in half the time with two men and a horse, but it hadn't moved in a spell. Andrew hoped it wasn't permanently busted. The grass stretched out a fair distance ahead and with only scythes, it would take *days* to harvest it all.

Back in Carroll Town, he could hunt to earn his keep and pawn off the work on the family's fields on those who wouldn't get bored and distracted easily. David in particular was good at the sort of dull, necessary tasks that would drive Andrew mad.

He reproached himself for his attitude. He owed the Merrills for saving him in the desert, and they were his best shot at punishing the Flesh-Eaters besides.

Still, his arms and back were getting sore, the back of his neck was sunburned, and he was having difficulty focusing.

Maybe pondering the better aspects of the situation would make things easier. Thanks to the drought, the hay would dry quickly and it wasn't likely to be ruined by rain. That meant the horses and cattle had fodder.

But thanks to the drought, the hay was sparse. Rumor had it the grain fields cut into the sod elsewhere were worse. If the harvest were anything like Carroll Town's would have been, the Merrill camp would hunger during the coming year.

He kept that bleak thought to himself. If only David had more sense.

"This is awful," David grumbled ahead of Andrew. "How are thousands of people and horses going to eat —"

Will struck him on the shoulder. "Shut the hell up, you dumb shit. Nobody needs to hear that now!"

Andrew glanced over to the nearest group of workers. Most were women and kids, but it looked like another squad had been detailed to help. Those men were giving David powerful ugly looks.

Andrew looked straight at them and shook his head. Most returned to work. The other, a man a foot taller than Andrew and bulkier besides, returned his look. Andrew did not lower his gaze.

"But it's true!" David said. "There are two thousand people at this camp and —"

The man who met Andrew's gaze narrowed his eyes. Any fight'd likely turn into a riot. Everybody'd be lucky if they just had to do gaspers until they collapsed.

The man took a step forward. Andrew raised a finger.

"Hold on," he mouthed. The other man nodded, though he didn't return to his work. Andrew turned toward David and Will. "Both of you stuff it. That fella over there already wants to fight. We've got work to do."

"Yeah," Owen added. "I'm not interested in more gaspers or a spell in the stocks."

Hank nodded his agreement. Will shrugged and returned to work. David scowled. "All right."

Once everyone was cutting again, Andrew looked at the big man and nodded. The titan nodded back and slowly returned to work.

Looks like that's taken care of.

After a few more minutes, someone shouted from the machine. It was Zeke, crawling out from under the reaper.

"Simmons! Get your ass over here!"

"Yes, sergeant." Will set the scythe down and headed over with a slight spring in his step. Andrew reckoned he didn't cotton to cutting hay either.

"What's he doing?" David asked. "Zeke wouldn't let him shirk."

Andrew recalled the battle with the Flesh-Eaters. "He was good with the mortar. Maybe he's good with machines. That reaper'll get all this hay mowed right quick. And after that, it can get cracking on the wheat. Maybe we'll have it all done in a few days."

Of course, one reason the machine could harvest so quickly was because there simply wasn't a whole lot *to* harvest.

Gears began turning in Andrew's mind. The fields around the Merrills' hideaways weren't their sole food source. They raided the Flesh-Eaters when they could, stealing food or loot they could sell to the pikeys. If the harvest this year couldn't replenish the army's food supplies, they'd need to raid the enemy a hell of a lot more.

A smile spread across his face. He'd have the chance to kill Flesh-Eaters and maybe find Cassie and Sarah.

ALONZO WIPED the sweat from his forehead as he entered the spacious tent where he met with his advisors. The others rose from their wooden benches. He gestured for them to sit. "Harvest's taking longer than I thought. One of the reapers broke down again."

The camps and refuges making up the present Merrill domain had only perhaps a *dozen* reapers, all horse-powered to avoid the smoke that would bring Flesh-Eater dirigibles. Most were about to fall apart. Harvesting by hand meant more work and less return. Father had done his best to make sure it wasn't too bad working in a factory and the Shoemakers repaid the favor by doing their damnedest to keep him supplied with manufactures, but the Flesh-Eaters kept a sharp lookout. Dozens of Shoemakers had ended up on the cross or the barbecue grill. And getting equipment to the Merrills' camps meant more deals with the trading folk, who drove hard bargains.

"We've been discussing the information you asked us to collect," said white-haired Gideon Paul, who'd been his father's treasurer. The Merrill cause was not exactly rich at the moment, so he handled logistics in general and not just money. "You won't like our conclusions."

"I haven't liked your conclusions since the war started. That don't mean I don't need to hear them."

The old man nodded. "We've had to tighten rations twice last year and that was with much better crops. This year is going to be even worse."

Alonzo swore. "How does it break down?"

"Well, we have five thousand men and six thousand women and children. Three horses per man, the sheep and cattle…" He paused. "We're going to run out of food. Spring at the earliest and we definitely won't survive summer."

Alonzo closed his eyes and took a deep breath. Was this it? Did he survive Fairmont and Pa's death just to starve in the high plains? Was the last living Merrill going to be Catalina, soiled by a tyrant? Was the Merrill line going to be stained forever by some wicked Sejer?

He ground his teeth and clenched his fist. To hell with that. He'd send all the women and children in small groups west. The lord of Hamari needed workers and tended not to ask questions. Then he'd take all the men and ride for Jacinto or, if a way around the Pass's defenses could be found, Norridge, for death or glory. It would be the end, but it would be a far better end than eating one's own boots before dying of scurvy or, Good Lord forbid, eating the dead.

"We can cull the livestock, of course," Paul continued. "That'll free up hay to sell to buy food for people, and we can sell the meat or give the people a feast to keep up morale. But that presents its own problems. Culling means much less milk, leather, and wool in the long run. Hungrier people and less trade."

Alonzo knew what was next. "We can't cull the horses. We'd all be dead five times over if it weren't for the troopers all being mounted."

"Damn right," said Major General Thomas Hutton, the last of his father's commanders. Sweat shone on his bald head. "Mounting up everyone barely got us out of Fairmont. If we have to *march* every-where, we might as well hop on the barbecue grill now and get it over with."

"What do you propose?" Paul asked. "Each day, the Southern Wall gets stronger and the airships come farther south. We won't be able to raid for supplies much longer. If we don't starve, they'll come down here and finish us."

Hutton's brown eyes narrowed."Trying to breach the Southern Wall where it's strongest is suicide. But so long as it's being built, there's food headed there, payroll —"

"We've been raiding *that* to keep ourselves alive and keep pressure on the Flesh-Eaters," Alonzo interrupted. "I propose we step up some."

In order to get the food and fodder — or the gold to buy more — to survive the next year, they'd need to steal colossally. Thus far, he'd contented himself with pinpricks, hitting isolated Flesh-Eater troops or filching supplies. This kept them in the fight but did no serious damage. A raid big enough to get what his folk needed would provoke serious Flesh-Eater reprisal or even intervention by the Leaden and Bloody Alchemy Hosts. At worst, Grendel himself might come south with the Obsidian Guard.

This might be a swift end by bullet or bomb instead of a slow one by hunger and sickness. It'd be the final victory for the sons of bitches who'd butchered his family and stolen his country, a victory they'd get without bleeding for it.

Well they'll bleed for this one all right. Oh, they will bleed.

IMPOSING PEACE

Garbed in his full armor, Grendel sat in a carved oaken chair on the dais in the stone and timber great hall of Stilesboro. The town council had wisely offered him their meeting place and made themselves scarce. Guardsmen as still as statues flanked him; others formed lines on either side of the dais. Below him to his right stood Clark in his military garb, barely-repressed eagerness on his face.

Enjoy this glory while it lasts. I'm raising you up only to dash you to pieces. The higher the climb, the worse the fall.

The oaken double doors opened. The bright light outside framed Travis "Mangle" Steuben, the first to arrive, and his bodyguards.

Despite the heat outside, Mangle wore a hooded cloak. Crimson eyes peeked out from underneath. His hands, one blackened and twisted and the other made of metal and clockwork, remained at his sides. What Mangle did to himself in the years he had ruled north of Norridge made Grendel uneasy, but he would not show this weakness.

And like Mangle, his bodyguards were also unusual. Mangle's men were huge and twisted, looking like they had bulls in their pedigrees. Hell, one even had horns.

The terrible man who once tended the wounds of Grendel's soldiers — and tortured his enemies — walked toward his master across the hardwood floor. Fifty feet from Grendel, the guards stopped and stood at attention. Mangle came forward alone.

"My lord." His voice had more than a hint of machine in it.

"Where is Quantrill?" Grendel asked.

"Here, my lord," Stephen Quantrill called from the doorway. A tall and slender man with a receding hairline, he wore a simple blue coat that reminded Grendel of his own preference for black. He came with only two guards, men wearing dark blue with light blue scarves

Grendel examined his pocket watch. Quantrill was on time, but only just. And arriving later than Mangle, symbolically keeping Grendel waiting. Grendel frowned. Though he was certain who started this war, Quantrill was not helping his cause. The second warlord approached Grendel's seat, leaving his guards behind the same way Mangle did.

"So glad you could join us, Quantrill," Grendel rumbled. "Now that we are all here, we can get straight to business."

And I can get back to Norridge in case another fire breaks out while I'm dealing with this bullshit.

Quantrill nodded but remained silent, watching Grendel with his dark eyes. Sweat shined on the exposed skin of his head and moistened the white hair fringing it. *He should be afraid.* Though the Blood Alchemy Host started this war, that did not mean Quantrill did not merit a reminder that pride came before the fall.

"As I'm sure you know, I have the Obsidian Guard, two Hosts, and the Flesh-Eating Legion ready to grind both of you into dust if you two do not cooperate. And my son has been itching for a fight lately. He is well to the rear, so do not think treachery will save your hides."

"I intend no treachery," Mangle intoned. "I have been your loyal man for many years. Unlike him."

"Don't let him poison your mind against me, my lord," Quantrill spat. "The fact he has served you longer does not affect the fact his wolves have been raiding *my* border, carrying off *my* people to be mutilated or to fuck monsters to make more!" He glared at Mangle. "You're trying to make it hard for me to mine the coal, hoping I'll cede it to you for less than it's worth."

Grendel's spies had been about since the messages from Norridge silenced the guns. The locals reported raids from the west. The attackers did not bear the bloody heraldry of the Blood Alchemy Host, but the dead they had left behind did not always look right.

Deformed, freakish soldiers were Mangle's stock in trade. Mangle was not stupid — Grendel would not have made him his man if he were. But not using his normal soldiers was a fatal error.

"The coal does not solely belong to you," Mangle retorted. "The veins abut my border and your works cross over. I have offered you those best-suited for such work, but your miners do not tolerate them and you don't make them."

Grendel knew "best-suited" meant the biggest and strongest of the horrors Mangle's breeding pens spawned, as well as the ones able to crawl into tight spaces or see in the dark. When Quantrill accepted a previous offer the miners went on strike rather than work alongside "freaks." Quantrill swiftly crushed the unrest, but dead men mined no coal. He had probably refused further offers from Mangle and offended the deformed man.

Grendel frowned. The welcoming feast in Hamari and the arguments between the Leaden Host and the Flesh-Eaters took valuable time, time for the situation in the north to erupt. Who knew what might happen if he dawdled too long far from Norridge? He would end this quickly. "When my children fight over a toy, I take it away from them *both*. I would much rather not treat you, my brave and clever men, like children, but in this case, you have *earned* it."

Grendel turned to Clark. "For services rendered in the fight against the Merrill pests, I award you the disputed region. The center of the territory will be the coal mines with the bounds thirty miles in all directions. It is yours until I conclude these gentlemen have earned it back. Use its resources widely."

Clark grinned. "I am honored, my lord."

As usual, Clark played right into Grendel's hands. His gladness meant he would likely send quality soldiers, not the sweepings, to this faraway post. It would be easier to suborn or destroy them once the time came to turn the Flesh-Eater realm over to his son.

Grendel turned back toward Quantrill and Mangle. Mangle remained inscrutable as ever, but Quantrill looked pissed.

"I defended myself," he grated, eyes angry in his narrow face. "And defended the people I rule in *your* name. Your treating me as equally at fault is unworthy of a wise ruler such as yourself —"

"Do not worry," Grendel interrupted. "I know who is responsible and who is not."

Grendel's gaze fell on Mangle like a thunderbolt. The twisted man's red eyes widened. "You will return *all* prisoners and pay Quantrill three hundred gold dollars each. Depending on what you have done to them, they might not be much use as workers."

"My lord," Mangle said. "That could run into many thousands —"

"You should have considered that *before* you attacked Quantrill instead of bringing the matter to me. Pawn some of your Old World gear to Alexander or rent out your aberrations if the cupboard is bare. I have supplied you with rebels and the sweepings of the jails for years now, so it is not like you are going without."

Mangle nodded. "Your will be done, my lord."

"It *will* be done. Falki will be staying here with the Obsidian Guard to make sure." *That* should ensure his decree would be followed without problems.

Meanwhile, it was time for Arne to start receiving direct lessons in ruling. The boy was sixteen now and if some other crisis required his attention while Falki was up here, he would be unprepared to rule in his stead.

"Both of you are to remain in the area to supervise the transfer of territory," Grendel continued. "Clark is needed elsewhere, but he will be sending a representative to handle his interests here." That should keep them busy and, more importantly, under Falki's guns.

"It will be done, my lord," Mangle said.

"Aye," Quantrill said, a bit slower than Grendel liked. Falki would need to keep an eye on the man.

"Good," Grendel said. "Dismissed."

———

GRENDEL SAT in his cabin aboard the *Nicor* and sipped his mead. Alrekr watched from his cage. A folder full of reports about the brief war lay open in his lap.

There had been two days of sustained combat with twelve regiments involved. This had been preceded by raids from Blood Alchemy territory into Quantrill's realm and some retaliatory attacks. Total casualties amounted to two thousand dead and four thousand wounded soldiers, with six hundred dead and nine hundred wounded civilians and two thousand taken captive. Small as far as wars went, but worse than the border skirmishes between the Leaden Host and the Flesh-Eaters.

His firm response should have nipped the problem in the bud. But if it did not, the next one would be worse.

Someone knocked on the door. "Father."

"Come in."

Falki, wearing the dark uniform of an Obsidian Guard captain, stepped inside and sat in a chair across from Grendel.

"I assume you have received my orders?"

"I'm to assist with the evacuation of the Legio Mortis and the Blood Alchemy Host and the establishment of the Flesh-Eater garrison in the buffer zone. I'm to delegate the duties as a company commander I can no longer perform to Lieutenant Nahed."

Grendel nodded. "It would be better if you were to continue your ordinary duties until this whole situation blows over, but I need to return to Norridge in case another fire starts." He paused. "This is different from hunting bandits. Mangle and Quantrill are dangerous, in different ways."

Falki nodded. "Quantrill is like Clark. He isn't one of your loyal men like Alexander, but someone you forced into submission."

Grendel nodded. "He might strike at me through you, hoping to ruin me in the long run by killing my most capable heir. He knows what will happen if I figure out who did it — he would attempt to make it look like an accident or pin it on Mangle. If the man had a birth family, I would take hostages. Hell, if he had a daughter or sister pretty enough, I would take them into my bed. More fun that way, plus any children are ready-made pretenders."

"No birth family," Falki repeated. "No parents, brothers, sisters. Like you?"

The boy was sharp, but Grendel did not laugh. Ejnar Irontooth took his family away. Blood-eagling the bastard and his men had not brought them back.

"Not quite. I do not lack for potential successors, but he does not seem to have *any*. Maybe he is bent, Odin cursed him with a limp cock, or there is somebody hidden away I do not know about. However, he rose to power the same way I did. If I had not put him in his place, he would have gotten stronger and stronger. It would not have been just the Camrose Confederation threatening Norridge."

Falki raised an eyebrow."No spies in his country?"

"Not reliable ones. He did not get where he is by being careless. Communications in and out are heavily monitored and he likes to rotate key people around, even his territorial lords. He claims it is to ensure his subordinates are well-rounded, but it limits my ability to make connections in his territory."

Falki laughed. "Clever bastard."

"Aye. He will be more dangerous than Clark when you put on my cloak. Clark is predictable and too straightforward for his own good and we hold Havarth over him, besides. Quantrill is smarter and a damn sight closer to Norridge, and the only leverage I have is I can beat the absolute shit out of him." Grendel paused. "Now, onto Mangle. He has been with me for thirty years, but that presents its own problems."

"Familiarity breeds contempt. He might take liberties, banking on his past service to you."

"Might? He just did. Since I gave him territory, he has become more and more absorbed in his science projects. He sends the tribute to Norridge, obeys the law on Old World weapons, and until now has never defied me, but maintaining assets in his territory is tricky. Unlike Quantrill, I lack pretexts to send outsiders to inspect the place as often as I like."

Falki raised an eyebrow. "You can't simply make him allow inspectors? Especially after *this*?"

Grendel frowned. "The lands I do not rule myself I gave to my followers, to rule as they see fit provided they follow certain rules. If I break this agreement, that risks insurrection. This arrangement is a two-way street."

"Mangle's little war has given you an excuse. Why not take it?"

Grendel pursed his lips. Between his handling of the conspiracy against the governor and now this, the boy showed he knew how to spin crises to the family's benefit. But this train of thought went to destinations better off avoided.

"That is a good idea, and I will consider it. However, you still need to tread carefully to avoid internal war. I could have contented myself with Sejera and had a free hand, but Sejera could be attacked from the Basin or from where Alex rules now. I took everything between the mountains, the desert, and the seas to create a realm that could not be attacked from outside, even if it meant I needed to delegate."

Falki nodded before changing the subject. "Any luck suborning those born to the area?"

Grendel shook his head. "The threat of the breeding pits is not just something I use to control the Basin. There is something in the land or in the air near that Old World" — he searched for the word — "reactor that makes children quickened there wrong. Nobody up here wants to sire monsters or have their mothers, sisters, and daughters bear them."

Falki raised an eyebrow. "That's deterred *everyone*?"

"Everyone who matters. The higher you rise, the more you have to lose." Falki nodded. "Keep Nahed and your company close and do not go *anywhere* alone. This is a subtle battlefield, but it can be just as lethal."

"Have you been monitoring Lenora's correspondence? She's probably hoping I don't come back and it's only Arne who's between Logmar and succeeding you."

"You are obsessed. Lenora's relations are flatlanders living in Hamari. If I had taken her from Quantrill's or Mangle's realm, you would have much more reason to be concerned." Grendel poured more mead. "I intend to leave for Norridge in two hours. I will leave half the Obsidian Guard here to deter Mangle or Quantrill from making trouble. General Hakonsson will have overall command, but he will delegate many tasks to you as my deputy." Although Falki's comments were troublesome, the old general should be able to manage him. "You should be here no more than a few weeks. Dismissed."

"Wait." Grendel raised an eyebrow. Falki continued. "You've humiliated Mangle and Quantrill today. The troops you're leaving will be able to take on one of them, but if they join forces, do you think we could handle *both*?"

That was unlikely, but Falki was clever to see it. "Do not worry. When I forced Quantrill into submission, I used Mangle's troops for the most part and gave him some of Quantrill's territory afterward for good measure."

Falki raised an eyebrow. "You deliberately created a rivalry between them to keep them from joining forces against you in the future."

Grendel nodded. "Between that and this recent war, there is too much bad blood for an alliance. And I used Quantrill to force Clark into submission, so I doubt they would join forces either. Now, *dismissed.*"

Falki nodded before leaving. Grendel returned to his drink and his thoughts. It had been four years since he broke the armies of James Merrill, destroying the last rival in the Northlands. Four years since the men who served him had a real enemy. Although many settled down to run their estates and lordships, others grew restless. The war Grendel aborted was the largest eruption yet. Another could easily erupt soon.

The expedition across the desert he pondered would take a long time to assemble. Another internal war could erupt in the meantime. In order to properly attack, Grendel would need to reconnoiter. This would require dirigibles, since probing with his largely idle navy risked provoking Everett, jealous of its monopoly on trade between north and south. He did not need a sea war he would not likely win, nor any warning to their trading partners of the coming storm. However, the airships were necessary for hunting bandits and Merrill raiders.

The Merrills. Instead of an expeditionary force to the regions south of the desert, he could order units from the most difficult Hosts into the desolate regions where Alonzo Merrill laired. That would give them something to do and dispose of the last opponent of his new order.

That was an *extremely* short-term solution. The Merrills would be easy prey. Grendel would be back where he started in a year at most. And deploying other armies into territory the Flesh-Eaters claimed could cause problems.

Crossing the desert it is then.

HARVEST FESTIVAL

The Merrill stood on the platform below which gathered almost every resident of the camp. "Thanks to your hard work, we've brought in the crops in record time," he called out so even Andrew could hear him. "Our granaries are no longer empty, and the horses that take us to war will be eating well. And so tonight, *we'll* be eating well!"

Andrew joined the cheering. The last few weeks' rations had barely been enough to keep body and soul together. There'd even been *scurvy* in the camp. He ran his tongue over his teeth. None *felt* loose.

"Rations will be increased, and I've given orders to slaughter cattle. Supper tonight will be more than hardtack and lard!"

The cheering grew louder. Andrew allowed himself to imagine fresh beef slowly roasting over the fire. It would be juicy, it would be tender, there'd be a whole lot more of it…

He frowned. Alonzo's speech made sense, but something about it didn't add up. Cattle provided milk, which meant butter and cheese. Having meat now was all well and good, but butter and cheese would provide more food in the long run. It would be wiser to keep as many cattle as possible.

Why slaughter now? The more he thought about it, the more his heart sank. The camp had more people than Carroll Town and Carroll Town would've starved even if the Flesh-Eaters hadn't killed everyone.

The Merrill wasn't killing cattle to celebrate the harvest — he was killing cattle they couldn't feed.

HANK ROTATED two spitted racks of beef ribs over the squad's small campfire. Rather than serving everyone at the mess tents, the quartermasters handed out food and the men prepared it themselves. Hardy had come around and talked with all of them and was now probably doing the same with some other squad.

Andrew watched the cooking from a trunk the former Flesh-Eater had found for them to sit on. Hank had also found a jug of corn whiskey. Hopefully that would lighten the darkness engulfing his heart whenever he pondered just *why* they were killing cattle. Somebody played a guitar in the distance. That, at least, brought a small smile to Andrew's face.

David watched Hank cook. "This is right excellent. Two rib racks right there. That's two cuts from one cow. There's a lot more where that came from and —"

Andrew ignored David, who obliviously chattered away. On top of the two racks of beef ribs being roasted, there were six steaks, one for each of them and the last to be split up. And there were hot rolls, the first made with the wheat from the new harvest, as well as carrots and potatoes and even some greens…

"You boys mind if I join you?"

Andrew's head snapped up. Alyssa stood there, holding a package under her arm. Though it appeared she addressed the whole squad, her gaze fixed on Andrew. His heart skipped a beat.

"Howdy," Andrew said. "Haven't seen you in a long while. What brings you hereabouts?"

"Well…" Alyssa kept eye contact with Andrew. "I haven't seen you boys since we seasoned the turncoats and I figured I'd see how you were doing." She shrugged. "By the way, I brought something."

She handed Andrew a package. Meat juice dripped onto his pants. His mouth began watering. "What's this?"

"Well," she said. "Before the wars, most of the Merrill cavalry punched cattle, and we brought in the cows over the last couple of days. We take them to the butchers and sometimes they're nice to us." She smiled. "Open it."

Andrew's jaw dropped. It was short loin! "Th…thanks," Andrew stammered.

"We had plenty, so I figured I'd share."

Andrew suddenly felt David peering over his shoulder. "That's a hell of a lot better than rib racks, not that those are bad by any means. Give it here. I'll have it cooked real nice."

Andrew turned and David all but took the package from his hands. He stepped over to the fire and busied himself with the rationed seasonings and the meat.

Will cocked his head. "What the hell's he doing?"

"He's a damn good cook," Andrew said. "The way he's into food, it'd be a right shock if he wasn't."

Will looked at David skeptically. "Yeah, but that's a goddamn *short loin*. Hank usually cooks when it's up to us and —"

Given how Will ragged on Hank for having been a Flesh-Eater, a body might think *he* of all people wouldn't want Hank anywhere near his food.

"He won't cook it all at once," Owen interrupted. "How the hell can he? Hank's already cooking the ribs."

"All right," Will grumbled. He turned his attention to David. "That's good meat. Don't bugger it up."

David scowled. "I won't."

Andrew turned back toward Alyssa and gestured to the meat. "The cowboys won't object?" He didn't want Alyssa to get into trouble for her generosity.

She shook her head. Owen passed Andrew the jug of whiskey. He handed it to Alyssa. She took a swig and sat on the trunk next to Andrew, far closer than he expected. Andrew's heart beat faster. She acted toward him the way he might act toward a woman he fancied.

Surprisingly, he didn't mind. But he *did* mind doing Cassie wrong, wherever she was.

Well, part of him did. Another part remembered the ambush of the

Flesh-Eaters. They *both* could have been killed. Hell, either could die the next time. And Alyssa *was* a looker.

Hank began taking the ribs off the fire. "Dinner's ready."

They all dug in. David, however, ate his kneeling next to the fire. He'd carved off a piece of the short loin for each person, seasoned and spitted them, and now turned them over the flames. Though Hank was absorbed in his food like the others, he still kept an eye on David.

"So," Andrew said. "They had the infantry in the fields along with the women and kids. I assume you were with the cowboys?"

"Yep. Brought the last cattle in for butchering today."

Andrew leaned closer, voice low so only she could hear. He already had his suspicions, but she could confirm or deny. "Why're they killing the cattle? I don't mind steak, but wouldn't it be better to have milk and cheese, eat it ourselves or trade to the pikeys?"

Alyssa sighed. "Most of the time, yes." She lowered her voice. "But fodder's sparse, even with the harvest. There's not exactly a lot of grass hereabouts. We culled the herds and hoped for the best. What we don't eat tonight's going for jerky."

Absolutely fucking wonderful. The morbid thought hit him. They were culling animals now. What if they had to cull *people?* They wouldn't eat them like the Flesh-Eaters would, but they'd still be dead.

"Steak's ready," David cheerfully announced. "How about Alyssa go first? She's a lady, and she brought us the meat in the first place."

"Why thank you, David." Alyssa sounded rather pleased.

He took a skewer off the fire and held it toward Alyssa and Andrew. Alyssa pulled a knife from her boot, buried it in the first steak, and pulled it free. She tore a smaller piece off with her fingers, apparently unbothered by the heat, and popped it in her mouth. She chewed thoughtfully and grinned. "Marvelous!"

David turned red and grinned. Owen slapped him on the back.

Will stepped forward. "Let's see just how good it is."

He set a steak down on his metal plate and carved a piece off with his knife. He let it cool a moment, then popped it in his mouth. His eyes grew wide. "Shit, that *is* good. Where'd you learn to cook?"

David beamed. "My grandma. She was the best cook in Carroll Town. Got a blue ribbon every year at the town fair."

Andrew felt a twinge. The fair took place every year in Carroll Town's square beneath the mooring tower. He could still remember the troupe of performers from further north who'd come with a clockwork carousel and spinning baskets one could ride in. He'd scrimped and saved for months before they came so he could ride at least twice. And David's grandmother cooked for everyone, a different dish each year.

The performers had stopped coming when Jacinto fell. The pikeys filled in as best they could, but they didn't have the wonders from the cities. But David's grandmother could still cook and the folk of Carroll Town didn't *need* outsiders to entertain them.

He remembered the last one. Everybody was glad the harvest had come in and was hopeful the next year's would be even better. The possibility there'd be a killer drought hadn't crossed anyone's minds. There'd been dancing and music. It was where Andrew met Cassie, while Sarah met Elijah.

He closed his eyes. Elijah was dead because of him, while Cassie and Sarah were in the hands of the enemy.

"Grandma had a book," David continued. "It was called *The River Cottage Meat Book*. Not sure where River Cottage actually *is*, but it had some right good recipes in it. I learned it better than my sister…"

His voice trailed off. He squeezed his eyes together. The other boy's pain sent hurt stabbing in Andrew's own chest. He remembered Sarah, sarcastic but kind. If she were still alive, she no doubt wished she weren't.

"I learned it well," David finished. "I can show you, if you want to learn too."

"Maybe later." Will grinned. "Right now, I want to finish this."

Andrew kept looking at the ground. Alyssa laid her hand on his. He inhaled sharply.

"Something's bothering you," she said bluntly.

Andrew slowly nodded. "He's not the only one who's got a sister."

Alyssa leaned close. "What was her name?"

"Sarah. She's my twin. The Flesh-Eaters took her." Alyssa winced. "They took my girl Cassie, too," he quickly added. "She'd tried to run, but was hurt." Maybe if Alyssa knew about Cassie, she'd lose interest in him. He wouldn't need to worry about staying faithful to Cassie if the biggest opportunity to do her wrong disappeared.

Alyssa closed her eyes. "That's awful. I had a sister once. Her name was Ellie." She paused. Her voice dropped to a whisper. "Ellie'd broken her leg trying to get away from the sons of bitches. Once they'd had their fun with her, they cut her open and left her for the rippers." Andrew's stomach lurched. Despite not wanting to encourage Alyssa, Andrew laid his other hand atop hers. She looked straight at him. "I wouldn't put too much hope in Cassie being alive."

This hit Andrew like a hammer. Based on what the officer said in Carroll Town, he reckoned the Flesh-Eaters kept their female captives around and only ate men that couldn't work. Cassie and Sarah were probably alive. Someday the Merrills might be able to rescue them.

"When was this?"

"Three years ago, after the fight with Carroll Town."

Hope arose unexpectedly inside Andrew. Maybe the Flesh-Eaters who'd killed Ellie had died in the fight at Carroll Town. Their replacements *might* be saner.

"They might not be dead," Andrew repeated. He took his hand off hers. "I can't." Hopefully that got the point across.

It looked like it did. Alyssa withdrew her hand. "Suit yourself." She sounded almost sad.

She rose and moved around Andrew, sitting closer to Will. Hank's lip curled in distaste, but she ignored him.

"So," she began. "Saw you liked the meat. What was it that was so good?"

Anger rose in Andrew's heart. Why the hell was she talking to Will now? She'd seen him antagonize David over the meat, the meat she'd brought in!

At least she wasn't flirting with Owen. He was swell — even if he was a pikey — but that wasn't something he wanted to see.

Alyssa glanced back at Andrew. She nodded to Will and then stepped over to Owen, avoiding Hank entirely.

Andrew clenched his teeth.

Well shit.

DEVELOPING THE PLAN

The new electric lights shone brightly in the room of Grendel's concubine Cora Wilkes. Not only was electricity safer than gas but it did not flicker. This afforded Grendel a much better view of the naked blonde lying beside him. Cora was in a good mood, discussing their daughter Rose's reading progress with her tutor while Grendel was away, how the sunny weather had been good for the flower garden she had on one of the balconies, and other news, besides.

Though Grendel toyed idly with her curly hair and made the appropriate single-syllable responses, his thoughts were elsewhere. He had developed his plan further coming home, but it had not fully congealed. Mounting an invasion of a distant country across some of the most hostile terrain in the known world was not something done lightly, but he did not see any long-term alternative but civil war.

Cora must have picked up on his not paying attention. She snuggled closer, her breasts pressing against his chest.

"Is something wrong?"

"Nothing you need concern yourself with."

Cora did not immediately respond, at least with words. Instead, she let her hand drift toward Grendel's crotch. Grendel exhaled at her touch, but his reaction was somewhat exaggerated. It was true he was sensitive there — no man alive was not — but he wanted her to think she really was manipulating him.

"My lord," Cora purred, her hand becoming more active. "If I knew what was bothering you, perhaps I can help you feel better?"

"Can you keep my men from fighting each other?" He allowed only the barest hint of enjoyment of her ministrations to reach his face. "If it does not stop, all this could come crashing down." He gestured toward the room around them and, by extension, to the palace and city beyond.

Her movements slowed. Grendel knew she did not have an immediate answer. This did not bother him — it was Isaac's job to help solve problems Grendel could not.

Isaac. Isaac would help work out the details of his plan.

"Catalina's folk are still making trouble, aren't they?" There was an edge to Cora's voice. Catalina had given Grendel a son. She hadn't. "Perhaps some of the men unhappy with the peace can go down there. They can help that savage Clark fight what's left of the Merrills."

Grendel smiled, an expression bearing a fair amount of sincerity. He had not taken Cora into his harem for her brains, but she *did* have them. She had been a camp follower, daughter of another camp follower, but her mother did not raise a fool.

Cora's hand moved faster. Grendel's breathing increased, an unfeigned reaction this time. He was sorely tempted to let her continue and talk to Isaac later.

He covered her hand with his. He had not gotten where he was without learning to bridle his desires.

Business before pleasure.

"Not now. If I return within an hour, we will pick up where we left off. Otherwise, go to sleep."

Cora sighed. She withdrew her hand and rolled onto her back. Grendel leaned over and kissed her on the forehead. Helpfulness should be rewarded.

Isaac sat across the table in his study within the citadel, an untouched glass of mead in front of him. Two guardsmen stood like statues just beyond the doorway. "We both knew this was coming," the older man said.

Grendel nodded. For a moment, he wished James Merrill had bothered excavating the Old World cities beneath the sands, at the least ones he could readily reach. The survival of a foe powerful enough to provide a good fight whenever a commander had the itch but not too powerful to threaten Grendel's rule would have prevented all this.

"Other than a few spots of banditry and the occasional revolt, the only enemy north of the Iron Desert is Alonzo Merrill," Isaac continued. "And he's not much better than a bandit himself." He laughed at his own joke.

"I had thought to send the restless men south, to finish him off. What do you think about that?"

Isaac pondered Grendel's words. "It won't keep them busy long. The Flesh-Eaters have reduced the Merrills to a gaggle of refugees. If you send the other Hosts, this contretemps will end all the faster." Isaac paused. He scratched at his substantial salt-and-pepper sideburns with his right hand, a sure sign he was thinking. "If you sent in Mangle's people, it might end all the faster. The Blood Alchemy Host passed through the land once before. The people must surely fear its return."

Grendel frowned. He had used the Blood Alchemy Host to force James Merrill to divide his armies, but kept Mangle's army under strict supervision afterward. If he wanted an army of monsters to kill all the men bearing arms and drag everyone else to their overlord's repulsive breeding pits, he would unleash the Blood Alchemy Host. But ravaged lands paid no taxes. Maintaining Havarth and his sons afterward would require a population loyal to the Merrill bloodline and grateful to be liberated from the Flesh-Eaters. Settlers from elsewhere would not do.

Still, it was not as though the Blood Alchemy Host was his *only* option.

"What are the most recent estimates of Merrill strength?"

"The most recent information indicates only a few thousand active combatants. The plan to cut him off from resupply and recruitment has been bearing fruit. With the help we've been giving them, the Flesh-Eaters can probably finish the job themselves." He paused. "Of course, *that* won't deal with the short-term or the long-term problem."

"Isaac, while I was on the way north, I had an idea and I have been pondering it some more. I would like your opinion."

"Yes, my lord."

"Everett's ships have traded in the west for generations and caravans cross the Iron Desert from the south. All bring goods not made here, goods that are in many cases higher quality." He paused. "Including that most precious commodity, coffee." Chuckling circled the table. *Good.* "Those goods have a source."

"Are you proposing we invade, my lord?"

"Not yet. There are maps of the desert and what lies beyond, but they are old. Some might even date back to the Old World. If we do not want to shove our dicks onto a clockwork saw, we will need more information."

"Reconnaissance, then?"

"Aye. Getting spies into the caravans will take time. Everett doesn't hire foreign sailors on principle and will certainly complicate any naval probe south. Airships will allow us to keep our recon secret, but deciding whose airships to borrow could prove…tricky."

If he sent dirigibles belonging to commanders he trusted, that would weaken those men. If he sent airships belonging to commanders whom he did *not* trust, they would interpret that as a move to weaken them. He wanted to heal the cracks in his realm, not deepen them.

On the other hand, if he made it sound like an honor and offered them the rewards of conquest, Clark at least would not look the gift horse in the mouth. Quantrill *might* not. This would leave his loyal commanders at full strength and weaken the less trustworthy, and they would be none the wiser.

"Let's start with Clark, then. He's on the Iron Desert and he'd likely interpret that as a gesture of your confidence in him. Especially since you gave him territory in the north." He paused. "However, the Flesh-Eaters don't have many airships and they need them to hunt the Merrills. Might be better to start with the Blood Alchemy Host."

Grendel pursed his lips. That would weaken Mangle, but at the same time, it would look suspicious. The Blood Alchemy Host's territory was far from the Iron Desert. They were not a logical choice for an extended reconnaissance mission.

"If you send Blood Alchemy *and* Legio Mortis dirigibles, it'll look like a team-building effort," Isaac continued. "Be sure to send only men with families on the mission. Extra incentive not to be killed or captured, and they *definitely* won't defect."

A reconnaissance mission could give the more restless men something to do. And it would provide the first real intelligence about the territory south of the Iron Desert in centuries. The trading folk and the sailors both local and Everetti provided some information, including at least one book, but firsthand intelligence was always better.

Isaac smiled. "A longer war also presents its own possibilities. The unemployed will take your dollar and the threat of the press gang will keep workers from striking. And if you manage to conquer even part of the south? Not only will Everett's trading monopoly be broken, but you might be able to fully centralize power."

Grendel nodded. If the cities where these manufactured goods were produced could be brought under his direct control, this would be a vast source of wealth and, consequently, power. He would keep Alexander and some others for old times' sake, but he could be rid of Quantrill and Clark — and Mangle if he fucked up again — forever.

"Begin gathering the needed resources, including dirigibles. You speak with my voice."

Isaac leaned forward. "You want the reconnaissance started now? What about the Merrills?"

"As you said, the Flesh-Eaters can take care of the Merrills themselves. Besides, if Alonzo Merrill thinks we are distracted, he might stick his neck out enough we can swing the axe."

Isaac nodded."Provided enough troops stay behind to do it."

Grendel nodded. "Enough will." He rose from his chair, drinking the last of his mead. "I want all the Host commanders, Falki, Quantrill, and Clark here as soon as possible."

A MOST INTERESTING NIGHT

Falki and his company rode across the broken and blasted ground back to their base camp. The wind had blown the day's coal smoke away at last and the stars shined brightly overhead. "That's one more problem solved," Falki remarked to Nahed. "Getting the goddamn Flesh-Eaters to dig their latrines farther from the goddamn lake will keep them from getting dysentery."

Nahed nodded. "Or cholera."

Falki frowned. He knew all about cholera. It had come to Norridge when he was six, not long after Father had made the city his capital. His younger full brother Delun, a year old and barely walking, had died in the first days. Then it was Falki's turn. He'd shat water, drunk more, and then shat it out again. And the water he didn't shit he vomited. It got to the point they'd laid him on a bed with a hole under his ass and put needles in his arms. They'd done the same with Mother a few days later.

She'd died, but he'd clung to life like a leech. He was just walking again when Father had blood-eagled the men who'd overseen Norridge's sewage and water-treatment plants.

"Sorry, sir," Nahed said. Falki frowned. He must've let his face show his emotions.

"It's no matter. The past is carved in stone. All that can be done is to learn from it."

And that he had. His soldiers' water was always boiled before drinking and clothes were kept free of the lice that brought typhus. The guardsmen under his command had the fewest deaths from disease.

This meant *everybody* wanted his advice on keeping their own men healthy. According to his tutors, disease had killed as many men as bullets during Father's wars. The fewer men who sickened, the more could fight. He'd learned that for himself when he'd seen the filthy camps of bushwhackers and piles of amputated limbs after battle.

"Tomorrow morning, want to hunt? I've seen pterosaurs around, and raptors. Scuttlebutt's some miners went up in the hills with rifles in case Quantrill agreed to bring in Mangle's creatures. Hunting's hunting, two legs or four."

It wouldn't be the first time he'd done that. Counterinsurgency was a lot like hunting, especially when dogs were involved. And although Falki took the lead, it wasn't like Nahed lacked enthusiasm. If some of Quantrill's miners thought they could decide with their guns who they worked alongside, they'd learn a permanent lesson.

"Sir, there are still requests for information from the other commanders. Those shouldn't be left to wait. We might get an outbreak."

Falki stiffened. He had no fewer than *five* left. Two came from the Flesh-Eaters, but the rest came from the Legio Mortis or Blood Alchemy Host.

The ones I'm supposed to be getting out *of here.*

Half of both armies had already left, but the rest were taking too damn long. Maybe it wouldn't be so bad if typhus broke out in a couple of their camps. That'd get them back to their mountains and out of his hair all the faster.

He frowned. Lots of things worked in the short run and caused problems later. Deliberately giving the Legio Mortis and Blood Alchemy bad advice would damage his reputation. He'd need support outside of the Obsidian Guard lest the lands beyond Sejera and the Basin fall away when Father died, or if he needed help from outside if the half-flatlander Logmar attempted treachery.

"That's a good point." He thought for a moment. "The Legio Mortis and Blood Alchemy have more steam-powered machines, which can boil the water for drinking and washing. The Flesh-Eaters don't have a lot of gear, but they do control the coal now. I think an arrangement can be worked out."

Nahed nodded. "Seems sensible. It'll keep the soldiers healthy and your star will rise in everybody's eyes. The hunting will still be there when you're done."

The Old World bunker set in the side of a gray stony hill Falki used as a headquarters came into view. Falki brought his horse to a stop and dismounted. Falki walked across the stony ground toward the steel door.

A soldier met him there. "Sir, you have a visitor. From Mary Grace." The man pointed down the hall toward the tall flatlander woman standing in front of the room he'd claimed as an office.

She wore a long teal dress that clung to her slender form. Over her shoulders hung a blue shawl whose shade reminded Falki of Quantrill. Her hair was gold. Falki's heartbeat accelerated. A large wrapped package sat by her feet.

"This her?"

"Yes, sir. She's got a gift for you." Falki raised an eyebrow. Sending a woman was unusual. "Should I have her leave it here?"

Falki would still get the gift if she left it there, but he wouldn't get the chance to find out why the nearby town sent a woman to deliver it. He smiled. Perhaps the woman was part of the gift. *That* would be an excellent excuse for neglecting the paperwork.

"I'll discuss it with her."

He stepped into the office and sat at the desk. The woman followed, carrying the package. She set it down and bowed.

Falki drew his knife from the sheathe on his calf. He doubted his men would allow something dangerous to be brought that close to him, but it didn't hurt to take precautions. Especially when there was someone in Norridge who wouldn't mind him dying if it brought her own son closer to Father's steel throne. "Open it."

She took the knife and with practiced ease cut through the thick brown paper. Falki raised an eyebrow. She handled the blade like a trained soldier would.

She pulled away the brown paper, revealing a mining pick. Lines of gold ran along the head and handle. A gemstone Falki didn't recognize sat at the top where the wood would otherwise emerge. She set the pick on the desk and stepped back, obviously watching for a reaction.

"What's the occasion?"

"The freaks raided Mary Grace. They carried off some of our people. Your father stopped them and got our people back before that monster Mangle could hurt them. And you're making sure Mangle gets out of our lands. The city council wanted to express its appreciation."

As the son of Grendel, Falki didn't want for much, but it was always nice when people gave him gifts. "The people of Mary Grace have my thanks. Miss..."

"Rosalyn. Rosalyn Pleasant."

"Well, that's certainly a pleasant name." He smiled at his own joke. She smiled back. Just a smile, not laughing to obviously curry favor. This wasn't something he saw much at all.

Falki rose and gently set the pick in the corner, next to a long spear whose shaft was edged with gold. That got Rosalyn's attention. "What's that?" She pointed at the spear.

"It belonged to Ejnar Irontooth. Not that useful in battles waged with guns, but it has a certain psychological effect."

Rosalyn raised an eyebrow. "Do tell."

"Father comes from Sejera, in the northwest. The Sejer — his folk — worship a god called Odin. If you throw a spear onto the battlefield before the fighting starts, you're dedicating the enemy to him. No mercy." Falki smiled. "I don't believe in Odin. But I do believe in drama and I do believe in fear. No quarter means your enemies won't surrender in the short run, but it generates fear in the long run. Each battle may be bloodier, but there'll be fewer of them."

She nodded. Falki raised an eyebrow. He'd expected his candor to make her uncomfortable, but it didn't seem to bother her at all.

"Have you ever used the spear that way?"

"Once. There was a group of rebels in the Basin, freeholders Father had cleared out to make room for Guard veterans. They'd killed Wang Fai — he was one of Father's supporters from Sejera. Every single man died that afternoon." He smiled. "*Ho la Othinn.*"

That wasn't all you did. Falki grit his teeth and took a deep breath. *Keep your focus on the present.* On the Pleasant, specifically. But the niggling, damning phrase "blood eagle" still floated in the back of his mind.

Rosalyn pursed her lips. "Is something bothering you?"

Falki shook his head. "It's been a long day." That part was true at least. And the best lie was one that was at least partially true. A future first lord of the Northlands had to be good at that.

"So tell me, what's Mary Grace like?"

"It's to the east of here. The coal ran out when Ma was a girl, but we adapted. We grow food for the areas where the mining's still going on, especially if it's in places where it's hard for the miners to feed themselves."

Falki nodded appropriately. It was good to see the people in Mary Grace knew how to land on their feet when things changed.

When things changed. Like when you let your goddamn temper get the better of you...

Rosalyn's eyes widened. "Did something I say upset you?"

Falki sighed. If he didn't get it off his chest, he wouldn't enjoy the night at all. "Tell me," he began. "Have you ever heard of the blood eagle?"

She leaned forward. "Blood eagle?"

Falki paused. What the hell kind of woman wanted to hear more about the *blood eagle* of all things? She didn't have any objection to the throwing of the spear. But he wouldn't tell her about *that* blood eagle.

But there was another...

FALKI STOOD on still-wobbly legs in Father's shadow. Father wore his black armor, complete with the tiger-skull helmet, and his wide face was like solid rock.

They stood before the mottled yellow and brown sandstone trapezoid behind Norridge's citadel. Between Falki and the huge tomb holding his mother's and brother's ashes — they'd been burned together on a longship on a lakeshore in Sejeran fashion — stood several wooden posts. Five naked men were bound hand and foot to each. Huge gongs flanked the wooden line. Black-clad guardsmen surrounded them. Beyond swarmed thousands of Norridge's residents. Murmurs raced through the crowd. Occasionally someone shouted something. Falki had learned the flatlander tongue along with Jiao and Sejer, but the crowd was talking so fast he couldn't understand them. He *could* tell the men standing before him were not liked.

Father summoned two guardsmen in Jiao. The two men — amber-skinned and dark-haired, like Mother — stepped forward. They struck the gongs with huge mallets.

The gongs' thunder abruptly silenced the crowd. Father waited until the last vibrations ended and then started speaking flatlander. "Citizens of Norridge," Father shouted. He spoke more slowly than the city folk. Falki could understand him. "Hundreds of your kin have died from cholera." The murmuring broke out again. The Jiao raised their mallets. The crowds fell silent. "You are not alone in your grief. My wife Lin Cao is dead, as is my youngest son."

Father's voice was steady. Falki had seen him weep beside the beds of his wife and youngest son. Weeping in private was fine, but not in public. *Never* in public.

"Today, their ashes were interred here. And today, justice will be done for the cholera."

Father unrolled a scroll. The men had taken something called "bribes" — Falki would have to ask what those were — to hire workmen who didn't do a good job fixing the city's water and sewer systems after Father had taken the city. Germs got into the water and that made people sick. Made Mother and Delun sick. Made *him* sick.

Anger screwed up Falki's face. They'd *killed* Mother and Delun and they'd *hurt* him. Father was going to punish them.

"Where I come from, those guilty of the highest crimes are sentenced to the blood eagle. Now see how I protect my own, and punish those who harm them."

Father ordered ten guardsmen forward in Sejer. Two stood behind each man bound to the posts. All drew long, curving knives.

The men bound to the posts wept and rattled their chains. They didn't even beg to live, but only to be spared the blood eagle. Piss streamed down some of the posts.

Something inside Falki pitied them, but he pushed it away. Mother and Delun were *dead*. Whatever came next, they deserved it.

Then Father gave new orders. The guardsmen buried their blades in the bound men's backs. Blood flew. The men screamed.

The screaming and the blood and the stink of piss were too much. Falki turned and ran, but a strong hand gripped his shoulder before he could hide behind Father.

"No," Father said. "You need to know what this looks like. Someday you'll have to give this order." He pushed Falki forward, toward guardsmen and their grim work. "Keep your eyes open. I will know if you do not."

Falki watched as the guardsmen put away their knives and jammed their thick fingers into the cuts they'd made. The men screamed louder.

CRACK! Bones splintered. The screaming rose even higher. Falki squeezed his eyes closed. "Falki," Father rumbled. Falki opened his eyes. It was just Father and him now. He wouldn't let him down.

The screaming stopped. The guardsmen were pulling something out of the bound men's backs now, two red things that looked like bags. Falki remembered the word his tutors had taught him. "Lungs." The guardsmen were pulling the men's lungs out. They stepped back, their work done. The lungs hung out of the men's backs. They fluttered once, twice, and stopped. The men's bodies relaxed. Falki crinkled his nose at the smell.

"This is what happens when you make mistakes and my people die!" Father shouted. "This is the law of Grendel!"

FALKI FINISHED HIS TALE. Most women would have been horrified by what he'd described — and *that* time it wasn't even him doing it — but she just watched, her green eyes attentive.

"That's certainly one way to get the point across," she said. "I bet Norridge hasn't had a cholera epidemic since."

Falki shook his head. "There was one more after that, but it was a lot smaller and wasn't due to corruption. In fact, Father greatly honored the people who ended it. Carrot *and* stick."

It was then Falki noticed she leaned closer to him.

The pick's definitely not the only gift.

Falki lay his hand atop hers. She didn't flinch or pull away. Maybe she feared offending the son of Grendel, but she didn't look uncomfortable at all. In fact, she looked rather flushed. Definitely a good sign. He would be having fun tonight.

Of course, that was tonight. Tomorrow would be different. He'd never taken a woman outside the Basin. He couldn't leave her here, where he couldn't keep an eye on her once he returned to Norridge. If he got her pregnant, that would cause problems, and he'd need to be the first to know. If he fucked her, he'd have to take her home.

Of course, he couldn't marry her. Father wouldn't kill *him*, but death was an effective way to end a relationship.

He shrugged. Father was not the only one who could have a concubine. Grendel took Signe soon after Mother died. He never married her — although *that* would have been nice — and he hadn't married any of the succession of women he'd brought into the citadel either.

Women like Lenora, women who'd borne potential rivals. He'd keep Arne around, but Logmar was dead meat. The younger boys might need to die as well. He didn't want to inflict such a grim necessity on his own children.

He rose abruptly. Rosalyn touched his arm. "Is something wrong?"

"I'm going for a walk," Falki snapped. "I won't be long."

He strode past Nahed down the long hall and out into the cool night. "Captain Grendelsson," Nahed said from behind him.

Falki whirled. "Yes?" Nahed stepped forward, but Falki raised a hand to stop him. "I'd like to be alone."

"Sir, your father's orders —"

"I'll only be gone ten minutes. I doubt any of the things he fears will happen in that time."

THE LIGHTS of the Obsidian Guard camp were a distant glow when Falki stopped. The flat, open land around him was empty except for the nighttime sounds of bugs and other small animals. The full moon looked down on him like the eye of one of Sejera's gods. The ever-present stink of coal-mining was all but gone.

He sighed. Then he started reproaching himself. *You goddamn weakling.*

A woman upset him, and yet *he* left? He'd *run away*? If he didn't want to take her, he should have sent her away.

Fortunately nobody other than Nahed and maybe a few guardsmen had seen. If word reached Mangle or Quantrill, they might think him weak enough to be challenged. They would not dare while Father lived, but he wouldn't live forever. And thanks to Father's inability to keep it in his pants, any troublemaker would have their choice of figureheads.

He scowled. He'd cross that bridge when he came to it. Until then, he'd need to show himself strong, to make up for this lapse. He turned back to camp.

Then he realized the night had fallen silent. He looked down. A faint shadow surrounded him.

"Fuck!"

He threw himself to the side and rolled, his hand diving for his revolver. Something huge slammed into the ground where he'd been a second ago.

An elongated head stabbed at Falki as he rolled. The sharp beak sliced Falki's right shoulder, cutting through the scarring a freeholder bullet had left a year ago.

His gun snapped upward. He fired.

The huge brown pterosaur lunged, moving on its feet and elbows. His bullet punched through a vast membranous wing. The predator screeched. Falki's lips skinned back from his white teeth. He'd have the bastard stuffed and mounted.

The pterosaur lunged. He leaped sideways and fired as the head stabbed through where he'd been. The beast screamed as the bullet carved a furrow atop its head.

CRACK!

His third bullet caught the pterosaur in its narrow chest. It screamed again, blood spraying from its mouth. Despite its wounds, it still lunged, beak reaching for Falki's throat.

Falki stepped to the side. The slash that would have killed him missed. The pterosaur recoiled, but Falki clamped his left hand around its long beak. It shrieked as best it could with a closed mouth, bright red blood dripping from the corners. It tried to twist free, but it was weakened and Falki's grip was like iron.

Falki locked eyes with the dying monster. *Want to finish this with minimal damage to you, my pretty little killer. I want to show you off to my friends.*

The pterosaur lashed with its wing-claws, scoring Falki's left arm. He ignored the pain and gave the head a hard twist, snapping its neck.

———

FALKI SAT in a chair outside his command post, an Obsidian Guard surgeon stitching the larger wounds closed. Rosalyn stood a respectful distance away.

Nahed shook his head. "I *did* warn you not to go out alone." Beyond him, guardsmen dragged the winged horror into the circle of light provided by the gas lamps.

Falki frowned but said nothing. However infuriating that was, Nahed was right. Instead, he focused his attention on the pterosaur.

From wingtip to wingtip, it was roughly fifteen feet. Its neck was at least four. The terrible head was three and bore a feathered crest. Down covered most of its brown body.

Despite the pain from his wounds, Falki smiled. In his free time, he'd hunted rippers, raptors, saber-cats, and dire wolves. He'd slain tyrant lizards and brought their young to zoos and parks, wiping them out in all but the most isolated parts of the Basin. However, the smaller beasts were relatively easy to kill if one had a big enough gun, and he'd never killed a tyrant lizard by himself.

This creature had the drop on him and was a damn formidable opponent. But he'd defeated it *alone*. That'd build respect for him among the guardsmen.

"I want it packed in whatever ice you can requisition and put aboard the next dirigible," Falki ordered. "Send it to my taxidermist in Norridge. This son of a bitch will be decorating my wall."

The guardsmen nodded and bore away the fallen pterosaur. Some remained, watching the surgeon work. Once the stitches were done, Falki rose. "You're dismissed," he ordered. Most of the remaining troops returned to their tasks, leaving Nahed, the two men guarding the bunker entrance, and Rosalyn. Falki's gaze fell on her. He had a victory to celebrate.

"Lieutenant Nahed, bring her in."

Falki returned to his office, with Nahed escorting Rosalyn. He sat at his desk and faced the beautiful woman. "The timing works out *quite* well, don't you think?" Falki locked eyes with her. "You arrive with your gift and the heir of the Northlands is nearly killed. I'm no fool — I know one can train a pterosaur."

Rosalyn's eyes were wide, but her voice remained steady. "I had nothing to do with that! They're everywhere after a battle, and it hasn't been that long since the fighting ended. I'd expect *you* of all people to know that."

Nahed learned forward, expression dark. "Treat the heir of Grendel with more respect."

Falki raised his hand. "Thank you for your concern, lieutenant. I think I can handle one woman." A woman who could stand up to him, even when he all but accused her of plotting to murder him? This was a rare treat.

"Yes, sir."

"In fact, I'd like to continue the questioning alone."

Nahed frowned, but nodded. He saluted, stepped outside, and closed the door. Falki turned his attention to Rosalyn. "You didn't leave when I did, even though you'd given me the gift," he demanded. "Why?"

"Well..." She toyed with her blonde hair. "You said you wouldn't be long."

Falki grinned. "And I kept my word."

He rose and swept around the desk. His heart raced. His uniform trousers were tighter than usual.

"Help me get out of these bloody clothes."

Rosalyn grinned. "Gladly."

He kissed her fiercely, and she returned it with equal passion. He tore her shawl away and threw it on the floor. She went to work on the gold buttons of his uniform.

Then someone knocked on the door.

Goddamn it.

"For you, sir." It was Nahed. "Priority telegram from Norridge."

Falki pushed Rosalyn aside. "Come in."

Nahed obeyed. Sparing an ominous glance for Rosalyn, he handed Falki a telegram.

Falki smiled as he read the new orders. A dirigible was coming from Norridge. He was to return to the capital due to "urgent business." General Hakonsson would handle everything now.

His smile grew wider. However much he enjoyed field command more than politicking, overseeing the disputed zone was far less interesting than fighting down challenges to his family's preeminence. Someone with a greater tolerance of minutia would do the job far better than he.

Falki put the telegram in his uniform jacket. "When will the airship arrive?"

Nahed examined his pocket-watch. "I'd say within four or five hours."

Falki grinned. "Excellent. I will be ready to leave when the airship arrives. Lieutenant Nahed, you are dismissed."

Nahed saluted, and Falki returned his salute. Once the man was gone, Falki turned his attention to Rosalyn.

"Now where were we?"

THE GREAT VITTLES GRAB BEGINS

Hutton unrolled the map across the wooden table in the same tent where Alonzo had learned about the coming starvation. Paul closed the tent flap against possible eavesdroppers before taking his seat. "The Southern Wall is weakest in the west," the general said. "And the crops north of Pendleton will be in. The Flesh-Eaters will take their cut, which means a lot of tax collectors running around and full supply depots."

Alonzo nodded as he examined the map. The Southern Wall crept ever westward, shrinking the raiding corridor and bringing dirigibles ever closer. But there were still opportunities.

Alonzo pointed to the westernmost forts. "They'll expect us to attack there. We've been attacking the wall as they built it. When was the last time we attacked east of…" — he put his finger on the map, on the portion of the Southern Wall one hundred miles below the bend in the Grand River — "…there?"

Hutton shook his head. "The forts are closer together, better able to support each other. Assuming we don't get spotted from the air, we might be able to slip through, but the soldiers aren't coming back." Hutton looked at his commander. "I didn't take your dollar to needlessly send our boys to their deaths."

Alonzo frowned. "I wouldn't dream of having our soldiers die without need, *general*." He turned his attention to the map. The plan he had in mind required hitting the eastern parts of the Southern Wall to divert Flesh-Eater attention from his planned breakthrough in the west. Of course, the Flesh-Eaters weren't idiots. Any diversionary attack would need to be large enough to look *real*. And *effective* enough.

He slid his finger westward. "Here's a good target. It's close enough to the thickest clusters of forts it'll make the bastards reckon we're trying to engage their largest army on the wall. The defenses are thin enough we might manage a local breakthrough, but it's far enough away our boys will be able to hit *and* run."

Hutton peered at the map. "Forts Taylor, Stirling, and Deming. Striking thereabouts seems sensible. Some of the riders've reported troops pulling out and heading north." He paused. "The problem is putting enough soldiers there to make the Flesh-Eaters think it's the real attack *and* breach the Southern Wall in the west. Not only that, but hold it open long enough to get the supplies."

"And making sure they've got enough supplies to do their jobs," Paul added. "Every single rider we send is going to need ammunition, food and fodder, and a right lot more besides."

The irony nearly made Alonzo laugh. In order to get the supplies they needed to avoid starving to death, they'd *need* to expend most of what little they had. And although they'd bartered much of the meat and leather from the animals they'd slaughtered to the pikeys, it was still dicey whether they had enough. "How many effectives do we have?"

Hutton thought for a moment. "As far as people we can send attacking, I'd guess around five thousand. But gathering them with the enemy in the sky will take time."

"Five thousand troopers. That's a big *brigade*."

A big brigade *against multiple Flesh-Eater* regiments *all along the length of the Southern Wall, and that brigade'll need to be* split. *This is* insane.

But on the other hand, a bullet or bomb was quicker than hunger or scurvy.

Alonzo returned to the map. Those three forts lay fifteen miles west of where he'd initially wanted to attack. The Flesh-Eaters' strength was infantry, not cavalry. The Merrill horse could handle their Flesh-Eater opposite numbers, and it would take close to a day for their footsloggers to arrive.

And there was open country beyond the forts, green country the Merrill horsemen could maneuver in *and* keep their horses fed. It would seem right plausible the Merrills would try to crack the Southern Wall there.

"All right." Alonzo pressed his finger down on the three forts. "The diversionary attack will hit here. We'll need to recall the *Asherton* from counter-patrolling and send it after Fort Hartford. That'll draw the enemy away from Fort Deming and then the troopers'll hit Deming and Stirling. How many troopers do you think it'll need to fool the bastards?"

Hutton raised an eyebrow. "Trapping the enemy within their forts is one thing. But if you want to take them, you'll need artillery."

"Artillery," Alonzo repeated. "Something we don't have a lot of." He looked at Paul. "Any pikeys selling artillery or gun parts?"

"Parts, maybe," the older man said. "But whole guns? I doubt it. If the Flesh-Eaters even *suspected* they're selling us cannon, they'd crush them, no matter how useful they are trade-wise." Alonzo swore. He didn't think the pikeys could fully revamp the Merrill artillery corps, but he'd hoped they could at least manage *something*.

"Still," Hutton said. "I'd guess we've got maybe fifty galloper guns and a few bigger pieces."

"How many antiaircraft guns do we have in movable condition?"

"One Old World four-barrel gun, but not a lot of ammunition. Some balloon-poppers."

"We'll take the big one with us. Once they figure out it's me leading the raid, we'll *definitely* have the type of company that flies."

"Sir, about that. This isn't like you ambushing a column or raiding the Southern Wall. The Flesh-Eaters will *massively* respond to this. I'm willing to lead this one —"

Alonzo shook his head. "The men'll fight better knowing I'm with them."

Hutton frowned. "I remember your brother saying much the same —"

His words physically *jerked* Alonzo. Grendel's freak general had sent John's body back in mock courtesy, in such condition the first man who saw it vomited. They had to close the casket for the funeral. Alonzo bared his teeth. Hutton's eyes widened slightly. "And if John hadn't been there, the army might've broken earlier and might not have hurt the Blood Alchemy freaks like they did. More of them would've meant more of our people being mutilated or dragged off to *fuck* monsters."

"With all due respect, sir, a member of House Merrill is more valuable —"

Alonzo scowled. "General, this matter is closed." Hutton fell silent. "How long do you think it'll take you to prepare?"

"Two weeks. If we want to rob the Flesh-Eater tax collectors, we can't wait. But the men will need more training and moving at night will slow things."

Alonzo turned to Paul. "Requisition the supplies Hutton needs, anything he asks for. Strip the camps bare if you have to."

"Yes, sir."

Paul left the tent. Alonzo returned his attention to Hutton. "Now, where should the main blow fall?"

———

THE BUGLE BLEW in a dark lit only by a few small fires. Andrew joined the files of men marching across the dusty ground beneath the watching moon to where both companies' wranglers gathered the horses. The pack full of supplies for the saddlebags bore down on his shoulders. For the second time since Andrew had been rescued from the desert, the entire unit would make the long ride to war.

Zeke loped alongside the squad, already wearing the duster with the sergeant's stripes. Hank followed close behind. Beyond them were Wyatt and his men. As they streamed toward their mounts, Andrew brooded.

Both companies had been assigned to attack Fort Deming, part of the Southern Wall. Zeke wouldn't say why – and Andrew dared not eavesdrop on Hardy – but he reckoned they were after supplies. It was the smart thing to do after the piss-poor harvest and the cattle-killing.

To prepare, the squad's patrol duties were halved and even camp chores were neglected. Instead, they'd been drilled on the use of grenades and fighting supported by artillery.

Two cannon mounted on large wooden wheels — "galloper guns" — had been rolled out. Close behind came a long upward-pointing gun the others called a "balloon-popper." The gunners were already hitching them to the horses.

It would have been nice if we'd had those ambushing that Flesh-Eater column, Andrew thought glumly. *We could've punched some right big holes, maybe taken out a couple mortar teams.*

But artillery would have slowed them and it was *speed* they'd needed, to hit and run before help arrived. That didn't seem to be much of a concern this time.

The drilling in protecting the artillerymen wasn't hard. Assaulting fortifications, *that* was hard. They'd thrown dirt, scrap wood, and other odds and ends into something approximating a Flesh-Eater fort and then attacked it. Not only was it hot, heavy work, but it gave Andrew a damn good idea of the butcher's bill they'd have to pay.

The soldiers began mounting up. The horses reminded Andrew of Alyssa. *She* was another bushel of grain entirely. They'd started drilling harder two days after she'd come by and he hadn't seen her since. The fact the squad was so busy meant the others weren't seeing her either, but that wasn't much of an improvement.

He closed his eyes. She was right fascinating — a woman as tough and ornery as any man. What if one of them died today and the last thing they'd done was fight?

He shook his head. She had just as much chance of coming out alive as he. Hell, she probably had *more*, fighting from horseback and all. Maybe he'd look for her later, after the battle...

He tensed. What the hell was he thinking?

He tried to force Alyssa out of his mind. Maybe Cassie was at the fort. Maybe they'd rescue her from the cannibal bastards. She and the other girls from Carroll Town counted on the Second Pendleton to get them out.

But if Cassie wasn't there, or if he was too late? Had he pushed Alyssa into the arms of someone else for no reason?

"Something bothering you?" Owen asked.

Speak of the goddamned devil.

Andrew looked away. The fact Alyssa'd put her cap out for Owen — a pikey, even though he obviously wasn't selfish or greedy — had made things worse.

Owen sighed. "We're about to attack a goddamn *fort*. I've done this before, and they're a right bitch, even with cannon. If you're distracted, you or one of us might end up dead."

Hank rode up alongside. Resentment flared. Andrew didn't want someone *else* poking their nose into the situation.

"Owen's right," the former Flesh-Eater said. "I've been in forts under attack. The butcher's bill without cannon is right huge and" — he gestured toward the company's two cannon — "that's not much. We'll have to storm." He swallowed.

Owen laid his hand on Andrew's shoulder. Andrew forced himself not to flinch. He locked his dark eyes with Andrew's. "What's coming is going to be bad enough without your mind wandering. So what the hell's eating you?"

Andrew sighed. He couldn't argue with that, pikey or not. "I had a girl back in Carroll Town. I'd met her at the fair about a year ago. She's swell, but I didn't want to marry her." He drew a breath. "Then the Flesh-Eaters came. I guess you don't know what you've got until they take it from you." He paused. "And now I meet Alyssa, who's after me like I was after Cassie. But Cassie might still be alive." The next words were like pulling teeth. "And anyway, it seems Alyssa wants *you* now."

Owen stared at Andrew. Then he started laughing. Hank joined in. Andrew scowled. "What's so goddamn funny?"

"For someone who's got a twin sister, you don't seem to know much about women," Owen said. "She's playing with you."

Hank finally managed to stop laughing. "Yeah."

The thought had never occurred to Andrew. He'd seen Sarah flirt with Elijah, but he'd never seen her use another man to annoy him. And Cassie had never done the same to him.

Looking back, it all made sense now.

When she flirted with Will, she was looking at me.

"Oh." Andrew drew a breath. "So you and her aren't —"

Owen laughed again."Nope." Then his expression hardened. "She knew flirting with me would piss you off. Don't think I haven't heard you say 'pikey.'" Andrew swallowed. His jaw worked. Owen was his friend. Owen had saved his life. And yet he'd said something that hurt him. He searched for words, but they didn't come.

"*Menceir* is better," Owen continued. "That's what we call ourselves. 'The trading folk' will do. But *not* 'pikey.'" Andrew nodded. Owen smiled. "By the way, I prefer brunettes."

Despite the awkwardness of the situation, Andrew laughed.

The bugle blew again. All three snapped to attention. While they'd talked, all of the soldiers had mounted up and a detachment of cavalry arrived. Andrew saw long blonde hair among the new arrivals.

Alyssa!

He was glad she came along, but knowing they'd bleed for the fort dampened his joy.

The burly, deeply-tanned major emerged from the shadowy horsemen and faced the column. "All right, boys," he called out. "We're going to Fort Deming. We're going to crack that nest of cannibals open and serve them a breakfast of lead!" He paused. "Now ride!"

The troopers thundered through the two vertical logs marking the entrance of the Merrill camp. A pillar of dust rose behind them. Those few left behind cheered. Many troopers shouted back or pumped their free hands into the air. Will and Owen were among them. Even Hank joined in.

Andrew remained quiet as the darkness deepened around them. David did the same beside him. It hadn't been that long since they'd ridden out of Carroll Town to face the Flesh-Eaters on the hills. He'd ridden with Sam then, and it was Sam who'd died, gutted like a fish from the river.

His eyes narrowed. The men of Carroll Town rode into the teeth of a much stronger foe, knowing they'd die but hoping that'd buy their kin time. The Merrill host was — probably — riding out to capture the food the Flesh-Eaters denied the residents of the camps, leaving them all but starving.

Good Lord willing, the Merrill troopers' sacrifice would be more effective than the Carroll Town militia's had been.

A MEETING OF MINDS

F alki sat on a fine wooden chair carved with serpents beside
Father's steel throne. The rising sun barely pierced the
skylights above. The weak light glinted on the interspersed
swords and rifles of Father's enemies that haloed the top of the
mottled green and brown chair. Father's throne had been forged from
the remains of the Iron Horse, the Old World machine that had nearly
killed the man when Falki was twelve.

That would have been just lovely. A frown crossed Falki's wide face.
*Most of our armies would be gone. The Camrose Confederation would have
claimed the whole Basin.*

Falki would still be lord of Sejera, and Alexander would have
backed him. However, Father had only recently subdued Quantrill.
The opportunistic bastard would have thrown in his lot with Camrose.
Then things would have gotten ugly…

He shook his head. Great doings were afoot. Once he'd returned,
Father had told him the entire scheme. It was clever, so many of his
plans. Give his subordinates a new enemy to fight, all while accumu-
lating territory and resources under Norridge's direct control. Central-
ization of power without civil war. And Father was too busy with his
plan to notice Rosalyn.

And Falki wasn't going to be in Norridge long. The latest settlement of Guard veterans had displaced some freeholders and they were

causing trouble. Unless Father *really* wanted to discuss the issue, he was going to be out of sight and out of mind soon enough.

"Do you know what's going on?" his younger half-brother Arne interrupted from his right. Like all of Grendel's children, he had Father's gray eyes. Although his hair was dark, it curled like his mother's. He was also fair-skinned like his mother Signe, and his eyes weren't narrow like Falki's.

"Your tutor's working with Astrid," Falki said. "You're going to learn directly from Father now."

He gestured to the round mahogany table edged in gold set before them. Around it sat the Host commanders and the once-independent warlords. A motley crew all united by the blood on their hands.

Falki's hand tightened on his holstered revolver. Mangle and Quantrill had not made trouble while he was in the north, but Father had not gotten to where he was by trusting people. The guardsmen in the room would make quick work of anyone threatening Grendel or his heirs, but it was always best to err on the side of caution.

"Today's lesson is going to be about keeping an empire once you have got it."

GRENDEL STRODE in through the hall's great double doors, wearing his full armor for effect. He nodded to each man at the table before taking his seat on the throne. "Good morning. I imagine most of you are wondering why I summoned you here."

Nods circled the table, stopping at Alexander to his left. Grendel had entrusted his blood-brother with the plan earlier, as he had Falki. He briefly described the recent fighting between the Blood Alchemy Host and the Legio Mortis. Quantrill smiled triumphantly when Grendel assigned the blame to Mangle. *That is probably not the only reason the son of a bitch is happy.*

"I have considered requiring you to demobilize most of your standing troops," Grendel began. "That should limit anyone's ability to cause trouble."

Although no one spoke, Grendel could feel the tension in the subtle frowns, the tightening of hands and mouths. Demobilization meant unemployment and depressed wages, strikes and unrest. Sending soldiers to crush men they'd fought beside risked mutiny. And those demobilizing first would be vulnerable to those demobilizing later. Mangle's stupid attack on Quantrill was no doubt on everyone's minds.

The guardsmen could kill anybody who make a stink, but that would mean war with their successors across the entire realm. He would win, and that war *would* give him absolute power over the entire Northlands. But he had no desire to rule a ruin, nor pass one onto his sons. And the plan he would reveal today would make him the same gains at home — and abroad as well — *without* civil war.

"However, I thought it might be better to put your skilled and brave soldiers to something more suitable than farming, mining, or working in the factories."

"What might that be, my lord?" Alexander played his part in the drama.

"An expedition across the Iron Desert."

No one responded. Some looked at each other. Grendel made a note of those that did — potential co-conspirators, if they thought him mad. Those he could not trust he had taken pains to set against each other, but Quantrill in particular was intelligent enough to put aside old grudges if it benefited him. And with what he suspected Quantrill had done, he would be the most dangerous one of all.

"Since the Fall, many believed the Iron Desert extended to the end of the world. Educated men like ourselves know this a lie. Everett has traded with us for centuries and no matter how tight-lipped they are about their homes or tight-fisted they are about their monopoly, their goods have to come from *somewhere*."

The doors to the throne room swung upon. Servants in black carried a pallet bearing foreign goods brought to Norridge as trade or tribute. Most were from lands under Leaden Host control. Still playing his part, Alexander rose and made space for them to push the pallet onto the table.

Although southern goods were not difficult to acquire if one had sufficient means, seeing so much at once was rare. The assembled warlords leaned forward at the sight of the stacks of gold bars marked with the image of a globe, anchor, and eagle, clothes assembled far more precisely than any northern factory could make them, and lenses whose smoothness exceeded any ground even in Norridge itself. And there was something else, something Everett's sailors said was new even in their homeland.

It was a large box with a round black disc on it. The merchants called it a "gramophone." Alexander leaned forward, placed the box's metallic arm on the disc, and turned a crank on the side. Jaunty music began playing. Grins broke out all around the table.

"For too long, the Northlands fought itself. Nobody had the resources to challenge Everett's sea monopoly. Even now, building a fleet to match theirs would ruin us. Invading the south and bringing these goods — and those who produce them — under our control will break Everett's monopoly without lifting a finger against them."

That should quiet any potential troublemakers. War with Everett risked Alexander's ships and cities. Those who resented Grendel's yoke might think Alexander might turn against his old friend. No risk to the western coast meant they could not hope to have Alexander as a co-conspirator.

Quantrill opened his mouth. Of course *he* had to throw a spanner into the works. "My lord, all this is well and good, but do we have any idea what we're facing? Superior goods mean superior technology, which typically means superior weaponry. Whatever lies south of the desert could be as superior to us on land as Everett is at sea."

Grendel, of course, had thought of this. "Agreed. I have just begun probing with my own dirigibles. My agents have been trying to loosen some tongues, to figure out what kind of armies and weapons will be waiting for us on the other side. Too much reconnaissance risks losing strategic surprise, but we have established the peoples south of the desert, like Everett, speak something like the flatlander tongue. There are even Jiao, although they do not seem to have had contact with their kin here. They use airships and trains for transportation like we do." Quantrill nodded. That put him just where Grendel wanted. "Since you are concerned, I will borrow some of your airships for further reconnaissance. Once they return, you will have *firsthand* information on what we will face."

He had just hoisted Quantrill on his own petard. If the man tried to drum up sedition by claiming Grendel put his dirigibles specifically at risk, the others would tell him to be careful what he wished for. And with much of his fleet elsewhere, he would be less likely to cause trouble with Mangle or put into action any covetous thoughts toward the Basin.

Even if this goes nowhere, I'll have gained something.

Quantrill nodded. "It would be an honor, my lord."

Either Quantrill did not know Grendel's intent or he played his cards *very* close. Grendel suspected the latter.

"All of you are to return to your domains and gather your armies. Clark, Mangle, Quantrill, I want thirty-five thousand soldiers from each of you. You will be the vanguard and will have first crack at the valuables. Alexander, seventy thousand. The rest of you, fifteen thousand each. I have gathered supplies and I am sure all of you have as well. Now is the time to use them."

The combined armies would number well over two hundred thousand, *before* Grendel sent in the Obsidian Guard. Even with the stockpiles, provisioning them would prove a challenge. Rail would be best to ensure a continuous flow of supplies.

He would summon engineers to see where best to build or extend rail lines. There were plenty of prisoners and conscripts to build them. He would summon farmers from their fields if necessary. Thanks to gas and electric lighting, work did not have to stop at nightfall.

Alexander leaned forward. "Airship reconnaissance is well and good, my lord, but it would be prudent to have boots on the ground. Infiltrators would also be less conspicuous than airships with strange markings poking around."

Again, Alexander played his part well.

"An excellent point," Grendel said. "It will take time to mobilize that many soldiers and build the needed infrastructure. Therefore, in addition to aerial reconnaissance, the airships will deliver scouting parties to sound out the territory in advance. They will find the best targets to attack when we have strategic surprise and the best choke points to hold the enemy at bay when they counterattack. Even if we cannot advance beyond what we initially take, we should be able to keep what we seize."

Grendel paused. "Not only will I supply Obsidian Guard for the task, but I believe Quantrill has some of the finest infiltrators and saboteurs in the Northlands." He turned his gaze toward Quantrill. "He would not skimp on them when the rewards for being in the vanguard are so great, would he?"

Quantrill smiled. "It would be an honor."

This was too easy. The bastard *had* to be up to something.

"Does anyone have any questions?" None did. "Excellent. You have your orders."

Grendel's subordinates rose and filed out, leaving Grendel alone with his guards and his sons. Now was the time for other business. "Step outside," Grendel ordered the guardsmen. They obeyed.

"I'm staying behind, I take it?" Falki asked as soon as it was just the three of them.

Grendel nodded. "I have left you to govern for days before. Now you will rule for weeks, months, maybe even years. If there is trouble, send Arne and plenty of guardsmen." He looked his eldest son in the eye. "Do not be eager. If I die across the desert and you die chasing bandits or punishing some bored soldiers, Arne will become first lord. He is younger and unblooded." Out of the corner of his eye, Grendel watched his younger son's reaction. He didn't object like Falki would have. *Good. Wise for his age.* "Somebody who would not dare challenge you or me may try their luck against him. And then there is Lenora."

Though Falki was unnecessarily paranoid about Logmar, Grendel would take the younger boy on the campaign. Logmar was only fifteen, but he could work the supply lines or carry ammunition to the cannon. It would also reduce the odds of the boy's mother causing trouble and would keep Falki from trying to arrange an "accident" despite Grendel's warning. He had just shown himself prone to temptation, after all.

"Hopefully with most of the soldiers crossing the desert with me, there will not be trouble like we have had the last few weeks."

Falki raised an eyebrow. "Most of the soldiers? Hopefully you won't take too many. The vets we've settled in the Basin might not be enough to hold it, and a lot of your commanders aren't exactly popular."

"I will not strip the Northlands bare. And I will take larger numbers of the troops I cannot trust out of your hair. They will not make trouble here and I will have enough Leaden Host and Obsidian Guard to keep them from making trouble over there. The other Hosts will contribute of course, but more will stay home."

Falki nodded. Arne looked bored. Grendel's gaze fell upon him. The boy's attention returned immediately.

"And before I go, there will be another printing of that booklet describing what goes on in Mangle's breeding pits and the worst of the mines. I may pardon some lesser offenders to further spread the word. The bards will be singing songs about my victories and what happens to my enemies. And I will make sure the informers I have among the soldiers remaining behind keep a close eye out for treason."

Grendel turned to Arne. "You understand why I am doing this?"

"You don't trust some of your men. You want to weaken them."

Grendel smiled. "That's a good lad. We use other men as our weapons, but some might turn on you. The weapons you trust least, you use first."

Arne cocked his head. "Won't they figure that?"

"Make it sound like an honor. First into the breach is first pick of the loot and women, if they survive. In case they *do* figure that out, they will be far away from their supporters here and I will have loyal soldiers surrounding them."

Grendel paused. What happened next needed to be kept as secret as possible.

"Arne, we are going to review the process I have set up to appoint district governors in the Basin, but I need to talk to Falki first. Go get ready."

Arne nodded and left the room. Grendel turned to face his eldest son.

"Yes, Father?"

Grendel was old, but he was still quick. He backhanded Falki before his son could react. He put enough strength into the blow to cause pain but not inflict significant damage. Falki stumbled backward, barely catching himself on the table.

"What the hell!" Falki snarled, murder in his eyes. Grendel hoped the boy was not foolish enough to raise a hand against him. He would hate to have to cut the offending hand off.

"May Odin have your guts to feed his ravens, Falki!" Grendel roared in Sejer. "May the Midgard Serpent swallow you whole! I thought you were fucking smarter!"

"What?"

"*First*, you wander off by yourself when I told you to *never* do that. You are lucky Quantrill sent just one trained pterosaur after you and not two or more. Otherwise you would be *dead*!"

"Quantrill? Why do you think it's him? There was a war there! The place would be full of pterosaurs!"

"I did not get here by trusting 'coincidence'! That woman shows up, you go for a walk, that thing attacks you, and lo and behold, you bring her home!"

"Well, once I'd fucked her, leaving her there would be a goddamn stupid idea! If she got knocked up, that'd be a grandson of yours under Quantrill's or Clark's control. Hell, he could find a flatlander kid with a Jiao grandmother and claim it's mine."

Grendel paused. It seemed his son *had* been thinking with something besides his cock. But there was still too much cock and not enough brain on display. "So instead of abandoning a potential successor to my least trustworthy men, you brought a likely spy into Norridge. That is an improvement, but not by much."

"I've already ordered her correspondence monitored. *Assuming* she's a spy, I'll know what she's telling Quantrill. Hell, I can lie to her and she'll pass it on."

"A spy you know about is an asset. Her purpose, however, is probably more than passing along pillow talk." Falki raised an eyebrow. "He knows I intend to marry you to Nora Matthews. Alex and I combined are unbeatable and I intend for that alliance to last after we are gone. A political match would go a long way toward making that happen."

"She's not my first girl —"

"I goddamn well know that. Do you think I do not keep an eye on you, to make sure you do not do *anything* that could cause me problems? The difference is *you never brought them home.*"

"They were all in Norridge. I didn't need to —"

"Shut up and *listen!* I already had to send messages to Alex to make sure he knows you are still going to marry Nora and not this little mountain flower."

Falki's eyes widened. "You think Quantrill is trying to disrupt relations between you and Alexander?"

"He is not dumb enough to think he will ever manage that. But making sure relations between our successors are not as tight is entirely different." Grendel's scowl deepened. "If that thing killed you, I would have lost my strongest heir. And now there is a likely spy in your bed. This will not go unpunished."

"You're going to start a war over this? Without proof? You told me to tread carefully with subordinates and respect their legitimate rights and now you're going to —"

"No. The expedition to the south will go forward, but Quantrill will leave with me. He will not return alive." Had there been more time, he would arrange for a tragic dirigible accident. "I already planned on eliminating him sooner or later. This advances the timetable a bit."

A smile slowly spread across Falki's reddened face.

"Now, if you were to send this Rosalyn back, Quantrill will know we know her purpose. Keep her here and pretend nothing has happened. In case she asks about your face, tell her you were sparring with Arne and he got a lucky hit. Do not even drop the slightest *hint* about our suspicions." He locked eyes with Falki. "I am going to let you keep her. But your son and successor will be borne by Nora Matthews. Make sure you and this Rosalyn do not have any before then, or I will."

He would err on the side of caution. The staff would dose her food with wild carrot and a bit of pennyroyal. They would continue until after Falki had gotten a son by Nora, after they were wed.

"You look like you are eager to go somewhere. Back to your bedroom, I assume?"

Falki shook his head. "The latest Guard settlement is running into trouble. General Chan has requested reinforcements."

Grendel frowned. Another revolt. Just what he needed. If Quantrill was behind the attack on Falki, he might have other tricks up his sleeves. Funneling arms to the dispossessed in the Basin would be doable from his territory. Although Quantrill dared not mastermind Falki's death while he and his entourage were easy targets in Norridge, Grendel could not take the chance.

"Given how you dealt with the ones who killed Wang Fai, I would be glad to send you, but you are staying here until Quantrill and most of his army set off. I will find other work for you to do. With the expedition, there will be plenty of it."

"Father —"

"Falki, shut the hell up."

Between Falki's foolishness, Quantrill's treachery, and the rebels' stubbornness, Grendel was in a foul mood. For a moment, he considered unleashing Falki. He had brought *peace* across the entire Northlands. The goddamn flatlanders did not appreciate the effort he put into keeping his ambitious men under control. They would most certainly deserve the punishment Falki would inflict.

But Grendel would not risk his firstborn son on something so minor, not now. Falki still gaped at him. "I need to think. Go fuck Rosalyn or drill your company."

Falki nodded, turned on his heel, and left.

TO BATTLE

The Second Pendleton rode single-file across the brown, stony ground beneath a wide sky turning pink with the sunrise. Andrew clenched the reins. Hours in the saddle, even in the dark,, had left his mouth dry. His throat was tight, but it wasn't solely from thirst. His eyes locked straight ahead.

This wouldn't be like the ambush on the Flesh-Eater column where they killed a right big chunk of the enemy in the first volley. Even if the Flesh-Eaters didn't see them coming, the two companies of the Second Pendleton would still be taking a fort by storm.

His gaze leaped to the front of the column. The cavalry — including Alyssa — were off scouting. They'd bring back word of any Flesh-Eater patrols.

Assuming the Flesh-Eaters didn't get the better of them, of course. The image of the Flesh-Eaters killing the cavalry or worse, capturing them and tearing them apart at their leisure, rose unbidden to his mind.

"Andrew," Hank said. "Don't drift off like that. You're going to need to stay on your toes."

Andrew nodded. He tried to force himself to keep his eyes peeled for any movement. Alyssa and the cavalry might return soon or the column might run into a Flesh-Eater patrol that had gotten between them and the scouts.

For a long time, nothing moved in the distance. Then, something appeared atop one of the hills on the column's right. Several somethings.

Andrew's heart leaped into his throat. His rifle hung in its loop on the saddle, and he'd practiced snatching it quickly. But no order had been given and it didn't seem like anyone else was grabbing their weapons.

The new arrivals grew larger. Andrew exhaled in relief. It was the scouts. Alyssa was among them.

The five riders made their way down the hill and approached the column. The major raised his right hand. The column halted.

Andrew tensed. Something was about to happen.

Muttering raced up and down the line of men. As the conversation rolled toward him Andrew heard "Flesh-Eater" and "patrol."

"Quiet, all of you," Zeke snarled. Other sergeants and corporals joined in, including Wyatt.

Orders soon rolled down the column. Zeke rode up to the front along with the other sergeants. After conferring with the others, he returned to the squad. "There's a Flesh-Eater patrol a couple miles ahead, heading west. We'll let them pass."

Will leaned forward in the saddle. "Why the hell don't we kill them?"

Zeke's gaze fell on Will like an avalanche. Will sat up straight in the saddle, eyes locked ahead. "The L-T didn't see fit to say, but I'm going to bet that picking a fight risks warning the fort. Now hobble your lip."

The cavalry went out again. The column waited. Sweat beaded beneath Andrew's hair. He took a swig of water mixed with a bit of corn liquor to prevent sickness. *Best not drink too much.* That risked an inconvenient need to piss during the fight or having less water in case they got scattered.

He remembered the desert. The shimmering air, the killing heat, the stone tearing through his pants to bite flesh when he fell. These badlands weren't as harsh, but they were no place to be without water once the sun finished rising.

Time passed. Andrew looked around. The other soldiers didn't look particularly happy, either. How much longer was this going to take?

The cavalry once more appeared over the hill. Once more they approached the column to confer with the officers. Zeke rode forward and quickly returned. "Looks like the Flesh-Eater patrol's gone. Get moving."

The column rolled out. They soon came across a tall wooden pole. Wires ran in both directions. Andrew's gaze followed the line to a similar pole atop the nearby hills. The wire connected to another pole and from there to more as far west as Andrew could see.

Will laughed. "Telegraph lines. Jackpot."

The column stopped. Zeke emerged from the column and looked the pole up and down. "Let's see what they have to say."

A soldier shimmied up the telegraph pole to the first of a series of metal spikes. He climbed to the top and went to work. A soldier from another squad did the same to one of the poles to the left. Andrew watched the men on the poles. Hopefully whatever they were doing wouldn't alert the Flesh-Eaters.

"Traffic's normal," one soldier called down. "They're asking about supply wagons and the *weather*. If they knew we were coming, they'd be talking a lot more." He paused. "Want us to cut the lines?"

"No," an officer called out. "Mount up and let's get moving."

The men came down from the poles. David leaned over to Andrew. "You sure this is a good idea? If we don't cut those lines, they'll call for help when we hit them."

Zeke shook his head. "The lines go down, they'll know something's up." His tone brooked no argument.

The two soldiers had barely mounted up when Hank pointed to the west. "Dirigible!"

Andrew's gaze followed Hank's finger. His throat clenched as soon as he laid eyes on it. Had tapping the telegraph line somehow called the airship in?

The dirigible was far away, but Andrew reckoned it smaller than the one at Carroll Town. It was painted blue, not red and black like a Flesh-Eater airship. The fabric-tearing sound of dirigible guns rose into his memory. His hands trembled on the reins.

The troopers had a balloon-popper and the numbers to fight a single airship — maybe. But it'd kill a lot of them first.

Muttering raced through the column. "All of you, hobble your goddamn lips!" Zeke shouted. "Behind the goddamn hills! The thing's far enough away it might not see us!"

The riders spurred their horses and rushed over the lowest hill. Andrew glanced back. Dust clouds rose behind them. Bile burned in the back of his throat. The dirigible crew *had* to have seen that.

"Dismount!" Zeke ordered as soon as they were — presumably — out of sight. "Prepare to receive dirigible!"

Andrew and the others formed a square around the balloon-popper, the horses and wranglers behind them. The troopers raised their rifles, aiming for where the dirigible's balloon would appear over the hill. The gunners pushed the regiment's galloper guns up the hill, barrels reaching for the sky. Andrew hoped all this would actually *work*.

The soldiers stood with rifles raised for what felt like an eternity. The temperature crept upward. A single bead of sweat trickled down Andrew's side. His arms began to tremble. He grit his teeth. He couldn't lower his rifle. If *anybody* lowered their weapons even an inch, they couldn't hit the airship when it came over the hill.

Other soldiers wavered. One was David.

"Keep the damn rifle up, Court!" Zeke ordered.

"Yes, sergeant!" His gun, which had drooped a couple inches, returned to its original position. His gaze and arms were locked. Sweat trickled down his face.

Other sergeants shouted similar orders. The waverers returned to position. The soldiers continued to stand.

At the word of a sergeant Andrew didn't recognize, one soldier broke ranks and crawled atop the hill. Hopefully the airship wasn't floating close enough to shred anyone who showed their face. The dirigible's commander would be right clever to dial down his engines, make the Second Pendleton think he'd gone, and wait until they'd let their guard down.

The soldier peeked over the top of the hill. The tearing-fabric sound of the dirigible's guns didn't come. Instead, there was only an awful silence. Andrew's arms burned. Another bead of sweat dripped into his right eye. He tried to blink it away. That didn't work. But he couldn't wipe it without lowering his rifle...

The soldier scrambled down and ran over to the major.

"At ease!" the major called out. "We're safe!"

Thank the Good Lord. Andrew lowered his rifle.

The major turned to his staff. Orders flowed once more. "All right," Zeke said. "The airship's damn near out of sight and still going south. We're going to keep goddamn moving."

The scouts headed out again. The column rolled north on the other side of the hills, parallel to their original course. The combination of the breeze from the movement and the sweat from before was right refreshing. Andrew smiled despite himself.

Ahead lay a gap. Could the column turn through and find its earlier course? The dirigible would have to be long gone by now...

A group of Flesh-Eater horsemen nosed through right in front of the column. All bore the dark tattoos of fanatics under their eyes.

Andrew's hands clenched on the reins. His heartbeat raced. How'd the Merrill cavalry not find them first? Did the Flesh-Eaters get between them and the column?

A darker thought flew unbidden across his mind. The Flesh-Eaters might've encountered the patrol first. Killed them. Killed Alyssa.

His expression darkened. If they'd done that, they were *dead*.

The column came to an abrupt halt. The Flesh-Eaters did the same. Several enemy horsemen fled through the gap. They *had* to be heading for Fort Deming.

Andrew frowned. Fanatics *retreating?* If they were smart enough to retreat when they were in a bad spot, that made them even more dangerous.

Gunfire broke out. The remaining fanatics charged the Merrill column. Flesh-Eater bullets snatched Merrill troopers from their horses. The harsh smell of spent gunpowder filled the air.

Andrew freed his rifle. A carbine would have been better, but he was still a good shot even from horseback. If the enemy horsemen delayed the Merrill column long enough to alert Fort Deming, the coming attack would be a bloodbath.

CRACK! The bullet punched through a Flesh-Eater horseman's armpit. He fell from his horse, which dragged his body across the rocky ground.

The sound of gunfire vanished. One Flesh-Eater bolted. The rest fed the brown earth with their blood.

Andrew's stomach lurched. He remembered the fall of Carroll Town, how one man's escape caused the death of all he'd known and loved. All because he'd hesitated...

He aimed for the fleeing rider. He would hit the man right in the center of his back and...

CRACK!

The Flesh-Eater tumbled from his saddle. Relief flooded Andrew's chest. He laughed. That man at least wouldn't be warning Fort Deming.

"Good shot, Andrew!" David called out. Andrew grinned.

The Second Pendleton's officers and sergeants buzzed with orders once more. "Spur your damn horses!" Zeke ordered. "Now!"

The Merrill horsemen began moving, faster than before. The remounts and their wranglers rushed to catch up.

The column had only gone a couple of miles when the cavalry drew near. Much to Andrew's relief, Alyssa was among them.

The major stopped the column and conferred with the horsemen. Andrew couldn't hear the words, but from their lips and gestures, he reckoned they'd killed fleeing Flesh-Eaters.

He grinned. The fort wouldn't know they were coming.

The riders' report filtered through the column. Zeke laughed. "We'll catch them with their goddamn pants down."

MISSION CREEP

The disguised Merrill ranks approached Fort Cochrane's open gates. A grin split Alonzo's narrow face as he watched through his field glasses. Not only had the column of false Flesh-Eaters kicked up enough dust to mask the mounted men following them, but the enemy clearly had no idea what was coming. Even if the Flesh-Eaters realized their "fellows" were frauds, they couldn't possibly close the gates in time.

Had he known it would work out this well, he'd have tried it all along the Southern Wall. That'd double the territory under his control at a stroke and have a strong bulwark against Flesh-Eater counterattack or any move from Grendel. The realm Pa ruled would live once more...

He shook his head. He'd plan for the future once he'd gotten that *food*.

A Flesh-Eater officer stepped into the open gate. Alonzo's grin vanished. With telegraph lines spreading like snakes across his land, pulling this gambit was damn tricky. He'd had soldiers tap the lines and send the fort messages supposedly from elsewhere on the Southern Wall, but the yellow armbands the disguised soldiers wore to minimize friendly fire would raise the suspicions of any officer worth a damn. If the timing wasn't perfect, there'd be a bloodbath.

There were few men atop the wooden walls, so it looked like he'd hoodwinked the enemy commander.

Hutton, mounted on his horse beside Alonzo, cleared his throat. "We can't wait much longer."

Alonzo nodded. The Merrill troopers were already at a disadvantage – they couldn't simply reduce the fort to rubble with the artillery they'd brought with them without hitting their own men. And though the horsemen were well behind the disguised infantry, there was the risk the Flesh-Eaters atop the walls would see them.

The infantry halted before the Flesh-Eater officer. The breath caught in Alonzo's throat. Each passing second increased the risk the plan would unravel. More Flesh-Eaters appeared on the walls. The officer looked the disguised infantry up and down, eyes narrow.

Well shit. "NOW!" Alonzo shouted. Beside him, the bugler blew the note signaling the first ranks of the horsemen to charge. Before the Flesh-Eaters on the walls could react, the disguised infantry rushed the gate.

The repeaters carried by the first mounted ranks — including most of Alonzo's personal guard — chattered as they raked the Flesh-Eaters atop the walls. Enemy bullets cast men from their saddles. The charge continued. They had to get close, give the enemy enough of a chance to hit them they couldn't focus on the footsloggers actually taking the fort.

Alonzo unslung his own repeater. Hutton leaned forward in his saddle. "Sir, there's no need —"

Alonzo squeezed his legs. The horse surged forward, leaving the rest of the sentence behind him. Men followed, joining those already circling the fort. Gun smoke lapped at the bottom of the walls, while more clung to the top.

As Alonzo drew near, he spotted a Flesh-Eater atop the wall. The man had fired on the horsemen but now turned inward.

CRACK! An Old World bullet that had been buried in some hill for centuries now went to its final repose in some cannibal's back. Alonzo fired on another Flesh-Eater, this one carrying a repeater. He missed. The Flesh-Eater's weapon chattered. Bullets snapped by Alonzo's head. Someone shouted and tumbled off their horse behind him.

Alonzo squeezed the trigger again, but the man fell to another bullet before his repeater bucked in his hands. The gunfire aimed at the riders vanished as the enemy found they had more immediate problems. Now all the Merrill horsemen had to do was kill every man with his head above the parapets.

Something whistled overhead. Alonzo's throat clenched. The Flesh-Eaters wouldn't use their mortars against the disguised Merrills inside the walls for fear of hitting their own, but the horsemen outside...

The ground shook. The shockwave threw Alonzo sideways. Only his feet firmly hooked in the stirrups had kept him mounted. Lines of pain skipped across his sides. He righted himself. A quick look showed thin lines of blood on his clothing. He glanced right.

The mortar shell had torn a huge gap in the second rank of horsemen. Gutted animals screamed and thrashed on the ground. So did mangled men. In the cacophony of pain, men and animals sounded the same. Ralston, his lower half gone and his intestines streaming behind him, still dragged himself toward the fort. Alonzo closed his eyes. Ralston was dead and didn't know it, but he was still loyal to his commander, still trying to fight the Flesh-Eaters.

Fort Cochrane would be named Fort Ralston when it was over. He owed it to the man who'd died for him.

The gunfire inside dragged Alonzo's attention back to the battle. Alonzo checked his desire to order the horsemen into the open gates. It would be hard to tell the true Flesh-Eaters from the false until the fort was taken.

The gunfire inside the walls faded. Alonzo aimed his repeater at the gates. If anyone in Flesh-Eater uniform spilled out, the horsemen would only have a split second to look for yellow armbands.

A man in a red and black uniform appeared amid the smoke atop the wall. Men raised their weapons, only to be shouted down by their sergeants.

The man raised his fist, revealing a yellow armband. Scattered whoops broke out among the horsemen. Everybody cheered when another soldier appeared beside him and unfurled the Merrill banner.

ALONZO STILL SMILED as the soldiers carried supplies from the fort's open gates to those tasked with rushing the loot back to the mule trains. Crates of desiccated vegetables, hardtack, beef jerky, potatoes, cornmeal…

And that was just *food*. The troopers also carried boxes of ammunition, Flesh-Eater uniforms, and shoes, wonderful *shoes*. Alonzo's boots had held together for years, but he'd seen bloody footprints and knew not that every Merrill trooper was so lucky.

An actual supply depot deeper in enemy territory would be even richer. He reached into a bag hanging from his saddle and pulled out a fistful of grain his horse eagerly consumed. Alonzo understood the principle of not muzzling the ox that treaded out the grain.

Behind the supplies came a dozen captives. Some were men. Whip-scars marked them as conscripted laborers, helping put the finishing touches on the fort. But most were women with Flesh-Eater jackets draped around them to conceal what the immodest clothes the bastards made them wear didn't. Their staring eyes and in some cases pained gait made it clear what they'd experienced. One was pregnant.

Alonzo's stomach lurched. Catalina suffered a similar fate at the hands of Grendel. He grit his teeth. His hands clenched. He'd kill the old Sejer bastard, kill him and the monster he'd spawned on his little sister…

He closed his eyes. He forced himself to think about the supplies. The haul didn't seem as good as it was the last time the Merrills hit the Southern Wall. They'd taken a supply convoy then, *tons* of food and ammunition. If it had been awhile since the fort had been resupplied, the lack of vittles and ammo made sense. But the farmers and cowboys under the Flesh-Eaters' rough thumb had seen a train come by on the tracks behind the fort three days prior.

Two dark-haired soldiers approached from Alonzo's left "Sir," one soldier said. "The telegraph office is secure. We've found something."

ALONZO SAT in the wooden chair in the telegraph office. Before him lay documents spattered with the blood of the Flesh-Eater who'd been trying to burn them when the Merrills stormed in.

Old World weapons. An Old World hoard. Just sitting *out here.*

Most of the ruins from before the Fall that hadn't been picked clean lay deep in the Iron Desert. The countryside northwest of Fort Cochrane didn't have sand pushed by the wind, so it shouldn't have been easily buried.

He frowned. Pa had spent so much time keeping the peace between the factory owners and the workers he didn't bother searching for Old World weapons. If House Merrill found this, it could have won the war the first fucking time.

He continued reading. *Crates* of repeaters and ammunition had been recovered. Half were sent to Jacinto, while an eighth went to Norridge. The rest were still on-site.

And there was *more.* Four-barreled antiaircraft guns, the kind that could rip a dirigible in half. And missiles. Those could only be fired line of sight, if they could be fired at all, but something that big flying that fast could rout even the most disciplined.

He shook his head. All that'd be moot if the Flesh-Eaters weren't convinced by the messages he'd sent out after taking the fort. "Any word back?" he asked the soldier who'd brought him the reports.

"Fort Hurd's commander is offering to send a dirigible and cavalry to 'pursue the fleeing Merrill dogs.' Fort Marshall's bossman wishes he could, but Merrill horsemen have been spotted near Forts Stirling and Deming and a dirigible's hit Fort Hartford."

Alonzo grinned. His divisionary attacks were working. "Tell Fort Hurd we've sent out our own cavalry and they should sit tight." He'd rather suggest they reinforce Fort Deming, but that'd need approval from an enemy bigwig who might see through it.

The two soldiers from before returned, carrying a Flesh-Eater wearing colonel's eagles. One arm was crudely splinted and bandaged, but the blackened eyes and bloody nose looked fresh. This had to be the fort's commander.

"Sir," one said. "We were questioning this lowlife here about where we could find more supplies and learned something you should know."

"Yes?"

One of the soldiers put his knife to the captive officer's throat. "Tell him," he ordered.

The man said nothing. Alonzo shook his head. "Such defiance. Such loyalty to the ones who would kill you for deploying your patrols so poorly that *most of my army* could approach your position undetected, for allowing two companies to approach your gates without a shot being fired, and for not holding more than ten goddamn minutes. Disobeying me won't gain you anything, but if you help me, you *might* survive."

Alonzo nodded to the soldiers. One struck the Flesh-Eater in the middle with his rifle butt. The blow would have doubled him over if the blade to his throat hadn't given him a powerful incentive to keep his back straight.

"Now you understand the stakes, let's get started." He held up the telegrams. "Where are these weapons going?"

The colonel didn't answer. The soldier dug the knife into the skin beside his windpipe. Blood trickled down the blade. "All right," the colonel grated. "The weapons're going to Jacinto."

"I know that. Anything else?"

"Clark'll decide who gets them once they're there. The troopers on the Southern Wall and the airship infantry have first priority."

Alonzo's throat tightened. If those repeaters got there, the wall'd become right impenetrable. Any enemy raid would cost him ten times as many. And his cause would be doomed.

"You've done a service to House Merrill." Alonzo looked to the soldiers. "Truss him up." The man seemed to know a fair bit about the enemy's inner workings. He might have more beans to spill. Not only that, but a colonel might make a right good hostage. "Then get me General Hutton."

The men disappeared with their captive. A few minutes later, the general, dirtier than before but unhurt, arrived.

"Change of plans," Alonzo said. "There's an Old World excavation site northwest of here. Antiaircraft guns and repeaters that're being distributed along the Southern Wall. We're going to hit that."

Hutton frowned. "Bad idea, changing the mission in the middle." His frown deepened. "But it doesn't look like we've got a choice."

A grim smile crossed Alonzo's face. "Great minds think alike."

SUCCESSFUL SO FAR...

The column drew near the hills before the Flesh-Eater fort when the scouts appeared in its path. The column came to a dead stop. It wasn't long before the sergeants moved their squads to various points at the bottom of the hill. Then Zeke delivered the bad news.

"The fort's alert. That means they're calling in help. We won't be able to wait for the artillery to smash them before we go in." He paused. "Our company'll blast the hell out of those towers. Next, the other company will ride around the fort and set fires while we suppress the men on the walls. Then we advance down the hill while *they* lay down suppressing fire."

"How the hell did they know?" Will snarled. "Hank, does eating people give you clairvoyance?"

Before Hank could open his mouth, Zeke silenced him with a raised hand. The sergeant's gaze leaped from man to man. "Simmons, you're manning the mortar. Gollmar, you're spotting. The rest, up the hill. Stay out of sight, and wait for the signal."

Andrew crept forward, bent down lest some observant Flesh-Eater see him. The enemy knew they were coming. Once the attack began, they'd unleash the mortars. He wouldn't be able to shelter behind the hill then. No, he'd have to stay atop the hill, come hell, high water, or fiery death from the sky.

He swallowed. "Anybody got any corn?" The bit mixed in his canteen didn't cut it.

Owen shook his head. "Pretty sure what we didn't drink before went into our canteens. Probably for the best."

Andrew nodded. What felt like a huge rock squatted in his stomach. The enemy was alert and behind walls. They'd have to charge those walls or wait for the artillery to knock them down while getting shelled themselves.

He hadn't seen Alyssa since the officers' last palaver with the scouts. She must be with the other company. The company that would go in first. His grip tightened on his rifle. He'd kill as many Flesh-Eaters on the wall as he could. Each one he killed wouldn't be able to hurt Alyssa.

Beside him, several gunners rolled up cannon. The major, still mounted, rode behind the troopers spread out below the hill. His hard gaze flitted from soldier to soldier. He closed his eyes for a moment and nodded to a boy holding a battered bugle. The boy raised the bugle to his lips and blew it twice. The gunners shoved the two cannon over the crest of the hill. Mortars erupted behind Andrew.

"Forward!" Zeke ordered. "Give them hell!"

Andrew and the rest of the squad scrambled over the hill. The enemy fortress lay spread out below. Walls of raised timbers formed a five-pointed star. Towers with six-barreled rotating Sawyer guns rose at the corners. In the center of the star, well above the armed towers and back from the gate, rose a tall mooring tower shelled in wood rather than being open to the air like Carroll Town's. Attached to the tower was a dirigible that no doubt carried even more guns.

Andrew suddenly had to piss. Behind him the cannon thundered, drowning out the whistling mortar shells and the crackling rifles. One round punched through the top of the left tower overlooking the fort's barred gates. Screams erupted. Mangled men and shattered equipment fell. The other round flew through the space beneath the tower's enclosed top and vanished.

Then the mortar rounds started landing. Pillars of smoke and fire bloomed within the fort. The chorus of screams grew louder. Andrew grinned.

New whistling filled the air. Andrew's eyes bulged. His gut churned. Images of Carroll Town and the ambush rolled through his head.

A pillar of flame erupted to Andrew's right. Now it was the Merrills' turn to scream. Flesh, blood, and metal flew. Andrew glanced around. Three shells had fallen amid the troopers. Shattered bodies surrounded where the explosions had bloomed. Some of these bodies screamed. Most didn't.

Chunk-chunk. The Merrill mortars were firing again. Andrew squeezed the trigger, hitting a Flesh-Eater visible amidst the smoke topping the wall. He toppled off the wall before the shells landed. Another shell exploded at the shattered left tower's base. Wood cracked as it toppled into the fort.

Rather than falling onto the dirigible, the tower toppled straight backward, bridging the gap where the walls narrowed into the point of a star. *Fuck.* It didn't look like it had even crushed any Flesh-Eaters

Gunfire crackled behind Andrew. Flesh-Eater horsemen burst onto the scene, blasting aside the Merrill flank guards. Andrew's mind raced. The fort must've sent men out ahead of the attack. He scrambled back down the hill, shooting as he moved. A bullet sliced across the rider's side. He shouted in pain, but continued his charge. His saber sang from its scabbard.

CRACK! Zeke's bullet took him in the chest. He tumbled off his horse. The horse kept going. Will dropped the shell he was loading as the enormous animal bore down on him.

With a roar, Zeke threw himself over Will. Both hit the ground as the maddened horse rode over them. Andrew sighed in relief as both men rose after the horse passed.

Something whistled overhead. Andrew threw himself down. He'd barely hit the dirt when the ground shook. A wave of dirt and stones slammed into him. Something metal sliced across his forearm. Andrew looked up once the world stopped spinning. Will was on his feet and loading another shell. A few Flesh-Eater raiders fell back. Several lay dead, but they'd killed Merrill soldiers and, worse, kept some of the mortars quiet.

"Sutter!" Zeke roared. "Stop gaping and start shooting!"

Andrew scrambled back up. Smoke shrouded the fort below. The top of the right tower over the gate had been utterly smashed.

But the dirigible floated serenely amidst the clouds of smoke and dust. Andrew frowned. *Maybe* it wouldn't come out to fight them, but if the men inside could find their assholes...

The cannon roared again. Andrew's gaze jumped to the sound. This time the towers on the far side of the fort received their attention. One looked to have already taken mortar fire from the other company.

A mortar round exploded in the open space around the fort. Andrew swore. A second round exploded atop the large building he assumed was the barracks to the right of the mooring tower.

"No more shells!" Will shouted.

Andrew looked back at the fort. Three towers out of action. That left the tower directly behind the dirigible and the one behind the barracks to hose the horsemen with bullets if they circled the fort. Hose Alyssa...

A bugle blew in the distance. The other company, all mounted, erupted through the space between the hills. One hundred horsemen — and some horsewomen — surged toward the fort.

A repeater chattered from the wall. Two Merrill soldiers fell from their saddles. Andrew's heart leaped into his chest as he saw long hair on one. Was it Alyssa? Was she hurt?

The injured horseman — horsewoman — pulled up onto her knees and right hand and crawled, dragging her left arm behind her. It was hard to tell the hair color from this distance. Was it just blonde or was it Alyssa's distinctive honey color? He tried to rise.

"Stay goddamn down!" Zeke shouted. He grabbed Andrew by the sleeve and yanked him to the ground.

Andrew could still see the fighting below. The horsemen turned and rode parallel to the wall. Many fired on the Flesh-Eaters above, gun smoke streaming behind them. Others reached into their jackets. They lit something in their hands and threw them at the wall.

Fires bloomed where they struck. When the firebombs hit stone they quickly burned out, leaving black, ugly smears. When they hit wood the fires caught. Smoke darker than that from the mortars reached for the sky. The dirigible and mooring tower remained visible, but the black clouds hid much of the fort from Andrew's sight.

Will appeared behind Andrew and handed Owen and Zeke clay containers with wicks.

"What are those?" Andrew asked.

"Firebombs like the cavalry got."

Andrew looked at Owen and Zeke. "Not everybody gets one?"

"Probably too dangerous," David said. "Fort's made of wood. Too many people throwing them around and we'll cook like the Flesh-Eaters. And there probably aren't many of them and —"

"I got it."

The trumpet blew behind Andrew. "Forward!" Zeke shouted.

The company rushed down the hill toward the battered gate. Gunfire crackled as the horsemen covered their advance. If there were any Flesh-Easters nearby, they were staying quiet.

The heat rose around them. Embers blew on the wind, falling like burning snow flurries. Sweat beaded on Andrew's exposed skin, but there was no time to go for his canteen. Ahead lay the gate. His grip tightened on his rifle. He reckoned there were Flesh-Eaters lying in wait –

Something whistled overhead. Andrew flinched. The shell landed behind the gate, explosions visible through holes torn in the thick wood. Smoke choked the gateway. That took care of any lurking enemies. Hopefully.

The first Merrills at the gate reached through the mangled wood and wrestled with the bar. "Keep a goddamn eye out!" Zeke ordered.

Andrew looked for any flicker of red and black. Metal glinted. A rifle barrel peeked out of a gash in the wall. Andrew fired. The enemy gun jerked. The bullet that might have hit someone instead buried itself in the ground. Andrew grinned.

"It's open!" someone shouted. "We got it open!"

The battered gates swung wide. Several men fired into the smoke before the rest streamed in.

Andrew had wondered what the inside of an enemy fort was like. Were there prisoners nailed to the walls? Did giant stewpots sit by the barracks, reeking of human flesh?

He didn't see any of that. The fort opened up beneath the smoke-crowned – but clean — walls. Dead Flesh-Eaters lay scattered about. Directly before the gate, between the advancing Merrills and the base of the mooring tower, the enemy had heaped shattered wood into a barricade. The mouth of a cannon heavily scratched by the bombardment glared at the oncoming troopers like an evil eye.

"Hit the goddamn dirt!" Zeke shouted. The other sergeants echoed his words. Andrew slammed into the ground as the cannon roared.

Not everyone was quick enough. Several men in front of Andrew went flying. Not all of them hit the ground in the same place at the same time. The mixed stench of gunpowder and ruptured bowels filled Andrew's nostrils. His guts churned. His ears rang.

It took a second to realize he was wounded again. Blood trickled down his left arm and the side of his face. He moved his arm to check. Pain flared in his forearm, which he expected, and his shoulder, which he didn't. A quick glance showed a bloody tear, but no shrapnel peeked out.

The cannon disappeared behind the smoky barricade. The prone Merrills were firing, but most of their bullets buried themselves in the wood.

"Gollmar, cook the bastards!" Zeke shouted. "The rest of you, look for someone to shoot!"

Andrew's gaze swept the savaged parapet above. Mangled bodies hung from the wooden platforms. Below one a brass halo of bullets surrounded a dropped ammunition box. *Shit. Too far to grab.*

Shouting and screaming tore his attention away. Zeke and Owen had thrown their firebombs. Flames erupted on the barricade. The Flesh-Eaters momentarily abandoned the cannon to douse the fire. The remaining Merrills surged forward. Blades flashed. Rifle butts rose and fell.

CRACK! A bullet caught a man in the head. It'd come out of the smoke to Andrew's right. Andrew fired back, but there was no sign he'd hit anything.

More soldiers streamed through the gates behind them. Zeke pointed at the brick barracks. "The balloon-popper'll be coming in soon. We'll need to keep whoever's in there bottled up!"

Something clanked above Andrew's head. He looked up. Amid the smoke, steel shutters opened in the dirigible's gondola. Long, lethal Sawyer guns and wide-mouthed cannon emerged.

"Oh *fuck.*"

STORMING THE TOWER

"Sergeant!" Andrew pointed upward. "Look!"

Zeke's eyes widened. "Everyone, forward!" Andrew joined the nearest troopers as they rushed out of the line of fire. They'd barely gotten to safety when the guns erupted over their heads. Men fell behind them. Some resembled shredded meat in uniforms rather than people before they hit the ground.

"Fall back!" someone shouted. The soldiers pouring into the gate abruptly changed course. Some retreated in good order, stopping to fire before moving again, but others fled pell-mell, knocking over their fellows. Their bodies sometimes shielded others when the bullets found them.

Now the only living Merrills inside the fort were either under the dirigible or hiding amid debris from the bombardment beneath the walls. Among the first group was Wyatt. Andrew scowled.

Goddamn it. Why'd he *have to survive?*

"Where's Sergeant Thompson?" Zeke asked. Wyatt pointed to a corpse wearing sergeant's stripes lying atop the blazing barricade. "That leaves me in charge then." Zeke looked at the soldiers. "The balloon-popper's outside and won't be shooting that thing down if it stays where it is. And if it stays where it is, nobody else is coming in or getting out. If the sons of bitches in the barracks or whatever hidey-holes they've got find their heads, we're going on the goddamn grill."

Andrew swallowed. The men beneath the dirigible were a right pitiful few. If there were many Flesh-Eaters still in the barracks or if the airship crew started dropping grenades, they'd be in boot hill in an eyeblink.

Zeke pointed toward the base of the mooring tower ahead. "The only way we're going to survive is if we get up there and take that dirigible." He looked from soldier to soldier. "Who's got grenades? Stairs are a right bitch without them."

One of Wyatt's soldiers raised his hand. "I've got two frags and a smoke."

Nobody else had anything. Zeke swore. "Here we go. Wyatt, your squad covers my boys. We'll cover you."

Before Andrew had time to think they rushed the mooring tower. A slit opened in its wooden side about two stories up. A gun emerged. Instead of a single cracking shot, however, the gun chattered. A bullet slammed into the earth in front of Andrew. The next two rounds yanked David's left leg out from under him. He slammed into the ground. His rifle bounced away. "My leg!" There were tears running down his face. "My leg! They shot me in my fucking leg!"

The chattering gunfire wasn't finished. One of Wyatt's men fled panicking from under the dirigible.

"You run, you fucking *die!*" Zeke shouted. He pointed to the tower door. "Get under the gun! He won't be able to do jack shit!"

Now it was Wyatt and his men's turn to run. Something moved within the barracks. Rifles peeked out of firing slits. Andrew shouldered his rifle and fired. His bullet ricocheted off the brick, but the gun abruptly pulled back.

"Pin them down!" Zeke shouted. The rest fired at the barracks. The enemy retaliated, but couldn't hit shit with the squad hammering at them.

Wyatt dragged David screaming to the base of the tower. The soldier bringing up the rear, the one who had the grenades, took a round in one side and out the other. Blood was already streaming from his mouth when he hit the ground.

"Shit!" Owen swore. "Shit!"

"Not now!" Zeke shouted. "Gollmar, Simmons, break that

goddamn door! The rest of you, keep the bastards in the barracks busy!" Zeke pointed at one of Wyatt's soldiers, a dark-haired boy who reminded Andrew uncomfortably of the young Flesh-Eater he'd gut-shot at Carroll Town. "Get those goddamn grenades!"

Andrew kept looking for a way to get a bullet inside a firing slit. The enemy inside would eventually learn not to flinch if a bullet hit too close. Then the Merrill soldiers outside were dead meat...

Movement flickered to Andrew's right. Were more cannibals joining the party? Andrew twisted, raising his rifle...

It was a dark-haired woman in a Merrill uniform sheltering behind some barrels. "Don't shoot, goddamn it!"

Andrew nodded. He looked up at the dirigible. If the Flesh-Eaters above hadn't known they were there, they certainly knew now. They would be dropping grenades any minute...

When death came, it wasn't from above. The thick wooden doors of the barracks popped open. There was a Flesh-Eater there with a rifle.

CRACK!

The bullet caught Hank in the chest. He dropped abruptly. By the time Andrew had his rifle aimed, the doors had slammed shut.

"No!" Andrew screamed. He started shooting at the door. The bullets harmlessly buried themselves in the thick wood. That didn't stop him. He'd drill through the door, put a hole in the head of that goddamn murderer...

"Sutter!" Zeke shouted. He grabbed Andrew by the shoulder and shook him, cutting through the red haze of his anger. "Sutter, don't waste your goddamn ammo! Check on Evans!"

Andrew knelt by his fallen friend. The bullet had punched straight through Hank's breastbone. Blood trickled from his mouth. His eyes were wide and staring. He'd realized he'd been shot before he died.

"No!" Andrew whispered. "Not again!"

He hadn't known Hank long or well, but he'd helped Andrew look for Sarah. The enemy had made him a Flesh-Eater, but he hadn't let them rot his soul. He'd escaped the bastards, fought for the right side...

And now he was dead. Andrew clenched his fists, digging his

fingernails into his palms. It wouldn't be just for Sam he'd kill all the cannibal devil-worshipping bastards…

Wood cracked. "We're through!" Owen shouted.

Zeke pulled Andrew away from Hank. "It's too late for him!" He pointed to David. "Get him inside!"

Andrew dashed over and grabbed David's left arm. He pulled the arm across his shoulders and pulled David up. David moaned. "Keep your weight on your good leg," Andrew ordered. "Keep hold of the gun." David nodded weakly.

Andrew carried David through the door, one last bullet from the barracks speeding his passage. As soon as they were inside, Zeke slammed the door shut and replaced the bar the soldiers had jarred free.

"Put him down," Zeke ordered. When that was done, he cut open David's bloody pants to examine the wounds.

"We're going to have to tie this off or you'll bleed out."

"Tie it off?" David babbled. "Tie it *off*? That means they'll have to *cut* it off…"

While Zeke cut strips from David's pants and tied off the wounded leg, Andrew reloaded. He didn't plan on running dry before killing the son of a bitch who'd murdered Hank. Pain lanced through his arm as he worked. He scowled and did his best to ignore it.

Once he finished the tourniquet, Zeke pulled David to the bottom-most step. "Anyone who comes through the door who isn't us, shoot him." Zeke pointed to one of Wyatt's troopers. "You stay with him. The rest, up the stairs. By twos!"

Two of Wyatt's men rushed upward, pausing before the landing. One peeked around the corner. "Clear!" The rest followed. Once they'd gathered at the landing, Zeke picked two more to make the next leg.

They didn't run into any trouble until the fourth landing. A grenade bounced around the corner and clattered down the stairs. Andrew froze. If it got any farther, they were all dead…

Owen stepped sideways and kicked the grenade hard. It flew off the steps, struck the wall behind them, and rolled around the corner.

"GET DOWN!" Zeke shouted.

The soldiers threw themselves down on the stairs as the grenade exploded. Wood splintered below. Heat washed over them. Something slashed across Andrew's back. Andrew turned to the young soldier with the grenades. "Give me one!" he snarled. The man quickly obeyed.

"Pull the pin and wait a second," Zeke ordered. Andrew nodded. He didn't want the grenade thrown back. He obeyed, waiting a moment, then threw. "Down!"

They all ducked. An explosion cracked beyond the corner. Someone screamed. A hot wind carrying splinters roared down. Someone snarled in pain and anger.

"FORWARD!" Zeke roared. The squad rounded the corner. Blood pooled on the wooden stairs. A mangled guardsman lay beside a hole in the tower's side. Enough of him remained that Andrew could see he had amber skin and dark hair like Eric Tan from Carroll Town.

"Good job," Zeke said. "That was one of the Obsidian Guard."

Will laughed. "One of them? Grendel's personal troops?" He looked at the body. "That wasn't that hard."

Zeke clenched his teeth and locked eyes with the redhead. "He was one against seven and we're damn lucky he didn't wax us with that grenade. I've fought the Flesh-Eaters, the Blood Alchemy monsters, and the Obsidian Guard. The Guard's the most dangerous." He paused. "They're probably guarding the dirigible. There'll be more." Zeke turned to the corpse. "Good thing that repeater's still intact. We'll need it."

AN UNPLEASANT SURPRISE...

The trooper Alonzo had sent in under a white truce flag trudged across the dry earth back from the excavation site. As the ranks of the assembled Merrill troops parted to allow him through, Alonzo frowned.

When the Merrills had arrived, the site was alert. The four towers armed with Sawyers were manned. The buildings clustered behind and between the two front towers — probably worker housing and barracks — had riflemen lining their roofs. The soldiers left at the fort hadn't successfully whispered sweet nothings into the cannibals' ears.

For a moment, he'd considered calling it off. A frontal assault against the towers would be a bloodbath, even if they won. *Hundreds* of good men would die. They wouldn't have the numbers to take back the loot they'd paid in blood for, even with the handcarts sitting on the new rail line spilling like a tongue from the excavation site.

Instead, he'd sent one of his smoothest-talking troopers to palaver with the enemy. Hopefully his artillery — he'd stripped the refuges of most of it — and his possession of an enemy colonel as a hostage would cow the Flesh-Eaters. As the man passed through the first rank of soldiers, Alonzo could see the dejection on his face. *Fuck.*

"Sir, they're not interested. Their commander says beat feet before they put us on the grill."

Alonzo gestured to the captive colonel mounted beside him. The man's feet were lashed to the stirrups and his hands tied around the horn of the saddle. He'd been gagged lest he warn his comrades. "What about him?"

"They said those who die for the Howling God will be served in the afterlife by those they killed. He should be glad."

Alonzo looked at the colonel, whose face was transfixed by anger. "See how little you're worth to them? Best pray to that devil you call a god you survive riding beside me." He ordered the soldier back to his unit and turned to Hutton. His heart hung heavy in his chest. A lot of good men were going to die soon. But if he left those weapons in enemy hands, those men and more were dead anyway. "Begin the attack."

Hutton disappeared into the ranks of troopers drawn up behind them. Alonzo returned his attention to the excavation site. Was this dragon's hoard something Father could have found?

Alonzo had sent his personal troops to comb the desert for Old World artifacts and used the monies he controlled as the Merrill's second son to buy relics from the pikeys, but that was peanuts. If John had some Old World artillery at Bluebell Creek, he could've torn the Blood Alchemy Host a new one as they rested and watered their troops. And if Father had more Old World antiaircraft guns at Fairmont, he could've brought the dirigibles down on Grendel's head...

Orders rippled through the first line of soldiers. It wouldn't be long before he gave the excavation site a taste of his artillery.

CRASH-CRASH! The two howitzers thundered behind Alonzo, the shots throwing the wheeled guns back. CRASH-CRASH! Galloper guns shouted in the gaps between the infantry squares, shells flying horizontally into the teeth of the enemy defenses. The first Flesh-Eater dead hadn't even hit the ground before the howitzer shells landed, smashing the top half of one of the towers to splinters. Wood and metal flew. Men screamed. The smoke and screams grew worse when the second rank joined in, their mortars savaging the low-slung buildings and the remaining tower.

It was almost like music, the storm of fire and steel. Lots of cannibal bastards were heading to boot hill today. More would die later at the hands of Merrill troopers armed with Old World weapons...

A cloud of dust and fire bloomed in the open space before the excavation site. Alonzo's gut clenched. He figured the Flesh-Eaters would have mortars, but the explosion was too big. Howitzers. He hadn't planned on ordering the advance until both towers fell, but enemy artillery left him no choice.

The first rank surged forward. Hutton must've had the same idea. Their only hope would be to get ahead of the falling shells.

That hope failed. Two shells landed just behind the oncoming soldiers. The explosions tore into the center of the line. Men screamed. Dirt and body parts fountained. Through the clouds of dust, Alonzo saw a vast and bloody hole open in the ranks. He closed his eyes.

No battle plan survives contact with the enemy.

New orders echoed through the second rank around him. The soldiers scattered, their mortars easier to maneuver than the howitzers the third rank manned and protected. Mortars popped. Alonzo prayed they'd get the Sawyer gun atop the towers before the troopers entered their line of fire. The rotating guns chattered. *Fuck.*

Many in the first rank fell, but some got below the enemy guns. The surviving Flesh-Eater sharpshooters sent more bodies sprawling, but now the Merrills were close enough to shoot back.

More explosions sent clouds of dirt and flesh flying. The howitzer shells continued marching toward the Merrills' big guns. Alonzo swore. If the third rank didn't get their asses moving, the Flesh-Eater counter-battery fire would rip them apart. The sweat-slick horses were already dragging the galloper guns out of the smoke. The howitzers and the four-barreled Old World antiaircraft gun were taking longer. Too much longer.

A two-toned whistle filled the air. Two fireballs roared over the howitzers. A wave of heat slammed into Alonzo. His horse stumbled. Men and animals screamed. Blood and metal flew.

"Goddamn it!" Alonzo roared. The vanishing fireball revealed one howitzer mangled beyond repair. The gun's massive barrel was torn free of the wheeled carriage and lay broken on the ground. The crews' torn bodies lay draped over the wheels and the barrel or strewn about. Blood sizzled on the hot metal.

The other howitzer and the antiaircraft gun were barely clear of the blast. The rearmost soldier attending the howitzer lay on the ground, a huge piece of shrapnel sticking out of his head.

The soldiers erected the remaining howitzer once more. Shouted orders echoed through the second rank. Though the Flesh-Eaters in the tower still cranked their Sawyer gun, the dust and smoke promised a less bloody advance. The men moved forward in stages, some hanging back to continue firing the mortars. Alonzo watched them rush over the mangled remains of the troopers in the first wave killed by the howitzer. These men would do better.

As the troopers disappeared into the whirling smoke and dust, the howitzer lobbed a shell over the fort's walls. No Flesh-Eater guns replied. Maybe they'd destroyed them, or the enemy had run out of ammunition? The howitzer fired two more times, explosions leaping upward behind the walls. Once the troopers got through the gates, they'd have a much easier advance. But the Sawyer in the tower continued firing. Men screamed, bodies piling in the open ground in front of the gates. Where the fuck were the mortars?

Twin fireballs bloomed atop the tower, answering his question. The damnable Sawyer finally fell silent. Alonzo grinned. He turned to the captive Flesh-Eater. "Enjoying yourself?" The Flesh-Eater turned purple. Alonzo laughed.

Alonzo returned to his attention to the battle. The crackle of rifles pushed through the ringing in his ears. Through gaps in the smoke, he saw the remains of the first rank and most of the second pour into the excavation site. The Merrill artillery slowed. Between limited ammo and the risk to the footsloggers, they'd be done soon.

He gave his horse a squeeze, sending it trotting forward. He'd never ask any of his soldiers to take risks he wouldn't take himself. His personal guard followed, pushing the captive Flesh-Eater along with them.

Thunder cracked behind him as his horse trotted forward. The shell whistled down seconds later, raising more smoke and debris. He frowned. That shell had landed a little too close to where he expected his troopers to be. If there'd been any fratricide, he'd have Hutton give the artillerymen a few stripes to remember them by.

By the time he reached the smoke-shrouded buildings, the fighting had moved forward. Alonzo led the horsemen along a dusty path deeper into the Flesh-Eater base. Everyone had their repeaters up, guiding their horses with only their feet.

They soon found a trooper barely old enough to shave limping toward them from between another set of buildings. Blood seeped from bandages on his arms and forehead. One arm hung limply. The man saluted as soon as his gaze took in Alonzo, his movement as crisp as any seen on the parade ground. Alonzo returned his salute.

"At ease. What is your unit, and how is the battle going?"

"Fifth Jacinto, sir. Don't know what's going on the right, sir, but we were advancing on the barracks on the left." The trooper paused. "Slow going. Bastards had barricades with a Sawyer on top, but the mortar boys took it out, sir. Once that was gone, we advanced..." He voice trailed away.

Something was wrong. "What is it?"

The soldier looked up, eyes wide. "Two more goddamn Sawyers on the roof! We rushed the barracks, but they opened up on us. We pulled back but left most of us behind."

"No more mortars?"

"Out of shells." He gestured to his useless arm. "They sent me to find more."

Alonzo nodded. Hopefully the officer overseeing the attack on the barracks had the good sense to hold a perimeter and wait for artillery.

Men shouted from where the wounded man had come. He looked back. "The Flesh-Eaters are coming, sir!"

Two bodyguards surged past the wounded man. They fired at something Alonzo couldn't see. Alonzo squeezed the horse with his legs. His mount carried him to just behind his followers.

Several Merrill soldiers rushed toward them, not bothering to shoot and scoot. More – and better disciplined — Flesh-Eaters pursued. The guards' repeater fire slowed them, but not by much. Wheels turned in Alonzo's head. The breakout from the barracks had to be contained, lest they get around the troopers on the right.

He turned to the wounded soldier. "Go find the mortars!"

"Yes, sir!"

Alonzo turned to the guards who'd remained behind. "To me! We'll hold the goddamn cannibals here!" He shouldered his own repeater as his remaining bodyguards crowded forward. The mounted men sealed the gap. Before the Flesh-Eaters could react, Alonzo and his bodyguards added their fire to the first two. Flesh-Eaters fell. The fleeing Merrills stopped as though they were hitting a brick wall. One gasped, dark eyes wide in a narrow face. His lips moved. Alonzo couldn't hear him over the noise of the battle, but he recognized the words "the Merrill."

The retreating soldiers turned. Some threw themselves onto the dusty ground, while others rushed back the way they'd come. The Flesh-Eaters pulled back, shooting and scooting. Beyond a log barricade that must've been part of the Merrill perimeter lay the brick barracks. Flesh-Eaters moved like ants on top.

Alonzo's ears caught a lethal whistling sound. His throat clenched. "Forward!" The horsemen and the infantry they'd saved advanced. The Flesh-Eaters opened fire, their bullets toppling footsloggers and throwing a rider from his saddle. Alonzo and his guards' repeaters replied. The enemy died or cowered behind their barricade.

The ground shook as a mortar shell exploded behind them. Even through his duster, Alonzo felt the heat. The horses whined in fear and pain. They wouldn't advance farther with the Sawyers intact and staying made them a target for mortars.

"Fall back!" Alonzo ordered.

As Alonzo's group retreated, the Flesh-Eaters rose from behind the barricade. Alonzo swore. Clark and the officers had to be insane, but he'd hoped the conscripts cared more about their own skins.

Another whistle filled the air. Alonzo clenched his legs around his horse. They were still in the open, still vulnerable...

The barricade exploded, wood and dead men flying. Alonzo grinned. The wounded man must've found his mortars after all.

More whistling. Another shell landed beyond the first. The third shell exploded in front of the barracks, shrapnel gouging its crimson brick flesh.

Alonzo looked behind him. More Merrills emerged from the smoke. If the mortar had neutralized the Sawyer, the Flesh-Eaters left behind were doomed.

"The Merrill!" the troopers shouted as they saw him.

"Don't just stand there!" Alonzo shouted. "Go into that barracks and drag them out!"

The men rushed around Alonzo and his guards. A second later, another mortar shell exploded, this one atop the barracks. *No more trouble from the Sawyers.*

Now he had to find the Old World arsenal. The maps at Fort Cochrane showed the barracks west of the excavation. "Come on!" he shouted to his guards. By the time they came to the edges of the vast hole torn in the brown earth, gunfire sounded in the pit itself.

Alonzo's gut clenched. The Flesh-Eaters had to know the game was up. He whistled at a nearby captain. "Get General Hutton." If the Flesh-Eaters were killing prisoners, he'd show them no quarter.

"Yes, sir."

The captain soon returned with Hutton. Ash and blood smeared the general's face, but he didn't seem hurt. "We're on the edges of the pit in places, sir," Hutton said. "Pushing down onto the ramp."

The news brought a momentary smile to Alonzo's face. They'd have their hands on the enemy's treasure soon enough. But the crackling rifles reminded him that something darker than honest battle was happening.

"They killing laborers down there?" Alonzo asked, voice hard.

"I don't know, sir. Knowing them, probably."

Alonzo gave his merciless order, ignoring the captive colonel's protest. Hutton nodded and relayed it to the captain. The officer vanished into line of men heading toward what Alonzo guessed was the ramp. The gunfire continued.

Alonzo looked to his guard. "They may need our repeaters." He pointed to the captive Flesh-Eater. "One of you stay here with him."

By the time Alonzo, his guards, and Hutton arrived at the ramp, the gunfire had stopped. Troopers spread out below. What lay within the pit took his breath away.

Two cylindrical metal hulks, their gray steel streaked with rust, lay exposed to the air. Something had broken their backs long ago. The front ends were rounded nubs, their broken windows like a cluster of eyes. Long wings, each bearing two massive propeller-tipped engines, lay in the dust beside them.

He'd heard stories of the days before the Old World had ended in blood and fire, how men had flown without the aid of hot air or hydrogen. Based on the huge rear doors opening up beneath vertical and horizontal fins, Alonzo guessed these were transports that could carry the load of a hundred dirigibles.

Merrill soldiers surrounded the two fallen titans, disarming the few Flesh-Eaters that had surrendered and seeing to dozens of men in ragged clothing. Only one civilian, a man with a pistol in his clockwork hand, lay dead beside the corpse of a Flesh-Eater. Alonzo brought his fingers to his hat in a momentary salute.

A little too soon for your own good, but at least you brought one down with you.

He rode down into the pit. It wasn't far from the ramp to the fallen flyers. Up close, they were even bigger, their open rear doorways revealing cavernous interiors. One was *still* half-full of crates the documents said brimmed with repeaters. He counted the crates and whistled. There were enough guns here for several regiments — *real* regiments, not gutted companies mixed together. They could *win* with this many weapons, not just prolong their defeat.

The other aircraft was mostly empty, its interior illuminated only by shafts of light from the open door of what must be its cockpit. A huge wheeled vehicle topped by two Old World missiles and another four-barreled antiaircraft gun squatted inside. How many horses would it take to drag *them* up the ramp and onto a train car?

Alonzo pointed toward the aircraft containing the crates. "Get everything out of the pit and onto handcarts. Start rolling them toward Fort Cochrane."

Dealing with the missile launcher would take time, but looting the repeaters and grenade launchers was simply a matter of having enough strong backs.

"Yes, sir!" There was real joy in the soldiers' voices. A chain of men began passing the crates up the ramp. The rescued civilians were especially enthusiastic. Bayonets made sure the surviving Flesh-Eaters didn't shirk.

Alonzo took the moment to wind his clockwork fingers. The longer it took to loot the site, the more likely they'd have to deal with Flesh-Eater reinforcements. It wouldn't do for one hand to stop working right then.

He returned his attention to the missile launcher. If stripping the other aircraft of its cargo took too long, they might simply have to dynamite it.

Alonzo had counted a hundred crates ferried up the ramp when shouts of fear from above stabbed his ears. Men stood on the lip of the pit, pointing north. One word was clear amid the different conversations at the edge of Alonzo's hearing.

Dirigibles.

"Stay here and keep the men from panicking," he ordered Hutton. "I'll reconnoiter."

Before his general could object, Alonzo spurred his horse up the ramp. He rushed through the outlying buildings to where the ruined towers marked the edge of the excavation site. His bowels filled with ice water at the sight of six airships painted red and black bearing down out of the bright blue sky. One was bigger, a dire wolf ruling a pack of its lesser kin. Four huge propellers drove it forward. It had two gondolas instead of one. Alonzo's heart sank. Clark's personal vessel, the *Bailey Mines*. It carried Old World artillery.

Clouds of dust rose behind them. Enemy cavalry and footsloggers had come along for the ride. The airships would be there in minutes.

Even if he ordered his men to retreat immediately, an airship could outrun a horseman. He doubted they'd make it back to Fort Cochrane.

He closed his eyes. *Goddamn it.* This would be just like Fairmont, except Father's trapped horsemen had charged the Obsidian Guard and broken the first rank before they fell. All Alonzo's troopers could hope for was to die quickly.

He thought back nearly two decades, to the gardens of the Merrill citadel in Jacinto. He, John, and Catalina, when she could be pulled away from those spinning put-together toys she loved, would play there for hours. John was faster, but he'd keep going, his will driving him to catch his older brother. And Catalina did her best to catch them both. Those were innocent days then, before Ma sickened. Before Grendel's shadow had fallen across their lives. Before John rode to his death at the hands of Grendel's most monstrous slave, before he'd fled Fairmont to save part of the army, before Grendel had claimed Catalina for his bed.

His hand flew to his long braids, the ones he'd cut when he killed Clark and Grendel. He would never get the chance now.

He forced himself to focus. The dirigibles drew closer. The longer he waited, the more fear would spread. Panic was what killed armies.

He grit his teeth. If this ended the unspoiled Merrill line, he would make it a battle worthy of his family. A victory as many of their enemies as possible would not live to enjoy. That would not happen if the soldiers died like goddamn *sheep*.

He spurred his horse back toward the pit.

"This is the Merrill! Prepare to receive dirigibles!"

RACE AGAINST TIME

Z eke had been right. Owen had peeked around the corner of the stairwell opposite the gangway and immediately leaped back. A repeater chattered. Three bullets passed through where he'd been.

Shit.

Zeke turned to the soldier with the grenades. "Give me a fucking smoke! Gollmar, light them up!"

Zeke struck a match and lit the smoke grenade. When the smoke hissed out, he tossed it around the corner. The repeater chattered. Bullets sliced through the smoke filling the space ahead. Zeke raised his manacled hand, keeping the men from rushing forward. He waited another moment, eyes narrow.

"GOLLMAR!" Zeke threw his hand down.

Owen eeled up the last stairs on his belly. Once in front of the gangway, he unleashed the repeater. The weapon kicked and bucked in his arms, but muscles straining, he kept on target. Men screamed. Bullets ricocheted off the metal above Owen.

The soldier with the grenade scrambled past Andrew into the smoke. The grenade clattered on the metal of the gangway and exploded. More screams. Owen's repeater kept firing. "HERE WE GO!" Zeke shouted. Owen rose into a crouch, giving the sergeant room to crawl. "SHOOT AND SCOOT!"

The troopers surged. Will crouched by Owen, firing down the gangway. Someone fired back. A bullet ricocheted off the wall and slashed across his face. Will screamed. Teeth and cheekbone flashed. Andrew winced.

Several men had already disappeared into the smoke. Andrew followed on his hands and knees. He nearly tripped over a corpse wearing a brown Merrill uniform haloed in blood. There were three holes in the chest, but the face was still recognizable. Wyatt.

A Flesh-Eater moved in the smoke ahead. Andrew pressed himself down beside Wyatt's corpse. Hot blood worked its way into the entire length of his sleeve. Bullets cracked over his head. The enemy soldier ahead fell backward out of sight.

Andrew pulled himself forward on his elbows, grip tight on his rifle. The wound in his arm burned with every move. More bullets cracked overhead. A repeater chattered. More screams.

A breeze began pushing the smoke away. Andrew's throat clenched. He fired into the dissolving smoke before someone could spot him. Zeke stepped over him, firing into the gondola. Owen came behind. Andrew rose and followed the two into the narrow steel box.

"EVERYBODY ON THE FUCKING FLOOR!" Zeke roared. The trio rushed over several Merrill and Flesh-Eater bodies. Most of the surviving crew, Flesh-Eater and Obsidian Guard, obeyed. One man hesitated long enough for Will, blood still trickling from his wounded face and eyes alight with pain, to decorate the wall with his brains.

A Flesh-Eater leaped toward Zeke, knife in hand. Zeke had his rifle pointed toward the end of the gondola. Even if Zeke turned, the Flesh-Eater was too close for him to bring his rifle to bear…

Zeke solved that problem with a blow from the manacle. Blood and teeth flew. The Flesh-Eater sank to his knees. A solid kick to the chest put the Flesh-Eater on his back.

Meanwhile, Andrew spotted two legs in black trousers emerging from behind the steel supports holding up a gun. Blood slickened the floor around him. The guardsman was wounded. Wounded animals were the most dangerous. He stepped closer, rifle up. The man didn't move. "Throw your repeater down," Andrew ordered. "Put it down and I won't kill you."

The Obsidian Guard were Grendel's best. That one could have obliterated the Merrill squad if he'd let them into the airship and bushwhacked them. He should shoot him first. Otherwise, he'd get up and kill them all.

Another step forward. The fallen man stayed put. Andrew's arms started aching. Sweat dripped into his eyes, adding an unwelcome burning pain. He blinked the sweat away. His rifle grew heavy in his hands. He sighed.

Now or never.

He leaped around the gun. The guardsman lay on his back, blood pooling around him. Short blond hair clung close to his skull. Shallow breaths painted his lips and teeth red. He smiled as Andrew drew near. "Ho la Othinn." His repeater snapped up.

Andrew leaped forward. His bayonet sank into the wounded man's gut. The blow slammed the man's head into the steel wall. His repeater clattered to the ground. Andrew tore the bayonet free. A length of intestine came with it.

Around him, the gondola grew quiet. Zeke rushed to a nearby open gunport, pushing the barrel aside to accommodate his size. He forced his head into the open air.

"This is Sergeant Ezekiel Thaxton! The dirigible is ours!"

The Merrill soldiers taking cover around the fort cheered. The cheering soon spread outside.

Andrew looked out the window over one of the guns. With the airship in friendly hands, the Merrill soldiers poured through the gates unimpeded. They rushed through the fort and up the ladders onto the parapets. Here and there gunfire popped. They soon ringed the barracks. Occasional shots rang out from the firing slits, but the men within weren't shooting like before.

A Merrill officer rode up. He drew a white sash from his pocket and handed it to one soldier. Holding it above his head, the trooper approached the barracks. Nobody fired. Andrew held his breath. Would the Flesh-Eaters make this easy or hard?

The scarred wooden door slowly opened. A skinny Flesh-Eater officer clutching a bloody rag to his forehead stepped out. Andrew couldn't hear him, but he looked tired, like he didn't care anymore.

Andrew leaned forward, eyes locked on the man. Someone like that might surrender!

The soldier returned to confer with the officer. The officer nodded. The soldier called back to the Flesh-Eater, who stepped back inside.

A moment later, unarmed Flesh-Eaters began filing out. Behind the dozen or so soldiers came several women. Some, the younger-looking ones, looked around with wide eyes. Others, older and more beaten-down, didn't look like they cared about anything. A couple had blonde hair, but none were as tall as Cassie or had the straw-colored shade he and Sarah shared. His heart sank.

Then Andrew's hopes surged. Weeks in enemy captivity could have changed things. Maybe the goddamn cannibals dyed their hair. He headed for the gangway.

Zeke's voice stopped him dead. "Sutter, where the hell you think you're going?"

"They're taking the women out of the barracks," Andrew babbled. "My sister and my girl back home were taken by them. I have to —"

"You have to stay right where you're at." The force of Zeke's words crushed Andrew's will to disobey. Zeke frowned. "And now I'd like to know why the hell the dirigible crew didn't join the fight."

He reached out and grabbed a short, dark-haired Flesh-Eater technician by the collar. "This thing's a death machine. Why didn't you send it out?" The technician did not respond. Zeke shook him. "Answer the goddamn question!"

The man's jaw worked. "We were finishing up an engine when the shells started falling," he finally admitted.

"What's left to be done? Can this thing *fly*?"

The thought of possessing the dirigible brought a grin to Andrew's face. He looked up and down the rows of guns lining the gondola. With something like this they could scourge whole Flesh-Eater columns! They could even smash *forts*!

"Just a little bit more!" the technician babbled.

Zeke grinned."Magnificent. Simmons, come with me. Let's get this bastard flying."

Zeke dragged the technician toward a ladder in the middle of the gondola. Holding a cloth over his disfigured face, Will followed. Will forced the technician to follow Zeke up before ascending himself.

Shouting erupted below the dirigible. Andrew stuck his head out. A trooper rushed from the barracks with a sheaf of papers in hand. He showed it to the officer. The man immediately yelled for troopers and pointed to the mooring tower.

The soldiers on the ground surged inside. Soon they rushed onto the dirigible itself. Hardy was among them. Andrew and his squad rose to salute.

"At ease," Hardy said. "Flesh-Eater command just said to mount up as many as possible and send them west. Ride the horses to death if they have to." Everyone winced. "They've got the Merrill pinned down with dirigibles along with a lot of our boys. Jasper Clark *himself* is there aboard the *Bailey Mines*. Our airship the *Asherton*'s too far away. That leaves us."

Andrew's eyes widened. Jasper Clark. The lord of the Flesh-Eaters. The man he failed to kill in Carroll Town. The evil mind behind the army that destroyed all he loved now attacked the Merrill!

Hardy's attention fell on Andrew. "Who's in charge here?"

Andrew's mouth worked for a moment. "Sergeant Thaxton, sir. He took one of the enemy up there" — he pointed to the ladder — "to do some work on the engine. He said that's why it didn't join the main fight."

Hardy nodded. "Get him."

Andrew scurried up the ladder into the cavernous balloon interior. He climbed onto a long metal walkway rolling like a tongue through the airship. Metal struts rose like ribs around him. "Sergeant!" His words echoed.

"Sutter?" Zeke replied. Andrew followed the sound to a doorway in the side of the balloon. At the end of the walkway were Zeke, Will, and the captive technician. A shrapnel-riddled corpse had been pushed to the side.

"The L-T sent me. The Merrill's in trouble." Zeke shot upright, using a combination of swear words Andrew had never heard before. Andrew's mind whirled. "He wants us to go help."

"Simmons, get him finished on that engine-double quick. If he tries anything kill him." Zeke eyed the technician. "He's good with machinery, so he'll know if you're up to something. Take a look at his face. He's in no fucking mood."

The technician quickly nodded.

Zeke's steps boomed down the walkway. Andrew followed him through the hatch. "What are your orders, sir?" Zeke asked Hardy.

Hardy smiled. "We're going to leave a skeleton crew here and head west as fast as possible. Relieve the Merrill and use this here dirigible to kick some cannibal ass."

Muttering echoed behind Andrew. Zeke turned away from the lieutenant. "Silence in the ranks!"

Hardy looked at Zeke. "He" — gesturing toward Andrew — "said something's wrong with the ship's engine. Can it fly?"

"One of my boys is working on it with a technician. They were finishing up when we dropped in." Hardy raised an eyebrow. "Simmons has an eye on him," Zeke continued. "If the prisoner's treacherous, he'll fix him good and proper."

Hardy nodded and turned to Andrew. "Check on the status of the engine."

Andrew had barely touched the ladder when the technician started climbing down, Will close behind.

"Can it fly?" Hardy asked.

Will poked the technician with an elbow. Slowly the technician nodded.

"Excellent news." Hardy turned to Zeke. "The major will command the ground troops. The dirigible's mine. We'll swap out as many enemy personnel as possible and pair the pilot and technicians we can't replace with troopers to keep them honest. Our platoon will man the guns and the fire extinguishers."

Grins broke out among the soldiers. Andrew joined them. They'd all run from airships. Now it was time to turn the tables.

THE SHARP STINK of spent gunpowder was overpowering, but it didn't entirely mask the metallic scent of spilled blood. Alonzo watched the smoke-shrouded dirigibles floating over the excavation site through a broken window and brooded over just how they'd gotten into this pickle.

His good, loyal men had met the dirigibles as they approached the excavation site. Pillars of smoke rose from where the Old World gun felled two airships. One went straight down. The other carved a furrow into the stony ground, leaving a trail of small fires. Alonzo whooped with the others, hoping they just might live through this.

Then the *Bailey Mines* pulped the priceless gun. The remaining dirigibles' Sawyer guns swept the front of the excavation site, shredding men or forcing them into cover. Clark's heavy guns then smashed their refuges. Those who survived *that* fled into the storms of Sawyer fire.

He and his guards had scrambled into the telegraph office, stepping over the bound corpse of the captured Flesh-Eater colonel. They'd barely avoided a burst that shredded a trooper behind them.

Now the dirigibles floated overhead. Their gondolas and balloons bore scars from the surviving balloon-poppers, but none were damaged *enough*. The snarling Sawyers tore through the hot, smoky air. Occasionally a bigger gun sounded, either one of the heavies on the smaller dirigibles or one of the monsters on the *Bailey Mines*.

Alonzo scowled. By dusk, the Merrill army would be dead. And he would have nobody to blame but himself.

Had he ordered the Old World weapons destroyed — they had the artillery and explosives for the task — they *might* have been able to flee before the dirigibles arrived. But he'd gotten ambitious. He'd hoped to arm the entire Merrill host with Old World kit make them the equal of the Obsidian Guard.

Had he succeeded, they could have sent the Flesh-Eaters scrambling for their lairs in the hills. Hell, if the rumors were true about slave gangs building railroads in the west, arming those men would have shaken Grendel on his throne in Norridge!

But he had failed. Now he and his men were trapped beneath the guns of four airships. If the enemy didn't simply level every building and then stamp on the fleeing men like boys killing bugs, they could keep the Merrills pinned until Flesh-Eater ground troops arrived. The thousands who'd followed him to their doom would be lucky if they died in some last stand rather than being crucified or offered to the Howling God.

His own death, even if it meant the bloodline stretching back to Charles Merrill and the days after the Fall would only survive in the spawn Grendel forced on his sister, would be a fair payment for his foolishness. But the skeletal regiments who'd followed him to his doom didn't deserve that.

THE DRY COUNTRY rolled away beneath the dirigible as its propellers drove it toward the excavation site. Below lay a rail line running beside the black traces of an Old World road.

Alongside these roads stood wooden pillars. Nailed to the pillars were men. Some wore ordinary clothes or, more rarely, brown Merrill uniforms, but others had been crucified naked. Vultures and ptero-dactyls gnawed on the faces of those *hopefully* already dead.

Andrew's stomach roiled. Maybe survivors of Carroll Town ended up on poles if they made too much trouble for the Flesh-Eaters. Although the dead below were all men, the image of Cassie and Sarah dying by inches rose unwanted into his mind.

"This the first time you've seen this?" Will asked. Though his wound had been bandaged, pain crossed his face with every word. Andrew nodded. Will looked down at the bodies. "Maybe some're still alive. Our boys on the ground will cut them down. Sickness'll take most, but there're men in this army who've came down off the posts."

Andrew continued looking out the window. Behind and below, the Second Pendleton pursued the airship. Individual horsemen periodi-cally broke off from the main body to swing by the crucified men. Several gathered around one. Andrew looked for Alyssa. No luck. "Hopefully they'll get that done quickly," he muttered. "We might need them."

"Leave no man behind, either for the cross or the barbecue grill." The soldiers below were pulling a man down. "Good Lord willing, we'll catch some Flesh-Eater honcho and put him up in that one's place."

Andrew didn't mind that at all.

AN AWKWARD GATHERING...

Grendel and his commanders gathered on the iron balcony overlooking the great rail yard in the heart of Norridge. Most of them at least. Clark had wished to return to his domains, citing the risk of increased Merrill activity after the harvest. He claimed his presence was more needed now that ten regiments were hundreds of miles away.

Grendel frowned. Did Clark suspect? He did not need the cannibal potentially allying with Quantrill.

He turned his attention to the rail yard. Below the gathered warlords, steel rails split and snaked across the vast plain of gravel like the arms of a kraken. Ordinarily, passenger and freight trains filled the yard, bringing the commerce, tribute, and ambitious of a continent to the heart of Grendel's realm. But he had ordered traffic diverted to the lesser rail yards to accommodate a special purpose.

While servants kept the alcohol flowing, Grendel watched the guardsmen drive lines of chained prisoners into waiting cattle cars that would take them to Hamari. There, the rail line supporting Grendel's planned expedition slithered south into the Iron Desert.

The convicts who did not move fast enough got a taste of the lash. One man fell to his knees and despite repeated blows could not rise again. The guardsman kept at it. The whip tore through the man's gray prison shirt. Blood painted the gravel around him.

Grendel frowned. A couple blows were a good motivator to get thralls moving, but beating them immobile defeated the entire purpose.

A sergeant stopped the guardsman. The kneeling man wept. The weeping grew more intense when the sergeant unshackled him.

CRACK!

The man's forehead and what was behind it decorated the ground. He slumped forward, his shattered face sinking into the slurry of meat and gravel. Alrekr hooted appreciatively and dropped from the railing, gliding across the rail yard toward the still-warm snack.

"Keep moving!" the sergeant shouted in the flatlander tongue. The line of convicts resumed shuffling into the car. Chains banged on metal as they marched up the ramp. Men — and a few women, who would keep the men entertained on the long, hot ride — disappeared into the maw of the car like little fish swallowed by a whale.

The rail line ate up laborers, especially the expendable prisoners. Alexander had standing orders to feed them more than the bare minimum, in order to keep them alive and working as long as possible. He probably delegated the task to the known soft-heart Mifshud. But working the three shifts needed to get the project done quickly ground men to dust.

The convicts spilled back out onto the ramp. Guardsmen lashed them, trying to force them onto the train. They did not succeed. Eventually the sergeants intervened, pulling back the lines of prisoners. The cars disgorged them like a sick dog vomiting until it was possible to close the door.

"Do you think this will be enough?" Grendel asked Alexander. His old friend stood beside him, mug of beer in hand. "I have emptied the jails all across the Basin and put out the call for troublemakers the jailers missed."

"And the breeding pits have contributed their fair share," Mangle rumbled from behind Grendel. "This year's crop will be much smaller. Fewer fathers to sire and mothers to bear."

Grendel turned to face his misshapen subordinate. He smiled, making sure it reached his eyes.

"But they will talk all the way to Hamari. Think of the fame this will bring you."

And the fear that will sow in the entire realm, he added mentally. *With fewer soldiers left behind, keeping control will be harder than before.*

"Eighty prisoners per car and there are fifty cars on that train," Alexander said. "Assuming most make it, this should make up for the losses we've taken in the past weeks."

Grendel nodded. More workers equaled more rest and fewer deaths. Convicts were cheap but not unlimited. Once they ran out, he would need to conscript laborers. *That* would stir unrest.

Meanwhile, Quantrill stood alone, watching the trains much like Grendel had. That he was not politicking with the others meant whatever treachery he had brewed had not gotten far. No matter how unsettlingly close he was to Norridge, he could not beat Grendel alone.

Booted feet and, incongruously, the clacking a woman's shoes would make, sounded in the room behind the balcony. Grendel's ears perked up. The latter meant a woman, unless one of his commanders had odd habits.

He turned to see Falki, in his Obsidian Guard dress uniform, emerging onto the balcony. Behind him came Rosalyn, wearing a long, black skirt fringed with gold and a silver leaf-patterned vest. She wore her golden hair up.

Grendel frowned. *When it rains, it pours.* Falki was no simpleton and his battlefield exploits showed tactical skill. But the gang leaders and two-bit warlords he had swept aside had *that*. To rule, one had to be a warrior *and* a politician. Flaunting his souvenir before the man whose daughter he was supposed to marry was *stupid*.

Alexander stirred beside Grendel. He looked Rosalyn up and down. His eyes narrowed. He stepped toward the two, boots loud in the sudden quiet.

Grendel's gaze snapped toward Alexander. *Falki is my son. This is my business.* Alexander took one look at his master's face and stopped abruptly. *Good.*

Grendel stepped over to Falki and, placing his hand on his shoulder, dragged him away from Rosalyn. That left the girl alone with his warlords, but he doubted any harm would come to her in a few minutes. No loss to him if any did.

"Falki, did you leave your brain in your bedroom this morning?" he snarled in Sejer when they were off the balcony and out of earshot. "Bringing her here, into the presence of Alexander?"

"Alexander is your friend, Father. And he wouldn't be so foolish as to try anything in your presence if he weren't."

"It is a needless reminder you slighted his daughter. Rosalyn may be your concubine and nothing more" — Falki's expression darkened at the word — "but concubines can bear sons just as well as wives."

"Oh, I've learned *that* lesson well enough."

Grendel shoved his son against the wall. "As I've told you before, my life is no concern of yours. I *will* have you note I have not fathered nearly as many sons as I *could* have."

Pennyroyal and other herbs were not always reliable, but they worked well enough. He had an heir, a spare, another spare, a boy he intended to unseat Clark with, and many marriageable daughters. Another son would not be too problematic and would help ensure his line continued in the event of disaster. But too many risked a dynastic war that could ruin everything.

He released Falki. "Now, what is done cannot be undone, and you bringing her here has the silver lining of letting Quantrill think his scheme is working. But when we are through, take Rosalyn back to the citadel. Do not *ever* bring her *anywhere* she will cross paths with Alexander *again*. Even when I am gone. Do you understand?" Falki nodded. "Good."

He would need to keep a closer eye on the boy. Falki had complained about his personal life before, but never this vehemently.

Grendel had a very good idea of the cause. Before, he assumed Quantrill simply wanted to spy on Falki or disrupt relations between himself and Alexander. That this woman intended to set his eldest son against him had never crossed his mind.

"Falki." Halfway to the balcony door, Falki froze. He turned to face his father, as pale as his skin would allow. "Do not be too eager to put on my cloak." Falki's jaw worked, but no sound emerged. "You *helped* bring down the Merrills and killed a lot of bandits and rebels. That is all well and good. However, the men outside all achieved much more. Even if you were to *replace* me, you could not control them."

Falki looked hurt. "Father, I —"

Grendel stepped past his eldest son back onto the balcony. He noted Quantrill's gaze was the first to fall upon him. He nodded, his politeness masking his wrath.

It had been a long time since he killed a foe worthy of him. Although he had joined the guardsmen in practicing with live targets before, those were easy prey, barely armed and desperate.

He closed his eyes, remembering the last battle with James Merrill, the repeaters tearing and the cavalry crunching against his defenses. Grendel had found the dying James Merrill amidst the heaps of dead men and horses and took his head with his axe in the old manner. Then he returned to his throne in Norridge and left the necessary head-breaking to his subordinates.

The bloodlust he suppressed so he could rule wisely rose like a water-monster from the western ocean, spiky teeth ready to tear through flesh. He could throw Quantrill off the balcony. His bald head would shatter on the ground, his brains mingling with those of the dead thrall.

He shook his head. *Patience.* There were many ways for a man to die on campaign.

RELIEF ARRIVES

The first faint boom of the enemy guns twisted Andrew's guts. It grew louder as the captured airship approached. Andrew's heartbeat rose with it. Rifles and galloper guns soon played counterpoint from the ground. The four enemy dirigibles swelled from dark specks in the blue sky into enormous red and black engines of destruction raining death onto the trapped Merrills. Andrew forced himself to watch the enemy as the stolen dirigible drew closer.

The vessel came in above four Flesh-Eater craft and far too many enemy infantry and horsemen on the ground. Three of their flying foes were the same size as the intruder, but one was vastly larger. Guns far smoother and streamlined than anything made in a modern forge emerged from not one but *two* gondolas. Whenever those guns spoke, a huge fireball erupted from where the target used to be.

The sight of what must be the *Bailey Mines* made Andrew need to piss. Four on one was bad odds, even with the advantage of height and surprise. He looked over his shoulder toward one of the back windows. There was no sign of the *Asherton*. He returned his attention to the gigantic airship below. Clark's flagship made it all *worse*.

On the other hand, Clark's presence cut both ways. If they killed him, maybe the whole Flesh-Eating Legion would fall apart. He frowned. *If.*

Two smaller airships floated below the *Bailey Mines*. The other dirigible floated above and behind the Flesh-Eater flagship. Andrew frowned. There went dropping it on the bigger dirigible.

"Get men on the guns and the fire extinguishers upstairs!" Hardy ordered. "The rest, open the windows and get those rifles up!"

The troopers obeyed, scrambling for the gun emplacements or the ladder leading up into the balloon. Will manhandled one of the Sawyer guns toward the first enemy airship. A cruel grin formed on his wounded face. New blood darkened his bandages. Andrew allowed himself to imagine the gas holding up the airship spewing from the holes the gun would make, some lucky spark igniting the whole mess.

Andrew stepped to an open window and set down his familiar rifle. He picked up the repeater he'd taken from the guardsman. Below, signal flags ran up and down the sides of the dirigible guarding the *Bailey Mines*'s rear. Andrew didn't know what they meant, something that sent fear crawling up his spine and spreading over his scalp. The dirigible slowly turned their way. He tensed. Images of gunfire and fiery death rolled through his head.

Hardy swore. "Wreck its engines now!" Andrew squeezed the trigger. The repeater kicked against his shoulder much like his rifle, but there was no smoke. The Sawyers drowned out the chattering as Will turned the crank beside him. Smoke poured off the weapon as it spun.

Sparks danced on the enemy airship's engines. Their distant rumble took on a painful, twisted tone. Rounds that didn't tear into the engines slammed into the rear of the balloon. The holes merged into flapping mouths puking lifting gas. The bag shrank. The dirigible sank. But instead of plummeting straight down, its damaged engines drove it toward the *Bailey Mines*.

Will laughed. "Keep going you bastard! Keep going!"

Andrew laughed too. Hopefully the balloon wouldn't deflate *too* quickly.

The *Bailey Mines* was turning now. Andrew leaned forward. Would it get away? Would it get away and then rise up and kill them?

Something flashed within the smaller airship's balloon. Will shouted. Andrew did too. Fountains of fire tore long rents in the bag's red and black fabric. Flames snaked across the balloon as it careened downward. Metallic ribs shined through the burning cloth.

Despite the fiery display, Andrew kept watching the *Bailey Mines*. It was moving now. If the dying dirigible missed and the monster turned its guns their way, they'd all *burn*. Just like the Flesh-Eaters below.

The burning dirigible did not slam into the tyrant of the air like Andrew hoped. Instead, its blazing balloon entangled the enormous engine on the lower left of the *Bailey Mines*, beyond its rearmost gondola. An explosion flashed amid the burning morass of fabric and metal. Serpents of fire crept upward along the big airship's side. Andrew grinned. Hydrogen was a real bitch.

But the fire wasn't *fast* enough. The *Bailey Mines* kept turning. Andrew's heart sank. One shot from a big gun could smash their gondola. The enemy vessel's huge guns rose away from the battered excavation site. Andrew swallowed. It wouldn't be long now...

Then the rearmost gondola exploded. The *Bailey Mines* bucked like a maddened horse. Beside Andrew, Will laughed.

"Ammo cookoff, you sons of bitches! *Burn!*"

A pillar of fire burst through the balloon. The airship's remaining engines drove it nose-first toward the ground. The Flesh-Eater soldiers besieging the excavation site scattered. Ballast fell like iron and stone rain. One piece crushed a fleeing Flesh-Eater's skull. The burning dirigible began pulling out of its dive. Its front gondola skimmed the brown earth.

The rest of the dirigible slammed into the ground. The front end snapped upward. What was once the king of the Flesh-Eater aerial fleet settled onto the stony ground. Small fires erupted all around as flaming debris rained over the excavation site. Black smoke rose into the sky, nearly shrouding the remaining enemy airships.

Andrew laughed. They'd done it! They'd killed Jasper Clark! They'd avenged Carroll Town! More cheers erupted throughout the gondola.

"That's for Ma!" Andrew shouted. "There's for Sam! That's for Sarah! That's for Cassie!"

"Sight on the next one!" Zeke shouted, his words silencing the cheering. "They'll be moving up to meet us!"

The two remaining Flesh-Eater dirigibles surged upward. A bow gun boomed on one. The stolen dirigible shook. If they couldn't put the enemy craft in boot hill right quick, they were dead. Hell, if the enemy craft got too close before exploding, *they'd* die.

Will strained to turn the gun right. Andrew set the repeater down and grabbed onto the hot metal. Pain flared in his fingers and palms. The gun clanked into position. Andrew released the weapon, giving his reddened hands a bit of relief, as Will cranked the gun.

The third dirigible buckled and shuddered as the captured dirigible's guns tore into its balloon. Flames spurted from holes torn in its sides. Still it kept climbing, absorbing hit after hit. Andrew snatched up the repeater, ignoring the pain in his hands. How much more would it take to kill the damn thing?

Eventually *something* important got hit. The wounded craft slewed sideways, debris falling from its gondola. It carved a huge furrow into the ground as it crashed.

The last one kept coming. Andrew's heart sank. The next fight would be a battle of equals.

Thunder cracked. The dirigible shook. Andrew tumbled to the floor and rolled up against the ladder that rose into the balloon. A fireball bloomed at the front of the gondola, blowing away the smoke the troopers' guns had made. Something whooshed overhead. Cold white foam dropped from above onto Andrew's body.

Andrew had barely dragged himself to his feet when another shell slammed into the gondola. The roaring explosion sent daggers into Andrew's ears. He nearly fell. Metal flesh split open like a sideways mouth. Two screaming men tumbled out, along with the heavy gun they manned.

"Sutter!" Zeke roared over the gunfire. He sounded so far away. "Get over there!"

"Yes, sergeant!"

Andrew grabbed both his weapons and crawled toward the yawning gap in the gondola's side. The enemy airship was parallel with them now. If it got higher, its gunners would hole their balloon just like the Merrills had the others. Every man aboard the captured dirigible would burn alive on their way down.

The huge mouth of a heavy gun yawned directly in front of the hole in the gondola's side. Behind it, soldiers in red and black shoved a shell into the breech.

He grit his teeth. *Not today!*

He squeezed the trigger. The repeater bucked in his hands. One Flesh-Eater went down with the shell. Another Flesh-Eater grabbed for it. Andrew pulled the trigger again.

The gun clicked empty. The Flesh-Eater picked up the shell and shoved it into the breech.

Goddamn it!

Andrew had never figured out how to reload an Old World repeater. This was no time to learn. He threw the repeater aside and snatched up his familiar rifle.

Thunder cracked. Andrew threw himself onto the metal floor. No heat filled the gondola. Had the Flesh-Eater *missed*?

The gondola tilted. Andrew slid toward the yawning hole. It was a long way down. He scrabbled for anything that could stop him. The repeater vanished through the gap.

His shoulder and side slammed into the metal wall. His feet kicked in empty air. He screamed and grabbed at the supports of a Sawyer gun. Pain stabbed his palms. He briefly gripped a metal spar before his hand slipped on what was probably blood.

A hand grabbed onto his wrist. It was one of the soldiers from Wyatt's squad. The trooper pulled Andrew to safety as the dirigible righted.

Andrew looked out the gap. The captured airship now faced the prow of the enemy gondola. A single Sawyer pointed at them. That was nothing to sneeze at, but now all their airship's guns could be brought to bear against just one of the enemy's.

Andrew grinned as the Merrill guns roared. The Flesh-Eaters' forward gun vanished in fire and smoke. The entire front of the airship crumpled inward.

The enemy dirigible began its slow descent. The soldier beside Andrew whooped. "We must've taken out the pilot! It's going to crash!"

"Into us if we don't bring it down!" Zeke roared. "Start putting rounds into the goddamn balloon!"

Andrew knelt before the huge hole and fed the last of his bullets into the ammunition tube. He squeezed the trigger over and over and over, the rifle butt pounding his shoulder raw.

Another salvo drowned out the crackling of his rifle. The captured airship rose. A wave of bullets and shells slammed into the enemy balloon.

Flames burst from wherever the ammunition touched. A wave of hot air slammed into Andrew's face. Something flew past his arm, the heat palpable through his duster. The dirigible hurtled toward them like a burning train. Andrew closed his eyes, not wanting to see his death coming...

Cheers broke out around him. Andrew slowly opened his eyes. The burning airship passed under the gondola. He whooped. They were going to live through this!

The soldiers rushed over to the other side of the gondola, tilting the dirigible with their weight. Andrew peered over taller men's shoulders to watch the burning airship plow into the front of the excavation site. The remaining structures splintered like matchsticks.

Andrew whooped with glee. They'd won! They'd taken out four enemy dirigibles! They'd saved the Merrill!

And then news got better. Out of the east came the Merrill horsemen.

ALONZO GRINNED as the last Flesh-Eater airship crashed into the front of the excavation site, hopefully atop the oncoming Flesh-Eater foot-sloggers. Although gunfire continued, the calculus of the battle had changed entirely.

He turned to the nearest officer. "Order the troopers to fall back. Let the bastards think we're running. Then we'll rip them a new one!"

The officer grinned. "Yes, sir!"

ANDREW WATCHED the Merrill soldiers flee their hiding places below.

The Flesh-Eaters on the ground followed into the maze of buildings. Gunfire crackled below as they moved, different squads covering each other. Why were they running away? The dirigibles were gone!

As the Merrills below formed into squads and squads formed into platoons, their retreat came to an abrupt halt. The pursuing Flesh-Eaters began hitting choke points even their numbers and ferocity couldn't break.

Andrew laughed. Good trick!

"Don't just gawk!" Zeke ordered. "*Kill* those sons of bitches!"

Will cranked the Sawyer. Andrew raised his rifle. Crackling gunfire filled his ears and the sulfur stink of gunpowder filled his nose. The enemy below fell like wheat before a reaper. Will grinned despite his wound. So did Andrew. *These* Flesh-Eaters would never hurt anyone the way their comrades had ravaged Carroll Town.

The surviving enemy scrambled into the buildings the Merrills had sheltered in before. The airship's heavier guns took care of those. Explosive shells blew off roofs, showering the men below in lethal shrapnel. A sound a lot like a hammer hitting metal echoed over and over again as flying debris bounced off the gondola.

More heavy gunfire sounded from the right. Andrew's gaze jumped to the sound. Something huge passed between the captured airship and the sun. Another dirigible, bigger than the one they'd hijacked. Andrew's vision swam. Were they going to die anyway?

Then he saw the bag was brown and bore the green heraldry of House Merrill. "The *Asherton!*" someone shouted behind him.

Will scowled. "Took them long enough."

The other dirigible floated beside the stolen enemy craft. With two sets of heavy guns floating overhead and the Merrill troops rallying on the ground, the Flesh-Eaters below had no chance. Their gunfire soon petered out. Andrew whooped.

We've won!

TO THE VICTOR GO THE SPOILS

A hellish scene greeted Alonzo and his surviving guards as they rode out of the ravaged excavation site.

The airships' fall had sown debris and burning balloon shreds like seed across several acres of the open ground. The stench of the burning fabric and fuel rose together with the barbecue-smell of burning flesh to create a miasma of horror. Dozens of Merrills and Flesh-Eaters lay burning all around. Some still moved.

And in the center of it all lay the ruined *Bailey Mines*. The two gondolas lay crumpled and twisted on their sides like tyrant lizards with broken backs. Beyond them, rags hanging from the balloon's metal skeleton still burned. Some of the great dirigible's Old World artillery pieces pointed at the oncoming Merrills. It would be right ironic if, by some dark miracle, some Flesh-Eater survivor killed Alonzo at the moment of his victory.

Alonzo snorted. Anyone inside the gondolas would have been roasted alive. It would just be a matter of stripping the thing for metal and valuables and then –

A repeater crackled from somewhere inside the *Bailey Mines*. Alonzo slammed his body down onto his horse. The bullets passed through where his head had been. He swore.

"What the hell?" a trooper shouted. "Nobody could have survived that!"

"Well somebody did!" a wit shot back.

The repeater chattered again. A trooper went down.

The Merrill repeaters shouted back. Something moved inside the gondola, like a red and black tongue inside a mouthful of shattered glass teeth. A trooper rode by the gondola, throwing grenades through the open windows. Alonzo led the rest toward the door at the far end. Anybody who didn't want to get pulped by the grenades would come through there.

The door slammed open. A grenade flew out. The Merrills recoiled. The explosion that would have killed the foremost horsemen failed to kill any.

On the heels of the explosion came a ripper. One eye socket was a bloody ruin. Blistered flesh showed where fur had burned away. It knocked a trooper off his horse and tore his throat out.

A repeater cracked. The ripper stumbled off the man's still-twitching corpse. It raised its mangled head at the Merrills and snarled.

Alonzo's own weapon chattered. Three rounds through the head and the ripper went down.

Then Jasper Clark emerged.

Alonzo did not know how the man still lived. His bald head and mad face were scorched black. Red meat peeked through split skin. His eye patch was gone, revealing the sunken grave of an empty eye socket. His red armor was torn and even *melted* in places. His hands were beet red, but their grip on the repeater was steady.

"Well-played, Merrill," he snarled through jagged broken teeth. "Well-played. Y'knew I couldn't resist repayin' your pa for Judy and Roddy by ending th'Merrill line myself." A flash of anger in his eye accompanied the mention of his dead kin. "Except for your sister, of course, and her boy."

Alonzo saw red. His finger slammed down the trigger. The gunfire walked up Clark's chest, throat, and mouth. Blood flew. His huge body slammed into the ground, raising a cloud of dust.

Alonzo dropped from his horse. He approached the fallen tyrant, repeater up. He had enough rounds to finish the bastard if he *still* hadn't died.

Clark lay unmoving. Alonzo narrowed his eyes. Springing forward like a sand snake snagging an unlucky traveler, he buried his foot in Clark's groin. Though the Flesh-Eater's balls pulped like grapes beneath his toes, the man did not move.

Alonzo laughed. "He's dead!" he shouted. "Jasper Clark is dead!"

Behind him, the troopers roared. Alonzo let his repeater hang from his shoulder by its strap and drew his saber. He bent over and sank his left thumb into Clark's empty eye socket.

Two swings of his blade and the tyrant's head came free. He turned and showed the men the head of the man whose army had ravaged their homeland, who had killed or conscripted their men, carried women off as slaves, and made children into fanatics. That man would never hurt anybody ever again.

He let the soldiers cheer for another minute, then set the head on the ground and raised his hands. Silence fell.

"Take his carcass and burn it on what's left of the buildings over there." He gestured to the shattered buildings of the excavation site. His Old World artillery had made them kindling. It was fitting that be his pyre.

Two soldiers bore away the fallen tyrant. As they left, Hutton rode out. Even more ash and blood stuck to him than Alonzo, but he wasn't hurt.

"He's dead," Alonzo repeated. "He's dead."

Hutton grinned. "It's better than that. Those Flesh-Eaters who got away are carrying the news. Once the telegraphs pick it up, it'll be everywhere. They'll *crumble*. You didn't just strike a blow against the Flesh-Eaters. You struck a blow against Grendel himself."

Alonzo grinned. The bastard deserved more than just a blow. He deserved a saber to the throat. Maybe to the crotch first.

His smile faded. Grendel would come. He'd come with multiple Hosts, with the Obsidian Guard. The coming battles would be far worse than the one he'd just fought, even with his new arsenal.

His smile returned. Clark was dead. Alonzo drew his saber and took one of his two long braids in his free hand. A swift cut and the braid fell onto the ground.

Once Clark's carcass was disposed of, he would see to the Second Pendleton.

ZEKE and the rest of Andrew's squad stood over David's cot in the stuffy medical tent. The gash in Will's cheek had been cleaned and stitched back together, leaving him with an odd permanent half-smile. But David's case was more serious. Although his wound had since stopped bleeding, the white-haired surgeon old enough to be Andrew's grandfather said the leg had to go or it'd mortify.

Zeke handed David a stick. "Put this in your mouth. Bite down when it comes. It'll make it easier." David trembled, drenched with sweat, but nodded and obeyed. "Gollmar, you hold his arms. Simmons, his legs." The two obeyed. Zeke sighed. "Remind me to look for chloroform next raid. Get this done."

The surgeon stepped forward, setting his scalpel, several pieces of thread, and the ugliest saw Andrew had ever seen on the table beside the cot. David's eyes bulged. He went rigid. Fearful sounds emerged from around the stick in his mouth. Zeke looked gravely at the rest of the squad. "Don't let him up."

Owen and Will tightened their grip. The sawbones took the scalpel and knelt by the cot. David lurched against the other two young men, but they held him fast. The surgeon pulled up the leg of David's trousers, exposing the messy wounds. They yawned open on his leg like morbid mouths with teeth of splintered bone. Tears ran down David's cheek.

The surgeon started cutting through the flesh above the wound. David screamed around the stick and started thrashing against Will and Owen's grip.

"Sutter, grab that leg!" Zeke ordered.

Andrew knelt by Will and the surgeon, doing his level best to ignore David's cries of pain and the hot blood spilling onto his still-tender hands. "String," the surgeon demanded. Zeke obeyed. The sawbones took the string and swiftly made a cut.

Blood spurted, spattering Andrew's face. He winced. His grip loosened. David started kicking around.

"HOLD ONTO THE GODDAMN LEG!" Zeke roared.

Doing his best to ignore the red, sticky heat around his eyes and the pain in his hands, Andrew forced the leg back down. The sawbones quickly tied off the gushing artery.

"There'll be two more of these," the surgeon said.

David passed out. Cutting and tying off the remaining two arteries was much easier.

The sawbones set the bloody scalpel on the table before cutting into the bone with the saw. The awful grating made Andrew wince. He looked away until it finished. His stomach lurched.

Owen looked at Andrew. "Your first time helping with an amputation?" Andrew nodded weakly. "You're doing better than I did. I upchucked on the poor man."

Despite the situation, Andrew laughed.

The surgeon set the saw down and cut away the rest of the leg with the scalpel. He threw it into the corner of the tent, then began stitching down a flap of skin. "Let him rest. Give him plenty of water, and beefstock to heal. Hopefully fever won't set in."

"What kind of duty will he be able to do?" Zeke asked. "It's not like we can discharge him."

"If we can find him a clockwork leg, he'll be back with you boys. But those're scarcer than hen's teeth even in the cities. We'll probably give him a peg-leg and take him off the front lines."

Zeke frowned. "I was afraid of that."

"I'm sorry, sergeant." The surgeon smiled. "But I'm sure you'll have plenty of replacements. Jasper Clark's dead and most of their dirigibles went down with him. With the enemy in disarray, people will be flocking to join us."

Zeke nodded. "Good Lord willing."

The tent opened. Andrew and the others jumped to their feet as Alonzo Merrill appeared. "I heard you boys were the ones who captured that dirigible," he said. "You saved my bacon and dropped Jasper goddamn Clark into my lap while you were at it."

"Yes, sir," Zeke replied. "Thank you, sir." He looked at Andrew.

"Got to give credit where it's due. Sutter here spotted the airship arming up. We got under the guns before they started shooting."

The Merrill smiled and clapped Andrew on the shoulder.

"Excellent job. Good thing I decided to rescue you back when I thought you were a Flesh-Eater." He stepped back. "Everyone who helped take that dirigible will get medals, of course. And although we don't know how many repeaters we've captured today or how much ammunition we'll have, every man in the Second Pendleton will get one!"

Owen whooped. Will grinned, although it soon turned into a wince.

All of us with Old World weapons, Andrew thought. *We'd be damn near unstoppable.*

NIGHT HAD FALLEN on the excavation site, but this time fires were lit with no fear of dirigibles. The *Asherton* and the captured Flesh-Eater airship had returned to make sure. Everywhere rang with the sounds of celebration. There was singing, laughing, and the playing of drums and fiddles. There was food, too, from the looted Flesh-Eater stores.

But Andrew wasn't hungry. Instead he sat at a wooden table inside a building smelling of spent gunpowder and blood. Ignoring the smell and the aches the day had left, he scraped out his rifle. The amount of shooting that day had done a number on it. He didn't want to take the chance he'd miss in the scraps to come. That, and there'd likely be inspection beforehand anyway. Zeke'd make them all do gaspers if their rifles weren't clean, and they'd deserve it.

"Sutter," Zeke said in the doorway behind Andrew.

The suddenness made him jump. He spun around and saluted.

"Sergeant!"

Zeke smiled. "At ease, Sutter. Not for long though." Before Andrew could open his mouth to ask, Zeke smiled. "After we fixed up Court's leg, I had a talk with the L-T and the Merrill himself. They're giving me a battlefield commission."

It took Andrew a second to make the connection. "They're making you an officer?"

"Aye. It won't take effect right away, not until we recruit enough men to fill out the regiment." He smiled again. "Looks like I'll be working for a living for a bit longer."

"Congratulations si...I mean, sergeant." That was well-earned. If Zeke hadn't had the initiative to storm the airship, everybody would have died that day. The soldiers at the fort, the Merrill, the whole army. Whatever was left would be easy prey for the Flesh-Eaters.

"You're welcome, Sutter." He paused. "That's not why I'm here though. The L-T wants you."

Andrew stowed his cleaning gear in pockets, collected his rifle, and followed Zeke to a shattered wooden building. They found Hardy in what looked like a former storeroom lit by a flickering kerosene lantern and shafts of moonlight through a shell hole in the roof. Zeke and Andrew both stepped forward and saluted.

"At ease, boys," Hardy said. "Sutter, come here."

Andrew approached the low table Hardy used for a desk. Hardy reached into a shirt pocket of his brown uniform and drew two patches. Two sets of paired golden triangles, one atop the other.

Andrew's eyes widened. His jaw worked, but no sound emerged. Those were corporal's patches! A corporal was just below sergeant!

"Sergeant Thaxton recommended you and I talked to the captain. You haven't been serving long, but if it weren't for you, the Merrill would have died today." He frowned. "And a lot more than just him."

Andrew finally found his voice. "What about Owen and Will?" He immediately closed his mouth. The other two young men might have seniority, but he'd just argued with an officer!

Hardy smiled."Their time will come. Gollmar will be the first and Simmons second if he can control his mouth. We'll be moving north to put our new weapons to the test and we'll be recruiting heavily. A corporal helps the sergeant drill the new soldiers, and there'll be plenty of that."

"I'll learn you your new responsibilities over the next couple weeks," Zeke said. "In the meantime, finish cleaning your rifle and go enjoy yourself."

Zeke stepped out. Hardy looked at Andrew. "You heard the sergeant, *Corporal* Sutter."

Once Andrew returned to his table, he set his rifle down and picked up the patches. He'd have to sew them onto each shoulder of his duster. But he wasn't much for sewing. Ma and Sarah had typically taken care of that, much like how he was the one who did the hunting...

He closed his eyes. Ma was dead, and if Sarah wasn't dead, what was happening to her didn't bear pondering. And Cassie likewise.

Of course, that might change soon enough. They'd be moving north, not running back to their camps. They'd exterminate the cannibals, make that old tyrant Grendel tremble on his throne. Cassie and Sarah hadn't been at the fort they'd broken today, but they might be at the next one, or the one after that.

The thought brought a smile to Andrew's face.

"Hey there, handsome."

Andrew's head snapped up. Alyssa stood in the door. Although she'd been in the battle too, the only thing marring her looks was a cut on her temple in front of her left ear.

"May I come in?"

Andrew nodded quickly. "Sure."

She sauntered over and sat on the bench beside him. "Was wondering where you were at. The old bastard's dead and everyone's celebrating. Owen and Will didn't know where you were, but I ran into your sergeant a few minutes ago." She leaned over, her shoulder brushing his. She picked up the stripes and whistled appreciatively. "You a corporal now?" She saluted, then grinned. "Sir."

Andrew laughed, a grin spreading over his face.

"Yep." He told her the tale of the capture of the dirigible and how they rode to the Merrill's rescue. Somewhere during the tale, she slid an arm around him. Andrew's heart began pounding. Cassie's face rose into his mind, but he pushed the thought back down. He laid a hand on her thigh. Her fingers soon locked with his.

"I was impressed with you boys taking the mortar during that ambush. But taking a whole dirigible and saving the Merrill's bacon? That's another bit of business entirely."

Andrew's heart pounded in his ears. She was so warm and so *close*. Cassie might still live, but Alyssa was right *here*, so *alive* in a way that Hank and so many others weren't. She wanted him and he wanted her and there might not be a tomorrow…

It happened so quickly. Their lips locked together. Andrew didn't know how long the first kiss lasted, but it was Alyssa who pulled back. She wore a big grin on her face.

"Worth waiting for." Then she kissed him again.

This went on for awhile. Andrew's hands slid forward, pushing her duster down from her shoulders. Pity there wasn't a door, but with everyone else celebrating, that shouldn't be a problem.

Alyssa's hands caught his wrists. "Don't you worry, there's plenty of time for that." She winked. "Right now, there's the party of the century going on out there, and I bet you'll be the hero of the hour." She pulled him to his feet. "C'mon. It's not right, you hiding in here."

They barely got ten feet from the door when someone started clapping. It was Owen. Will stood nearby, smiling as much his bandaged face would allow.

"Took you long enough," Owen said. Will laughed.

Andrew had to agree.

TRIUMPH, BUT...

"Jasper Clark is dead," Falki said flatly.

The younger man stood at attention before Grendel's vast desk. Grendel nodded before handing him a pair of telegrams that had arrived that morning. Falki's eyes widened as he read them.

Grendel already knew what they said. The first came from one of the archdeacons who presumed to speak for the entire Flesh-Eating Legion. It recounted the death of Jasper Clark and the events leading up to it.

Grendel would mourn the loss of the very expensive airships more than the cannibalistic vassal he intended to betray, but his death did not end the problem. The Merrills now raided as far north as Pendleton. The archdeacon was sending soldiers from the Flesh-Eater core territory in the northeast to deal with this. All would be well, he said.

The second came from a Flesh-Eater officer Isaac had suborned even before the death of James Merrill. The man was mostly interested in land and money and paid only lip service to Clark's lunatic religion. Grendel had expected this telegram would be more honest. He was not disappointed.

The Merrills carried Old World weapons. The officer estimated Pendleton would fall before Grendel received the telegram. Flesh-Eater forces *were* rolling southwest, but they had slammed into a popular insurgency spread by Merrill outriders. The army and clergy could not agree on how to handle the crisis. That made the situation even worse.

Falki looked up after he finished reading. "How is this possible? The Merrills only have a handful of regiments. They couldn't possibly —"

"Now you see why I lecture you about putting just the right amount of weight in your hand. Clark was too hard. As soon as the opportunity came the people revolted. That handful of regiments is going to grow *ten times* soon enough."

Grendel had anticipated the Merrills might be more problematic for the Flesh-Eaters if Clark had to garrison the north, but not a reversal of this magnitude. He would need to recall those men immediately.

"Is it time to send Havarth? He's young, but with a trusted man to rule until he's old enough —"

Grendel pursed his lips. "That is a possibility. But first things first."

"Ironic, isn't it? You'd planned to kill him, but now you have to avenge him."

Grendel smiled. The boy was learning even the most powerful man in the Northlands still did not have complete freedom of action. "Regardless of the weapons they carry, the Merrills are still few. They will overextend themselves. Once we turn the tables, they will be trapped above the Southern Wall and annihilated."

"We?" Falki asked. His incomprehension faded, followed by eagerness. "Both of us at the same time? I thought it was risky."

"Consider this a learning opportunity. Your company will be part of a much larger force and facing a much more dangerous foe, especially now. They will be much, much more challenging prey." He paused, then allowed a measure of irritation into his voice. "You have been blooded before, but not enough. Your recent cock-up has likely damaged you in the eyes of many. Some victories under your belt will help fix that." He fixed his son with a hard look. "Do not make me regret this."

Falki nodded. "I will not."

"Good." Grendel paused. "This also factors into the invasion of the south. I have not called up this many since the wars with Camrose. This will work out any problems coordinating, blood the younger men, and keep the armies busy while the railroads are built. And if Quantrill eats a bullet or shell, so much the better. That would be two long-term problems solved, not just one." Grendel smiled. "Alonzo Merrill thinks he has won a great victory. We will show him one can win a battle and lose a war."

Falki leaned forward. "How soon?"

"The armies were already mobilizing. The first airships can be there in a week, two at most."

The last time he had gone to war himself, it had been against James Merrill. Now it was time to kill the son just as he had the father and pave the way for his own blood to claim the Merrill patrimony.

CATALINA PACED the confines of her small room, knee-length black skirts swishing when she came to a wall. She sat on her bed and tried to leaf through an engineering book John had given her just before he'd left for Bluebell Creek, but the window overlooking Norridge kept reclaiming her attention. Above the tallest buildings floated the black dirigibles of the Obsidian Guard. Soon Grendel would send them south. Send them to war.

The tyrant had been gone for several days and hadn't told her what he was up to. However, Cora had been all too willing to fill in the details. That shrew said Grendel intended to finish the Merrills once and for all. She'd asked Grendel to bring Alonzo's head back, to set it up in his bedroom.

To watch next time Grendel summoned Catalina.

She closed her eyes. Slowly, she forced that horrible image from her mind. She returned her attention to the airships.

A dirigible flotilla could move only at the speed of the slowest. Once the fleet left, it shouldn't take long for them to arrive in the realm her family once ruled. She ran what she knew about the speed of a big transport dirigible through her head. Her heart sank. Once the big propellers started spinning, they'd be in Jacinto in *days*.

Catalina clenched her fist, her nails digging into her palm. If only she had a way to warn her brother! She doubted he could defeat the gathering armada — their father at the peak of his power couldn't — but if he knew the hammer was going to fall, he could prepare.

But she wasn't loyal like the rest of Grendel's whores. She was a prisoner of war, only her prison was a well-appointed apartment in Grendel's citadel rather than the mines of the western Basin or those damned cotton plantations the Flesh-Eaters had on the Grand River. She wasn't allowed to send letters.

Maybe the others could help? She shook her head. None would risk their comfortable idleness for her sake, but maybe if she figured some way to trick one...

She shook her head. When Grendel had first taken her captive, she'd kept to herself, not befriending his other concubines. Most of *them* were camp followers or other trash and *she* the daughter of a cattle-king, even though at seventeen she was youngest. And when Hayes was born, she focused all of her attention on him. She'd dealt with the other women mostly on matters pertaining to their children.

Damn it.

She'd put herself at a major disadvantage. She had no real friends, not even allies. And she was in a poor position to make them now, with her reputation of unsociability, and lacking even the others' limited freedom. And a sudden attempt to be sociable would look suspicious.

And with Grendel away, the petty intrigues of his harem would worsen. Lenora wanted Logmar to become first lord. She'd take advantage of Grendel's absence to intrigue against Falki and Arne. Or worse, plot against Hayes so he couldn't threaten Logmar the way Logmar threatened the elder two. The thought of the Obsidian Guard bayoneting her little boy at that whore's instigation sent a shudder rolling through her.

Then the ghost of a smile appeared on her face.

Jessamine was new to Grendel's harem and wouldn't remember Catalina's earlier unfriendliness. Should the old monster put her in a family way, her child would be young and vulnerable just like Hayes. The next time she saw Jessamine, she would go out of her way to talk to her.

"Mama, where's Pa going?" Hayes walked through the door,

carrying the stuffed cat toy Astrid had given him and wearing a black romper suit Catalina had trimmed with green. He looked toward the window and the gathering airships, curiosity lighting his gray eyes. Those damned gray eyes...

She grit her teeth. *He's a little boy,* she told herself. *My little boy, not just his. And he misses his pa, however much a complete son of a bitch the man is.*

"He's going south, Hayes." She stepped to the side, allowing her son to approach the window. He climbed onto her bed to get a better look at the dirigibles.

"What's he doing?"

This was tricky. If Catalina told him the truth, he'd spill the beans to Grendel when he returned. This wasn't like telling him about what *should* have been his homeland or even teaching him to treat others as he'd like to be treated. Grendel would kill her for telling Hayes his father intended to murder his uncle and kill his people. Then who'd teach the boy proper values? Certainly not his father, his brothers, or his collection of wicked stepmothers.

"He's visiting your Uncle Alonzo." As she spoke, she examined his clothing. The black Grendel insisted he wear made him look far too pale, although the green he allowed her to add brightened it up a *little*. There was some dirt on it. He must've been playing in the garden with his sisters Lin and Rose. *Lenora's and Cora's daughters. Delightful.* She'd have to check with Astrid to see how they got along.

"Is he coming home soon?"

She shook her head. "It may not be for a long time, chickabiddy."

She *hoped* it would be for a long time, and that he returned empty-handed. If Grendel returned with her brother's head, she doubted she could stop herself from trying to kill him at first chance. Even if it meant Grendel would kill her or Falki would kill Hayes.

She closed her eyes. *Kill those cannibal bastards, brother mine, and dig in. All hell is coming for you now.*

She didn't expect him to kick Grendel's tailbone up between his shoulder blades, but maybe he could keep the tyrant busy, keep him away from Norridge.

Away long enough for her to finally cause some trouble.

THE PEOPLE of Pendleton roared their adulation as the mounted Merrill host streamed through the open gates into the vast city. The captured Flesh-Eater airship floated overhead, green and yellow Merrill heraldry already painted on both sides.

Hundreds crowded the streets beneath red brick buildings taller than any Andrew had ever seen. Others leaned out of open windows, throwing flowers and paper confetti. Gunfire crackled here and there.

The reports about the enemy garrisons being depleted were true. The Southern Wall forts the Merrills had attacked fell far more easily than Andrew had expected. The Flesh-Eaters had abandoned other outposts to avoid getting crushed in place. The marvelous repeaters from the excavation site, farther-reaching than his old rifle and lighter to boot, enabled the Merrills to devastate Flesh-Eater forces they'd previously fled. And Clark's death fucked up enemy morale.

Ahead amid vast open space lay Pendleton's towering concrete citadel. The green Merrill flag fluttered from atop a spire studded with artillery. Andrew snorted. If the Flesh-Eaters had retreated inside and barred the gate, it would have been a right bitch to deal with, Old World weapons or not. They must've been spread out through the city and, when word of the approaching Merrill army arrived, been torn apart where they stood.

Serves the bastards right.

The gates of the star-shaped fortress lay open. A group of burly men, some with clockwork limbs, waited there. They held in their hands things Andrew couldn't make out, things dripping blood.

At the head of the column was the Merrill. He rode up to the men in the gates, who all went to one knee before him. They lifted whatever was in their hands in offering.

Something twisted in Andrew's stomach. The men were offering the Merrill severed heads!

"Who're those guys?" Andrew asked, leaning toward Alyssa.

Alyssa leaned forward. "Shoemakers, I reckon. We're not the only ones fighting the Flesh-Eaters."

The Merrill said something to the men. They rose to their feet and filed off, still carrying the heads.

Andrew watched the men disappear into the citadel. "Who'd those heads belong to?"

"Probably the Flesh-Eaters in charge or locals that kissed their ass. They'll be decorating the walls soon."

Andrew couldn't object to that.

AFTERWORD

Thank you for completing my novel *Battle for the Wastelands*. I hope that you enjoyed the experience. If you're looking for more content from me, you can visit my Amazon author page at shorturl.at/ptzK1. If you'd like exclusive content and the progress of future books in the series, you can sign up for my newsletter at shorturl.at/gxHJO. A Falki novella "Son of Grendel" is slated for release in the near future, while I hope to have the second full novel in the series released sometime in 2020.

Good or bad, all reviews are appreciated.

ACKNOWLEDGMENTS

Special thanks to the Writers of Metro Atlanta and the Lawrenceville Science Fiction and Fantasy Writers Group for spurring me to get this done in a timely fashion and helping me refine it. Also thanks to Matt Cowdery, Mikio Murikami, and Jason Sizmore for helping me refine and package this yet further.

ABOUT THE AUTHOR

Matthew W. Quinn (b. 1984) grew up in Marietta, Georgia. After graduating from the University of Georgia with a dual degree in magazine journalism and history, he had an extensive career in Atlanta media before moving onto social-studies education. Throughout all of this, he has written science fiction, fantasy, and horror. His first sale was the short horror tale "I am the Wendigo" to the webzine CHIMAERA SERIALS and he later wrote licensed fiction for the BattleTech science fiction universe. 2017 saw the publication of his horror novel THE THING IN THE WOODS, while 2019 saw the publication of his horror-comedy novella LITTLE PEOPLE, BIG GUNS. He is a member of the Atlanta chapter of the Horror Writers Association.

Matthew is also a regular participant in the podcast MYOPIA: DEFEND YOUR CHILDHOOD in which the movies you enjoyed as a child are put on trial to see if they hold up. He can be reached at mquinn1984@gmail.com.